Praise for
Reservations for Two

"Lodge has created yet another sumptuous story—full of intrigue, humanity, tantalizing tastes, and true love, in its myriad forms. She gracefully leads us into kitchens, restaurants, and hearts, not to mention sensorial visits to France, Italy, and the tensions of WWII Paris. Poised on a knife's edge, Lodge left me yearning for her next story and for time in the kitchen to test some of her tempting recipes."

—Katherine Reay, author of the critically acclaimed
Dear Mr. Knightley and *Lizzy & Jane*

"*Reservations for Two* is a foodie's delight, peppered with great dishes and references to European culinary landmarks. Lodge's sparkling dialogue adds levity to the book's more serious moments and kept me flipping pages well into the night. But fair warning . . . readers will be hard pressed to choose between turning to the next chapter and running to the kitchen to try one of the many delectable recipes."

—Carla Laureano, RITA Award–winning author
of *Five Days in Skye* and *London Tides*

"Endearing, witty, delectable. Hillary Manton Lodge's second installment in the Two Blue Doors series is as delicious as her first, even for a non-foodie like me! I especially appreciated the seamless transition from Juliette's current life and travels to her grand-mère's WWII past, a captivating angle that added the perfect hint of mystery."

—Melissa Tagg, author of *From the Start*

"Through a clutch of discovered letters, which I read as compulsively as did our heroine, Juliette D'Alisa, and her large Franco-Italian family, we discover that circumstances can be as bitter as baking powder or as delightful as powdered sugar. Both, however, are required to produce the very best madeleines, as well as a deeply satisfying life. *Reservations for Two* is a touching, page-turning novel, which brings home that each day, no matter its troubles, can be filled with good things, especially *chocolat et bisous,* chocolate and kisses, if we freely offer them to those we love. I read, wanting happiness, ultimately, for the delightful Juliette, as much as she wanted it for everyone else."

—SANDRA BYRD, author of *Let Them Eat Cake*

"Hillary Manton Lodge has done it again! From the exquisite prose to the twists and turns of a delicious—pun intended—plot, *Reservations for Two* is a complete delight. Though this story picks up where Lodge's freshman novel *A Table by the Window* left off, this book easily stands alone as a do-not-miss treat! From the lavender fields of Provence to Paris, Memphis, and the Pacific Northwest; from recipes for Rosemary Fig Focaccia to Nasturtium and Spring Greens Salad; from the 1930s to the present . . . this novel is a delight for the senses, a trip through time and kitchens, far and near. Kudos to Lodge."

—KATHLEEN Y'BARBO, best-selling author of The Secret Lives of Will Tucker series and *Firefly Summer*

"With a palate of rich characters, vibrant flavors, and vintage-inspired romance, Hillary Manton Lodge's *Reservations for Two* is a feast for the senses. From the fragrant lavender fields of Provence to Tuscany's golden hills, Lodge takes the reader on a journey that is about both discovery and coming home. It's *très chic* and enchanting—a recipe of *amour* for the reader's heart!"

—KRISTY CAMBRON, author of *The Butterfly and the Violin* and *A Sparrow in Terezin*

"Hillary Lodge has done it again! Picking up where *A Table by the Window* left off, *Reservations for Two* is another delectable story filled with romance, intrigue, witty dialogue, exquisite prose, and delicious recipes. This one is sure to charm readers every bit as much as the first!"

—KATIE GANSHERT, award-winning author of *A Broken Kind of Beautiful*

RESERVATIONS *for* TWO

Books by Hillary Manton Lodge

A Table by the Window

RESERVATIONS *for* TWO

A Novel of Fresh Flavors and New Horizons

HILLARY MANTON LODGE

WATERBROOK
PRESS

RESERVATIONS FOR TWO
PUBLISHED BY WATERBROOK PRESS
12265 Oracle Boulevard, Suite 200
Colorado Springs, Colorado 80921

The characters and events in this book are fictional, and any resemblance to actual persons or events is coincidental.

Trade Paperback ISBN 978-0-307-73177-7
eBook ISBN 978-0-307-73178-4

Cover design by Kelly L. Howard

Published in the United States by WaterBrook Multnomah, an imprint of the Crown Publishing Group, a division of Penguin Random House LLC, New York.

WaterBrook and its deer colophon are registered trademarks of Penguin Random House LLC.

Library of Congress Cataloging-in-Publication Data
Lodge, Hillary Manton.
  Reservations for two : a novel / Hillary Manton Lodge. — First Edition.
    pages ; cm
  ISBN 978-0-307-73177-7 (paperback) — ISBN 978-0-307-73178-4 (ebook)
  I. Title.
  PS3612.O335R47 2015
  813'.6—dc23
      2014047950

Printed in the United States of America
2015—First Edition

10 9 8 7 6 5 4 3 2 1

For Danny, who is constant.

1

While there is tea, there is hope.

—Arthur Wing Pinero

The Provençal breeze tousled the ends of my hair as I tried to organize my thoughts. "I'm beginning to figure out what I want," I told Neil, my voice echoing slightly over the cell connection.

"Oh?"

"When you hang up and listen to the message I was leaving, you'll hear all about it."

He chuckled, and my heart squeezed in my chest. Neil McLaren had the best laugh I'd ever heard—low and warm. If I closed my eyes, I could see the way his eyes crinkled at the corners, the way his lips turned up.

Not that I'd gotten to spend that much time looking at his eyes during our on-again, off-again long-distance relationship, but his short visit to Portland had left a lasting impression.

It was a laugh I never thought I'd hear again.

"You want me to hang up?" he asked.

"Nope, never."

"So why don't you tell me what you want?"

I shrugged and looked out onto the lavender waving in the breeze. "I want the impossible. I want my job at the restaurant, and I want to be with you."

"Cool."

"Cool?" I lifted an eyebrow. "What are you, fifteen?"

Neil sighed. "Sometimes I feel like it."

"The restaurant—I gave up my job, my normal, stable-ish job at the paper to open this restaurant with my brother. I've always, always wanted to run a restaurant, and I'm not ready to give that up."

"I wouldn't want that for you."

"But—," I started, ready to remind him that he worked in Memphis and that instantaneous travel remained a figment of *Star Trek*'s imagination.

"Here's the thing," Neil said, interrupting me. "I have vacation days I haven't taken because all I've done for the last few years is work. I have thousands of frequent flyer miles built up, just sitting around."

"Aiming to get your name on the side of a plane?"

"Not yet. I'd rather use them. And I'm at a good place to pause at work. Do you want company?"

All of my counterarguments about work, travel, and romance dissolved in an instant. "What?"

"I'll fly out there. You want us to be together? So do I, and spending time in Europe doesn't sound so bad."

"It's not a vacation," I told him. "It's a trip to see family, when I'm not meeting with investors or poking around in my grandmother's history— though I suppose that's still family related. There will be family dinners and people with opinions. And if you decide to come with me to Italy, those opinions will get even louder."

"Do you want me to come?"

"Yes, but—"

"Then I'll see you there."

I snorted. "You don't even know where I am."

"I know you're at Chateau de l'Abeille. I also know how to use Google."

"Well . . . fine. Be all smart like that."

"I love you, Juliette. I want you to know that."

Joy blossomed inside my heart. "I love you, Neil."

"Guess what?"

"What?"

"I'll see you soon."

From: Letizia Adessi, ladessi@cucinadiletizia.it
To: Me, jdalisa@twobluedoors.com

Ciao, Juliette!

Can't wait to see you! You must remind me when you are arriving on the train. Nonno and the rest of the family are delighted to see you, though we're very sad that your parents won't be able to make the journey. How is your mother? And when does your new restaurant open?

Letizia

From: Me, jdalisa@twobluedoors.com
To: Letizia, ladessi@cucinadiletizia.it

Dear Letizia—

Looking forward to seeing you as well! I'll be a few days with my mother's cousin here in Provence, then planning to take the train to Rome. I have a few scheduled meetings with suppliers for the restaurant, but the rest of my time is all yours. The plan is still to travel together to Montalcino for Nonno's party, yes?

My parents are doing okay for the time being. Mom's cancer was diagnosed at stage three, so she's had surgery as well as chemo, with radiation planned next. With my mom's health we're hopeful, but the doctors have warned us that ovarian cancer is usually chronic, and never really goes into remission. But we have hope.

My father is having a difficult time, but he's a wonderful care-taker, and the rest of us are filling the gaps as we can, both at home and at D'Alisa & Elle. Business is doing okay at the restaurant, at least.

The preparations at Two Blue Doors (the new restaurant) are going well—we're looking to open on July 25th. It's been a few years since his last restaurant closed, so Nico's excited to have his own place again, though if he changes the menu one more time, I might have to murder him (just kidding—they're always great changes. He really is a talented chef. It's just that the ordering budget is something Nico views as an abstract idea, rather than a hard and fast set of numbers).

I've been living above the restaurant in the apartment, along with my friend Clementine, who's the pastry chef—that's been fun, and waking up to pastry experiments has been lovely. With everything on my to-do list for the opening, I haven't had time to miss working at the newspaper, though I do wish I saw work friends more often.

I just got to Montagnac, where I'll be staying with my mother's cousin Sandrine, her husband Auguste, and my great-aunt Cécile for a few days. It's a lovely spot—the family chateau where my grandmother was raised and my mother grew up. Now it's an inn as well as a lavender farm—Sandrine and Auguste run the place. I'll be sure to take pictures to share. And if my plans shift at all, I'll let you know as soon as possible. There are a couple variables here (one in particular) that I'm not entirely sure about.

Can't wait to see you! Is there anything I can bring from here for Nonno's party? Give my love to everyone!

Juliette

I spent the next thirty-six hours expecting to get a phone call, an e-mail, or a carrier pigeon telling me that it wasn't going to work out, that Neil wouldn't make it for any number of wholly practical reasons.

There was no denying the chemistry we'd felt when we were together, but the distance had taken its toll, and we'd broken up.

But now we were back together, or as together as two people who had broken up over the phone and gotten back together over the phone could be. Our breakup before my flight to France still felt fresh—fresh enough that I expected news that Neil had come to his senses more than I expected the man himself.

As the hours passed, though, my phone didn't buzz with a text or e-mail revealing that he'd changed his mind, that some immunology crisis had emerged, that an unexpected summer tornado had hit Memphis.

And I knew, because I'd checked.

Instead, I was setting the table for lunch when I saw a moving cloud of dust come down the long road toward the chateau.

"Either that's the German guests who haven't checked in yet," said my cousin Sandrine, watching the window from over my shoulder, "or your *copain* has arrived."

"Eh?" her husband Auguste intoned, setting aside the radio he'd been tinkering with to have a look out the window for himself.

We watched together as Neil—all six feet and three inches of him— unfolded from his tiny rented Fiat.

"*Ah, c'est l'Américain,*" Auguste noted, turning to me. "*Bonne chance.*"

"Oh, *la.*" Sandrine pressed a hand to her heart. "*Très beau.* How did you meet?"

My heart fluttered with happiness. "The Internet," I said, my eyes trained on Neil. The moment he spied me through the window, a grin spread across his face.

I raced out the door and into his arms. "You came!"

Neil pressed a kiss to my forehead and held me close. "I told you I would," he said. "All you had to do was ask."

I looked up at him, taking in his gold hair, his gingery beard.

We returned to discover that the lunch table set for three had become a table set for two; Sandrine and Auguste had disappeared. Two candles flickered at the center of the table.

"I think Sandrine and Auguste feel invested in our having a happy reunion," I remarked dryly.

"I can live with that." Neil tipped my chin upward and placed a gentle kiss at the corner of my mouth.

My fingers wove into his hair as I kissed him back.

We might have stayed like that forever if the sound of Neil's stomach hadn't broken the moment. "Sorry," he said. "I ate a croissant after landing. That was a few hours ago."

"Do you want to eat lunch?"

"It smells really good," Neil admitted sheepishly.

We sat and portioned food onto our plates; Neil poured the wine Sandrine had left open, a rich, full-bodied Bordeaux. I told Neil about my time with Sandrine's mother, *Grand-tante* Cécile, how she'd remembered the war years just long enough to tell me about Gabriel Roussard, *Grand-mère's* first husband, my grandfather.

"That's incredible." He shook his head. "Really, Juliette—all of this because you found a photo in your grandmother's cookbook."

I nodded. "So now we know for sure who he was, and why he looked like a clone of Nico. And Cécile confirmed that he was a Jew. That's why their family wasn't happy about it." I shrugged. "And then Cécile got up to make tea, and when she came back—it was gone. She was gone, at least the version of her that remembered her teens."

"It'll come back."

I shot him a wry glance. "I don't want to bank on her Alzheimer's feeling cooperative. She may well not remember, at least not before we leave." I shrugged again. "I shouldn't be greedy—I still found out more in that conversation than I would have on my own. Anything more is gravy."

Neil lifted an eyebrow. "I think I know you pretty well, and I doubt you'll be satisfied with just a slice of the story. You won't stop working until you know it all, from the filling to the crust."

"That's very poetic of you."

"Thought you'd like that."

"I'm impressed." I smiled flirtatiously. "And you're right, I'm just . . . trying to pace myself. Set realistic expectations."

"Fair enough. Tell me more about who all lives here. Your great-aunt and your cousin?"

"Technically Sandrine is my mom's first cousin. Auguste is her husband,

and they manage the chateau together. Cécile is Sandrine's mother—she was Grand-mère's younger sister."

"I'd like to meet them."

I grinned. "Let's tidy up and go find them."

"Let's," Neil said, leaning in for another kiss. "But maybe not just yet."

We spent the day together, catching up on the details surrounding Two Blue Doors, my mother's health, and Neil's latest research. We explored the chateau grounds and simply enjoyed spending time together, in person.

That evening I baked a batch of lemon-scented madeleines for our evening visit with Grand-tante Cécile. Neil and I brought the cookies to her sitting room on a tray, as well as a pot of strong black tea and an appropriate number of cups and saucers.

"*Bonjour,*" said Cécile, putting her paperback novel down when she saw us.

"Bonjour," I echoed back, showing her the tray. "Would you like some tea?"

"Oh yes," she said, and I stilled in cautious anticipation. Cécile's English came and went along with her memories. If she spoke English, she was more likely to remember a time when she'd used it.

We made small talk, and I gently reminded her who Neil and I were. After Cécile and I had each enjoyed a madeleine and Neil had eaten four, I ventured a question. "Where exactly did Mireille and Gabriel meet?"

"Paris," Cécile said, setting down her teacup. "Mireille wrote me letters, but kept him a secret from our parents as long as she could."

I sat up straight. "Letters?"

"*Naturellement.* Mireille and Gabriel wrote letters too, after she returned to the chateau. How else would they continue their attachment?"

"Um . . . a telephone?"

"Too expensive, calls from Paris. And besides, Papa wouldn't have it. Mail—she pretended to be writing a girlfriend she'd met in the city."

"Letters, then." I pleated my skirt between my fingers and tried my best to sound casual. "Tell me about them."

Cécile's eyes widened. "They were *very* romantic," she said, leaning forward. "Passionate. I traveled to Paris after she went back, telling our parents that I needed new clothes when really Mireille wanted me to meet him. She married him just a couple weeks later. Everyone was shocked, of course, but not me."

Neil squeezed my hand.

"What happened to him?" I asked. In all likelihood, I already knew the answer. "How did he die?"

"Die?" Cécile's face went blank. "Who told you that?"

"Well . . ." My voice trailed off. Come to think of it, I had no records. I opened my mouth to say as much but Cécile interrupted.

"I had a letter just last week from Mireille. She's with child, you know. They're so excited. He's dead? Are you sure?"

"No." I patted her hand. "I must have been mistaken."

"Never speak lightly about such things! And Mireille with child . . ." She shook her head. "*Ce serait un désastre.* They love each other so much."

"So—Mireille and Gabriel are happy?"

"*Très joyeux.*" She shook her head. "My heart longs for a man to look at me the way Gabriel looks at her. Or," she added, her voice coy, "the way this gentleman looks at you."

My face turned pink. Neil winked at me.

So many emotions fought for dominance—relief, happiness, frustration. Cécile remembered Gabriel for the first time in days, but only half the story.

I crossed my legs together at the ankle and tried to reorganize my mind into a new line of questions. "So what is Gabriel's occupation?"

"He is a pastry chef. Mireille assured Papa that he is a very important pastry chef, working at Maxim's. Not that Papa cared."

"What is he like?"

"Handsome—très beau. They look well together, he with his dark hair, Mireille with her blond curls."

I smiled. From what I'd seen in the photo of Gabriel I'd found in Grand-mère's cookbook, his resemblance to my brother Nico was uncanny. "And they wrote letters. Did Mireille keep them all, you suppose?"

"She kept all of the letters I wrote to her in Paris—she showed me. All tied up with a pink silk ribbon. She read them when she was lonely, she told me. I can't imagine she would part with Gabriel's letters."

"Where do you think they might be?"

"I imagine she has them with her in Paris."

"Of course," I said. "When you were girls here, did she have a hiding place for things in the chateau?"

"The window seat in the north garret, of course," Cécile answered without pause. "It's where we kept all of our secrets away from Papa. The seat sticks until you know how to lift it just right."

"How is that?" Neil asked.

"I couldn't say," she said with a coy smile.

One last try. "Is there room for me to hide something? In the window seat, I mean?"

She patted my hand. "I'm sure you can find a new place to hide something, dear. And besides, you wouldn't want me to find it, would you?" Cécile leaned forward and took another madeleine from the plate. "These are very good. Mireille is such a good baker—I'd know her madeleines anywhere."

"She's very good," I agreed, while a mixture of pride and frustration stirred in my heart.

Neil and I tidied up Cécile's sitting room before we left; Sandrine arrived to assist her mother to bed. We wished them both a good evening and slipped out of Cécile's rooms and toward the rooms my grand-mère had used in her youth.

The garret above Grand-mère's rooms had been designed for use as servants' quarters, but had since become the storage nook for stray linens, pillows, lamps, and old clothes.

Neither Neil nor I spoke as we picked our path to the window. "Do you think this is it?" I asked.

"If it opens easily, I imagine not," he said. "But don't worry, I brought this." He reached into his pocket and pulled out a sturdy flathead screwdriver.

My eyes widened. "I don't want to damage anything—do you think that'll help?"

"It's a screwdriver. They can open lots of things."

"You're referencing *Doctor Who* again, aren't you?"

He winked at me. "Let's take a look."

We knelt in front of the ledge, and I removed the chintz cushion. I tried to lift the seat and it didn't budge.

"I think we've got the right one at least," Neil said, reaching for it. He jiggled the lip of the seat back and forth, and then side to side.

As he shifted it to the left, the hinge seemed to loosen. We looked at each other and grasped the seat together, pushing it to the left and then up.

"Oh," I breathed as the lid raised without argument and revealed its contents.

Letters. Bundles and bundles of letters.

Food is never just food. It's also a way of getting at something else: who we are, who we have been, and who we want to be.

—MOLLY WIZENBERG

I scooped out one stack of letters with careful hands and examined the envelope until my eyes confirmed what my heart knew to be true. "Look," I said, holding one out for Neil to see. "It's addressed to my grandmother. Look at the return address."

"G. Roussard."

I ran my finger over the brittle envelope. "My grandfather wrote this, my real grandfather. Look at his handwriting!"

"It's very neat," Neil observed.

"But confident, don't you think? Confident but unpretentious."

Neil nudged my shoulder. "True, but there's a hint of cynicism in the way he dots his *i*'s."

"Don't tease." I held the stack closer to the ceiling light and squinted. "I don't know—it was only a few months ago that I found this man even existed."

"Are you going to take all of the letters with you?"

I hesitated. In my hands I held my grandmother's letters. I felt strange removing them from the house without telling Sandrine, but a part of me worried about her response. Without much self-examination, I knew I would smuggle them out of the country under my clothes or behind my suitcase lining if I had to.

Not that such lengths would be necessary. "I'll take them back to my room tonight and figure out what all is in there—that's a lot of paper, and they may not all be Mireille's."

"Cécile said it was their spot."

I shrugged. "Sometimes people stash things in strange places. You wouldn't believe the things my sister Sophie keeps in her glove compartment. Let's just say—not gloves."

"I'll keep that in mind."

"Anyway, I'll look at them tonight and ask Sandrine about them in the morning."

With little effort I found a mismatched chintz pillowcase that made an adequate antique mailbag. We walked hand in hand back down to the family wing.

Neil pressed a kiss against my temple. "I'm glad I get to be here with you."

I turned my head for a real kiss. "I'm glad you're here too. I just . . ."

"Yes?"

"We're here. At a French chateau. I worry that all of this . . . as wonderful as it is . . ." I sighed. We'd reached my door. I opened the door and put the letters on the bed gently before wrapping my arms around Neil's neck. "Real life is waiting for us. All of this is like an episode of *The Bachelor*. You know"—I waved my hand—"without the excessive drinking, crying, and filmed confessionals."

"You don't know. I could be going back to my room only to spill my heart out to my webcam."

"True."

Neil stroked my cheek with his thumb. "One day at a time?"

I nodded. "One day at a time."

"One very good day at a time," Neil echoed before he lowered his lips to mine.

I lifted my chin to meet him halfway. As we kissed, I breathed in his scent, enjoyed the feel of his arms around me. This was his superpower—as long as he held me in his embrace, I truly believed that everything would be okay. I believed we would have a future, that we would be able to work through the massive challenges that our relationship faced. Distance, culture, work—none of it mattered when Neil's hands entwined in my hair and his lips crushed my own.

We parted with breathless reluctance. "Sleep well," I said, looking up at him shyly.

"Good night," Neil said with a nod, his eyes still on my lips. He turned and left for his own room before either of us could change our minds on an encore.

With my toes still tingling, I closed my door and turned to my bedtime reading. Sitting on the bed with crossed legs, I removed each tied bundle from the pillowcase and spread them out over the quilt. One by one, I carefully untied each stack to evaluate the contents.

Some were letters both to and from Mireille, between her and Gabriel. Others were addressed to Cécile.

Next I began to arrange each bundle by date, but discovered quickly that they'd already been in chronological order and bundled per month. Curious.

In the end, I painstakingly laid out each bundle, took a picture of each letter, and then retied the stack before moving on to the next. Once I'd photographed every letter—some of them containing multiple pages, all of them both front and back—I downloaded all of the photos onto my computer and began the painstaking process of ordering each letter according to the date.

I'd photographed the envelopes as well, so most of the letters consisted of three photographs. I organized the letter photographs into folders, and then ordered the folders by date.

I was nearly finished when I heard a knock at my door. "Come in," I called.

Neil's face appeared. "I heard typing and figured you were awake." He looked to me, looked at the letters on the still-made bed, and back to me. "Juliette—did you sleep?"

I looked at him. "Is it morning?"

He nodded, a bemused smile on his face. "Yes, love, it's morning. Did the letters keep you up?"

"I photographed and organized them so I could read them without worrying about damage." I looked out the window. Sure enough, morning daylight streamed past the edge of the curtain. "I guess I stayed up all night."

"You look a little cross-eyed. Cute," he amended quickly, "but cross-eyed."

"I . . . feel a little sleepy."

"I imagine so. Sandrine's making breakfast for the chateau guests and staff. Are you hungry?"

"Yes, I think so," I answered after thinking a moment.

"What had you working so hard?"

I stood and showed him my system. Neil's eyebrows lifted. "I'm impressed. I would hire you as a research assistant."

"Oh really?"

He dropped a kiss on my lips. "If you weren't so overqualified, yes."

I snorted. "Overqualified? You're funny. I don't know the first thing about immunology or lab work—I'd be the worst."

"I bet you'd be able to write grant applications like a pro, and if you cook, you've got a handle on basic chemistry. So, these letters—are you still wanting to keep the hard copies?"

"They're family history; they're important. It looks like most of them are between Grand-mère and Grand-tante Cécile, but some are from Gabriel. I don't have anything else of his. With the digital copies, there's no way they can be damaged by repeated reading." I sighed. "What I am disappointed about, though, is I didn't find any more photographs. I was hoping for, I don't know, a wedding photo or something."

"Would she have mailed it?"

"Maybe. Probably not. It was a nice dream, though." I looked up at him. "It does make me wonder if there's another stash somewhere around here of photographs."

"Didn't you ask Sandrine about that already?"

"I did. But then, she didn't seem to know about the letters. There're a lot of things in this house."

"So you need to be able to ask Cécile."

I nodded. "Probably. And who knows, maybe Grand-mère took them with her when she moved to the States. I've been through her belongings, though, and haven't found anything new. Maybe they're hidden somewhere I've not looked yet—she was certainly trying to keep it a secret." I ran a hand through my hair. "I wasn't trained to be a superspy."

"No?"

"Nope."

Neil tucked my hair behind my ear. "Let's get you some breakfast."

A quick glance at the mirror told me that I looked oily and red-eyed and a little wild around the edges. My vanity got the best of me as I pulled my hair back, used a blotting paper on my nose, and zipped on a lace-trimmed hoodie.

"Bonjour!" Sandrine sang out when she saw us. "I made American pancakes this morning. Would you like some? I am about to serve the first batch to my guests."

"I can make some for us," I said, taking in the batter, the greased griddle, and the bowl of sliced apricots. "You can go and fuss over the guests."

"*Ah, bien,*" she answered, loading a platter full of beautiful apricot-studded pancakes to take away. "Bon, I pour the batter and place the slices over the top just so. They're very moist because of the *crème fraîche,* and then I serve them with a *crème anglaise.*"

"It looks great," I said, taking the ladle in hand and stirring the batter, just to get a feel for the consistency. "Don't worry about us."

Sandrine grinned her thanks, and I turned my attention to breakfast.

"I can do that, if you want to sit," Neil offered.

I waved him away. "I can make pancakes in my sleep."

"I liked that she called them 'American pancakes.'"

"Well, they are. French pancakes are crepes, and German pancakes are a whole other deal altogether." I ladled four puddles of batter onto the griddle, enjoying the sizzling sound they made as batter met butter. "English pancakes are closer to crepes, just thicker."

"Reminds me of when I was in Toronto for a conference. I tried to order a Canadian bacon and pineapple pizza but got tongue-tied."

I laughed and began to arrange the apricots. "What did you do?"

"I said 'Hawaiian' instead. The guy seemed to know what I was talking about."

"Quick thinking."

"Thank you."

"In truth, between the crème fraîche and the crème anglaise topping, I think these pancakes are a bit more trans-Atlantic than American."

"I'll take your word for it."

He watched as I tested the edge of a pancake and then flipped it over with a decisive flick of the wrist.

I met his gaze over my shoulder. "What?"

"I like watching you cook."

"That's good, because I do it a lot," I said, flashing him a saucy smile.

A few moments later we sat down with breakfast. Tea for me and coffee for him, with plates of steaming apricot-laced pancakes smothered in chilled crème anglaise.

"I need the recipe for this," I said, three bites in. "Clementine would kill for this. Or reverse-engineer it."

"They're very good. Maybe you could make them for my parents when you meet them."

"Your parents?" My back straightened. "I thought they were in North Carolina."

"They are, but I think they're hoping to visit Memphis for a day or two to meet you. That is, if you're still wanting to come out to Memphis."

"When did they say that?"

"I talked to them a couple days ago."

"Oh," I said. "That's great."

As the words left my mouth, I tried to decide if I meant them or not. Sure, he'd met my parents. Sure, I wanted to meet his parents. But . . . despite the fact that we'd broken up and reconciled, our relationship was still early days. We were still getting accustomed to each other. His parents traveling to meet me? Suddenly it felt like a lot of pressure.

I cut another bit of pancake with my knife and fork. Who was I to talk about pressure? Back in Portland, I'd brought Neil to a dinner with my entire family. Personal questions had been asked. Had there been a podium, it could have looked like a press conference, just with better food and fewer camera flashes. There was no way his parents could prove to be more awkward than my family, en masse.

Could they?

"So," I began, trying to find the best way to broach the topic, "what have you told them? About me, I mean."

Neil's eyes gleamed. "Fishing for compliments?"

My face flushed. "No, I mean . . . I was just curious what you'd told them. About us." And me, by extension.

"I told them that you're smart," he said. "And lovely, and a wonderful cook, and one of the most creative, interesting people I've ever met. I told them we're dating, and that I'm very serious about you."

My heart swelled. "Oh," I said simply.

"Nothing you didn't already know."

"I don't know about that. I'm not sure you ever said, 'Juliette' "—I affected a lowered voice, which didn't sound anything like a man—" 'I am very serious about you.' "

Neil rolled his eyes before giving me an affectionate grin. "I'm not going to dignify that with a response."

"Then don't." I put my fork down. "So—we never talked about travel plans. I've got four days planned here, and then Italy next. I'll be in Rome first, then a few days in Montalcino for my grandfather's birthday before I fly home."

Neil picked up his espresso cup. "I've got the time off. If you think having me at your grandfather's party is too complicated, I can fly home."

I grasped his hand. "Of course I want you there. Are you sure you're ready for sixty-two Italians fueled up on espresso and cake?"

"You know I'm only in it for the cake."

"You're incorrigible," I said, but I couldn't wipe the smile from my face.

~ Apricot-Crème Fraîche Pancakes ~

1 cup whole wheat pastry flour
1/2 cup all-purpose flour
2 teaspoons baking powder, preferably aluminum-free
3/4 teaspoon fine sea salt
1/4 teaspoon nutmeg
1/2 cup crème fraîche
3/4 cup whole milk
3 tablespoons honey
2 large eggs
2 teaspoons vanilla bean paste or vanilla extract
2 tablespoons butter, to grease the skillet
3 ripe apricots, peels removed and sliced thin (if apricots are
    out of season, fresh raspberries are a delicious alternative)

In a small bowl, sift together the flours, baking powder, salt, and nutmeg. In a medium bowl, whisk together the crème fraîche, milk, honey, eggs, and vanilla.

Add the dry ingredients to the crème fraîche mixture slowly, stirring constantly, mixing only until just combined.

Melt butter in a large skillet over medium-low heat until it begins to froth. Ladle the batter onto a griddle using a 1/3 cup measure. Arrange 3–4 slices of apricot on top of each pancake. Cook for 3–4 minutes, or until the batter bubbles and the edges begin to firm. Flip and cook the opposite side until golden, another 1–2 minutes.

Serve pancakes immediately with crème anglaise ladled over the top. Refrigerate any leftovers. If you're not in the mood to make the crème anglaise (recipe below), simply serve with hot maple syrup.

Makes about 10 pancakes.

~Vanilla Bean Crème Anglaise ~

4 large egg yolks
2½ tablespoons sugar
1 cup whole milk
¾ cup heavy cream
1 teaspoon vanilla bean paste

Prepare an ice bath by filling a large bowl halfway with ice, then nestling a second bowl (ideally metal) inside the ice. Set a wire-mesh strainer over the second bowl.

Using a mixer, beat the yolk and sugar together for about two minutes, or until pale and creamy.

Combine the milk, cream, and vanilla bean paste in a medium-sized saucepan, and bring to a simmer over medium heat, stirring constantly to prevent scalding. Once the cream has just reached a simmer, remove from heat and reduce burner to medium-low.

With the mixer running on low, slowly pour ⅓ cup of the hot cream into the sugared yolks. Blend until well incorporated, then pour the remaining cream into the mixing bowl.

Transfer the custard to the saucepan, and return it to the stove. If it's frothy; the air will dissipate as it cooks. Stir over medium-low heat for 5–10 minutes, or until the mixture can coat a spoon. For thicker custard, cook a few minutes longer. If the custard resists thickening, increase the heat; avoid a boil, as the egg will cook and the sauce will separate. Once the custard has thickened, remove it from the stove and pour it through the mesh strainer and into the chilled bowl.

Chill the sauce in a covered container for three hours, or overnight. The custard will thicken as it cools. Makes about 2 cups.

Bread, milk and butter are of venerable antiquity.
They taste of the morning of the world.

—Leigh Hunt

*A*fter I'd finished breakfast and showered, I felt infinitely more myself. Without air conditioning, my long, dark hair dried twice as fast as usual. Once I'd dressed in a pale chambray shirtdress, I finished organizing the photo files and then set off to find Sandrine.

I tied my hair back as I walked. This time of day, Sandrine went through the guest rooms, tidying and refreshing linens. I found my cousin in the "bee room," which was decorated in golden honey tones with a honeycomb motif and accented in dark woods.

"Cou-cou!" I called from the doorway. "Can I give you a hand?"

"Bonjour!" Sandrine looked up from the bed she was making. "Of course."

I took the sheets on the opposite side and tucked them under the mattress. "Cécile told me where to find Mireille's letters last night."

"Ah, bon! That is good news. Did you find what you were looking for?"

"I did find letters," I said, "but I haven't been able to read them yet."

"But you must take them with you! You must have them."

"Thank you," I breathed, my smile wide and real. Probably tired as well. "I spent the night making digital copies, but there's something about the real thing, you know?"

Sandrine tugged the coverlet into place before replacing and fluffing the pillows. "I am glad you found them. Letters are an important part of a family's history."

"I was wondering if there were any family photos in the chateau. I noticed

I don't have any photos of Grand-mère before my mom was a toddler. For that matter, I'd love photos of my mom as a baby. Do you know if there are any?"

"It is almost a miracle that you found the letters, because this house holds its secrets well. I have some photos, but I don't remember seeing many of Mireille. You're welcome to look, but the house ate my own childhood photos long ago. The house is always open to you—if you would like to try to unearth more of the house's secrets, do try. It has always fussed at me when I've tried."

"The house fussed at you?"

Sandrine gave a French shrug. "It was for a boring and practical reason—I wanted to tap into the existing pipes to add another en suite bath. The house was not happy—there was a burst of water and a *petite deluge*." She held up a hand. "Clean water—*merci, mon Dieu*—but a mess, nonetheless."

"Oh my goodness," I said, noting as I listened how much her voice sounded like my mother's. The accent was much thicker, of course, but the resemblance certainly ran strong with the women of the family. Their facial features were similar as well, although Sandrine had inherited her coloring from her father, *Grand-oncle* Richard.

"Another time," Sandrine continued, "I went looking for some old clothes of my mother's, and I could not find the key to one of the closets. I thought between Auguste and me that we had all of the keys—I even tried an old skeleton key. The chateau—it is not haunted. I know Americans like their haunted houses, but it's not. It's just a large old house with opinions."

"Ah. Well, I will try to look and not cause a cave-in."

"I think the house likes you," Sandrine said, her voice lowered conspiratorially. "It likes your mother a great deal."

"That's . . . nice of it." I closed my mouth and smiled; any moment now and I would run out of reasonable responses. "Anyway, we'll be out of your hair in a few days."

"And on to Paris?"

"That's the plan."

"Auguste and I will miss you. I know *ma mere* has enjoyed having you for conversation. But you will enjoy Paris. And Neil? He is going too?"

I couldn't hold back that smile. "He is. And he's coming to Italy with me after."

"He is a good man, your Neil."

My Neil. "Yes," I said. "I think so."

We chatted about the chateau, Cécile, and the family's penchant for bichon frises (theirs had passed quietly of old age two months prior) as we finished up the rest of the rooms. After working on Grand-mère's building for so long, the simple domestic chores felt natural and easy, even relaxing. Make beds, dust, sweep, vacuum, repeat. Except this time I had the company of another woman.

As we began the last room, Sandrine shifted the conversation from family news to advice with the élan of a talk-show host.

"You must be good to him, your Neil," she said, "but do not be too accommodating. I have noticed that American women will do whatever a man wants. But that is not the French way. And you"—she pointed at me—"are French."

I decided against reminding her that I was half-Italian as well.

Instead, I nodded to indicate listening.

"You must not make things too easy for him, but do let him know that you appreciate him." She raised her eyebrows for emphasis.

I felt my cheeks turn pink. "I . . . We're not . . . I mean, we don't—"

Sandrine waved a hand. "You don't have to go to bed with him to keep him. The important part is to love him, but stay a little mysterious. Make him work a little."

"I'll keep that in mind," I answered, turning my face away until my flush subsided.

For lunch I decided to rummage through Sandrine's fridge to see what I could make. Inside I found crème fraîche left over from the morning's pancakes, celery, and an opened jar of olives. In the pantry I found a beautiful tomato, a lemon, shallots, and most importantly, packaged tuna. On the counter sat some beautiful croissants, left over from Sandrine's pastry offerings to her guests.

Neil stepped into the kitchen, face flushed. "Hi," he said, grinning when he spotted me. "I just finished patching up the roof over the shed with Auguste. It's gotten hot out there." He paused to kiss my cheek. "How are you?"

I returned his kiss with a real one, enjoying the way he smelled of sandalwood and sun. "I'm good. Are you hungry? I was just thinking of piecing together some lunch."

"Are you happy to be back in the kitchen?"

"Of course," I said. "I haven't cooked in so long my fingers are feeling tingly, and ladling pancakes doesn't count. Do you like tuna?"

"I like it if you're making it."

"Just be warned," I said, reaching for a chef's knife to begin chopping the shallot, "it's not your mother's tuna sandwich."

"No?"

"I'm thinking of something Provence-inspired. Tuna Provençal is very traditional here, made with fresh tuna steaks and vegetables. I was thinking of incorporating those flavors into a sandwich with the croissant."

Neil gave a crooked smile. "I like the way you talk about food."

I grinned back at him. "I just like you."

Another kiss, and he left to shower before the meal. I set to work chopping, juicing, stirring, and toasting. Sandrine stepped inside the kitchen. "What is this for lunch? So nice to have someone else cooking in here for a change."

"Provençal-inspired tuna sandwiches," I told her. "On croissants."

Sandrine wrinkled her nose. "A sandwich inside a croissant? That sounds very . . . American."

I pointed my spoon at her. "But tasty!"

Sandrine eyed my handiwork warily.

"Would you try just a bite?"

"I will try," she said, though I could see in her eyes she remained unconvinced.

The tuna salad came together simply enough once I finished prepping the ingredients. After spreading olive oil inside the cut halves of the croissant and toasting them lightly, I filled them with the savory tuna mixture. "Lunch is ready!" I called, hoping that either Neil or Sandrine remained within shouting distance.

Auguste arrived first, with Sandrine close behind. "So much yelling at my chateau," Auguste mused. "It used to be so quiet . . ."

I snorted. "I've heard enough stories from Grand-tante Cécile that I know that's not exactly true."

Sandrine laughed, while Auguste examined the sandwiches on the sideboard that I'd assembled. "So that is the sandwich?"

"It is." I plated it quickly, serving it with a pickle spear.

Neil appeared a split second later, his hair damp and slightly curly from his shower.

It was a good look for him.

"Hungry?" I asked, enjoying the opportunity to look at him.

"Always," he answered, grinning.

Sandrine winked at me.

We sat at the wooden farmhouse table together and enjoyed our sandwiches. At least, Neil and I did.

Sandrine bit into her sandwich with caution, and I watched, making an effort not to laugh. "How is it?" I asked.

"Different."

"Different good or different bad?"

"Different good," she conceded. "And yet I still believe a croissant is meant to be eaten only in the morning, and only with butter and jam."

"I agree," said Auguste, but I couldn't take offense, considering that he'd finished his sandwich and any remaining crumbs before I'd made it even halfway through.

If Nico were there, he would have railed that this was the problem with modern French cuisine, its inability to innovate, to try things that hadn't been around since the days of Marie-Antoine Carême.

But he wasn't there, and I decided that sometimes winning a small battle on the side of the tuna sandwich was good enough for me.

☙ ❧

To: Caterina, cdesanto@beneculinary.com
From: Me, jdalisa@twobluedoors.com

My dear sister,

So sorry to hear about your hall bathroom. Christian is a very enterprising child; I am hopeful these will be funny stories you tell at the cocktail party before he receives a marine biology award. Or something.

We'll be heading to Paris soon. I'm planning to stay in Provence longer than anticipated to get some extra time with Grand-tante Cécile. She remembers, some days, good stories about her and Grand-mère that I've not heard before. Missing Grand-mère, I've enjoyed hearing more about her, and being near Cécile is like having her nearer for just a little while.

As for Éric . . . it was surreal to see him in Seattle. You'd like his restaurant, and I don't have to tell you the food was good. I don't know, it was kind of one of those "if only" sorts of conversations where both parties are nostalgic and wishful, though no one's willing to make a change to make any of it a reality. He married and divorced and is single now, and while I certainly got the idea that we could pick up where we left off (or as much as a person can after, what, six years?)—I know Éric. He's only ever going to be married to his restaurant. So it was one of those "If only, but won't happen" kinds of conversations.

But the best part that came out of it was that L'uccello Blu's restaurant's closing wasn't my fault. When it happened, I felt very responsible—Éric was such an integral part, and I'd made him go away. Éric assured me that in fact there were other factors going on in the business end of things, and that wasn't something I needed to carry.

Which is nice, you know?

I'm not hung up on Éric at all (just wanted to make sure that's clear). Things are really great with Neil, though I am concerned about what's going to happen when we both get back to real life. Like I said, I'm committed to life in Portland right now, and he's pretty settled in Memphis. Trying not to worry about it too much . . .

Anything you want me to bring you back from Paris? Not that I'd mail it to you—you'll have to come to Portland for it (because I'm sneaky like that).

Love to you, Damian, and the twins. Speaking of . . . what's Luca up to?

J

To: Me, jdalisa@twobluedoors.com
From: Caterina, cdesanto@beneculinary.com

Oh, sweet Luca. Of the twins, he's always been the cuddly, quieter one. This is nice, on one hand, but it also means that it takes me longer to discover what kind of shenanigans he's into. Last week he very quietly decided to become creative in the kitchen. Applesauce and Elmer's glue were involved.

Something from Paris? I'll have to think on that . . . You'll be glad to hear I'm planning a trip out for July; I told Mom I'd be there for her second round of chemo. She gave me a song and dance about how I didn't have to bother. (I'm sure you've heard this. I think it's based on an Édith Piaf song or something equally plaintive.) Anyway, I'll be out with the boys, and Damian too if he can get the time off work. If so, I'd be happy to lend him out as a handyman.

Anyway, looking forward to seeing you! Let's take a trip to Anthropologie, if you can spare the time. And if I can be of any help with the restaurant, let me know (not Nico. Because he'd probably get dramatic over how self-sufficient he is and bless him, we both know that's not true). When are you getting your kitchen equipment? I can clean an oven like no one's business. My skills with an oven brush are slow-clap worthy. Children dream of one day being able to clean an oven like me. Old men weep.

Yes, I am tired, and it is late. How did you guess?

Love, Cat

P.S. Sandrine e-mailed me and said you made her eat a sandwich out of a croissant, like an American. Oh, you imperialist you . . .

~ PROVENÇAL-STYLE TUNA CROISSANT SANDWICHES ~

The key to these sandwiches is the quality of the ingredients, particularly the tomato, tuna, and the croissants. I recommend oil-packed tuna, a sweet, ripe tomato, and croissants from your favorite bakery. To toast the croissants without damaging the delicate pastry, use a preheated oven or a toaster oven. You can find crème fraîche in the refrigerated section of well-stocked grocery stores. In a pinch, you can substitute it with sour cream or mayonnaise.

1 clove garlic, minced fine
1/2 a tomato, seeded and diced
1/4 cup diced black olives
1/4 cup diced celery
2 tablespoons minced shallots

1 cup crème fraîche
10 ounces albacore tuna, drained
1 tablespoon *herbes de Provence*
1 teaspoon dill
Fresh lemon juice, to taste
Salt and pepper, to taste
2 fresh croissants
2 tablespoons olive oil

Add all ingredients—save the croissants and olive oil—in a bowl and mix together. Taste, and add lemon juice, salt, and pepper to taste.

Cut the croissants in half and brush the cut-sides with olive oil. Toast lightly.

Spread tuna mixture on the bottom croissant, cover, secure with a toothpick (if that's your thing), and serve immediately.

We are indeed much more than what we eat, but what
we eat can nevertheless help us to be much more than
what we are.

—ADELLE DAVIS

*A*fter lunch I poked around the house for a few hours, hoping I
might find a stray photo sticking out that would answer all of
my questions.

Not surprisingly, I found nothing.

I even tried the locked door Sandrine had described. For the sake of curiosity, I examined the door and its frame. I could see the hinges, but they were inset in such a way that I couldn't pull the hinge pins free without first dismantling the door frame. Even then, the door had a bolt, so in all likelihood I wouldn't be able to open the door without a fire ax.

After dinner Neil and I took a walk around the lavender fields. The late-evening light cast long shadows over the rows; a light breeze teased the ends of my hair.

"There's a locked door," I said. "At the chateau."

"Oh?"

"Sandrine can't open it, and none of the keys fit it." I looked out on the fields. "There was a key in Grand-mère's prep table. It looked old."

"You think it might fit the door?"

"Hard to say, but it's not like I brought it with me. Stupid."

"Hey." He elbowed me in the side. "You didn't know there would be a mysterious locked door."

"That's true." I took a deep breath. "I love the lavender. All problems seem smaller in a field of lavender."

Neil grinned and lifted his arm, leading me in a twirl. I spun, my skirt flaring out, my head tilted back with joy. "I think lavender makes me giddy," he said.

"I don't mind." I squeezed his hand as we continued down the row. "My tickets out of Charles de Gaulle are nontransferable, nonnegotiable, non-everything. There are things I want to accomplish in Paris, and I certainly can't dig into my Italy time, but . . ."

Neil's hand slipped to the small of my back. "I don't really want to leave here either. I keep thinking about what it would be like to stay."

"Yeah?"

"Do you think I'd make a good lavender farmer?"

"Oh, the best," I said. "Immunology is kind of like botany, right?"

"People have cells. Plants have cells. There's a lot of crossover."

"I'm glad we have that settled. So . . . Paris?"

"Parree," Neil drawled in his best fake French accent. Or worst. They were probably interchangeable. "The city of lights!"

I grinned at his enthusiasm. "Have you been?"

"Nope. But I'm glad I'm going with you. I get the feeling you know your way around the city."

"Not like some," I demurred. "My sister Cat is the Paris savant. She knows all the back alleys and roads, the best baguette stands, the best boutiques. I've only been a couple times, and it's been years." I paused. "I realize that sounds terrible. Most people haven't been to Paris at all."

"Not unless you're counting Paris, Texas."

"Or Paris, Illinois."

"Paris, Maine," Neil countered.

"Paris, Idaho," I added with a nod. "And Paris, Arkansas."

"There's a Paris, Arkansas?" Neil asked, eyebrows high.

"Yup. Kentucky too. And a couple others . . ."

"How do you know this?"

"A potent blend of *Where in America Is Carmen Sandiego?,* curiosity, and the Internet."

"Who said technology never offered anything useful?"

"I'm guessing victims of e-mail scams."

Neil snorted.

"Shall we head out tomorrow, then? Maybe around ten or so? It's not a short drive, and if we leave early we can take a break or something before dinner."

"You're the tour guide," Neil said. "When you come to Memphis I'll have more input, but here—it's entirely up to you."

"Ten o'clock, then." I slipped my arm into the crook of his elbow. "Let's go tell Sandrine and Auguste."

Sandrine was sad to hear we would be leaving, but understood. "You must visit Chez Paul, on Rue de Charonne. The charcuterie is very good. Ah! But we will miss you both. You will come back, yes?"

"Of course," Neil answered before I had a chance. And I knew, looking at his earnest face, that he meant it.

Auguste bade us good-bye with tears and kisses on each cheek, as well as jars of his prized honey and wedges of lavender-infused cheese.

Saying good-bye to Cécile felt more bittersweet. "Oh," she said, patting my hand. She paused as if she were considering something, and then patted my hand again. *"Bon voyage."*

I gave her a hug; for a small moment, it felt like hugging Grand-mère.

The drive into Paris felt interminable, with heavy spring rain that started after Riom and bouts of sluggish traffic that drove us both a little crazy—never mind the fact that we were driving separate rental cars for the first leg.

"I live in Memphis," Neil said after we turned in his car. "I didn't think people could drive any worse."

"It's not worse. It takes skill to drive close enough to someone to be able to shake the other driver's hand."

Neil shook his head. "All those *Top Gear* episodes. I thought I'd be better prepared."

We made it to the hotel just before dusk. At least I think it was dusk. At any rate, the sky shifted from wet and overcast to dark and wet and overcast.

Living in Portland, I considered myself fairly waterproof, but it was a lot of water for a summer evening. We schlepped our luggage inside through the rain, and retired to our separate rooms for a nap before dinner.

When I awoke, the rain had stopped. I stretched, fluffed my hair, and checked my e-mail, sitting up straighter when I realized I had an e-mail from Élodie Armant.

To: Me, jdalisa@twobluedoors.com
From: Élodie Armant, elodie@elodieenparis.fr

Bonjour, and welcome to Paris! I was so delighted to hear from your sister that you were in town. We must have tea and pastries—I know the perfect place. Do you have a mobile with you?

Bisous!

Élodie A.

By the time I met Neil outside the hotel, the clouds had begun to clear and a particularly Parisian variation of petrichor filled the air. We walked together under an umbrella—loaned to us by the *gardienne*—until we reached Chez Paul, where we dined on hearty bistro fare, balanced by a green salad spiked with dandelion greens and vibrant yellow dandelion petals.

"The secret of French food," I told Neil between bites, "is that nothing goes to waste. After so many wars, the French learned how to cook everything. Which," I noted, loading my fork with sole, "is usually in a large quantity of butter."

He chuckled. "Everything is better with butter."

"Well, to be technical, there are four mother sauces. But butter goes in most of them. Anyway, the dandelion greens—leave it to a Frenchwoman to decide they make for good eating."

"It was a woman who decided that?"

"Would a man get adventurous with weeds?"

"Good point."

We laughed together, and I reveled in the joy of being in Paris and having someone to share it with.

"Caterina helped me get in touch with a friend of hers," I said, changing the subject. "She's a food blogger here in Paris. We're working on plans to go to tea."

"I thought everyone around here drank coffee."

"They do, but tea salons are in fashion."

"Well, I'm glad you'll be able to meet," Neil said, his eyes crinkling at the corners. "How does Caterina know her?"

"The thing about Cat," I explained, "is that she knows everybody. Six degrees of separation and all that gets a lot slimmer when she's in the mix, and not just because she helped cater an event attended by a couple Kennedys. With Élodie, I think they went to school together at the University of Oregon. Cat went to business school after culinary school. Élodie was studying abroad at the time; I think they met in one of Cat's Italian classes."

"Cat didn't already speak Italian?"

"She did, but she wanted to make sure she could teach it, not just from a native speaker's perspective. And the form of Italian we grew up with has its own regional bent; Cat is nothing if not thorough."

"I'd like to meet her sometime."

"She'd like to meet you. You have no idea."

After a flurry of text messages, Élodie and I met the following day for tea and pastries at La Pâtisserie des Rêves, on Rue de Longchamp. "Juliette!" she said when she saw me approach. Despite having never met in person, we clasped hands and exchanged air kisses. "I would have recognized you anywhere!" Élodie exclaimed. "You look just like your sister." She looked over my shoulder. "And . . . you are alone?"

"Neil's at the hotel. He had some work to do."

Élodie's lower lip jutted. I would have looked ridiculous had I made the same expression, but it made her look charming and, well, French. "That is too bad. Caterina asked me to take a picture of him if he came. She's very jealous, you know, that I get to see him first."

"If she asked me," I said dryly, "I would send her a picture."

"Ah, but where is the fun in that?" She laughed. "Bon! Let us go inside."

We stepped through the glass doors and greeted the proprietor. While the front was borderline nondescript, the inside sparkled in citrusy sorbet tones— lime green, hot pink, and orange—with the palette grounded in crisp white.

The shelves along the walls were lit, highlighting the contents of each cubby—an assortment of shining *viennoiserie,* such as brioche and croissants, as well as packaged items such as brightly colored fresh marshmallows. In the center of the room stood an island, which featured domes suspended from cords connected to the ceiling.

Beneath the domes were beautifully arranged pastries, both protected and highlighted by the glass.

"It's incredible," I breathed, taking in the display.

"The domes are actually plastic, quite light," Élodie explained. "And see at the top? They're counter-weighted, so you can pull the cord. Underneath, you see, it is refrigerated slate to keep them chilled. *C'est bon, non?*"

"*C'est très, très bon.*" I looked around to figure out the system. Unlike most Parisian bakeries that kept all of their goods safe in a glass-enclosed pastry case, this bakery appeared to be mostly self-serve. I watched, curious, as another woman told a waiter she wanted one of the *tartes au citron* featured under a dome. The waiter left, disappeared to the back, and returned with a tarte on a plate for her.

Mystery solved, we made our choices. Élodie ordered a pot of tea for us to share. I ordered a Paris-Brest, daisy-shaped and filled with praline cream, as well as a chocolate-wrapped éclair.

I could always take up running when I got home.

We took our goods to the seating area, where white tables and chairs waited with inviting red and magenta-hued cushions.

"So tell me," Élodie asked as we sat at the last open table, "what brought you to Paris? Caterina was vague—not that you *need* a reason to be in Paris."

I told her about the restaurant that Nico and I were opening, and how we were using Grand-mère's *patisserie* space. "But the real reason I'm in Paris," I said, "is that I'm trying to find out more about our grand-mère."

"Ah, bon. What are you trying to find out?"

The waiter interrupted with our tea. I thanked him before answering.

"I know she went to pastry school," I said, "here in Paris, in the late thirties."

"Which school? Do you know the name?"

"L'école de Paris de Pâtisserie. It was rare, you know. Rare enough for a woman, but she came from a good family in Provence."

"Not working class, then."

"No—her father was a lower baron. But she loved working with pastry, so my great-grandfather allowed her to study. I'd like to find out more about her time—school records, that sort of thing. And"—I chose my words carefully, remembering that she and Caterina were friends—"she had a friend. Gabriel Roussard."

"A friend?" Élodie lifted an eyebrow.

"She mentioned him in letters to her sister. I know he was a Jew." I took a sip of tea to look casual. "I was just curious about him."

"And he was in Paris?"

"*Oui.* Also, I think he may have had a relative who worked at Van Cleef & Arpels. Anyway, I was hoping to find more information while here."

"You have how many days in Paris?"

"Three more."

Élodie pressed her hand to her heart. "You do *not* want to spend any of your three days in Paris waiting in line to talk to a record keeper who is not going to tell you anything. And while your accent is near perfect, you sound enough like an Américain that a particularly unpleasant individual might pretend not to be able to understand you."

"I know." I bit into a forkful of éclair. "This is really wonderful. This chocolate wrapping . . . it's perfect. Not too brittle."

"Monsieur Conticini is a genius."

"The waiting in line bit—I've braced myself for it. The rudeness too. What can I say?" I gave a shrug and took another bite. "My naiveté springs eternal."

"There are too many places for you to go, things for you to see—and eat! No, I cannot allow it. You must let me help."

I couldn't help but stare back blankly. "You want to help?"

"But of course! You are Caterina's sister, and my friend. If it were not for Caterina, I would not have passed my first Italian class and would have eaten at all the wrong restaurants. I owe her many favors, and since she is not here, I will use some of them for you. Now," she said, cutting into her *grand cru* decisively, "write down, please, the names of everyone you wish to find out about, and any information you have. Dates, places—anything at all, even if you do not think it is of use."

"Are you sure?"

"*Certainment.* And I have contacts and resources you do not have. Please, you must let me help."

"Thank you," I said, finding myself breathless. "Thank you so much!"

"I do require a small payment, though," Élodie said, holding her thumb and forefinger close together. "*Un petit prix.*"

"Yes?"

"You must take me to meet your Neil." Élodie's eyes sparkled. "And I shall take a picture. It's the least I can do for your sister."

"I'll give him a call," I said. "You're welcome to come with me in my car. He and I are sharing the rental."

"Then we shall drive to him."

I put my hand on Élodie's arm. "This research . . . I have not told my family much, because I don't know what it all means, not yet. I would appreciate your discretion."

"But of course," Élodie answered immediately, responding the way I'd hoped she would. To the French, discretion was next to godliness. "I will not say a word to Caterina."

"Thanks," I said, feeling both calmer and more excited. With Élodie's help, I might learn something new about my mysterious grandfather, Gabriel Roussard.

~ Nasturtium and Spring Greens Salad ~

For the salad:
1 generous handful mixed spring greens
2 strawberries, sliced and cut into matchsticks
1 tablespoon slivered almonds
1 ounce parmesan cheese, grated
Small handful nasturtium blossoms

For the dressing:
1 tablespoon champagne vinegar
1 tablespoon extra-virgin olive oil
1 tablespoon orange juice, preferably fresh-squeezed
1 tablespoon honey, to taste
$1^1/_2$ teaspoons dijon mustard
2 teaspoons poppy seeds, optional

For the dressing, whisk together all ingredients.

Toss greens and almonds with salad dressing. Sprinkle parmesan cheese and strawberries over the salad. Place blossoms over salad whole; serve immediately.

5

A clever cook can make good meat of a whetstone.

—Erasmus

To: Me, jdalisa@twobluedoors.com
From: Caterina, cdesanto@beneculinary.com

I CAN'T BELIEVE ÉLODIE GOT TO MEET NEIL!!!!! I knew she would try, but I thought you were wily enough to fend her off. AND SHE TOOK PICTURES!

I'm not offended. Not at all.

DO YOU HEAR THAT?? I'M NOT OFFENDED.

C

To: Caterina, cdesanto@beneculinary.com
From: Me, jdalisa@twobluedoors.com

That's very big of you. I'm sure Élodie was very ladylike and didn't rub it in.

If it would help, I can supply you with his last name, as well as some keywords that would help you when you're Googling him.

I'll be meeting his parents when I visit him in Memphis, hopefully in a couple months or sooner. If you're very helpful keeping this quiet w/ the family, maybe I can get my hands on a couple baby pictures for you.

Xoxo, J

To: Me, jdalisa@twobluedoors.com
From: Caterina, cdesanto@beneculinary.com

That's playing dirty.

But yes, on all counts. I want to know what my future nieces and nephews will look like when they're fresh from the oven.

C

To: Me, jdalisa@twobluedoors.com
From: Caterina, cdesanto@beneculinary.com

Thought of what to bring you from the trip. I made arrangements to source our olive oil from a supplier in Montalcino. He gave me two bottles—one goes to Nico (who will give it his final blessing and possibly set up a shrine to it—it's that good). You can have the other bottle. I'll mail it to you once I'm back, or hold it for ransom.

Xoxo, J

With Élodie's promise to scavenge through records for me, I used the time I would have spent in line waiting to speak with low-level government employees, in line waiting to get into restaurants or to speak with the proprietor of a cheese shop.

Neil and I ate dessert at Ladurée, bought crepes from street vendors, and spent a too-short afternoon at Musée Marmottan Monet.

We had a wonderful time, but all the while I knew it would soon come to a close.

The truth was, the longer I was gone, the more I was needed back home. The menus were back from the graphic designers and needed approval. The website development bids were in and needed to be examined. A pipe beneath the dishwasher had burst, requiring the immediate attentions of the family plumber, Gustavo. Frank Burrows, our primary investor, wanted to schedule a meeting after I returned.

Even Gigi, the bichon frise, had expressed her displeasure in my absence— Clementine wrote to tell me that Gigi had happily chewed through one of my shoes, to a point where, to quote my roommate, "I wouldn't have known it was a shoe if the other hadn't been four feet away, and that same yellow."

So I was down a matched pair of shoes, and no matter how many times I distracted myself with lavender macarons, I could hear the restaurant calling me home.

I began to pack my things that night, knowing we'd leave for Rome in the morning.

It made sense, I told myself. I'd pack up ahead of time, and then we'd go out for a fashionably late dinner.

It made sense, but I still felt sad. I didn't like it. The trip, being with Neil— packing reminded me of the fact that another leg of our trip had come to a close. In my head I knew we could never have stayed in France forever, walking in the lavender fields in Montagnac or exploring the nooks and crannies of Paris. We were normal people, Neil and I. We had work, and budgets, and families. We were grownups, and we had responsibilities.

And while I knew these things to be true, it didn't make the truth sting any less. Despite my efforts to bolster my spirits with practical reminders, my eyes began to fill with tears.

I was lost in my thoughts when Neil knocked on my door.

"Hi," I said, attempting a bright smile.

"Hi yourself." He took in my tear-stained face. After a moment, he nodded his head in the direction of the hall. "Let's go for a walk."

"I really should pack."

"Come on, Juliette. Let's go walk by the Seine."

So we did.

We started out at the Pont Neuf, Paris's oldest bridge. At first we admired it from afar, taking in the architecture and the details, the grotesque *mascarons* that decorated the structure. As the sun lowered, the bridge glowed, lit from below.

Neil held my hand in his. Neither of us spoke as we walked across the bridge.

He tugged me to a stop halfway across. "Let's look at the water."

"Sure," I said, tucking myself under his arm. The day had been warm, but now a chill breeze blew over the water.

"Stop worrying."

"I didn't say anything."

He pressed his finger to the space between my eyebrows. "Your brow is furrowed," he said. "I think that's the correct term for it."

I couldn't help but smile. "You learn that in Anatomy 101?"

"Something like that." He gave an approving nod. "Better."

"Glad you approve." I looked out over the water. "I don't want to go home."

"Me either."

"I'm worried . . . I'm worried this won't work once we get back to real life."

"Was it so bad earlier?"

"Give up seeing you every day? I'd say so."

He shrugged. "Touché. But for now, we'll make it work. We'll take trips. We'll talk. And later . . ."

I felt myself straighten. "Later?"

"What do you think about later?"

"I want there to be one."

He chuckled. "That was vague."

"You were vague too!" My voice sounded shrill to my own ears.

"Want to keep walking?"

I took a last look at the water from where we stood. "Fine."

We walked farther down the bridge and turned toward the Conciergerie on Quai de l'Horloge. "That's pretty, that building there," Neil said, pointing.

"It is pretty. It started life as a palace but got turned into a prison during the Revolution."

"Oh." Neil absorbed that information. "Nice-looking prison."

"It's a tourist attraction now. And it got a significant face-lift too during the nineteenth century. You wouldn't know it to look around, but the French love to remodel. Marie Antoinette's cell was refinished as a chapel in her honor."

"My sister made me watch the Sofia Coppola movie about her," Neil admitted.

"Oh?" I laughed. "What did you think?"

"Poufy."

I patted his arm. "Not your kind of movie?"

"No, but I got my sister to watch a Madame de Pompadour–themed episode of *Doctor Who* out of it."

"Well, there you go. The pastries in the movie were provided by Ladurée, you know."

"Where we went for macarons?"

"That's the one."

"Have you read any of your grandmother's letters yet?" Neil asked, slinging his arm around my shoulders.

"Not yet. I fall into bed exhausted every night—I want to give them my full attention." I snorted. "Not that I won't have distractions at home," I said. "But at least things will be a little quieter."

We continued walking down Quai de l'Horloge and turned on Boulevard du Palais toward the Sainte-Chapelle. "As for later—after this trip—I know that I want us to continue to get to know each other," he said.

"I'd like that."

"My job . . ." He paused, and I saw his thoughts pass over his face before he formed them into words. "I love it. Sometimes I think people criticize men for loving their jobs, but I don't care. I like what I do. I like who I work with, for the most part. I think God calls people to do different things, and he made me to be a researcher."

"I feel like you've had this conversation before."

He gave a sheepish grin. "I have. It's a favorite conversation topic of my sister's. I just wanted to be honest. We talked awhile ago about how I'm learning to be more comfortable with my feelings and not bury myself in work, but that doesn't make me love my job any less. That said, immunologists like me don't stay at the same facility through their whole career. Chicago has a large immunology scene, San Diego—there are research institutes across the country."

"Caterina's in Chicago."

"My friend Callan is originally from Chicago. All that to say, I might move somewhere else, but I don't know where that would be." He tilted his head up to take in the Sainte-Chapelle in all of its gothic, stained-glass glory, examined it, and then looked back at me.

I gave a sad smile. "With the restaurant, my family—my mom, and her health concerns right now—I don't see myself leaving Portland anytime soon."

"I didn't think so. It's challenging," Neil said. "But we found each other, didn't we?"

"We did."

We kept walking, neither of us speaking, and circled back up Quai des Orfèvres, back toward the bridge.

Once we got back onto the bridge, Neil led me to a clear spot where we could once again look out onto the river.

He squeezed my hand. "I know things are . . . not ideal. So we'll just hang on for now and see what happens."

"Yes," I said, dryly. "Specifically, to our cell phones."

"Hey." He spun me around until we were facing each other, his hands on my arms. Pedestrians parted around us, like a stream around a stone. "I'm all in, Jules," he said, his voice intense, his eyes locked on mine. "I'm all in, and I don't know how this is all going to work, but I want to find out. We are going to find out." Neil's mouth crooked upward in a half smile. "I don't know where we're going to be when we do, but right now, I don't need to."

I hugged him tight, resting my face against his chest. Despite the Parisian busyness surrounding us, I could hear his heartbeat through his button-down. "Okay," I said against the crisp cotton. "I believe you."

"And stop worrying. We're going to Italy," he reminded me. "You can't be sad in Italy."

6

Tomatoes and oregano make it Italian; wine and tarragon make it French. Sour cream makes it Russian; lemon and cinnamon make it Greek. Soy sauce makes it Chinese; garlic makes it good.

—ALICE MAY BROCK

We returned my rental car in Paris, and took the Eurorail train to Rome early the next morning. "We'll stop in Turin," I explained as we selected seats. "And then change trains to get to Rome."

He eyed the seats nervously. "These aren't reserved or anything?"

"Nope, just by section."

"That's . . . odd."

"Think of it as being like the subway, only with a first-class section. Or compartments—we might have one of those train cars later."

"Is there any way to tell?"

"Nope."

"And that doesn't bother you?"

"Don't be such an American," I told him with a wink before choosing a pair of seats. I gave Neil the window seat so that he'd potentially have a place to put his legs.

The other passengers settled into their seats; tourism being in high season, the seats opposite us filled quickly. But both passengers turned to their books, leaving Neil and I to our conversation.

"We'll stay with my cousin Letizia in Rome for a couple days before going to Montalcino," I explained. We'd been so focused on Sandrine and Cécile, on Grand-mère, on Paris, on each other, that we'd hardly discussed what would happen when we left France.

"Letizia offered me one of her cars," I continued. "And she'll pick us up from the station."

"One of her cars?" Neil questioned. "How many does she have?"

"Riccardo—her husband—is a car guy. You guys will probably get along like gangbusters, come to think of it. He likes to tinker, like my brother Alex."

"What do they do?"

"Riccardo is a *notario,* the Italian version of a corporate attorney. Letizia is a private chef. She's a lot like Cat, really, just more Italian."

"The sister I haven't met?"

"Right. So I guess that comparison wasn't particularly helpful. They're both chefs, both outgoing with a fearless streak."

"She'll probably remind me of you."

"Oh no," I said, shaking my head. "I'm boring and I second-guess myself. Letizia is the sort of person you invite to a dinner party full of accountants— she's smart and engaging, and she'll get everyone around the table singing the theme song from *Rocky,* in Italian."

Neil leaned close, eyebrow lifted. "You're not boring, and if you second-guess yourself, it just means you're prone to self-examination, which is a good thing. And I think you're smart and engaging, even if you don't encourage singing around the table like a hobbit."

I giggled. "A hobbit?"

"That's what hobbits do: they eat, they sing, they eat and sing at the same time."

"I don't remember that from the movies."

Neil tilted his head. "Tell me you've read the books. Of course you've read the books."

I gave a regretful shake of my head. "Sorry."

"Why not? The hobbits feel the same way about food as you do. You'll feel a kinship."

"There was a guy I dated," I said, "in high school. He was really into the books, kind of ruined it for me."

Neil shook his head. "You're what, twenty-eight now? Don't let one bozo ruin classic literature for you."

"Bozo?"

"We can read them together, once we're back in the States," he said. "Talk about them."

"Because we won't have anything else to talk about?"

He shrugged. "It's just an idea."

I looked at him. The light from the window caught the red-gold tint to his hair, highlighted the smile crinkles at his eyes. He had high cheekbones and a bold nose. It wasn't a warrior's face, but a scribe's face.

A good face. I sighed a little on the inside.

"My Italian relatives are going to love your red hair."

Neil raised a ginger eyebrow. "That's . . . good."

"We can read the books," I said. "I trust you. And it'll be nice to have something that's not the restaurant to think about. Heaven knows it's going to take over my life once I'm back."

Neil squeezed my hand. "You'll enjoy it."

I couldn't stop my smile. "I will. Now, let's see—what else should we talk about? I want to get the whole *Before Sunrise* experience in before we arrive."

"We could. I was also thinking of getting some work done."

"Fair enough. I'm . . . a little tired."

"Just a little?"

"Maybe a lot," I answered, with a crooked smile that probably made me look punch-drunk.

"You can rest on my shoulder," Neil said. "Close your eyes for a little bit."

He didn't have to say it twice.

The train journey took eleven hours. We chatted, read books, sent e-mails—to others, for once. Our knees touched, our arms touched.

Being in his presence, I felt like a leaf absorbing the sunlight.

We arrived in Roma Termini at once exhausted and restless. We navigated through the sea of strangers to collect our luggage and work our way to the street. I hailed a cab, speaking to the driver in firm Italian while keeping an eye on the meter. I tossed our luggage in and climbed inside. Neil ducked inside behind me.

"Buckle up," I told him. "We're in Italy now."

My *zia* Matilde—my father's younger sister—and *zio* Alessio waited at Letizia's modern apartment, along with Letizia's husband, Riccardo, Riccardo's sister Noemi, and Noemi's sprawling family.

Neil and I were pulled inside with grasping, insistent, loving hands. Our cheeks were kissed, arms patted, faces admired. Neil's in particular—his reddish beard was considered a grand success.

Matilde left to start the pasta water, and shortly after, the hugging and the greeting and the tugging pulled us in the direction of the dining room.

The Fronzoni dining room table waited for us, set for twelve.

"I guess we're eating now," Neil observed.

"Anything worth doing should be done over food," I told him with a cheeky grin.

We took our seats and spent the next few hours enjoying bruschetta, fried squid, heaping plates of penne puttanesca, and *saltimbocca di pollo*. Being full wasn't an option—the meal only ended once we'd proved consumption of a slice of olive oil cake.

I fielded questions about the new restaurant, my mother's health, the weather in Portland, and if I thought I would marry Neil.

The last question was, at least, posed in Italian.

Not that he'd have noticed, though, because he was just as busy answering questions about his work in Tennessee, his life in Memphis, if he'd ever seen Elvis (my uncle turned out to be a fan), and whether he came from a large family.

The latter, it turned out, quickly became the most popular conversation topic.

After an hour, *Zio* Alessio noticed I was about to tip over. "You must sleep!" he said, grasping my shoulders. "And you, Neil," Alessio added, his tongue audibly itching to add a vowel or two to Neil's name. I suspected Neil might wake in the morning to find he'd been christened with a new, more

Italianate name. "You must sleep as well, Neil. Letizia will show you to your rooms. And tomorrow, you explore Rome, *si*? Get some sun. Drink some real coffee."

"Go shopping," Letizia chimed in. "We must. Come this way, the rooms are here. Rest well, Giulietta," she said, using the Italian version of my name. "Ciao and sleep well."

I awoke the next morning to find Letizia sitting on my bed. "You are awake? Good. I unpacked your clothes for you," she said, flicking a hand in the direction of the closet.

"Oh," I said. I almost marveled over how heavily I'd slept—but it was beside the point.

"Yes, I unpacked your clothes, and I am very glad we decided to go shopping today. So get up, get dressed, and we'll stop for *cornetti* and espresso on the way." Letizia punctuated our plans with a smile and the clap of her hands.

"I just picked up new pieces," I said, sitting up.

"Yes, some of them are fine. But you need a short dress. And I am very concerned for your shoes . . ."

"I'm happy to go out shopping, Leti, but I have a very small budget, and the restaurant is eating away at it. And I shouldn't leave Neil—"

Letizia flicked her hand again, treating my fiscal concerns like a stray fruit fly. The gesture was so effective that I resolved to learn how to execute it myself. "It will be taken care of," Letizia stated. "You are so beautiful, and you have such a nice figure, and you are in Italy—we leave in thirty minutes. As for your Neil, he will be thankful."

Forty minutes later I had showered, dressed, and thrown on enough makeup to look fresh and almost rested. I had just enough time to kiss a sleep-tousled Neil good-bye before Letizia hurried me out the door. Before I knew it, we were strolling down the streets while Vespas zoomed around us.

We started at Letizia's favorite boutiques, ducking into some for no more than a minute if Letizia wasn't impressed with the stock, or much longer if she loved everything. Her gaze could assess a shop in thirty seconds flat—and when I remained quiet during the trip, she turned that gaze on me.

"You are in love," she said. "I can see it in your face, by the turn of your mouth. This Neil makes you happy? Do you think he'll be a good husband?"

"Not sure, but I know you'll tell me," I sassed.

"Ha! That man was made to be a husband. He'll never look at another woman." She handed me a short, cross-back black dress. "It is good to work for the attention, though—you need a little dress. This is good. You have good legs."

"Thank you," I said, though I doubted a dress would change much at all. But I didn't have the energy to deflect the comment or argue the way I would have if it were from Sophie or Caterina. Instead, Letizia kept tugging me in the direction she desired, and I reveled in having someone else to make the decisions.

While I considered myself a professional-level shopper in the States, Letizia was a woman on a mission. And clearly, price was not a part of the equation. From shelves and racks Letizia found me two Sophia Loren-esque minidresses that were just this side of decent, a cashmere pashmina, a cropped and tailored red blazer, a pair of very strappy, very high heels, as well as a pair of Gucci sunglasses.

I goggled at the price, but Letizia insisted, saying how nice they would look with Grand-mère's scarves, which she admired very much.

We stopped for lunch at Ditirambo, where I had the best tuna steak over a bed of arugula. Letizia chattered about Italian politics and the state of Italian film, followed by her thoughts on Paulo Sorrentino's *The Great Beauty*. "And so what of you?" she asked after taking a pause for breath. "You are in love, but your eyes are worried."

"There's not much to tell," I hedged. "He's a doctor. I'm trying to open a restaurant." I shrugged. "And we live across the country from each other."

"Love can motivate people to make difficult circumstances work," Letizia observed. "Is Tennessee so far?"

"It's about three thousand miles. Far enough." I took a sip of my rosé. "The truth is, I don't know what to do, and with everything with the restaurant, my mom's cancer—it's a little overwhelming. Or a lot. A lot overwhelming."

"But you don't want to give him up. You can't put love on hold forever."

"Mm. I've heard that."

"But you don't believe that. Do you want an *affogato*? I do." Letizia lifted her hand to flag the waiter.

"Oh, I believe it," I said, feeling more cynical than ever. "In theory. I'm just worried about how it's going to work in practice."

"Certainly you need an affogato, to sweeten you up." Letizia winked.

I scowled. "You think I'm bitter?"

"I think you frown too much. Cheer up—wear that black dress tonight. Just watch—Neil will have no reason to stay in Tennessee."

Letizia's sincerity stopped my snicker in its tracks. It was a nice idea, of course, but I had little hope that our long-distance conundrum would be solved by a short black dress.

After the shopping trip, Letizia and I returned to her apartment. She kissed my cheeks and left for work, leaving me keys to her husband's Alfa. "He took the Ducati today. The Alfa's full of petrol, not that you'll need it all. Dinner's at nine. Ciao!"

I thanked her for the keys and waved good-bye. I went looking for Neil and found a note that he had decided to explore on foot, and to text him when I returned. I pulled out my phone and sent him a brief missive.

In the guest room, I unpacked the new purchases. They were extravagant, but Letizia was right about one thing—they did look amazing with the Hermès scarf.

I dressed in the black minidress and topped it with the blazer, added the spindly heels, one of Grand-mère's scarves, and the Gucci sunglasses.

A glimpse in the mirror told me I looked even more Italian than usual.

I heard the slamming and pressure change of a door opening and closing. "Neil?"

"It's me," he called. "Did you have fun?"

I stepped out into the hallway in my new ensemble. "Letizia had fun dressing me."

Neil's eyes widened as they took in the look. "I'll say."

"Is it too much?"

He closed the space between us and kissed me soundly. "Don't go running off with any race car drivers."

"I don't think I'll be able to run very fast in these heels. I think you'll be able to catch me."

"Maybe. Riccardo loaned me a pair of his shoes."

My eyes widened. "He must really like you."

"Or he really hated my shoes."

"Footwear really is different this side of the pond. Less comfort, more style. I wouldn't have thought you two had the same size foot."

"Close enough." Neil lifted a foot. "There's practically no traction. Or padding. And the toes are so long . . ."

"They look nice."

"They hurt."

"You're very nice to wear them."

He shrugged. "I thought I'd try to please my host. When in Rome, and all that."

I grinned. "Literally. Well, now that we're both shod by Italians, want to go out? I want to see a man about some tomatoes."

Neil laughed. "Why not?"

With renewed confidence fueled by new clothes and Italian espresso, I programmed Riccardo's Alfa with my intended destination. Neil arranged himself behind the wheel, and we were off.

Our first stop was the rep for Dad's favorite tomatoes. Letizia happened to be right—with a little friendly flirting and a larger order, I managed to negotiate our tomato prices to a new, lower price. Afterward we visited two cheese-makers and a winery. This time I declined to commit, taking free and copious tasting notes, as well as samples to take with me.

I expected to be very popular at dinner that night.

A stop for gelato—we were in Rome, after all—and we drove back to the apartment.

By that time Neil had adjusted to the Italian drivers and attacked the roads more aggressively, *come un italiano.*

With an hour until dinner, we parted ways for a short nap.

I dreamed, unsurprisingly, of Neil. Also, of cheese.

7

Households that have lost the soul of cooking from their routines may not know what they are missing: the song of a stir-fry sizzle, the small talk of clinking measuring spoons, the yeasty scent of rising dough, the painting of flavors onto a pizza before it slides into the oven.

—BARBARA KINGSOLVER

We drove to Montalcino the next morning. At dinner the night before, Riccardo and Neil had traded their thoughts on each other's cars—apparently Neil had a BMW in Memphis. While we were planning to drive a rental car for the trip, Riccardo insisted Neil keep driving his Alfa Romeo. Neil accepted immediately.

We parked the car under a beautiful old oak tree; Neil looked around at the other parked cars and sighed. "Riccardo beat us here."

"What?"

"His and Letizia's Ducati. They got here first."

I gave his leg a conciliatory pat. "We'll chalk it up to home court advantage. Let's go in and say hello, shall we?" As I stepped out of the car, I could see where the setup for Nonno's party had begun—lights twinkled in the olive trees, streamers fluttered in the breeze.

Inside, it sounded like a restaurant kitchen at eight o'clock on a Saturday night.

"Wow." Neil paused at the threshold. "Are you sure it's safe to go in?"

"Don't worry," I said. "I'll protect you. *Buongiorno!*" I called out.

"Giulietta!" My zia Annetta poked her head out of the kitchen. "You are here! Come in, come in. Leave your luggage in the hallway; Donato will put it away for you. Come here and stir this *torta della nonna* custard for me."

"Okay," I called back. "Are you good at stirring?" I asked Neil.

"I feel pretty good about my upper body strength," he replied.

"Good, good. Just know that any of these women could out-stir you in their sleep. Zia!" I called once we neared the kitchen. "I have a friend with me."

"Si! Letizia told me." Annetta looked Neil up and down. "Do you think you could turn the pig?"

Neil stared at her blankly. "The pig?"

"On the spit. The *porchetta*." Zia Annetta pointed to the back of the kitchen, where there was a large, open wood oven featuring a stuck pig at the center.

I grinned at Neil. "Welcome to Tuscany."

"So much fuss," said a gravelly voice from the kitchen door.

"Nonno!" Annetta scolded as she browned the veal cutlets. "You should be napping."

"I napped earlier. What I haven't done is see my granddaughter."

I squealed and—once I'd seen my stirring duties passed to Francesca's oldest daughter, Sofia—jogged across the kitchen to wrap my grandfather in a hug.

As always, he smelled of rosemary and olive oil. In his face I saw a wizened version of my father. "Happy birthday!" I said, careful not to dislodge his cane.

"It is a day like any other except"—he put a gnarled finger into the air—"it is a day with a party!"

"I do love a good party. My parents wish they could be here."

He patted my arm. "Oh, I know, I know. I spoke to them both on the phone last night. It is very sad about your mother. Your father is doing the right thing."

"I think so."

"I am proud to call him my son. It's a pity he has to take out a second mortgage, but I am proud of him." Nonno didn't rest on sentiment; he spied Neil by the wood oven. "And this! This is your young man! He looks good at the spit. He is a chef, no?"

"No," I said with a shake of my head. "He's an immunologist. A doctor," I added, seeing Nonno's confused face.

"Ahh. Doctor. Eh, doctor is good too. Can he roast a chicken?"

"I don't know."

Nonno gave a sage nod. "You must find out. You can tell many things about a man by the way he roasts a chicken."

"What about a woman?"

"To know a woman, it is the soufflé. A shallow woman, her soufflé is too tall. A distracted woman, her soufflé will be burned."

"I thought a burned soufflé meant a woman was in love," I asked, playing along.

"No, no, that is not so. A woman in love will be making the soufflé for the one she loves, yes? So she will watch that soufflé very close. In fact, the soufflé may be underdone because she takes it out too soon, because she cannot stop looking at it."

"I see," I said, masking a chuckle. "I think Zia Annetta would be happier if you were sitting down. What do you think?"

"Annetta worries too much," Nonno said with a huff.

"Perhaps," I answered mildly. "The chairs in the dining room look comfortable. I could bring one in here. You could supervise."

Nonno leaned on his cane and considered the idea. "Your doctor friend might hurt himself unless he learns to put his back into it when he turns the spit. It's a pig, not a duck."

"True."

Nonno patted my arm. "You're a smart, smart girl. You know that, yes?"

"I'll be over here, stirring," I said, grinning as Nonno left to teach Neil the finer points of turning a pig.

"He may not have meant mortgage," Neil said later when I worried aloud about my parents' financial situation while setting the outdoor table. "Do you think it could have been lost in translation?"

"Nonno's English is pretty good. You know he used to be in spaghetti westerns, back in the sixties?"

"I didn't know that."

"Ask him about Clint Eastwood sometime." I sighed. "But with the restaurant . . . I mean, it makes sense. And he's been working a lot. I hope . . . I hope they're okay. I just . . . I try not to think about what might happen."

Neil opened his mouth, then closed it again. After a moment's thought he spoke. "I'm sorry. Cancer is cruel, no matter which way you look at it."

I shook my head. "We're in Italy, Neil—I don't want to think about it anymore."

Neil wrapped an arm around my shoulders and pressed a kiss to my temple. "I'm sorry, love."

I grasped his hand and clung tight, resting my head against his shoulder. "I haven't had time to read any of the letters."

"What?"

"Mireille's letters. I have to read them. Find out what happened. I don't know . . . I just need to read them. Soon."

As we finished out the table, my heart felt heavy. Thinking about the letters, my mom's cancer, the thousands of miles between Neil's home and mine—I felt as though there would never, ever, be enough time.

~ HOME-STYLE TIRAMISU ~

Tiramisu, translated "pick-me-up," is very popular throughout Italy. It's quick and easy to assemble, and easy to make for a dinner party. It utilizes the Italian tradition of making a "cake" by soaking something crisp in a full-flavored liquid. In this version, Italian *savoiardi* cookies or crisp ladyfingers are dipped quickly in brewed coffee and layered with a simple custard. The standard Italian version uses very fresh, uncooked eggs for the custard. Free-range, organic eggs are recommended; farm-fresh eggs are ideal if you can get your hands on them. The filling also relies on creamy mascarpone cheese, the Italian take on cream cheese. Look for it near the ricotta in well-stocked grocery stores.

6 very fresh eggs

$^1/_2$ cup sugar, divided

$2^1/_2$ cups mascarpone

$^1/_2$ ounce shaved dark chocolate (optional)

20–22 savoiardi or crisp ladyfinger cookies

$1^1/_2$ cups brewed coffee or espresso

1 tablespoon cocoa powder

Wash the eggs with soap and water before cracking. Separate egg whites into one mixing bowl and yolks into another.

Beat egg whites until stiff peaks form. Add most of the sugar and beat until egg whites are glossy, about another fifteen to thirty seconds.

Beat egg yolks until pale and creamy. Add mascarpone and remaining sugar and beat until well incorporated. Grate dark chocolate over mascarpone mixture, if using.

Fold the egg whites into the mascarpone mixture, folding gently until fully incorporated.

Pour coffee into a shallow bowl. Set out a 9x9 or equivalent-sized baking dish to assemble the cake. (Note: if you double the recipe, a 9x13 works great).

Dip the unsugared half of the cookies into the coffee and then place them snugly against each other until the bottom is covered, about ten or eleven cookies. If necessary, break cookies in half to fit.

Spread half of the custard mixture over the cookies, and repeat with a second layer of coffee-dipped cookies, followed by the last of the custard.

Cover and refrigerate for 1–2 hours. One hour leaves the cookies a little structured still, while two hours gives a fully softened cookie. Sift cocoa powder over the top. Keep cake chilled.

Serves 4–6.

8

There's a friendly tie of some sort between music and eating.

—Thomas Hardy

*M*ore than a dozen cars sat parked in the driveway and grassy area outside my uncle Ciro's home, as if the Alfa Romeos and Fiats had multiplied like fluffy little *conigli*.

My cousin Giancarlo's best friend Ivo's band played outside, in a combo which featured a lute, an enthusiastic tambourinist, and a noted love for dated American pop. Nonno held court near the large dance floor and a larger pile of gifts.

I should have been on the dance floor myself—how often does anyone get the chance to dance with her boyfriend in Tuscany, much less to the melodious strains of "Kiss from a Rose" sung in Italian?

At the very least, I should have been talking to one of my five dozen Italian relatives. But all I could think about was my parents.

And once I started worrying about my parents, worrying about my brother and our restaurant seemed like a natural progression.

I was still lost in concerned concentration when Neil reappeared at my elbow. "Here," he said, handing me my phone. "Call someone. Call Caterina, call Nico, call your parents—whoever you have to talk to."

"No, no, I'm fine," I protested, waving him off.

"You're frightening the little children with that scowl. Please? If you won't do it for me, do it for the children."

"It's seven thirty in the morning in Portland. Nico would kill me."

"Call Cat."

"She'll be at work."

"So wake up Nico."

I thought it over. "He might be awake."

"Call him."

"Fine." I pressed a kiss to his cheekbone. "I'll be back in a few minutes."

I walked away from the party, the music, and the chatter, and dialed my brother's number.

He answered groggily on the third ring. "Who died?" he asked, sounding more cranky than concerned.

"No one," I said. "Calm down."

"I couldn't think of any other reason you'd call so early." A yawn. "Party's today, right?"

"Going on right now. The band is playing a rendition of 'I'd Do Anything for Love,' so actually, I might die."

"Oh." He sounded impressed. "In English or Italian?"

"Italian, with feeling—oh, hang on." I took a second to get a handle on the melody. "Nope, now it's Sting."

"Stop stalling, Jules. What's got you so worked up that you're calling me rather than slow-dancing to a classic yet cheesy power ballad of the nineties?"

"I couldn't stop worrying about Mom and Dad."

"Worrying?"

"Panicking, maybe. How are they?"

"About the same. Mom's chemo sickness got worse, doctors put her on antinausea meds. She's better, for now."

"That's good, I guess? How about Dad?"

"Busy. Distracted. Worried about money."

"How can you tell?"

"He won't talk about it, but I know he's been keeping a very close eye on the numbers at the restaurant."

"Does he have reason to worry? Has D'Alisa & Elle been underperforming?"

"No, it's doing great. Plenty of covers, and as it turns out, Mario has real flare for using all of his ingredients and keeping costs down. Dad's been updating the interior some, and it looks sharp."

"Good, good, that's good." I ran a hand through my hair. "How about things at Blue Doors?"

"You'll have waitstaff to interview when you get back. Hope you're ready to hit the ground running, because this rocket is ready to launch."

"I know. But we'll learn things during the soft opening, and there's the tiny reality that we need to finish up all of the inspections. I think the electrician is coming the day after I get back. All that to say . . . I hope you're at peace with a soft launch."

"I will be, I will be—we're just so close! You're flying home in . . . three days?"

"Three days," I echoed, turning around to search for Neil. After a moment I found him, carrying platters for Annetta. I couldn't hold back either my smile or my tears.

"Who's picking you up from the airport?"

"Alex and I have it worked out."

"Well, if you need anything, you can give me a call."

"I'll let you know."

"Rumor has it that Neil's with you."

My eyes returned to him, now playing catch with Francesca's son Leo. "He is," I answered simply.

"So what are you doing on the phone with me?"

"Checking in," I said, "but point taken. See you in a few days?"

"Few days," Nico repeated. "Hey, Jules?"

"Yeah?"

"You happy?" he asked, sounding every bit the protective older brother.

"Yeah," I said, a smile stretching across my face as I looked out at the party, at Neil. "I am."

"I'm glad. Have a safe flight."

I hung up and walked back to Neil.

He smiled wide when he saw me approach. "Catch?" He tossed the ball to me.

I caught it with one hand and tossed it back.

He tossed it to Leo. "How's Nico?"

"He's good. My parents are okay—my mom's on antinausea meds. Nico's ready to open the restaurant the day I get back. Pretty much what you'd expect."

"Feel better?"

I slipped under his arm and hugged him around his middle. "Yup."

Neil pressed a kiss to my temple. "I'm glad."

"Blech!" Leo cried at the sight of our embrace. *"Che schifo!"* He scrunched up his face before turning and running away.

"And here I thought Italians weren't afraid of a little PDA," I joked. "Let's get back to the party—I want to be there when Nonno opens his gifts."

Hours later, the combination of evening chill and pervasive darkness chased off the last of the guests.

Several of them, however, were only chased as far as the inside of the house, so while the tipsy revelry continued, Neil and I grabbed our jackets and left for a walk.

My right hand clutched his left as we ambled into the night. "If I were really clever," I said, "I think I would have brought a flashlight."

"Eh, that's what phones are for."

I pulled mine from my pocket and hoisted it in the air. "To phones! What would we do without them?" I stumbled forward three more steps. "I think there was more than fruit in my aunt's fruit punch."

"I think that is a fair assessment."

"It feels good to get outside. I love my Italian family, but I feel like I've been listening to my uncles argue for the last three hours."

"You *have* been listening to your uncles argue for the last three hours. I've heard enough shouted Italian to be fluent."

"That's possibly very true," I said. "I enjoyed hearing you all talking about cars, though. They weren't expecting that."

"For an American man to love Italian cars?"

"More like an American knowing Italian cars the way you do. And in their heads they think Americans only like Corvettes and Mustangs."

Neil snorted. "Not this American."

"You impressed them."

"You were pretty impressive yourself. I like hearing you speak Italian."

"It was a really good party, though, don't you think?"

"The part where the dogs got into the roast pig—that was good." Neil lifted his arm, guiding me in a loopy, goofy twirl.

I laughed and played along. "You're fun. The roast was good. The aunts chasing the dog, chasing the roast—" I shrugged. "They're a viral YouTube video waiting to happen, bless them all."

Neil spun me closer, pulling me into his arms. "Come to Memphis, Giulietta. Come see my home, meet my family."

My heart beat hard in my chest. "You really want me to?"

"Come on," he said. "If I try to tell them about this beautiful, multilingual woman who cooks, they'll think I just made you up." He brushed my hair from my face. "I want to take you for a walk on the Rhodes campus. I want you to meet the people who are important to me."

For the first time, I looked into his eyes and felt no fear, no anxiety. "I want that too. When I get home, I'll buy a ticket."

"I'd like that," he said, a trace of his southern accent creeping into his voice. "I know finances are tight. Let me help with the tickets." He squeezed my hands. "And I'm happy to help with a hotel, or if you'd feel comfortable, my friend and his wife would love to have you at their place."

"Southern hospitality and all that?"

"That's right." He held my face. "I love you."

Rather than answer, I pulled his face to mine and kissed him. He tasted of summer fruits and butter cookies.

"Memphis," I said, my voice low and husky. "Memphis in about two weeks?"

"How does that work for your restaurant schedule?"

I calculated the dates in my head. "It gives me just enough time to get the restaurant ready and through the soft opening, visit you, and come back for the grand opening." I shook my head. "I must be crazy."

"Having second thoughts?"

"Strangely . . . no."

Neil whooped and danced an awkwardly charming little jig, then looked up at me with an abashed grin. "That was weird," he said. "If you told any of my co-workers that just happened, no one would believe you."

"It's Tuscany," I said, tilting my head back to take in the stars. "Anything can happen."

That night, Neil slept on a cot in a room with Francesca's boys. I slept in the attic loft, sharing the space with the family dog.

Despite the late night, the echo of voices began early the next morning. I persevered through the gauntlet that was the bathroom—showering with the last of the hot water while Letizia and Francesca applied their makeup and discussed their intimate relations with the husbands.

Neil went out on a drive with some configuration of the men; Nonno and I enjoyed a quiet breakfast over coffee in the sunroom.

I spent the afternoon brushing up on my pasta-rolling technique with Annetta, smiling when Neil tried his hand at it.

The next forty-eight hours sped by, and before I knew it we were saying emotional good-byes and waving out the car window as we drove away, folded into the back of Letizia's Alfa.

We flew out of Rome together, Neil and I. Since he'd booked his trip with an open-ended ticket, he'd been able to book one of the last seats on my flight.

With a little maneuvering, I convinced the gentleman next to me that his seat was not as good as the one Neil occupied, especially since a family with a two-year-old happened to be seated two rows ahead.

We crossed the Atlantic together, hands clasped, fighting sleep—neither one of us wanted to miss a moment of our time together.

Too soon, we landed at JFK.

He would fly to Atlanta, and then on to Memphis.

My flight would take me straight to PDX.

Neither of us said much—after all, we'd hardly slept over the past twenty-four hours. I had no idea what time it was, but breakfast sounded good, so we tracked down a place that served piping hot breakfast sandwiches, and another with a selection of not-too-stale breakfast pastries.

If I'd thought about it, the food offerings would have been a letdown after eating my way through France and Italy.

However, the point of airline food is to create a new baseline, making it possible to consume with a certain satisfaction anything we found at ground level. And if that meant stale croissants, then stale croissants we would eat without question.

Afterward Neil walked me to my gate.

We sat together in the uncomfortable seats, holding hands even as the first two zones were called to board.

"I'm not going to say good-bye," Neil said at last. "I'll see you soon."

"See you soon," I echoed.

A moment later, the flight attendant called out my zone number for boarding. We stood together.

"This is kind of old-fashioned," I said, wrapping my arms around his torso for a final embrace. "Getting to say good-bye at an airport terminal."

"You're right," said Neil. "It's very romantic in here. That smell of stale food . . ."

I snickered, and then pulled back to look into his eyes. "Until Memphis?"

"You got it."

A too-short kiss full of promises, and I found myself walking away, turning for a final wave before walking down the jet bridge.

9

A crust eaten in peace is better than a banquet
partaken in anxiety.

—AESOP

My plane touched down in PDX at 3:14 p.m. I'd spent the flight
in comfortable silence, seated next to a man wearing a North
Face jacket and lace-up Keens on his feet.

To offset the spate of tears that had hovered behind my eyes since I'd last
laid eyes on Neil, I pictured instead my cousin Letizia's hypothetical reaction
to those Keens.

That thought alone buoyed me enough to get me through the flight without falling apart. All I wanted was to drive home with my brother Alex—likely
while listening to U2—and fall asleep on my own bed.

I checked my messages just after the flight landed. One alarm message
from my phone, reminding me to find a power source soon. Four texts from
Neil, all of them saying that he was home, that he missed me.

Everyone else grabbed their belongings and prepared to launch themselves
into the aisle, but I sat and clutched my phone.

I missed him so much my heart ached in my chest. I squeezed my eyes shut
and thought about home, about sleep. For a brief second I indulged myself in a
fantasy where Neil had actually flown to Portland rather than home, and that
he was waiting at my apartment. He'd be there, and I could curl up on the
couch with him, rest my head against his chest, and fall asleep.

When had I become that girl—the girl who fell apart when she wasn't with
her boyfriend? In the short amount of time that we'd had together, I'd seen
Neil first thing in the morning and last thing at night, day in, day out. And
look what had happened.

I was a junkie with a dying cell phone battery.

As I finally disembarked, I reminded myself of how much I loved my little apartment over the restaurant, how much I'd missed Clementine, missed my dog, Gigi.

Heck. I had a whole closet full of clean clothes waiting for me. And new spices in my suitcase waiting to be introduced to the rest of my spice cupboard.

Alex had told me he'd park in short-term parking and meet me at the baggage claim. Once I made it to the carousels, I scanned the crowd for the top of my brother's blond head.

The head that appeared, though, was the one belonging to my oldest sister, Sophie.

I loved my sister, but I knew in my gut that my hopes and dreams for a quiet reentry into my normal life were, well, a thing of the past.

"Hi," I said once we were close enough to hold a conversation in a normal speaking voice. "Glad to see you." I hiked my computer bag higher on my shoulder. "I was expecting Alex."

"There was a catering emergency, so he called me. Dad's at the restaurant, trying to train the chef who's taking over from Nico. The guy came from a James Beard Award–winning restaurant, but you know Dad."

"I do."

"And Mom's still tired from her last treatment."

I winced. "How's that going?"

"It's chemo. What do you expect?"

Okay, then. I yawned, making a show of it. "Sorry," I said, belatedly covering my mouth. "Jet lag."

"You must be exhausted. I hate transcontinental flights. Want some help with your suitcase?"

"Sure." I swung the suitcase around my side and toward my sister.

She grasped the handle and began to pull. "What on earth do you have in here, Juliette?"

"Oh, you know. International contraband of various kinds."

"Don't say that!" Sophie hissed, looking from side to side to see if anyone had heard us.

I looked around myself, seeing one TSA agent who seemed to be very interested in the ceiling tiles. "Relax, Soph. It's just wine and olive oil. And honey. And chocolate. I left the unpasteurized cheeses behind."

"And your clothes?"

"Eh, I left them behind too."

"What?"

We finally made it out the doors, and I breathed in a lung full of Portland air. Or, more accurately, the exhaust of a thousand Priuses. "If I didn't know Chloé was a great kid, I'd think that motherhood made you high strung. The clothes are in there too, I promise."

"Sorry. It's just . . . there's a lot going on lately."

"Where'd you park?"

"That way," Sophie answered, pointing vaguely enough that I had no choice but to follow her questionable lead.

After a hike to the short-term parking, we loaded my luggage into Sophie's BMW X5. "Do you want water? There are bottles in the back."

"Yes, please," I said, selecting a bottle of near-body temperature water. "I get so dried out on planes. So . . . what all's going on?" I asked, knowing I could be dipping my toe into a dangerous conversational pond.

She sighed. "Nelson."

If I'd actually been able to take a drink of the water, her answer would have preceded a spit-take. "Nelson? Why? How?"

Sophie buckled her seat belt, her face stoic. "He's having a midlife crisis."

I frowned. "He's an accountant."

"Accountants have midlife crises too, you know."

"You don't—you don't think he's having an affair, do you?"

"Affair? Who said anything about an affair? Why would you say that?"

Deep breaths. "I'm sorry. You said midlife crisis. It was just a question. You can say no."

"Well, he's not having an affair."

"Fine. So . . . ill-conceived moustache? Sports car?"

"He's on a diet. He's not eating carbs."

Oh. "How do you feel about that?"

Sophie remained silent for two miles. "I'm already allergic to dairy—eliminating pasta is just mean-spirited."

"That would be a change."

More silence as Sophie changed lanes.

"What does he want to do?"

Sophie shook her head, laughing incredulously. "He's . . . he's taking up bicycle polo."

"Wait—what is this?"

"It's polo, played in a field. With bicycles, rather than horses."

"And this is Nelson? CPA Nelson? Folds-his-own-trouser-socks Nelson?"

"Nelson, my Nelson, coming home with scrapes and bruises because he's falling off his bike and who knows what else."

"Well . . . huh. It's like the Portland version of Fight Club, I suppose." I shook my head. "I left my brain somewhere over the Atlantic, so that's all I've got so far. I suppose it's good that he's exercising?"

"Why can't he just run around like everybody else? Of all people!" Sophie burst out, and then reined herself in. "If you marry Neil—that's his name, right, Neil?"

"It is his name," I answered cautiously.

"Right. Well, if you marry him, think of having him sign a prenup promising not to give up linguini. He might be—what is he?"

"A research immunologist. Say—do you have a phone charger in here?"

"Just an iPhone charger. You've got an Android, right?"

"And proud of it. Oh well. It was worth a shot. But yes, Neil's in medical research, and to hear him talk about it, he eats macaroni like it's going out of style."

Sophie snorted. "Give it ten years and he'll give it all up and start picking out Paleo recipes from magazines. And . . . he's gone a lot more, because of the matches. Reminds me of when I was growing up and I only saw Mom and Dad if one of them was coming or going."

Even through my jet-lagged haze, I could tell that not only was Sophie genuinely wigged out, but that she didn't mean much of what she was saying. Rather than deal with the crazy head-on, I patted her hand. "I'm sorry. This must be stressful for you." I looked out onto the road. "Was it that bad for you? Growing up like we did?"

"The restaurant came first," she said in a small voice. "If I wanted to see my parents, that's where I had to be. Some kids are fine with it—some love it. I've read the memoirs. But . . . I don't know. It was different by the time you came around."

"I know."

And I wasn't just saying that. I knew from stories over the years from my older siblings that while Mom and Dad loved each other, and loved each child with a fierce devotion, the restaurant simply took most of their time.

Sure, we all grew up to be independent self-starters, but I knew that Sophie in particular felt the loss keenly.

In that moment, her life made more sense to me. While I couldn't fathom most of her thought processes, her desire for a sense of bourgeois normalcy countered the often chaotic childhood she'd known.

I mulled over those thoughts as we continued down the freeway, right past the Burnside exit to my apartment.

"Whoops," I said. "Don't worry—you can take the next exit at 6th. There's a bit of backtracking, but it's not bad."

"It's fine," Sophie said, waving a casual hand in the air. "We have to pick Chloé up from dance."

"Oh. Where's her dance class?"

"Just over in Beaverton. It'll be quick. She gets out in fifteen minutes—we'll just make it."

"Okay," I said, but truly the only thing I could think of was my bed, and how nice it would be to be sleeping in it.

Twenty minutes later, we pulled up to Chloé's class, where other tween girls waited outside, dressed in leotards, tights, and wraparound skirts.

Chloé waved enthusiastically when she saw me in the passenger's seat. She bounded to the car and leaped inside. "Aunt Juliette! You're home!"

I grinned. "I am! I missed you." And I did—it was worth skipping my bed if it meant seeing my niece's bright, crooked smile. "Are you glad school's out?"

"Yes," Chloé huffed, "but I think I'll be just as busy this summer. Mom signed me up for all kinds of camps and classes."

"Which you asked for," Sophie pointed out.

"They all sounded cool," Chloé admitted.

Sophie and I exchanged glances.

"I think you'll have fun," I told my niece.

"I hope so," Chloé replied happily. "How was your trip? How was *Neil*?" she specified without pause.

"Who told you Neil was there?" Sophie asked her daughter.

Chloé shrugged. "Uncle Nico said so. He said *Zio* Ciro told him that they hope you marry Neil and move to Italy. You don't want to move to Italy, do you?"

"Not anytime soon, don't worry," I assured her.

On one hand, I knew Neil had made a good impression with the Italian family, but I didn't know it was *that* good. And on the other—Nico had no business telling our niece about my romantic life.

Sure, Caterina promised to keep quiet about Neil joining me on my trip, but even snipping one branch, the rest of the family grapevine seemed to function at high capacity.

"Neil is good," I answered at last. "We had a lot of fun in Paris, and visiting with Grand-tante Cécile and Cousin Sandrine."

"How is Cécile getting on?" Sophie asked.

"She's good. Mentally not always in the present, but well in body and spirit. She looks a lot like Grand-mère."

"And Neil liked Provence?" Chloé asked.

"He did. It worked out well for Auguste, to have an extra man in the house for chores."

"Did you do anything romantic in Paris?"

"Chloé! That's too personal," Sophie chastised. "Apologize."

"Sorry," she mumbled.

"We had a nice time." I looked at her over my shoulder. "We visited Ladurée . . . What are you doing?"

"Changing," Chloé answered as she shimmied into a T-shirt and out of her leotard. "I've got a game."

"When," I asked, though my intuition told me I already knew the answer, "is this game?"

"I don't know, like, now? Or fifteen minutes?"

I turned to my sister. "You're taking me hostage. I'm never going home, am I?"

"Stop being so dramatic."

"I get dramatic when I haven't slept in twenty-four hours."

"You haven't slept in twenty-four hours?" Chloé poked her head near mine. "That's cool."

"It's only cool when you're in college."

"It's not cool in high school?"

"You're growing in high school, so you actually need the sleep. College is that sweet spot when you've stopped growing and your energy's still high."

"Huh. Will you come watch my game anyway? We brought the good juice boxes."

"Well," I said, taking a deep breath, "as long as it's the good juice boxes." I picked up my phone to text Clementine about the change of plans, but my phone had gone black and refused to revive.

No phone and headed to a middle school girls' soccer game? I was living on the edge.

I spent the game on the sidelines, cheering with the rest of the soccer parents. I gave high-fives and may have yelled something at the ref about his unflattering socks.

My inhibitions were somewhere around nonexistent, but the excessive cheering must have paid off. Chloé's team won handily.

"We're going to frozen yogurt to celebrate!" Chloé announced breathily once she jogged off the field. "Can you come, Aunt Juliette?"

"Aunt Juliette's very tired," Sophie said. "I'm going to talk to Grace's mom and see if she can give you a ride home."

Chloé nodded and shrugged, trying to be a good sport but clearly disappointed.

"In for a penny, in for a pound," I said. "Let's go. I could use some dairy."

My flight had landed at 3:14, but Sophie's car didn't pull up to my apartment until just after seven.

"It looks like Nico's upstairs," Sophie commented as she shifted her car into park. "We'll come up and say hello."

"Sure," I said, reaching for my purse. Nico might have been waiting for me—or he might have been hanging out with Clementine, my pastry chef roommate, under the pretext of waiting for me.

I'd find out soon enough.

"You know you're welcome to come back to our place for dinner, right?"

"Eh, I'm here," I said. "If worse comes to worse, I'll order pizza or something. I think I had a frozen entrée from Trader Joe's in the freezer. I won't waste away."

Sophie hauled my suitcase upstairs, while Chloé slung my carry-on satchel over her shoulder.

I rapped on the door before turning the handle and stepping inside. "Hi," I called out. "I'm back."

A skitter of toenails over the floors, and Gigi was at my feet, trying to decide if she wanted to jump on my legs first or roll over for a belly rub. The belly rub won out. "It's official, then, is it?" I asked, kneeling down. "You chew my shoes, I rub your belly—it must be love." I used to think I wasn't a dog person, but that was before Grand-mère passed and Gigi had, eventually, come home with me.

"Did Sophie kidnap you?" Nico called from the dining room.

"I heard that," Sophie yelled back.

"I kidnapped her!" Chloé declared with pride. "I kidnapped her to watch my soccer game. It was all my fault."

"Okay, everybody freeze," Nico said, which made no sense until I'd put my things down and rounded the bend to view the dining room table.

Nico, Clementine, and Adrian, the sous-chef, sat around the sturdy French oak table, heads bowed over Bananagram tiles.

"Um . . . hi?" I said.

Clementine stood first. "We're frozen. Adrian—hand off that tile."

"I was just moving it away from the edge of the table."

She shot him a glare that would crystalize Jell-O. "Frozen." She turned to me. "Hey! I tried to call you. Your phone die?"

"It did. Long flight and all that." I gave her a hug.

"I imagine it buckled under the weight of all those text messages from Neil."

I blushed. "That too." I turned to wave clumsily at the other party in the room. "Hi, Adrian."

"Good to see you," he said, standing. He was a good-looking guy, no getting around it. His hair alone made him notable, with its black curls, never mind the tan and the eyes. But the trouble was that he knew it.

When we'd first met—right around the time Nico hired him as sous, he'd attempted to flirt with me. At the time, I hadn't been at all interested. Not only had his level of flirtation been off-putting, but having dated another one of Nico's sous-chefs, Éric, I had no intention of repeating that life experience.

I was with Neil now, of course, but still felt a lingering awkwardness around Adrian. "Nice trip?" Adrian asked.

"It was," I said. "Really nice. Ready to get back to work though."

Over my shoulder I could tell that Sophie and Nico had greeted each other, argued, argued more, and were wrapping up to say a companionable farewell.

"Thanks, Soph, for the ride home," I said, stepping forward to give her a hug. "And thanks, Miss Chloé, for letting me come to your game."

Nico snorted, but an elbow to the ribs ended it soon enough.

"I'm happy to stay, Juliette, if you need any help unpacking," Sophie offered.

The image of Grand-mère's letters tucked in my suitcase flashed before my eyes. "That's sweet of you, but no—you guys go home and get dinner. I'll be okay. See you guys for dinner on Sunday?"

"Dinner on Sunday," Sophie echoed, and with a last round of hugs they tramped back down to the car.

10

A cook is creative, marrying ingredients in the
way a poet marries words.

—ROGER VERGE

I turned back to the strange tableau before me. "So . . . game night?"
"Adrian and I were out looking at kitchen equipment. I came over to
welcome you back and Adrian here tagged along," Nico said. "But Clementine
said you weren't here yet. After an hour, I called Alex to find out that Sophie
was picking you up." He sat back down in his chair and leaned back, balancing
the chair on the back two legs. "I knew I wasn't going to see you for a while."

I groaned and rubbed my eyes. "I love my niece and I'm glad to have had
time with her, but holy mother, I'm tired. And starving—frozen yogurt doesn't
stay with you, you know?"

Clementine put her hands on her hips. "Let's find you something to eat.
You probably don't want caffeine at this time of night."

I waved her concern away and walked toward the coffee machine. "Nah,
caffeine just bounces off me. One of the benefits of my genetic material. I'll
make an espresso."

Clementine shook her head. "You sit down. I'll make it."

"Thanks. I should raid the fridge, though. I haven't eaten anything but
airplane food or frozen yogurt since . . . yesterday. I'll make toast or something.
There's always toast."

"You know what I think is funny?" Clementine asked. "How little chefs
cook in their down time."

Nico flailed his hands. "We cook all day—why should we cook all night?"

I filled a glass with tap water. "Éric cooked for me," I said, feeling brave and more than a little pleased with myself. After six years of silence, I wasn't going to hide my relationship with Éric any longer.

"Éric?" Adrian asked.

Nico shook his head. "My sous-chef at L'uccello Blu. Talented guy, beautiful plates. And my *sister* dated him. Never told me."

"I told you," I said. "I told you weeks ago. What you haven't told me is why you're playing Bananagrams at my kitchen table."

"When was all this with Éric?" Clementine asked after the coffee grinder ground to a halt. "You don't mean Éric Tovati?"

I nodded. "It was a long time ago."

"They dated for a year," Nico muttered bitterly.

Clementine gave an approving nod. "You're one for secrets. Good job. I met Éric a long time ago—he was hot. Talented, but, you know . . ."

I was so tired I couldn't stifle my giggle as I opened the freezer. "I know. I was young, it was fun. Hey, look—chicken tikka masala. Score."

"Now that's just sad." Adrian stood, crossed the room, and shut the freezer door. "You can't come back from Italy and eat freezer food. Sit."

"I'm fine," I protested. "I ate Picard's in France—leave it to the French to know how to freeze food better than the rest of the world."

Adrian shook his head at Nico. "I can't believe you'd let your sister eat a frozen entrée after all that."

"I cleaned her oven. She's in good shape," Nico answered, unperturbed.

I frowned. "You cleaned my oven?"

"They were just sitting around, waiting for you," said Clementine. "So I put them to work."

In my peripheral vision I could see Adrian pulling eggs, cheese, and vegetables from my refrigerator. "How did that go?"

"Gigi got a walk, and the oven's spotless."

"Good work," I said. I glanced from Nico to Clementine. My brother had it bad if he was willing to be talked into cleaning an oven that wouldn't be inspected by health services. "Caterina will be disappointed, though. She was looking forward to scrubbing out the oven."

Nico lifted his eyes to the heavens. "How did I wind up with you and Caterina for sisters?"

"I'm so sorry," I drawled, then turned back to Clementine. "So you figured after all that labor, they deserved a little fun?"

"Bananagrams, fun for young and old," she said. "And it's the one game I could find."

"Makes perfect sense," I said. "I'm going to plug my phone in so Neil doesn't think I died."

I took the opportunity to drag my luggage to my room and remove the spoils. I threw them all into a tote and carried them back to the dining room. "We can have a tasting party, if you like. I brought these back mostly for restaurant purposes, but y'all are here, so . . ."

"*Y'all?* Neil really is rubbing off on you," Clementine teased.

I shrugged. "It's a good word. You should try the honey and see what you think. It's the one that's made at the family chateau."

"Have a seat," Adrian ordered. "Your food's done."

I obeyed, and Adrian slid the plate in front of me. "That looks really, really good," I told him. "Thank you." He'd made an omelet, and a bite revealed ham, gruyère, and bright green spears of asparagus. A small green salad rested next to it, as well as a piece of baguette he'd found somewhere. "This makes it nice to come home."

Clementine set a cup of coffee near my plate and sat back down by her game tiles. "But you had a good time, though?"

"Yeah." I realized as I said it that I'd had a wonderful time, but now that I was back in my kitchen, with the people in my life, the time with Neil seemed like a dream. A strange, wonderful, but fleeting dream. "I took lots of pictures. I promise I'll be chattier about it once I've eaten."

"And slept," she added. "All right, you guys. Let's play!"

They were off. It took five minutes and several non sequitur exclamations until Clementine won the game, just as she'd said she would.

"I won, I won," she chanted. "I won, and now I'm going to taste the honey as a victory lap."

"You were lucky," Nico griped. "I picked up two *q*'s in the last thirty seconds."

Clementine shrugged and grinned.

Adrian rolled his eyes, then pointed at my plate. "You're done?"

I glanced down. The plate was completely empty. "I don't really remember eating all of that."

He stood, removed the plate, and placed it into the dishwasher. "That means you were hungry."

I sipped at the espresso and sighed. "The English have their tea—but this is the drink of my people."

"Did you sleep during your flight?" Nico asked.

"No, not really. Partly because the in-flight movie was the Wes Anderson movie I'd been wanting to see but never found time for." And partly because I'd been too busy missing Neil to be able to settle. Though now I had no doubt that I could sleep for a week solid. On that note . . .

"I think I'm going to go to bed," I said, yawning for punctuation's sake.

Clementine tilted her head. "You just drank an espresso."

I waved a hand. "It'll help me walk in a straight line to my bed. Otherwise, you would've had to carry me. I'll see you all sometime tomorrow, I'm sure. Night, all."

Gigi trotted alongside my heels. Together we traveled down the hallway to my most anticipated destination: bed.

I had hopes and dreams of sleeping for two weeks straight, but the date and time on my phone informed me that I'd only made it for six hours.

Quel bummer.

I got up and slipped into my lounge clothes. Gigi looked up at me from the bed, clearly perplexed over why I would get up while it was still dark outside.

I flipped on the bedroom lights before opening up my suitcase. If I couldn't sleep, I could at least make a dent in my unpacking. I threw clothes into piles before finally—and most importantly—unpacking Grand-mère's letters.

My mind wandered as I cleared a desk drawer out for the letters. I remembered the door at the chateau I couldn't open, and the memory of a key in the prep table.

No time like the present. I tiptoed into the kitchen, turning on as few lights as possible. It felt familiar, digging through the table late at night. What was it about this table that it didn't want to reveal its secrets in the light of day?

Only a moment's worth of digging revealed the key I'd remembered. I turned it in my fingers—it certainly looked like the sort of key that would have opened that door.

What I wanted was to get on a plane, fly back to Provence, and try the lock myself. The more practical and affordable solution, though, would be to put the key into an envelope and mail it to Sandrine.

I brewed up a quick mug of tea before returning to my room. Gigi lifted her head in acknowledgment, watching as I settled into my chair with my laptop. After a moment's consideration she leaped off the bed and onto my lap, snuggling close as I pulled up the photo files. Now that I was back, I considered the logic of printing the copies. As much as I wanted to touch and handle the original letters, I didn't dare risk any damage—my link to Grand-mère's past was tenuous enough.

"If she'd told you anything, you'd tell me, right?" I asked Gigi, scratching her ears. Gigi looked up at me and blinked. I nodded. "Thought so."

I continued to pet Gigi's soft white fur as I began reading the first letter.

August 16, 1938

Dearest Cécile,

Bonjour from Paris! I am fully moved into Tante Joséphine's pied-à-terre. Her housekeeper, Madame Giroux, is very kind, though I have my doubts about the cook. I am glad to be settled because the pastry school begins on Monday.

Anouk is contented here; Tante Joséphine has taken to her well (it helps that she does not shed); my only hope is that Tante Joséphine does not slip her too many treats, which may upset Anouk's stomach. We have taken a few walks out in the neighborhood and have found it to be very pleasant. I believe we will be very contented.

I hope things are well at the chateau, and that Papa is not working too hard. I have thoughts in my head about a chocolate tea cake for him, so moist that he will forgive me for going away and doing something so gauche as to go to pastry school.

Give Maman my love and tell her that I promise to be very properly dressed at all times. Between you and me, however, I bought three sturdy, sensible dresses for classes. I wear aprons, of course, but it only made sense. What I couldn't decide on, though, was if lighter or darker dresses made more sense. In the end, I decided that the presence of flour made lighter-colored dresses sensible (let us hope I don't spend an entire class pitting cherries. No one can come out of that unscathed).

Oh, my dearest Cécile, I miss you so. Please beg Maman to let you visit me soon! But only on the weekend, as I'll have classes during the week.

Bisous!

Mireille

I leaned back in my chair. Anouk—I'd heard about Anouk, Grand-mère's first bichon frise. I hadn't heard about Tante Joséphine, however. The tone of the letter made me smile—it reminded me of any number of e-mails to Caterina. I dove into the next letter, also from Mireille.

September 5, 1938

My dearest Cécile,

Forgive me for not writing. Tante Joséphine gave me quite the scolding (I believe Mother complained). I feel terribly, of course, but I shall tell you of my days.

I rise very early to bathe, dress, walk Anouk, and then take the metro to the 15th arrondissement, where the school is. On rushed mornings, I pass off the walking duties to the maid, Marie, which I suspect she enjoys since she offers every morning.

I attend each class—this term it's "Fundamentals of Laminated Dough," "Introduction to Chocolate," and "Understanding Rising Agents."

You know that I'm no simpleton in the kitchen, dear sister, but while I agree that I have things to learn (hence my enrollment), I'm nowhere near as delicate and scatterbrained as the gentlemen in my classes believe me to be.

Of course you must know how this irritates me.

So once I complete my courses for the day, I go to the markets to pick up whatever supplies I need and then return to Tante Joséphine's home.

For the afternoon, I prep the doughs and pastries that need to be begun. This requires the use of a portion of the kitchen, which has not further endeared me to the cook, but one must make sacrifices.

After dinner I finish off the pastries that I started before, and then set them to bake. Lately I've taken to working on my chocolates and truffles while the pastries are baking.

Tante Joséphine blames me for the fact that her frocks have grown tight. We are working to arrange a donation of sorts to some of the ladies' organizations. I would be very happy to provide the pastries for a fund-raiser or ladies' tea, as long as they don't care what they're getting.

I am getting better, however. None of my classmates would ever admit so much—they're too busy trying to hide my tools and salt things when I'm not looking—but my instructors have begun to chastise me less. I am getting stronger and much faster, and my small fingers are good with detailed work.

Anyway, after my evening baking I clean everything up (I do. The cook has no room to complain on that account), package up everything I made, and then fall into bed with an aching back and sore feet. Sometimes I take a bath first, if I'm wearing too much flour or sugar.

Mother will be pleased to know that I've located a very accommodating beautician who will cut and set my hair in the late afternoons. She is very kind, and she knows all the best confectioners in her arrondissement (the 3rd), so she's useful as well.

How is the honey crop coming? I would very much like a jar (or three) of the chateau's honey. It really is better than anything I can find in the city; poor souls can't even tell the difference.

You'll be happy to know I've posted letters to Maman and Papa as well. I have not told them how much I've been baking off-hours; I believe it would distress them both. Let's keep that between us, yes?

Bisous!

Mireille

11

All happiness depends on a leisurely breakfast.

—John Gunther

I took a catnap between seven and nine, and then showered and dressed for the day in a breezy cotton skirt and a V-neck tee. As much as I knew I needed a day or seven to catch up on sleep, I also knew that the restaurant's soft opening day loomed whether I liked it or not.

We'd gone back and forth over the soft opening. Some restaurants simply opened and carried on. But because we were looking to serve a higher-end clientele, we had no room for errors. Instead, we'd have a crowd of friends, family, and invited guests to come and dine with us. From there, we'd learn which dishes took longer to get out of the kitchen, which staff members needed more training, and how well the flow between the front and back of the house worked. The staff received more practice, and therefore would be less likely to make errors that we would otherwise have read about on restaurant review sites.

Nico had winnowed through the waitstaff applications while I'd been gone. Today I got to conduct interviews.

The day would start off, though, with a staff meeting. For the occasion, I baked up a blueberry cake with hearty buckwheat flour, using the blueberries I found in the freezer.

"Morning!" Clementine greeted me as I waited for the cake to bake. "How'd you sleep?"

"Great, until about 4 a.m. I'm on somewhere-over-the-Atlantic time." I nodded toward the oven. "I've got a blueberry buckwheat cake going for breakfast."

"Smells great," she said.

"If I'd known everyone was going to be over last night, we could have held the meeting then. Which," I added, "might have worked if I had the ability to string two sentences together. I'm going to make an espresso. Want one?"

"Sure."

I reached for the coffee beans. "You're good with strong espresso, right?"

"Do you make it like your brother?"

"Nico? I suppose about the same."

"Just as long as I know what I'm getting into."

I lifted an eyebrow. "Nico made you coffee?"

"About a week ago, while you were gone."

Interesting. My brother didn't make coffee for just anyone. I considered asking about it, but a knock sounded at the door before I could say anything. "Speak of the brother. I'll let him in."

Sure enough, Nico and Adrian stood on the narrow landing. "We've got pastries and coffee in here," I said. "What are you two contributing?"

"I brought nectarines," said Adrian, holding up a cloth bag.

"And I've got bacon," said Nico. "Which means I win."

I rolled my eyes. "Funny. Come on in."

"Can I borrow your stove?" Nico asked, waving a brown-wrapped package in the air.

"Oh, why not?" I answered breezily. "Clementine! The boys brought nectarines and bacon."

"Bacon?" Clementine wrinkled her nose. "I'm vegetarian, you know."

Nico stopped midstride. "Really?"

Clementine winked. "Gotcha."

I plucked the bacon from Nico's fingers. I gave him a significant glance, but his eyes never strayed from Clementine's face.

Adrian caught my expression, though. He grinned at me and clapped Nico on the back before setting to work cutting the nectarines into wedges.

Once all the food was ready, the four of us loaded up plates and took them to the breakfast nook.

I grabbed my tablet device from the living room and opened up the calendar. As we dined on the nectarines, bacon, blueberry cake, and espresso, we mapped out exactly what the next several weeks would bring.

Ordinarily the sous- and pastry chefs wouldn't have been involved in the process. But that was one of Nico's talents—involving people in such a way that they felt like they mattered, felt heard.

By working so closely with his sous, Nico created a stronger, deeper kitchen. Even chefs needed a backup, and if he worked this closely with his sous, Adrian, he could get sick or injured without bringing the entire restaurant to a halt.

As far as Clementine's involvement, it helped to break the usual barrier between the dessert offerings and the rest of the kitchen. As a result, the menus were better integrated, the ordering more streamlined.

And it gave Nico a chance to spend more time with her, which I suspected they both enjoyed.

"We're getting down to the wire for training," I said, looking down at the tablet calendar. "I'll be interviewing waitstaff this afternoon."

"For the love of bacon," Adrian pleaded, "no actors. Please?"

Clementine shook her head. "Actors don't like to wait tables anymore. They prefer working as personal trainers."

Nico's eyebrow quirked. "Really? When did that happen?"

"When they figured out the hours were more flexible and the pay was better. What?" She held her hands out defensively. "I dated an actor once."

"You mean you dated a waiter," Adrian corrected.

"Turned personal trainer." Clementine shrugged. "It didn't last. He gave up butter."

"Good riddance," I said. "More's the pity for him—the two of you guys could have built up quite the racket. Anywho, waitstaff. They're coming. Right now the soft opening is in less than two weeks, invitation only. Be thinking of who you want to invite. Ideally I'd like to see how we handle fifty covers and tweak things from there."

Nico nodded, picking up a piece of bacon. "Sounds good."

I watched as his bacon-holding hand lowered past his plate. "Don't give that to Gigi," I warned. "It'll upset her stomach."

"It's bacon! Dogs love bacon."

"There's fat in bacon, and she's sensitive. Eat your own bacon, or leave the leftovers with us. Anyway, we'll make alterations and prepare the press materials. In roughly four weeks, we'll hold the grand opening."

I released a breath before continuing. "The first weekend we'll hold a promotion with a buy one/ get one glass of wine, or half off a bottle."

"You don't think that's chintzy?" Adrian asked.

"Oh, I do, but it works." I reached for my espresso. "Even the wealthy enjoy having saved money."

"It's true," said Nico. "Dad did it from time to time at D'Alisa, worked like a dream."

I went back to my notes. "Social media campaigns will include a presence on Facebook, Twitter, and Instagram . . ."

"I must be old," Nico said. "I remember when people still used Myspace."

Adrian reached for another slice of cake. "I wouldn't bring that up."

"So far, we're on track," I said. "Which is good, because I'm going to be out of town the week before the grand opening."

Nico blinked at me. "Wait, what was that?"

"I'll be flying to Memphis," I said with all of the confidence I could muster.

"You just got back."

"And I'll come back again," I pointed a finger in the air for emphasis. "Really. I promise."

"C'mon." Adrian held out his hands. "It's not like she can go after the grand opening. Seriously, dude."

"Yeah," Clementine echoed dryly. "Seriously, dude."

"You don't need me. And we're miraculously ahead of schedule. All that's left on my to-do list at this point is the social media marketing, and I can do that on the road." I gave a bright smile. "I'll bring back barbecue sauce."

"Why a week?" Nico asked.

I reached for another nectarine slice. "It's eight-hour travel day. I want to maximize my time."

"You should go to Corky's Barbecue," Adrian suggested. "I went to the Nashville one, but I think they're based out of Memphis. Wet barbecue, rather than dry-rub style. Good barbecue," he said, drawing out the vowels.

"Sounds good," I said. "Clementine? Do you feel set for the opening?"

"I do," she said. "Menu's set for the opening, ready to teach it to the wait-staff. I'm working on a few new ideas as the seasonal produce shifts."

"Let's keep an eye on the weather too," I said. "If we wind up with a late July heat wave, let's be ready with plans for chilled soup, a nice light tuna—that's up for you to decide," I told Nico, "but there's wisdom in being weather appropriate."

Nico nodded. "My fish supplier is reliable; I've put in last-minute orders and gotten great product from him."

"My industrial ice cream maker is back-ordered, but it should arrive about a week before the opening," Clementine added. "I thought we might consider offering to-go quarts of ice cream for diners who otherwise decline dessert. We can tie a bow around them, keep it fancy, but still sell product."

"I like it," I said. "I'll price out containers. If we put an emphasis on our desserts, there may be wisdom to having a pastry intern. What do you think about that?"

"Help with grunt work? Sure, as long as he doesn't get underfoot."

I made a note. "I'll keep that in mind. Anything else? I've got interviewees coming shortly. Everybody good?"

Everyone pushed back their chairs. Clementine and Adrian carried plates back to the kitchen; Nico hung behind.

"I wish you'd asked me about the Memphis trip earlier," Nico said, keeping his voice low.

"As a brother or as a business partner? It won't affect the restaurant, promise."

"I worry about you," Nico said, after a moment. "I don't know about this long-distance thing. Has Neil thought about moving to Portland?"

"His job is in Tennessee," I answered with a sigh.

"Do you want to move to Tennessee? Is that what this trip is about?"

"I . . . I'm going to Tennessee to meet his parents and his friends," I said. "We haven't made . . . long-term plans."

"I want you to be happy," Nico said. "I just . . . I'm not sure how this is going to work out for you."

"Me either," I answered honestly. "When I'm with Neil, it's good. Good enough to stick around long enough to find out if we have a future."

"But if he's in Memphis," Nico said slowly, "and you're in Portland, and neither of you is willing to move . . . what then?"

I slung my arm around my brother's shoulders, pretending I didn't ask myself that question on a daily basis. "I'll let you know when I figure it out. Speaking of getting in each other's business," I added, glancing toward the kitchen, "you and Clementine. When are you going to ask her out?"

He glanced toward the kitchen, where it sounded as though Clementine was showing off Gigi's tricks for Adrian. "I'll leave you alone about Neil, you leave me alone about Clementine. Deal?"

I held out a hand to shake. "Deal."

With the meeting concluded, I considered trying to get some office work done before the afternoon of interviewees, but called my mom instead.

"Juliette! *Ma petite! Ça va?* How was France?"

"*Très belle,*" I replied before switching back to English. "Are you free for lunch today? Is Dad around?"

"Your father is at the restaurant, but I would love to see you." She paused. "I haven't been able to eat very much, or eat and keep it around for long."

"What if I bring lunch?" I suggested. "And if it gets eaten it gets eaten, and if not you can save it for Dad."

"That sounds nice. I can't wait to see you," she answered.

"I can't wait to see you either," I echoed before we said our good-byes and hung up.

I gathered my things and Gigi's as well—I couldn't bear to leave her behind just yet. I called in an order of my mom's favorite Vietnamese takeout and stopped to pick it up on my way over.

Gigi and I navigated the wooden steps to the door together, and I knocked before letting myself in with my key. "Hello?" I called. "I've got pho. And spring rolls."

"*Ah, bon, ma petite!*" Maman came around the hallway corner and appeared, her face a wreath of smiles.

The smile on my own face froze. She'd lost even more weight, and her eyebrows had drifted away. The dark circles under her eyes made her look as though she hadn't slept in weeks, and maybe she hadn't.

All of it made sense; none of it was easy to see. Not with my vibrant, strong mother.

Gigi jumped and gave a bark of delight, which gave us both something else to look at and me a moment to compose myself. Once Gigi had calmed, we exchanged careful hugs and air kisses.

I put the pho into bowls and plated the spring rolls, grabbed silverware, and made for the back deck. Off leash, Gigi raced out the door and set off to find a squirrel while Mom and I made a place at the large wooden table.

Mom sat in the sun, holding her bowl of pho close. "Tell me about your travels," she said. "How are Cécile and Sandrine? Is Auguste well?"

I nodded and reached for a spring roll. "Sandrine and Auguste are lovely, couldn't ask for better hosts. Cécile is well, but the Alzheimer's has taken its toll."

"I wish I could have seen them. I wish I could have seen the lavender. Does it still hum with bees?"

"It does. And I brought you honey from the most recent crop."

She clapped her hands together. "I helped with the harvesting when I was young. My hands smelled of honey for days! Sandrine and Suzette and I had so much fun putting the labels onto the jars and tying them with string and a sprig of lavender." She smiled. "Those were beautiful days. Having cousins my age made it feel as though I had sisters."

"And all of you grew up there together?"

"We did—my parents, me, and Henri, and my tante Cécile with Sandrine, Suzette, and Eléonore." She took a spring roll of her own. "What about your father's family? How is everyone? How is your nonno?"

I filled her in on the Italian leg of the trip, dancing around the topic of Neil until my mother pressed that particular topic. "Your Neil, he joined you for the entire trip?"

My face flushed pink, as it always did when the subject of Neil came up.

"He did. He's . . ." I searched for words. "He's easy to travel with, easy to get along with."

"Easy to love?"

My blush deepened. "It's still early. Early, but . . . yes. I do love him, Maman. At least, as much as I can after such a short period of time."

She smiled. "It did not take me long to fall in love with your father."

"Once you stopped arguing on the plane."

A shrug. "I never said we agreed about everything, only that we loved each other."

"How . . . how have your treatments been?" I asked, half afraid to hear her answer.

Her smiled faded. "They've been difficult, and my white blood cell count has been low. Our insurance plan hasn't been paying for as much of the treatments as we'd hoped."

"That's why Dad's been at the restaurant more, isn't it?"

"Money is tight." She reached out and squeezed my hand. "I don't want you to worry. We'll figure out what to do. And until then? We'll enjoy the sunny days and Vietnamese noodles and happy dogs napping outside."

I followed her gaze to where Gigi sprawled on the grass, belly to the sun, paws resting lazily. "She looks happy."

"You do too," she said. "When you're not worried about me."

"Of course I'm worried about you."

"Juliette, I don't know how many days I have here on earth—none of us do. There's no sense in being anxious during those days."

"I can't help it," I said in a small voice.

Her hold on my hand tightened. "Be strong with me."

I squeezed back, and worked as hard as I could not to cry.

Neil called just as I began the drive back home. Between the time with my mom and hearing the sound of Neil's voice, my emotions sat closer to the surface than I preferred. "Hi," I answered, wincing at the way my voice warbled.

"Are you okay?"

"I just had lunch with my mom. I'm fine, she's fine, she's just . . . she's sick. And I know she's sick, but that doesn't make seeing it a whole lot easier."

"I'm so sorry, Juliette."

I swiped at a stray tear that managed to trail down my face. "She's getting the best care and the best food, and her health is as good as it can be, considering—it's not like she already had some other chronic condition. She has faith. I—I have faith." I sniffed. "Sorry, I know you didn't call for me to fall apart on you."

"Just needed to hear your voice, that's all. No agenda."

"You poor thing," I said dryly. "Calling to be nice and look where it gets you. What happened, were there no easygoing, well-adjusted single women in Memphis when you opened your online dating account? You just had to date someone in Portland whose life was a mess?"

"What can I say? There were other candidates but they didn't have enough life challenges for me to commit," Neil joked.

"You're funny," I said.

"We've all had our challenges and baggage," he answered. "Mine just happens to be a few years ago."

I remembered the night he'd told me about his childhood best friend Felicia, who'd suffered from a rare degenerative disease, and whose death left a teenage Neil paralyzed with grief.

"You're right, I know. I just hate that it's a bit one-sided."

"I'll try to dig up something."

"Things are good with you? Work's all right? The DNA sequencer is working properly?"

"Yup, the tech came out and it's back online."

"Sequencing away?"

"It is. I miss you."

"I miss you too. I'll see you in a few weeks, and I can't wait."

Neil mentioned a few other things he couldn't wait for, which had me blushing in seconds. We said reluctant good-byes when I got home—if we wanted to see each other, I had work to do.

Two days later, our restaurant not only boasted a high score from the health department, but also a competent array of staff.

I'd hired three people to wait tables and two people to wash dishes. My first hire would probably irk Adrian. Braeden Stein, an operatically inclined voice student at Portland State. While not *technically* an actor, Braeden was charming and smooth with, admittedly, a lovely speaking voice. I had no aspirations of his sticking around in the long run, but I had a hunch that diners would find him charming and interesting. Even more, he had a singer's confidence, and when I gave him a list of specials to read, he managed to describe them in such a way that sounded familiar but not rote.

My second hire was Mallory Briggs, who was blond, gorgeous, and competent. She possessed the skill of being friendly but not uncomfortably familiar.

Many restaurants suffered from deep divisions between the kitchen and the front of the house, which is problematic when you're relying on cooperation to transfer an order into a dish that will need to be delivered. I knew I could rely on Mallory to charm the diners as well as the kitchen, which would help the front-of-house business run smoothly.

I also suspected she would catch Adrian's eye what with the pretty and the smiling and the blond hair.

Which was none of my business.

The third hire was Patrick Chen, who arrived in a perfectly tailored vintage suit, complete with pocket square. I admired his sense of hipster style and tales of his adventurous palate; before moving to Portland, he'd waited tables in New York and eaten his way through Singapore.

I felt good about the hires, but wished I could share about them to Neil in person. Instead, I had plans to meet with my friend and former co-worker Linn for dinner.

We'd have a good time, I wasn't worried—I couldn't wait to catch up with her and hear about the paper I'd left behind and the latest restaurant-scene dish. But my plans meant that Neil and I wouldn't have much time to talk, and it'd been a few days since we'd spoken at length.

Instead, we'd texted throughout the day, between appointments (on my end) and meetings (his).

We missed each other; most of our messages shared that sentiment.

I called him on my way to Linn's place.

Neil's phone rang, and I gave a sigh of relief when he picked up, and his voice filled my car via Bluetooth. "Hi, beautiful," he said.

My smile stretched wide. "Hi, yourself. Tell me about your first day back on the job. Texting doesn't cut it for me."

"Coffee," he said. "I remember the coffee. You?"

"A lot of coffee," I conceded. "And meetings and interviews and more coffee. Did I mention I told Nico about the Memphis trip?"

"I'm sure he was thrilled," Neil said dryly.

"Very," I answered lightly. "Also, late last night I dug up the key I'd found in Grand-mère's prep table."

"Oh yeah? So what's your plan for it?"

I navigated the roundabout on my way to Linn's Goose Hollow neighborhood home. "I'll mail it to Sandrine—that's all I can do. If I'm lucky, Sandrine will have time to give it a try and see if it works." Even saying it, my plan sounded thin. "Ideally," I admitted, "I'd go back and try it myself, dig around the house some more. The letters—they're incredible. There has to be more."

"You started the letters?"

"I did! Grand-mère's so young, such an adventurer. She has so much ambition, so much life. It's funny trying to reconcile the version of her that I'm reading and the version I remember."

"We know what that's like."

"True. But it makes me want to dig through the chateau that much more."

"You may have to go back," Neil said. "And I'm not saying that lightly. Sandrine has her hands full with the chateau and caring for her mother. She may not have time to go digging."

I winced. "That's true. But it'll be all I can do to make it to Memphis. I have no idea when I might be able to have the time, much less the money, to travel back to Montagnac. It's so much easier in books and films, you know. People can put their lives on hold, fly around the world." I passed Linn's house, looking for a place to park. "Sorry. I'm tired and cranky, and I'm about to have dinner with Linn and I'll probably be terrible company."

"You're superior company, even when you're tired. I should know."

"You're sweet," I said, though I suspected I had a sibling—or four—who would beg to differ.

"Are you still enjoying the restaurant? Are you glad to be back?"

"I am. We're getting close to opening, and I'm excited to put plans into action. I'm nervous," I admitted. "I know what kind of hoops reviewers are going to make us jump through. Being on the other side is . . . nerve-racking."

"You'll do great," he said. "And I'm not just saying that."

"No?" I asked, a goofy grin on my face. What was it about this man that turned me into a loopy fifteen-year-old?

"How are your parents? How's your mom doing?"

"I talked to them this afternoon. I'll see them for family dinner Sunday—they're out of town on a getaway this weekend."

"Good for them."

"That's what I thought. Mom's between treatments. She'll start radiation when she gets back, but until then they're taking a long weekend at Cannon Beach."

"Family dinner, then. Are you going to ask your father about the second mortgage on the restaurant?"

I sighed. "I haven't figured that out yet. Depends on whether I can get him alone. We'll see. Did it feel good being back in the lab today?"

"It did. I had dinner with my friend Callan and his wife, Tarissa, tonight."

"What did they think about your impromptu European tour?"

"Tarissa was jealous, but the coffee and caramels I brought back helped. If Callan doesn't take her to Europe within the next year, I fear for him."

"They sound great."

"They are. They're anxious to meet you when you come out."

"Yeah?"

"Tarissa's delighted that you got me to take time off. You're a winner in their book. Mine too," he added, "but you knew that already."

"I think you're pretty great too. Hey look, a parking space." I pulled to the side and prepared to reverse into the parking space. "Don't mind me, I'm just parking." Once I made it into a socially acceptable position, I threw the car into park, then grabbed my purse and the bottle of Bordeaux I'd brought for Linn before climbing from the car.

"Do you guys have a date for the grand opening?" Neil asked. "I want to be there, if I can swing it with my work schedule."

I laughed. "We'll have just seen each other."

"Not at your restaurant, we won't."

"I'd love for you to be there," I said, striding down the sidewalk. "We'll open on Friday the 25th. Mark your calendar."

"Consider it marked."

I stopped in front of Linn's townhouse apartment. Looking up, I spied Linn's face through the curtain. She waved, and I waved back.

"Well, I'm in front of Linn's," I said. "She has enough questions about you, and if she figures out who I'm talking to . . ."

"Say no more. Have fun, okay? I'll talk to you tomorrow. I love you, Juliette."

"I miss you, and I love you," I said, before ending the call and walking up the steps toward Linn's front door.

~ BLUEBERRY BUCKWHEAT BREAKFAST CAKE ~

This is a hearty, fragrant cake to serve friends for breakfast. Yogurt keeps the cake moist, while also adding protein to start the day.

1 1/4 cups buckwheat flour

3/4 cup unbleached all-purpose flour

1/2 teaspoon sea salt

1/4 teaspoon nutmeg

4 teaspoons baking powder

1 1/2 cups plain, whole-fat yogurt

1/2 cup whole milk

1½ teaspoons vanilla bean paste or pure vanilla extract

Zest of 1 orange

6 tablespoons butter, softened

²/₃ cup light brown sugar

2 eggs plus 1 egg white

1 tablespoon demerara sugar, for sprinkling

2 cups blueberries

Preheat the oven to 350°F. Coat a round springform pan with a thin layer of butter. Kitchen tip: you can use a leftover butter wrapper for this. Otherwise, place a half tablespoon of butter on a paper towel and wipe it around the inside of the pan.

In a large mixing bowl, whisk together the flours, salt, nutmeg, and baking powder. In a small bowl, mix the yogurt, milk, vanilla, and zest together, stirring until smooth.

In a stand mixer, cream the butter until pale and fluffy. Add the brown sugar, scraping down the sides of the bowl when necessary, and mix for another couple of minutes. Slow the mixer and add the eggs and white, one at a time.

With the mixer running, add half of the dry ingredients and half of the yogurt mixture. Then add the last of the dry ingredients and the last of the yogurt. Turn the mixer off just as the last of the yogurt incorporates.

Pour half of the batter into the springform and sprinkle half of the blueberries over the top, pushing some of them down into the batter. Follow with the second half of the batter and the blueberries. Sprinkle the demerara sugar over the top.

Bake for 50–70 minutes, or until the cake is golden on top and pulling away from the sides of the pan. You can serve it immediately, though it's even better the next day.

Serves 10.

12

A plate of apples, an open fire, and "a jolly goode
booke" are a fair substitute for heaven.

—LUCY MAUD MONTGOMERY

I curled up in my room that night, with Gigi on my lap, ready to read
more letters.

September 26, 1938

My very dearest Cécile,

*My classes have continued to go very well. Tante Joséphine is content because
we have found a very proper ladies' organization to which to donate my creations.
They are exceedingly grateful, and I may find myself the recipient of an award of
some sort.*

If they do, I shall send it home to Maman.

*Now, for the rest of this letter, I ask that you read it very much alone. The
beginning, I agree, is dreadfully dull, but I did it because I know that sometimes
Maman can be nosy with the correspondence, and I didn't want to begin with the
delicious details that I'm dying to share.*

Are you quite alone? Good.

*Do you remember when I said that one of my instructors paid me a grudging
compliment? I neglected to mention that he is the most scrumptious man I have
ever seen. I wonder if I were not at pastry school, if I would describe a gentleman
in a way that was not . . . well, edible.*

I suppose it's quite unladylike. May I remind you not to tell Maman?

Anyway, this instructor. His name is Gabriel Roussard, and he is young, perhaps twenty-four or twenty-five? A couple of the students are older than he is and thought that he could be bullied, but he is very, very good. According to Marcel (I overheard this, naturally—none of my classmates want to be caught taking pity on the girl), he studied under Maurice Pinon, and has created some of the most noteworthy desserts in the city. He teaches two classes a year—one beginning, one advanced—and spends the rest of the year at the restaurant, where he is a favorite with the English and American tourists.

While my instructors have ceased berating me for the texture of my pâte brisée, he seems to have taken an interest in me. He told me that my croissant dough was, in fact, very good. And just today, he asked how I spent my afternoons after classes. I told him, of course, how I shop for produce and supplies and go home to practice my technique.

He asked if he could join me at the market, where he would show me how to choose the best quality fruit.

I felt I was adequately prepared to shop for myself, but I wasn't about to shy away from the opportunity.

After my last class, we met at the front doors and we walked together to the markets.

Cécile, I wish you could have been walking behind us, taking notes! He asked how old I am, and where my family lives, my interest in pastry, and what I plan to do after I complete the program.

And as he shared what he knew about choosing fruit (I really did learn something), he told me about his brothers. One works in the city as a jeweler for Van Cleef & Arpels. The other is an Ancient Languages professor in Warsaw, specializing in Hebrew.

He seems smart, and kind, and thoughtful. He has a generosity of spirit, I think, that I found lacking in Gilles.

(Though when it comes to Gilles, it is very kind of him to visit Papa. I am forced to think well of him for that.)

This has become a very long letter, I shall give you a summary: I find my pastry instructor troublingly attractive, and I am improving in my classes. Oh, and the honey arrived perfectly, thank you, dearest. I have taken to heart your *recommendation for showing off my trim figure on my next visit home, and I am already planning which frock will set off my figure to its best effect. Two weekends from now, would you like to come and shop for hats? We'll need something on our heads to truly cut stylish figures, if we're to do it properly.*

Bisous!
Mireille

There it was, in Grand-mère's lovely, handwritten loops—Mireille laid eyes on Gabriel. And he admired her. They discussed fruit together.

My heart swelled with the charm of it all. I continued to Cécile's reply.

October 3, 1938

Dear Mireille,

I confess I enjoyed the lengthy description of your Paris adventures, particularly your handsome instructor. If this were a schoolgirl novel, of course, he would be a spy of sorts. Does he look like a spy? Or perhaps a tragic past. I do enjoy a good tragic past.

It does seem timely to remind you that you never told me much about why you ended your engagement to Gilles before you left. If I'm to rebuff any attempts at an attachment to Gilles, it might be useful to know more.

Thank you for the caramels! Maman had friends over for cocktails, and I passed them out. To her horror, you may have orders for more. Mme. Reyer was there, so I would expect the entire village will be singing your culinary praises.

Maman is determined to repaper half of the chateau; I believe this is how she is dealing with both missing you and not having a wedding to plan.

I confess I am deadly bored.

Maman has me busy with all sorts of charity work, of course. She's hoping, I think, to keep me firmly within her world so I don't go veering off into something as unacceptable as pastry. It is my job to marry well, to someone who will take care of the farm and the chateau.

(This is not to say that at some point you might decide to marry and have the chateau, but Maman is preparing for the worst.)

Maman is "helping" me throw a tea. If you would like to send more caramels, I would not argue.

Missing you, but glad you're enjoying your adventures.

Cécile

October 15, 1938

Dearest Cécile,

My apologies for your difficulties at the chateau, though I'm sure your tea will go swimmingly. If you're open to suggestions, make sure there is oolong tea for Mme. Proulx, and if you don't serve something with lemons to Mme. Masson, she'll simply sit in a corner talking about how nice and refreshing lemon is, and wouldn't everything else at the tea taste better with a touch of lemon? A lemon curd is a good start, or a lemon tart (if you can get good lemons).

Classes are fine. One of my classmates spoke to me this week—to ask if I would share my fleur de sel. You would be so proud, dear sister, to know how gracious your older sister can be. Yes, I did share my finishing salt.

No one's spoken to me since, but my classmates seem to be less hostile.

As for my handsome instructor . . . yes, it is very schoolgirl of me, I suppose. And he has been very professional. Too professional of late, but he has been very kind about my work in class. No more trips to market.

This has not stopped me from wearing my best hats on the way to class (with my sensible dresses—what am I to do?), but I recognize that at least he is a pleasant distraction from an otherwise grueling routine.

As for Gilles, it is simple enough, and yet . . . not simple. As time went on, I came to understand that Gilles's hopes and dreams for our life were not hopes and dreams that I shared. If I had loved him more, it would have bothered me less. If I had loved him, a quiet life like the one our parents have led would probably sound ideal.

But since I didn't love him that much, it sounded dreary and unpleasant. Gilles and I have known each other since we were small children—I hated ending our engagement. If he had been willing to move to Paris, Marseille, or even America, perhaps it might have worked.

Gilles, however, could not leave his land, his family. And that's fair. He was not kind, though, when I ended our engagement. And I suppose that's fair too, though he seemed more upset about our family's farms not being joined in holy matrimony than he was about not marrying me.

I'm probably thinking more ill of him than he deserves. But if he tries to convince you to marry him for the sake of the farms . . . for heaven's sake don't do it, not unless you're passionately in love with him.

Can't wait to see you when you visit!

Bisous,

Mireille

My heart beat faster reading her words about Gilles, the man my mother called father. Mireille certainly hadn't minced words. If that was how she felt, why did she marry him after all?

I wanted to stay up late reading, but work exhaustion, combined with travel exhaustion, forced me to bed.

Tomorrow. I would read more tomorrow.

13

But even modest restaurants offer the opportunity to become someone else, at least for a little while.

—RUTH REICHL

*S*aturday morning I managed to sleep until 6 a.m., which felt like an accomplishment at the time. After a walk with Gigi, I took my laptop, coffee, and a leftover piece of blueberry cake downstairs to the restaurant to work.

Gigi napped at my feet as I wrestled through creating Facebook, Twitter, and Instagram accounts for the restaurant. Alex had helped with the preliminaries of the website, securing the host and finding a simplistic enough platform that would allow me to maintain the website on my own.

While a part of me longed to hire out the web design, my ability to wear yet another hat would save the business more than enough money to make it worthwhile. I had just enough coding acumen to work within a web design platform and get it to do what I wanted, as long as I was prepared to sacrifice the time.

When I needed a break, I picked up the phone and called Nico. "Hey— you got a minute?"

"Gearing up for the lunch rush, what's up?"

"Could you write a chef's blog? Say once a month?"

"You think it's a good idea?"

"I do." I leaned back in my chair. "It makes you accessible. You can talk about the seasonal menu, your favorite ingredients."

"I'm a terrible writer."

"Too bad you don't know anyone who would edit you."

"I suppose if you were editing, it could work."

"Me?" I feigned surprise. "I was talking about Linn, from the paper."

"You're funny. This is really gonna happen, Jules. Are we ready?"

"Once the waitstaff learns the menu, yes. And we need dishwashers . . . soon. But we'll be ready."

I hung up, turning to look out the window and gaze out at the street view. The sun shone, the flowers in the front wide open to absorb the sunlight. I leaned forward toward Gigi to suggest a short spin outside when my eyes caught movement from the opposite side of the room.

I watched in horror as a mouse scurried across the floor.

Seconds after I had ended my blog-centered phone call with Nico, he received another phone call that could be loosely termed "hysterical."

I was all for feminism, but any attempt at an "I am woman, hear me roar" attitude stopped cold at the sight of a small rodent inside our nearly-open place of business.

Nico couldn't leave D'Alisa's lunch rush, but Adrian was both available and on my doorstep in twenty minutes' time.

"Not a fan of mice?" Adrian asked.

"We have a soft opening in a week," I said, fighting to keep from yelling, crying, or an indiscernible mixture of the two. "You could say that no, I'm not a fan."

"Have any friends with cats?"

"My friend Linn. Who reviews restaurants for a living—I'm gonna say no."

"Then we'll have to set traps. No poison, but traps."

I took a deep breath and nodded. "Okay. No, not okay. This is a disaster. We're going to have to push back the opening day. We'll definitely need to have another health inspection." I shook my head. "I'll have to postpone going to Memphis, but I already bought the tickets . . ."

Adrian held up a hand. "One step at a time. The construction across the street? Probably stirred up some nests, so they decided to come over here."

"There's probably a joke in there somewhere. A bad one."

"Nobody likes it, but these things can happen. You grew up at a restaurant, and you're telling me you never once had a breakout of ants?"

"My dad always handled things like that. What if a mouse dies in the wall? We'll have to close—we can't afford to close."

"Mice happen, you know this."

"But—"

"They're not like roaches—sometimes a stray finds his way in. Look. I'm no good with building or assembling things, but I've worked in commercial kitchens long enough to be really good at pest control." He put his hands on his hips. "I'll look around for entry points and fill them with black foam. I'll set out some glue boards and snap traps. We've all been working in the kitchen off and on for days—none of us have seen any droppings."

I groaned.

"No—no, that's good. It just means they haven't been partying, making a mess of things. It's gonna be okay. These things happen."

"Okay."

"We're going to be fine. It might even be enough to let Gigi there roam the downstairs for a day or two."

I looked down at Gigi. She'd been delighted, once she woke from her nap, to have something to chase, though the mouse made it out of sight before she had a chance to do anything interesting with it. "If she catches a mouse I'm going to have to brush her teeth, like, four times before I let her lick my hand."

"Fair enough."

"Okay." I repeated the word once more to try to pull my mind from panic-mode and into fix-it mode. "I'll send you with the business credit card. You can get everything you need, just bring back the receipts."

"We'll open," Adrian said, nodding toward the computer screen before meeting my eyes. "The website? It looks slick. You're good at this, all of it."

My cheeks flushed. "Thanks. I, um, I'm going to go . . . walk Gigi," I finished, once I remembered what I'd wanted to do before the tiny mouse had upended my life.

I all but stumbled out, phone, keys, and leashed dog in hand.

Thankfully the weather was lovely and it didn't look as though I'd regret the addition of a cardigan—or an umbrella, though life in Portland had certainly taught me caution.

A glance at my phone showed a text from Alex, asking how I was. Another text displayed Neil's name. I hit the call button and waited for the line to connect.

"Hello, gorgeous," Neil said a moment later. I felt the tension in my neck release, just the smallest bit.

"Hi."

"Enjoying your day?"

"Um . . ." I looked from side to side. The last thing I wanted was someone overhearing. "I was working downstairs. I saw . . . I saw a mouse."

"Oh no."

"Adrian's begun to take care of it; he's out buying traps." I shuddered. "I'm grossed out just saying it. Grossed out, worried it'll affect our opening date, overall jet-lagged . . ."

"Sounds terrible," Neil said cheerily. Perhaps too cheerily for my taste. "What are you doing now?"

"Walking Gigi. They say walking is good for stress."

"There's research in that direction, yes. How's it working?"

"Not. Not working. Neil, what if we have a terrible infestation? What if they die in the walls? What if we open and the mice aren't actually gone, and customers see them, and we end up with dismal Yelp reviews that we can't ever come back from?"

"You've put a lot of thought into this."

"Neil!" Tears stung my eyes.

"Juliette, deep breath. You're not being rational."

"I'm being plenty rational!" I shouted into the phone, drawing curious stares from passersby.

"The world is not going to end. I promise. You may have to hire a professional, but if your mice run out of food and shelter and can't get inside, they'll find someone else who's easier to bother. You might have to push your opening date out, but you're leasing from your parents, so your overheads are low, and if your investor's at all intelligent, you should have an emergency fund for this sort of thing. I'm sorry you're stressed, but I promise you'll still be able to go on, still be able to have success."

Somewhere in my head, somewhere deep, I thought he might maybe be right.

But the rest of my head raged that he wasn't taking me seriously, that he wasn't listening. "I'm sorry," I heard myself say into the phone. "I can't talk right now."

"Juliette—," I heard Neil protest, but my thumb was already en route to the end button.

Gigi and I had reached a park, which meant that there were lots of people to witness the tears rolling down my face. It also meant there were benches—I sank onto the nearest one before my legs gave out.

I felt ridiculous. I knew I was blowing the situation out of proportion, and that I'd behaved badly . . . and yet I couldn't stop crying.

A couple of people stopped to see if I needed help. I shook my head. An elderly woman handed me a tissue and patted me on the shoulder before shuffling on.

I thanked her and blew my nose.

My phone rang. Neil's face and number flashed on the screen.

"Hullo?" I said when I answered, my voice nasal from tear-induced congestion.

"Juliette, sweetheart, are you crying?"

"Yes," I warbled. "In a public park. It's not ideal."

He chuckled. "I'm sorry. I shouldn't be laughing. I just wanted to tell you that I'm sorry you're stressed, and I should have been more sympathetic."

"I really miss you," I said, a new wave of tears threatening release. "And I'm stressed about the restaurant, and I'm afraid of failure, and I'm really, really tired."

"You should go home and sleep, Jules. Don't make me talk about medical studies about sleep and brain function. It won't end well for either of us."

I giggled. "You're funny."

"I'm glad you think so."

"It's true. I also need to blow my nose again."

"Can you get home okay, or do you need me to call someone for you? Or a taxi?"

"I'm only about a mile away." I crumpled my tissue. "I'll be okay. I . . . I wish you were here."

"Me too. We'll see each other soon, though. And we'll talk."

"The next couple weeks are going to be crazy." I stood, beginning to walk in the direction of home. "We might wind up having to go back to e-mails, unless I'm lucky enough to get the occasional window."

"Then I look forward to your e-mails."

"I know I'll laugh about this later, but . . ."

"I know, sweetie. Go home. Rest."

"I'm already walking."

"Good. Call me or text me when you get there, okay? Unless you want me to stay on the line. I'm happy to talk you through the walk. If you want, you can tell me where you are and I'll follow your route on Google Earth."

I laughed again; my shoulders relaxed. "That's either very romantic or very stalker-y. I'm okay. I'll text you when I get back."

"Be safe."

"It's still daylight, silly."

"Don't walk into an oncoming car by accident, okay?"

"And I thought I was the one who was supposed to be irrational."

Neil gave a rueful chuckle. "I don't like it when you're upset. Makes me worry, okay?"

"I'll text you when I'm home. But you're right—it will be a perilous journey. The skateboarders are out today in full force."

"I love you, Jules."

"I love you too, Neil."

Twenty minutes later, I'd made it home in time to see Adrian unloading supplies from his car.

Adrian took in my reddened eyes and frowned. "Juliette? What happened? Are you okay?"

"I'm fine," I said, holding out a placating hand. "Took a walk, got overwhelmed. An old lady gave me a Kleenex." I held it up for him, unclenching it from the center of my hand. "I just need to go rest."

Adrian shook his head. "You and your brother, stubborn to the bone."

"Yes, well, we're in good company." I pointed to the bags. "Thanks for . . . doing what you're doing."

Adrian stood up straighter. "You're welcome. Anytime. I'll keep working—you go upstairs. I don't want to see you again."

"Right-o," I said, giving a mock solute.

I could feel his gaze as Gigi and I walked up the stairs to the apartment door. I unlocked the door and pushed it in. Gigi ran in ahead of me; I turned and waved to Adrian as I stepped inside. He waved back, giving me a warm smile and a wink.

I was too tired to dwell on it. Gigi drank from her water dish before dashing to my bedroom. She and I agreed on that account. It was time for a nap.

I woke with a start some time later—I didn't know how long. Gigi raised her head from the pillow, opening an eye just long enough to find out what I was doing before dropping her head back to its resting place. I reached for my phone to check the time: 4:43.

I listened for the sounds of other people, whether it was Clementine in the apartment or Nico and company below, but I only heard the occasional traffic outside my window.

And it was warm. For the sake of keeping the bills down, I'd kept the A/C off, but soon enough there wouldn't be any help for it. Fifteen years ago, Grand-mère had spent the money having the house retrofitted with energy-efficient windows and an HVAC system that was both more effective and more attractive than having window units in every single window. Before, the giant ovens at the center of the patisserie had kept the entire building swelteringly warm in the summers. The addition of the A/C had ensured that she sold plenty of ginger lemonade, iced hibiscus tea, and fruit tarts, even on the warmest of days.

Since everyone was out, I took Gigi out to relieve herself before putting her in her kennel, gathering my cleaning supplies and heading to the restaurant kitchen.

True to his word, Adrian had begun pest control. I could see traps placed in strategic locations all around the kitchen and the dining room. Unless one of them started rattling, I wasn't about to check them for occupants.

Instead, I set to work cleaning. I emptied out the pantry, checking for any evidence of chewed-through bags or packaging, and cleaned the shelves, walls, and floors. I moved on to the grill and the oven, pulling the appliances away from the walls and deep cleaning along the baseboards.

For better or for worse, everything seemed plenty clean. After all, we'd only finished our health inspection days before. The fact that we now had rodent visitors boggled my mind. Still, being on my hands and knees on the floor helped me to work out my frustration and anxiety.

I heard the back door open and slam shut, followed by voices. A moment later, Nico, Adrian, and Clementine towered over me.

"What are you doing?" Adrian asked, incredulous. "I thought you were going to take the afternoon off."

I sat back on my heels and rested my hands on my knees. "I did. It's like six now. Evening time."

Clementine laughed and shook her head. "Fair enough, though it looks like you cleaned my station."

"I did."

"It was pristine," she said, not sounding offended but merely reciting the fact.

"It was," I agreed.

"Feel better?"

"Yes, actually." I gestured at the three of them. "What are you all up to?"

"More pest control," Adrian said. "Checking for anywhere they might have gotten in."

"Are you sure it was a mouse you saw?" Nico asked, crossing his arms. "Because I haven't seen any evidence, anywhere."

I stood, setting my cleaning supplies aside. "You mean did I mistake a mouse for what, a cockroach? I saw a mouse, and even if it was something else, it couldn't have been anything that a diner would like to see running along a restaurant floor. Plus," I added, "it had a tail."

Clementine cringed. "Ew."

Nico turned to her in frustration. "You work in the food industry. How can you be squeamish?"

She stiffened. "Look—I can deal. But nobody said I had to like it."

I rolled my eyes and turned to Adrian. "Consider yourself the pest control foreman."

Clementine slugged his arm. "Just what you've always wanted."

Adrian shrugged. "Don't mind helping. If we all split up, this'll go faster. We have to look through the baseboards and the walls for any holes or gaps. If you do, we've got black foam to paste over it. Nico and I will start with the basement. Juliette, you and Clementine can work on this floor."

I nodded.

"It's six now," he said. "When we're done I strongly suggest we go out for pizza."

"Amen," I said, and we all set to work.

To: Neil McLaren, neil.mclaren.f1@netmail.com
From: Me, jdalisa@twobluedoors.com

Dear Neil,

I hope you've well recovered from my unfortunate meltdown this afternoon. After a nap, I know I did. I woke up and started working on the kitchen, with help from Nico, Clementine, and Adrian; Alex arrived around eight, and Nico roped the new line cook, Kenny, into helping as well.

(It feels funny calling Kenny "new"—he worked with Nico at the last restaurant, and has been working part-time for my dad for, like, ever. He's great, a hard worker, intuitive about food. Glad we've got him on board. So . . . he's our new regular line cook. I'll work on a better title.)

Anywho, we ordered pizza and ate in the apartment after.

Nico and Adrian did find some mousy evidence in the basement, but they said it looked more like the mice were just passing through and less long-term residents. Which makes sense, since there's the construction across the street, and we had a near-perfect score on our health inspection (I feel like I keep nattering on about it, but there it is).

So . . . I think we'll be okay. And I think the restaurant will open on time. And I'm very, very thankful that Adrian turned out to be handy with such things.

Thanks for sending the links to the Top Gear episodes! I'll be working on invitations for the restaurant soon, both the creation bit and the postage bit, so hopefully I'll have some sit-down time soon to watch.

Also hoping for time to get back to the letters. When I left off, Mireille was writing about how glad she was to have ended her relationship with Gilles. Since Gilles was the man I believed to be my mother's father, this is all very confusing. It's strange reading these letters, discovering the beginnings, knowing the endings, but having so little information about anything in between. I meant to read more last night but was too worn out, and I'm using the last of my energy to write to you.

Of all seasons of life, almost-opening-a-restaurant season is not ideal for genealogy.

But I'm just fussing again.

Write to me, N. I miss you.

14

A restaurant is a fantasy—a kind of living fantasy
in which diners are the most important members
of the cast.

—Warner LeRoy

To: Me, jdalisa@twobluedoors.com
From: Neil, neil.mclaren.f1@netmail.com

Dear Juliette,

Any mice in traps this morning? Are you brave enough to check?

Glad you have so many people to come and help. I wish I could have joined in, though I'd be more likely to find myself in a corner trying to test mouse droppings for hantavirus.

Staying busy here. The powers that be have decided to restructure the department, which leaves me with a stack of evaluations and paperwork when I'm not in meetings.

I couldn't care less, as long as my funding stays put and Callan and I can work together. He's been a good friend. I enjoy my work, but even I will admit that elements of immunology research can become tedious. Callan's company makes up for a lot.

My parents are excited about the trip out to meet you. I'm working out an itinerary for your visit; if there's something in particular you'd like to see, let me know. Rhodes College makes for good walking; my sister is a fan of the Dixon Gallery and Gardens. Of course, there's Graceland (though you strike me as

more of a Johnny Cash girl than an Elvis girl. Feel free to correct
me if I'm wrong).

All that to say—if there's something you want to do, tell me,
and if you want me to play tour guide, I can do that too.

Love, Neil

To: Neil, neil.mclaren.f1@netmail.com
From: Me, jdalisa@twobluedoors.com

Dear Neil,

Pleased to report that a) mice were caught in the traps, but
b) I was not the one to find them. So far, no new evidence of any
critters running about, which is positive.

Now that the Great Mouse Emergency has passed, life has
continued on as before. Yesterday I began training the waitstaff
on the menu, teaching them about each menu item. The benefit,
obviously, is that a diner can ask any question about the ingredients, the preparation, or the taste, and it can be answered by the
waiter.

All we have to do is make it through the soft opening. And
the grand opening. And the first two years . . .

One step at a time.

I'll be very honest, I haven't had any time to think about what
to do in Memphis, other than be very, very glad to see you again.
So if we spend half of our time sitting on your porch, I'll be more
than contented with that.

Love, Juliette

That night I prepared for family dinner, gathering up the small gifts I'd purchased during my travels. I had scarves for the ladies, belts for the gentlemen,
and a pretty beaded hair clip for Chloé, as well as some wine and olive oil to
share.

I gathered up Gigi's necessaries—leash, water dish, and ball — and packed the two of us into the car.

At my parents' home, we were met with a hero's welcome. As Maman folded me into her arms, I couldn't help but wince at the fragility of them.

"Did you have a nice weekend out?" I asked once she'd pulled away to study me for signs of health and/or fatigue.

"Ah, bon—we had a lovely time away."

"It's my turn," my father said, pulling me into an embrace of his own. "How was my family? Did they treat you as one of their own?"

"Above and beyond," I assured him. "They were wonderful. I enjoyed catching up with them."

"Well, you must come inside. You brought pictures, yes?"

"I did," I said, patting my purse. "I put them all on a flash drive."

The rest of the family waited inside; I found Chloé on the floor, giving Gigi a belly rub, while Alex and Nico discussed which of the family's Alfas needed to be repaired first. Within moments we were all gathered around the table, pausing in a moment of prayer before diving into the dinner my father had prepared.

As usual, my father had crafted a beautiful meal. After a warm July day, the grilled leeks with poached eggs tasted perfect. We continued to the grilled tuna served with a tomato bruschetta and generous servings of garbanzo bean salad.

While I ate, I fielded questions about the trip, what I saw, where I went, and which family members I spoke with, all while swallowing questions of my own. I was able to catch everyone up on the latest family happenings, give updates on the children, and recount each meal I'd eaten. But rather than create chaos, I decided to save my own questions for a later date.

For dessert, my father served warm, honeyed focaccia, studded with fresh figs and sprinkled with rosemary and pine nuts. "This is good," Sophie said, slice in hand. "Juliette, you should take some of this back to Clementine. Nico—why didn't you bring her along this week?"

"This week?" I turned an innocent glance toward Nico. "You brought Clementine last week? That was . . . nice of you."

Nico blushed and shifted in his seat. "I was working at the restaurant until coming here. Inviting her seemed like the polite thing to do."

Ladies and gentlemen, my brother, Emily Post.

"I'm sure she appreciated it." I cut another slice of fig focaccia. "She's great company."

"Oh, she is," Sophie agreed. "She's very, you know, 'Portland' . . ."

Which was Sophie's shorthand for piercings and a couple of small tattoos of Julia Child quotes. "But 'Portland' suits her," I interrupted. "Don't you think, Nico?"

"Sure," he said. "So when are you leaving to visit Neil in Memphis?"

Well played, Nico. Well played.

"You're visiting Neil in Memphis?" Maman asked. "Are you meeting his family?"

I licked the honey from my fingertips before answering. "His parents, I think, will be coming to visit. They live in North Carolina. I'm not sure whether his sister's coming. She lives in Jackson."

"That's in . . . Florida?" Sophie asked.

I shook my head. "Mississippi. Well, Neil's sister lives in Mississippi. I know there's a Jacksonville in Florida, that might be what you're thinking of."

"There are a lot of Jacksonvilles," Nelson, Sophie's husband, noted. "Isn't there one near Medford?"

Alex shrugged. "That's all right. Most of the country thinks Portland is a city of godless liberals who put birds on things."

I hid a delighted grin at the return of my oldest brother's dry humor. "Which is so silly," I said, reaching for my water glass. "Everyone knows we're decorating with bicycles these days."

"And owls," Sophie added. "Which are technically still birds."

Nico nodded. "And marijuana."

Sophie backhanded his arm. "Nico! Not in front of Chloé!"

Chloé rolled her eyes. "Mom, I know what pot is."

"Where did you learn about pot?"

"School."

Sophie wadded up her napkin. "Private school. We'll look into it."

"Mom!"

Nelson patted his wife's shoulder. "I'm pretty sure they know what pot is in private schools too."

"I'm pretty sure this conversation has veered wildly off course," I said, standing. "Who wants to see pictures?"

"Of pot?" Nico asked with fake innocence.

Sophie gave him a look that would have withered a cactus. "Enough."

"He's just bored." I slid a glance at Nico. "I wonder what Clementine's up to tonight."

"Is Neil going to propose in Memphis?" he shot back.

"Propose?" Maman echoed. "Isn't it . . . a bit early for that?"

"Nico's just joking, Maman," I assured her. Although now that Nico mentioned it . . .

Neil wasn't going to propose. We hadn't known each other nearly long enough, hadn't spent the time together, hadn't talked about life directions or future plans. Our lives and love remained in limbo, and I didn't know when and how that might ever change.

The week flew by. The mice disappeared as quickly as they appeared. We managed a last-minute reinspection, which we passed with flying colors. This time, I hoped it would stick.

Every night I fell into bed, asleep an entire second before my head hit the pillow.

The Friday before the invitation-only soft opening, I picked up the menus from the FedEx Office. I came home so elated, I set to work in the kitchen making cookies.

With a plate of warm cookies and a glass of whole milk, I settled into my favorite living room chair and allowed myself to relax with Mireille's letters.

November 3, 1938

Dear Cécile,

    I confess I've been quite desolate since you left. What fun we had! I have worn my new hats to class, where one of my instructors (sadly, not Monsieur Roussard) said that I looked quite pert that morning.

    The fact that I have been working harder than any of my classmates has slowly earned the respect of my instructors and a little notoriety from my classmates (in addition to the notoriety of being a woman). My classmates have, I think, begun to work harder than they would have otherwise. The end result is that the instructors of my classes have noticed that their students are altogether more dedicated; I overheard one professor state to another that he may have to add material to the class because the students have mastered the course material so rapidly.

    But I'm still working very hard, and the other gentlemen in my classes remain suspicious of my presence. I'm doing well in my chocolate (though sometimes it seizes up, but I'm getting there) and laminated dough classes, but the rising agents! I have struggled. I'm acceptable with baking soda and cream of tartar, but yeast can be capricious and difficult to please. The weather, lately, has not aided my efforts.

    I hope you enjoy the chocolates. Cook is quite disturbed by the number of things in the kitchen I have been dipping in chocolate, or mixing into my chocolate. My latest creation is a cardamom chocolate truffle, which is quite sophisticated. The challenge has been grinding the cardamom fine enough so that it's undetectable in a creamy chocolate base. Next term I'll be taking a course in creams and custards, which I'm very much looking forward to. My hope is to have ice creams and ices well under my belt before the heat of summer.

    We shall see. I've been so tired lately that I've drifted off at the dinner table, to Tante Joséphine's horror (in my defense, she is occasionally a tedious conversation partner). The important part is that I'm fully awake in my classes, so as not to miss a thing. I can't even imagine what might happen if my classmates saw me—the only female student—yawn in class.

    They would probably celebrate.

    Bisous,

    Mireille

November 17, 1938

Dear Cécile,

    Just a short letter this time. I have my final tests this week, which means I must make my very best chocolates and laminated doughs, and pray to the Lord above that my yeast doughs don't fall or rise sky high the way they were just last week.

    I must succeed at this, dearest. I don't know how I'd live with the disgrace, otherwise.

    Chocolate and bisous,
    Mireille

November 29, 1938

Dear Mireille,

    Praying for your tests! Mother lit a candle for you at the church. I'm sure you'll sail through, but know that I'll love you no matter the outcome.

    When the tests are over, please set your pastry tools aside, if only for a day or two, and catch up on your sleep. Wear something pretty, and let Tante Joséphine take you shopping.

    Bisous!
    Cécile

December 8, 1938

My very dearest sister Cécile,

    I passed all of my classes!! My breads were perfect, my chocolates smooth and unblemished, my laminated pastries so airy and buttery that M. Roussard sighed when he sampled a bite!

    After class he stopped and asked if I had yet visited Ladurée on Rue Royale during my time in Paris.

    I told him that I had, but that I hadn't been since I was young.

    My dearest sister, you know this to be a gentle stretching of the truth, since we visited there together just weeks ago. However . . . the preparations for the final tests aged me in a way that even Tante Joséphine noticed. The girl before the tests, indeed, she was very young.

And so when M. Roussard asked if I would like to return to Ladurée on Saturday, you must imagine how delighted I felt. I accepted, of course, and floated all the way home.

My new classes begin in two weeks. As I wrote before, I'll be taking a course on creams and custards, as well as the principles of candy making, and introduction to fruit.

I had believed that fruit and I were sufficiently acquainted for several years now, but I'm sure I will learn more. You must know what a trial it is for me to keep my impertinent thoughts to myself in class! I have worked to be a credit to Maman, and I believe that even she would consider my behavior to be beyond reproach. If only I could have achieved such results in a drawing room, rather than a kitchen—c'est la vie.

I will be departing for a visit home on Monday the 19th. I shall come bearing many sweets to distribute amongst our friends and, yes, even our enemies in the village, while wearing the dresses we bought together in the city.

Let them eat cake, I say!

(Although I won't move on to proper cakes for yet another term, no one has to know that.)

Bisous!

Mireille

December 10, 1938

My dear Cécile,

I'm in love with Gabriel, and I'm going to marry him. I thought it appropriate to tell you.

Mireille

My heart swelled with the last letter. I loved Mireille's certainty; I could see it in her handwriting, in the way she wrote, the way she signed her name. As I read, I couldn't help but wonder if I had that kind of certainty about Neil. I certainly hadn't written Caterina to inform her of an impending marriage.

Was it simply because Mireille lived in a different time? People didn't date for three years before marrying back then. Or was it because she'd had more time with Gabriel than I'd had with Neil? From the letters, it hardly seemed so.

A part of me wanted to wring my hands, to wonder, to worry. The more rational part (which I was simply surprised to find still awake) reminded myself that I would see Neil soon, in Memphis, and afterward, who knew?

Perhaps I would be e-mailing Caterina.

~ ROSEMARY FIG FOCACCIA ~

1 packet (about 2¼ teaspoons, or 7 grams) of yeast

½ cup warm water

2 cups flour

2 tablespoons olive oil, plus more for bowl and baking sheet

2 tablespoons sugar

½ teaspoon sea salt

About 9 fresh figs, washed and sliced into halves with
     stems removed

6 tablespoons honey

4 tablespoons butter, melted

1½ tablespoons fresh rosemary leaves

2 heaping tablespoons pine nuts

Scatter the yeast over the top of the water and set aside while the yeast bubbles, about two minutes. Lay out a pastry cloth and dump the flour into the center. Make a well with your fingers, pulling flour from the center to the outside, forming a ridge. Fill the well with the olive oil, sugar, sea salt, and yeast water. With your fingers, slowly work the flour into the liquid mixture until a dough forms. If it's running dry, add a few drops of water.

Knead the dough until smooth and elastic. Lightly oil a mixing bowl and place the dough inside, giving the dough a turn in the oil. Place a tea towel or dishtowel over the top of the bowl; allow the dough to rise in a warm place until it doubles in size, about an hour.

Preheat the oven to 350°F. Line a baking sheet with parchment paper, and gently oil the parchment paper.

Place the dough on the baking sheet, pressing and stretching gently until it measures about ten inches in diameter. Poke the dough with your fingers first, then pierce the top all over with a fork. You want lots of dips and valleys for the good stuff to sink into.

Press the halved figs into the dough, cut side up. If you want to get fancy, feel free to create a pattern with the figs.

Stir the honey and melted butter together with the rosemary. Glaze the top of the bread with half of the mixture. Sprinkle with pine nuts and sea salt.

Bake the focaccia for about 25 minutes, or until the edges have browned, the top is crisp, and the focaccia is cooked through. Remove from the oven and add another layer of glaze with the remainder of the honey, butter, and rosemary mixture. Serve warm. If you're feeling adventurous, crumble a bit of blue cheese on top.

Serves 6–8.

Popcorn for breakfast! Why not? It's a grain. It's like, like, grits, but with high self-esteem.

—JAMES PATTERSON

*T*he next morning I awoke to find a sweet e-mail from Neil in my inbox, wishing me luck for the day ahead.

I smiled through breakfast.

Clementine began her work well before dawn, prepping the puff pastry for the fruit galettes and stirring the custard for the ice cream.

I spent the morning making final touches, polishing the wood tables until they shown, and trimming back any of the flowers and greenery that reached too far into the outdoor deck seating.

Nico, Adrian, and Kenny filtered in later in the day and began the prep work, cutting piles of slim asparagus, translucent shallots, and sweet, glossy peppers.

An hour before the doors opened, I ran upstairs to dress for the dinner seating. I slipped into my little black dress, the one I'd purchased in Rome. A swipe of eyeliner, a little more mascara, and a layer of Nars Montego Bay, and I looked like . . . well, as close as I could get to Sofia Loren playing a restaurant manager.

In Oregon.

Without a tan.

I strapped on my watch, slipped into my heels, and promised my feet a long soak once the evening ended—they'd need it.

My heart swelled once I made it back downstairs and opened the two blue doors, the ones we'd named the restaurant for. Recently washed, the blue paint

gleamed in the summer sunlight. I found small knots in my stomach beginning to loosen, right around the time new ones formed.

My mind flew in thirty different directions as I tried to process all of the
things that I needed to do, the people who would be coming, and the food that
would be served. Instead of completely freaking out, the way I wanted to, I
focused on putting one foot in front of the other, completing tasks before the
guests arrived.

I stepped into the kitchen to check in. "How are things?"

"Good," Nico said, not looking up as he worked. "Real good."

Adrian, however, looked up. "Nice dress," he said, giving me a quick but
thorough once-over.

"Thanks," I said, feeling a blush creep over my face.

"You have to taste one of the cherry *zeppole*." Clementine called out. "The
choux pastry came out particularly well this morning. And the cherries—you
just have to taste one."

"Yeah?" I strode through the kitchen toward the pastry station. As I
walked past Nico and Adrian, I spied Adrian's gaze through the corner of my
eye. My dress wasn't anywhere near indecent, I reminded myself.

Just, you know . . . short. And snuggish. And . . . who was I kidding? If I
was going to wear it, I needed to *wear* it. As I listened to Clementine verbally
swoon over her pastry—and rightfully so—I squared my shoulders and stood
taller.

Clementine plated a zeppola for me; I used my fingers to lift the confec-
tion to my lips.

"Oh my goodness." I licked the stray powdered sugar from my lips. "If you
told me angels came down from heaven and made the choux pastry, I would
believe you."

"And the cherry filling?"

"It's perfect. This is going to be an instant classic, Clementine. Be excited."

"Oh, don't worry," she said. "I am."

The waiters tromped in a split-second later, one after another. I left the
kitchen to give the waiters their final marching orders. Before I knew it, guests
began to pour through the doors.

I knew most of our guests, but not all, as our primary investor, Frank, had invited friends and colleagues of his own. As the hostess of the dining room, I sat everyone at their tables, handed out menus, and assured each guest that their servers would arrive to take their drink orders and answer questions about the menu.

Maman and Papa entered, both very chic—Papa in an Italian suit, despite the heat, and Maman in a little black dress. She'd arranged to have her chemo port in her arm rather than her chest, so it stayed tucked away inside the sheer sleeve of her silk cardigan. They took their turns kissing me on both cheeks before allowing me to lead them away.

Sophie and Nelson came in a few moments later, with Chloé and Alex in tow. "We're on an uncle-niece date," Chloé informed me. "Could we have our own table?"

"Sure, sweetie," I said, looking to her parents. "You guys get a real date night! I'll be right back."

I led my brother and niece to a table in the sunshine and gave them menus. "Your server will be with you to take your drink order and answer any questions you might have about the menu."

Chloé giggled.

Alex shook his head. "We can't laugh, Chloé. Our Juliette has gone corporate." He looked up at me and winked. "It looks great in here. Grand-mère would have loved it."

I couldn't hold back my smile, not that I tried. "Thanks, Alex."

"You should get back to Sophie. She looks impatient."

Chloé snorted.

Alex raised an eyebrow at her. "You're getting in all sorts of trouble tonight."

I left the two of them to banter while I set Sophie and Nelson up at a lovely table with a view of the garden. I repeated my line about the menu and their server, and then left to help our next guests.

While I likely wouldn't have all three of my waiters working the dining room at the same time, tonight I scheduled all of them. I watched in pleasure as they worked their tables with smooth, charming efficiency.

Within moments the orders began to flood in. Drinks, appetizers, salads—Nico called out the orders, Adrian and Kenny each answering with a quick "yes, chef." Knives sliced and chopped, drink orders left the kitchen.

I watched over the front of the house, adjusting the temperature as the space warmed, quieting the music just a hair.

While most everyone had spent their first moments in the dining room looking around, taking in the views from the windows and checking out the interior décor, a hum now filled the dining room as people forgot where they were and simply began to engage with their dining companions.

Minutes later, appetizers began to leave the kitchen.

Nico and I had argued over an *amuse-bouche*. He'd liked the idea of sending out the tiny complimentary appetizer, but I wasn't convinced. In a day and age when so many people had specific dietary needs and desires—whether they were gluten-free, dairy-free, vegan, vegetarian, or Paleo—sending out the same complimentary bite sounded foolish. As a new business we couldn't afford the extra expense, especially if half of them wound up uneaten.

In the end he'd agreed, mainly because we agreed about the kind of restaurant we were opening.

It wasn't a shock-and-awe-type place—we weren't serving salad with a side of dry ice. Instead, we'd worked to create a menu that was special and notable but not yelling for attention—the execution would speak for itself.

Time would tell if our strategy would set us far enough apart to keep us in business, but until our Yelp reviewers wept for a measly amuse-bouche, we'd spend our time and energy on other things.

Like mousetraps.

Even though we hadn't had a single rodent visitor since our last inspection, I'd remained jumpy and watchful.

But so far, our diners were having a lovely time. Appetizers were passed around, and people smiled as they ate. By the time the entrees came out, I began to relax. Every table I visited—whether it was friends, family, or strangers—held happy faces and kind words.

We were going to pull this off. Everything was going to be okay.

My shoulders sagged in relief, and I cast a glance outside to admire the view.

And wished I hadn't. While our diners ate beautiful, carefully crafted dishes, seated on handcrafted leather chairs, sixteen unicyclists rode their wheels down the street, past the restaurant.

Naked.

My mother gasped.

Marti, my former boss at the newspaper, laughed out loud.

Alex, Sophie, and Nelson all flailed their hands toward Chloé, in an effort to shield her eyes.

Frank sat at his table and counted each unicyclist. Out loud. And when each one had passed, having literally ridden off into the sunset, Frank set aside his fork to applaud. The rest of the dining room joined in, with the exception of the members of the family who were trying to block Chloé's view.

In that moment, I realized something deep and true.

There would be mice. There would be naked unicyclists.

There would be so many things, all wholly out of my control. Things would happen—good things, bad things, funny things. Things that managed to be all three at once.

I had to listen to Idina Menzel and let it go. Not that I was planning to run around leaving mouse munchies on the floor, but there was only so much pre-planning I could do. The rest would just have to happen.

Trust . . . wasn't historically my thing. As the youngest in a restaurant family, I knew I was loved, but I also knew that my needs weren't top priority.

Most of the time, this was a good thing—I learned to become highly self-reliant at a young age. But as I stared down the end of my twenties, I found myself increasingly aware of the fact that self-reliance wasn't going to prepare me for every trial, mishap, or tragedy that came my way.

So I joined in with the laughter in the dining room.

I wasn't laughing at the unicyclists, bless their breezy bums. I laughed because they'd been the ones to finally crystalize the realization that I really, really needed to let God take care of our kooky little restaurant.

Hopefully the next time I needed a life lesson, it wouldn't require mass nudity.

Our patrons left the restaurant slowly, several of them lingering over dessert, coffee, and cheese plates.

My former editor at the newspaper, Marti, patted my arm on her way out. "Look at you, landing on your feet. You belong here. Well done."

Praise from Marti? I'd take it.

Linn pointed at my chest. "You. Me. Coffee. This?" She circled her finger toward the ceiling. "This is great. You look completely at home here."

I smiled in gratitude. "That means a lot coming from you."

"You've earned it. This place looks like you. It's meticulous—you've put a lot of work in here, and it shows."

"I'll be in Memphis next week—coffee when I get back?"

"Memphis?" Linn's eyes widened. "If you're going to Memphis, we just upgraded to lunch."

"Lunch, then. Let's do it." We hugged, I shook her husband's hand, waved good-bye as they stepped outside and into the dim twilight.

My parents, siblings, and niece were the last to leave, seasoning their good-byes with praise, well-wishes, misty eyes, and a particularly rib-crushing hug from my father.

By the time the doors closed after them, the busboys and waitstaff had cleaned the tables, and Mallory was hauling the vacuum out. With the front of the house ready for another day, I helped in the kitchen until it shined as well.

Nico "found" a bottle of champagne and suggested we take it upstairs along with the leftovers that wouldn't keep—soup, bread, and a smattering of desserts. Not wanting to risk a mess in the downstairs, I agreed, even though all I wanted to do was soak my feet for eight to twelve hours.

"A success!" Nico crowed as he poured champagne into flutes.

"Yes, it was," I said, happy to relieve him of a glass. "We'll have to prepare for more of the cherry zeppole and the goat cheese starters—I think those are going to be big sellers."

Nico carried his glass to the couch and sank into the middle. "Agreed."

"But we need to work on getting the duck out faster."

"Yeah, yeah. We'll get there."

Adrian took his glass and sprawled on the floor. "That was a rush. I'm starving. I'm too tired to eat." He covered his eyes with a large, callused hand. "Crisis."

Clementine surveyed the food offerings. "There's plenty of soup," she said, her suggestion drowned out by a chorus of male groans.

Apparently soup could not assuage the hunger created by a dinner service. While I had difficulty mustering sympathy—it had been a relatively easy, fully-staffed evening—we had plenty to celebrate.

I considered ordering pizza, but the thought made my soul shrivel. Instead, I opened our refrigerator and inspected the contents.

Fresh chicken breasts, summer Meyer lemons, mascarpone cheese, and spinach—add some pasta and I had the makings of a simple but satisfying dinner.

I tied on an apron and set to work. Adrian groaned when he walked into the kitchen and saw me standing over the stove. "You've been on your feet for hours," he said. "Let's just order in."

"Thought about it," I said, turning the chicken before settling the lid on the wide sauté pan. "Just seemed wrong."

"Cooks eat a lot of pizza."

"Former food-writers don't."

"Hey—you're a manager now. Live a little."

I arched an eyebrow. "Come on. Are you trying to tell me that a pizza that's been sweating in a corrugated cardboard box for twenty minutes is going to taste better than fresh food?"

"Never said it would taste better—part of putting up your feet after a night is to put up your feet."

I shrugged and began to zest a lemon. "I'll relax when this is done. Won't take long."

His gaze sharpened. "You don't relax much, huh?"

"Nope." I threw him a smile. "You can chop the spinach if you want."

"Slave driver."

Eye roll. "Whatever. Don't sprain your wrist."

"This knife is dull."

I laughed out loud. "Now you're making things up."

"Could be." He set the spinach aside. "What else needs to be done?"

"Not much. You can give the the pine nuts a light toast, if you like, but otherwise it's all drain and dump from here."

"I can toast pine nuts."

I nodded to the bag on the counter. "They're over by the flour bin."

With Adrian's help, the last-minute pasta really did come together quickly. I drained the pasta over the spinach leaves, saved some of the pasta water, and threw everything together. As a finishing touch, I squeezed a bit of lemon juice over the sliced chicken before layering it over the top of the pasta.

Adrian and I ladled it into bowls and handed them out. Once everyone had a bowl of pasta, I took my own bowlful, landed in a chair, and kicked up my feet with gratitude.

To: Neil, neil.mclaren.f1@netmail.com
From: Me, jdalisa@twobluedoors.com

Dear Neil,

Well, the opening went well. Full house, but except for a few odd bobbles, everything went smoothly.

Sophie sent her food back, and Nico threatened to send it right back, which would have resulted in a meltdown in the dining room that nobody needed. We ran out of the cherry-filled, Italian-style donuts (which were amazing, so I totally understood).

Everyone was complimentary, which was a relief. We had comment cards on the tables, which I will tackle Monday morning.

My one goal for tomorrow is to make it to church on time. Afterward I plan to do a bit of packing for Memphis.

I can't wait to see you! I miss you so very much.

Juliette

P.S. I've been checking the Memphis weather. Is there anything in particular I should pack?

To: Me, jdalisa@twobluedoors.com
From: Neil, neil.mclaren.f1@netmail.com

Dear Juliette,

You could bring mosquito netting. Not for your bed, but to wear around town.

Just joking. It'll be hot and humid, so . . . I don't know what that translates into as far as women's wear. You might want a sweater or two for the evenings.

As far as the mosquitoes go, you may want to pack repellent.

I'd like to take you out on a date (or two), so whatever you'd wear on a date, bring that. And we'll also be going to dinner with my parents at a nice restaurant.

Don't think that I'm worried about what you'll wear. I know you'll look fantastic. You could walk around in chef's whites (that's me, using kitchen terms) and you'd still be the best-looking woman in the room.

Do you have time for a phone call tomorrow? I love your e-mails but I miss your voice.

Neil

~ Meyer Lemon with Farfalle ~

Both creamy and zingy, the pasta sauce for this dish comes together quickly after a little prep work. It works well as a side dish or a light meal, but for a heartier version, feel free to add sautéed chicken, shrimp, salmon, or scallops. If you do decide to add a protein, increase the mascarpone from 1 cup to $1^1/4$ cups.

1 cup pine nuts, toasted
    (see instructions)
Juice and zest of two Meyer lemons
8 ounces mascarpone
$^1/4$ teaspoon freshly grated nutmeg
1 pound farfalle, or other short pasta
10 ounces fresh spinach, roughly
    chopped
$^1/2$ teaspoon fine sea salt
Freshly ground pepper to taste

To prepare the pine nuts:
Place the pine nuts in a large skillet and toast over medium-low heat, shaking and stirring occasionally until the majority of the nuts develop a golden brown shade. Remove from heat and set aside.

To prepare the sauce:
Zest the lemons into a small bowl, and then juice. In a medium-sized mixing bowl, stir together the zest, juice, mascarpone, nutmeg, salt, and pepper. Set aside.

For the pasta:

Boil in salted water for 11–13 minutes, until al dente. Prepare a strainer in your kitchen sink; place the spinach at the bottom of the strainer. Pour the hot pasta and water into the strainer and spinach. Return the pasta to the pot along with the spinach; stir in the sauce, followed by 3/4 cup of the pine nuts. Serve immediately, garnishing with remaining pine nuts and a grind or two of additional pepper.

Serves 4–6.

16

That's something I've noticed about food: whenever
there's a crisis if you can get people to eating normally
things get better.

—MADELEINE L'ENGLE

I awoke in the dark to the buzzing of my phone. Alex. "Hey, what's
up?" I asked groggily.

"Dad's taking Mom to the emergency room," he said. "I'm following in
my car."

"What's wrong?" I asked, dread coiling in my gut.

"She was running a fever. Cancer patients have to go straight to the ER if
they have fevers."

"Right. I remember that," I said. If only it had been food poisoning—I
would rather have sent a restaurant full of diners to the emergency room, braved
a dozen terrible Yelp reviews before opening, than have my mother face a cancer complication.

"The only reason they told me is because I'm in the garage apartment. I'm
following just behind. Would you mind calling Sophie?"

"I can call her, yeah."

"I'll try Nico next."

I sat up in bed. "Nico might still be in my living room."

"You guys know how to after-party."

"I had to give up around one. If he's here I'll wake him up, if not I'll call
him for you. Are you sure you want all of us down there?"

"Sophie will want to be there," Alex reasoned.

"Gotcha. I'll be there soon to run interference."

"Thanks."

I hung up, ignoring my aching muscles as I rose and dressed. After securing Gigi in her kennel, I flipped on the hall light and investigated my living room's occupants.

Nico lay stretched on the floor, on top of an assortment of throw pillows with my yoga mat for a base. To his left, Adrian slept on the couch, his arm thrown across his eyes.

I knelt beside Nico and gave his shoulder a gentle shake. "Nico. Wake up."

"What? Why?" he groaned.

"Alex called—Dad's taking Mom to the ER."

Nico's eyes flew open. "What's wrong?"

"Fever. Other than that, don't know yet. Alex is calling Sophie, I'll meet them down there."

"Should we call Cat?"

"Yes, but let's wait until we know something. It's not worth waking her until there's information to share."

"I'll go with you," he said, pushing himself onto a sitting position. "Your camping mat is terrible."

"It's for yoga."

"Explains the color."

"Shut up. When can you be ready to go?"

"As soon as I find my shoes. What time is it?"

"Three."

Adrian sat up suddenly, blinking at the light coming from the hallway. "Everything okay?"

"My mom's sick, headed to the ER," I said. Adrian's curls were sleep-tousled and uncomfortably attractive. I looked away.

Adrian swore under his breath. "Sorry. You guys are meeting them there?"

"Yeah," I said, pulling out my phone just long enough to text Alex to tell him that Nico and I were on our way. When I looked up, Adrian was on his feet, walking to my kitchen.

I fished my shoes from the hall closet before writing a quick note for Clementine with a request that she take Gigi out in the morning if I hadn't gotten back yet. From the flush down the hall, I gathered that Nico would be ready to leave momentarily. I placed Clementine's note on the table and turned toward the kitchen.

I'd planned to gather a few snacks for the duration, but Adrian was ahead of me. He'd found my New Seasons grocery bag and had loaded it with items from my snack stash—the cookies left over from my Friday night baking spree, dried fruit, and roasted nuts, as well as some protein bars.

"Thanks for that," I said, uncertain what else to say.

"No problem. Do you think you'll need anything else?"

"Tea," I said, reaching into the bin on the right side of my pantry. "I can't solve the coffee issue, but I can make sure that no one has to drink Lipton."

"Noble goal."

Nico stepped into the kitchen doorway. "Ready to go?"

"Yeah." I grabbed the bag by the handles. "Thanks for this, Adrian."

"You're welcome. Text me if you need anything else, okay?"

"I will," I agreed. "And you're welcome to stay," I added. "You don't have to leave just because of this."

"Thanks. Your couch is pretty comfortable."

"More comfortable than a yoga mat," Nico grumbled, and with that we traded the warmth of the apartment for the damp dark of the morning and the uncertainty that lay ahead.

Nico and I made it fifteen feet into the emergency room before we heard the voices.

"There they are," said Nico.

I didn't respond. Didn't need to. Sophie's voice rang out loud and clear. "What do we have to do to get a warm blanket around here? She's shivering!"

"We're here," I said, stepping through the curtain toward my mother. She lay on the bed under three thin hospital blankets, IV fluids running through narrow tubes into the central port on her upper arm.

Papa stood beside her, holding her hand, his face drawn and gaunt.

My heart clenched tight in my chest, and for a moment I couldn't breathe at all. But I summoned every last shred of courage I could find long enough to take her hand in mine.

She gave it a weak pat. "You didn't have to come. Alex shouldn't have called everyone. I hope no one told Caterina to board a plane. I'm fine, it's only a urinary tract infection."

"He was right to call," I said. "I'm glad to be here."

"Pish. You must be so tired after your opening."

"I'm fine," I said. Sophie and I exchanged glances. She looked exhausted, her fine blond hair tied in a careless topknot, worry carving new lines in her face. We both knew that even small infections could be disastrous, no matter how much our mother wanted to make light of them.

"I brought tea with me," I added, holding up my bag. "I'm sure there's hot water somewhere. Would you like me to make you some? I have chamomile. Rooibos too, you can choose."

"Oh, *cherie,* chamomile would be nice."

"Good. I have cookies too."

Maman brightened just the tiniest bit. "Cookies?"

"Chocolate chip."

"I could probably nibble on a small one."

I opened the bag and handed her a cookie before offering the bag to my father and Alex.

"I'll be right back with the tea," I said, nodding to Sophie. The tea would help keep Maman warm in the meantime, and I'd try to track down more blankets while I was out.

I wished Neil were here, somehow. He'd charm Maman, soothe Sophie, and figure out how to get the best care out of the staff. I considered texting him, but what good would it do? I'd have to use my own resources.

Five minutes later I returned with a paper cup full of tea and a hospital staffer willing to provide blankets. We tucked them around Maman while she sipped her tea.

An hour later the doctor stopped in; if he was surprised to see the four of us stuffed into Maman's little curtained room, snacking on cookies and tea, he didn't show it. He told us the tests had confirmed a UTI and that she would be on a heavy round of antibiotics to prevent the infection from spreading to her kidneys.

Sophie grilled him for additional details, extracting every last bit of information out of him that she could. She could be a handful, my sister, but she was also a crackerjack patient advocate.

We waited another hour for the discharge papers; I passed out snacks while we waited, making two more tea runs.

By the time we left, a damp dawn stretched across the sky. Each of us kissed Maman good-bye; Alex followed them back to the house.

Sophie and I hugged good-bye, and I climbed into the passenger seat of Nico's car.

Nico turned on the heat; I folded my arms tight across my chest.

"You okay?" he asked, not looking away from the road.

I realized then that he'd hardly spoken while we'd been at the ER. "You?"

"This is bad," he said, his voice raspy. "I hate it."

"I know," I said. "Me too."

"I'm tired, but I can't sleep."

"Me neither," I said. "I was thinking about going to the early service."

Nico mulled that idea for a couple of minutes and then nodded. "Sure. Mind if we stop off at my place? I'd like a change of clothes."

"Of course."

We got back to my apartment around seven, with Nico freshly showered and dressed and me feeling like one of Gigi's chew toys.

I pushed open the door to the apartment to find Gigi napping on the couch and Adrian and Clementine cooking—and arguing—in the kitchen. At least it sounded like arguing, but it stopped the moment the door squeaked open.

"How's your mom?" Clementine asked, eyebrows knitted together in concern.

"Bacterial infection." I knelt to pet Gigi, letting her sniff the hospital scent on my clothes to her heart's content. "It's treatable." I elbowed the snack bag, now half-empty. "Thanks for this," I told Adrian.

"Yes," Nico agreed. "No lives were lost in the pursuit of food."

"You're looking spiffed up," Adrian commented, taking in Nico's clothes and still-damp hair.

"We're off to church this morning," Nico answered.

"After your night?" Clementine's eyes widened.

I straightened. "It's not as if I'd be able to sleep if I went back to bed. You're welcome to join us," I said, my gaze widening to include Adrian. "Both of you."

Adrian shrugged. "Sure. Why not? When are you leaving? I have clothes in my car. Mind if I use your shower?"

I nodded toward Clementine. "It's her shower, she's the one you should ask. I'm off to get cleaned up, you guys. I feel . . . gross."

Thirty minutes later I'd showered and dressed, applied enough makeup to not look like a tuberculosis poster and pinned my braided hair to my head, rather than dry it.

Clementine sat in the kitchen, coffee in hand.

"That is a good idea," I said. "I think it's time for coffee."

"I'm not sure about this church thing," she said, looking away from me and out the window.

"Fair enough." I reached for the coffee beans. "This church might surprise you, though. Or it might not—I don't know what kind of churches you've been to."

Clementine drained her coffee cup. "I figured they were all pretty much the same."

"Every church is different," I said, searching for the right way to explain. Living in Portland, Clementine had a native's resistance to the brand of Christianity that either made media news or was shouted at her as she walked down the street. "You know how Memphis barbeque is different from Texas barbeque, and both are different from Carolina barbeque or St. Louis–style barbeque, but somehow they're all barbeque?"

"Missing Neil much?"

"Yeah," I admitted sheepishly. "I guess my point is that there are all kinds of barbeque, but they're all the same thing at the essence."

I supposed that if I wanted to take the metaphor a step further I could make a point about how chicken dredged in barbeque sauce, baked in the oven was in no way barbeque, even though a lot of people still thought it was, but I figured we'd had enough kitchen apologetics for one morning.

"That sounds kinda Universalist. And yes, I know what that is," Clementine added.

"Mm, a Universalist would say that we could call creamed corn barbeque. Which it's not."

Clementine studied my face for a full moment before giving in to laughter. "You're weird."

"Also uncaffeinated."

"So what kind of barbeque is this church?"

"Portland barbeque. Which means there's either coffee or beer in the sauce."

She laughed again, which I decided was a good sign.

Adrian emerged dressed and bathed a few moments later, which I concluded must have had less to do with any desire to be timely, and more with the fact that the hot water heater wasn't by any means robust.

A cup of coffee and a bowl of muesli later, I gathered my purse and jacket. The four of us folded into my Alfa, which was somehow the largest of the four available vehicles.

I felt like I was back in college, squashed into a car bound for World Market.

We made it to church safely and emerged in a fashion that I hoped looked more adult and less like a clown car.

Despite the odd start to the morning, we'd arrived in enough time to file in before the music started. Somehow I found myself seated between Clementine and Adrian. I shifted in my seat to make sure my gored A-line skirt didn't somehow wind up in his personal bubble.

Which . . . would assume that he had a personal bubble.

I had no idea about Adrian's personal faith, but as we began singing I found myself impressed with his baritone singing voice. And then hating myself.

What was wrong with me? I was days away from flying to Memphis to see Neil, a man I professed to love. Was my admiration of Adrian's singing an objective appreciation of beauty? I wanted to think so, but doubted it. Was it simply a symptom of being parted from Neil for so long, or something more?

I did my best to focus on the lyrics and then the sermon. Friends, family, and loved ones were greeted and parted with.

Adrian looked around at the sanctuary's interior. "I like it here. I may have to change churches."

"Oh?" I asked, trying and probably failing to mask my surprise.

"With my work schedule, I don't make it to church all the time. But this has a good feel. Friendly."

I nodded. "I like it," I said. "I'm going to go and, um, get a drink of water."

After promising Clementine I'd come right back, I strode out of the sanctuary as fast as I could.

I felt so ashamed. Because of Adrian's flirtatious, occasionally smarmy attitude months before, I'd assumed he couldn't be a person of faith.

As if. I'd certainly met my fair share of churchgoing guys who fancied themselves ladies' men—even if being a ladies' man, to them, meant inviting two different girls to coffee in a given week—with the attitude to go with it. And here was Adrian, smiling around the sanctuary, commenting on its friendliness—hours after helping me pack food to take to the ER—when I'd been waltzing around, assuming he had to be a faithless heathen.

Good one, Juliette.

I took a drink of water, filled my lungs with oxygen, and prayed for my blackened soul.

I spent Sunday afternoon prepping meals for my parents. I made a gingery Tom Kha Gai soup and a black bean soup, and added a sturdy kale salad, and when I tucked it into the fridge for later, I began work on the quick-cooking cassoulet.

While the bean, sausage, and duck confit dish wasn't exactly health food by any dietician's standards, it was also my mom's version of comfort food. What it lacked in antioxidants, it made up for in spirit-healing properties.

I packaged each meal, freezing the soups and half of the cassoulet.

Family dinner that night felt like any other night—with the volume turned halfway down. My parents looked exhausted, though glad to see their children.

Adrian and Clementine joined in tonight, and I wondered at the extent the family had begun to fold them in. Some families became more insular during times of stress, but ours seemed to grow and expand as loved ones pitched in. Clementine, of course, I had no qualms about making one of ours. But Adrian . . . he was becoming more complicated than I wanted.

"Such a good daughter! Truly I am a blessed man," my father said at the end of the night, pulling me into a hug and kissing both of my cheeks, European-style. "You know, you did not have to bring food."

"I wanted to," I answered.

I began to gather my things and run through the good-bye hugs. With travel on the horizon, I expected no less than three from my blood relatives, and a hearty handshake from Nelson.

"So you're leaving for Memphis this week?" Adrian asked once I'd made it within three feet to the door.

"Tuesday morning," I said, the familiar bit of anxiety unfurling in my stomach.

"Fly safe, and all that," he said, smiling.

"Thanks." I cleared my throat. "Anything you want me to bring back for you?"

"A bottle of Corky's Apple Barbecue Sauce," he said. "If you've got room in your luggage."

"'Kay," I said. "See you."

He tipped an imaginary cap. "Enjoy the trip."

On Monday I packed for Memphis with a mixture of excitement and apprehension. I couldn't wait to see Neil again, but the idea of another parting made my stomach churn.

On my nightstand, I'd arranged a tableau of photos of Neil and me together—a shot we'd taken of ourselves in Portland, on the riverfront, a photo that Sandrine had taken of us by the lavender field, and yet another at Nonno's birthday party.

We looked unbearably, incandescently happy. What would it be like if we were able to have a future together? And would I be this anxious about our relationship if we lived in the same city? Living so far from each other, every interaction seemed so . . . loaded. The instability made me nervous. If we both lived in Portland, would we feel more comfortable letting our relationship develop slowly? Closer, we could have been like risotto—adding a little stock at a time, letting it absorb until the rice became rich and creamy, plump with stock and wine.

Instead . . . I didn't know what we were. Stir fry, maybe. I could only carry the food metaphors so far.

I called Caterina while I stuffed clothes into my suitcase.

"Etta!" she said warmly when she answered. "Lovely to hear from you during daylight hours."

"Oh, come on, I haven't called after midnight since . . . since Mom was in the hospital. So not long ago."

"But once you're in Memphis, we'll be in the same time zone. That'll be exciting, won't it?"

"It will," I said, grinning. "I'll be sure to call you when I'm there. We can synchronize our watches or something."

"So what's going on? Is Mom okay?"

I sighed. "She's hanging in there. The antibiotics are starting to work. We're hoping they don't give her a yeast infection, but what can you do? No, I was just calling to chat."

"Why are you calling me instead of your fella?"

"He's at work. And he's great—really."

"Good. That's good that he's great."

"It's just . . . this whole long-distance thing. I'm not even there yet, and I'm dreading saying good-bye."

Caterina exhaled. "That's rough."

"And we see each other so little that every time we're together, it's so much more intense, like we have to make the most of every moment. Sometimes I feel that's good, even special, but other times it feels like we're setting ourselves up for failure. In real life, we can't live like that all the time. We have to have time doing normal people stuff, with one of us writing e-mails on the couch while the other watches TV, sharing a box of stale crackers."

"Is there something triggering this?"

If I was honest with myself, yes. With anyone else? No. "We need more normal. Mom's sick, things are crazy, and I'd just like to have him around, you know?"

"But stale crackers? Be real."

"You know what I mean."

"Oh, I do. But the rest of it, working on the couch with the TV on . . . it's the stuff of life, you're right."

"Is that weird? I want for Neil and me to be boring together. Instead we're in this high-drama, long-distance relationship, with no end in sight, and I keep thinking that I'm just not cut out for it. And I feel guilty—think of all the military families. Why can't I get it together?"

"I don't think setting every relationship to that standard is healthy. I knew I wouldn't like that kind of life, so I didn't marry a serviceman," Caterina said plainly. "It's not for everybody, and it's foolish to think it might be."

"You think?"

"I had a friend tell me off once, because I wouldn't date a guy who would spend most of his career on the road, but I figured—look, I'm not cut out for that life. I'm high maintenance and a lot of work, just ask Damian. No guy who travels needs to come home to that. So better that he marry someone autonomous and patient than a handful like me. I mean, think about it. We were raised in a crowd, with some assembly of loved ones nearby at all times. 'Alone' is not really part of our social vocabulary."

"I can see that."

"Look, if you want unsolicited advice, Sophie's your girl. But you called me, so I'll tell you that I think you should go to Memphis and have a great time. Don't overthink it, just let the trip happen. If it's everything you ever wanted and more, great. If you need to reevaluate, you'll be okay."

Will I be okay? my heart asked, but I knew the answer. I would be disappointed but not destroyed. I would start again, even if I didn't want to. I would carry on.

I sighed. "You're right."

"Your heart will go on."

"Look at you, quoting Celine Dion."

"She feels things. Do you have anything fun planned for Memphis?"

"We're going to dinner with his parents, who are traveling to Memphis from North Carolina." I cleared my throat. "I'm not at all anxious about that."

Caterina laughed. "Dinner with the parents? Really? You're anxious about that?"

"It's not funny!"

"But he met Mom and Dad, right?"

"He did. And you're right, I should just buck up and get over it. There's no getting out of it, no telling him I wish it were just the two of us. He's really excited about it. I just have to put on my big girl apron and deal with it."

"Does it have pockets?"

"What?"

"Your big girl apron. Does it have pockets?"

"Yes," I said, baffled but game. "Several."

"Good."

"You're loopy."

"I am. And it's even daylight—who knew? But the boys didn't sleep much last night, and my current class is a handful."

"Oh yeah?"

"I've got a classroom full of students—all ages, mind you—who want to be handheld every step of the way, and if their cuisine doesn't come out the way mine does, it's my fault. Always, always my fault. They burn the risotto because they weren't stirring, or their cakes won't come out of the pan because they skipped the buttered parchment paper step. Basically I tell them how to do things, and either they don't listen or they blow me off, and then when things don't work it's my fault and they're irate because they paid good money for that risotto."

"I hope someone really said that, that they paid good money for the burned risotto."

"Oh, she did."

"What did you tell her?"

"That I provided the ingredients and the instructions, but what she did with them was her responsibility."

"How did that go over?"

"Well, the upside of being obviously Mediterranean is that you can get away with being more forceful than would be otherwise acceptable. If I sound extra Italian and flip my hair around . . . I don't know. It changes the dynamic. Damian's better at it when he guest-teaches. He flirts."

"I miss you guys."

"Seriously, come on out anytime. I won't even make you baby-sit the whole time. But you're opening a restaurant, so I know your time is not your own. I'm going to try to come out for the opening, at any rate."

"Oh, do. Please come. We had a fleet of naked unicyclists for the soft opening, so I can only imagine what will happen when we open for real."

"Chloé told me about that."

"It was . . . a notable experience for her young life."

Caterina laughed. "I'm sure. Well, dear sister, I can hear the plaintive cries of my children in the next room as they beg for nourishment."

We said our good-byes, though Cat's "dear sister" wording had stuck with me. I'd been so busy I hadn't had time to read letters. With that thought in mind, I made sure that the scans of the letters were on my computer for the flight. I'd be traveling for nearly eight hours—plenty of time to catch up on Mireille's love affair.

~ DOUBLE CHOCOLATE CHIP COOKIES ~

$2^3/_4$ cups bread flour
1 teaspoon baking soda
1 teaspoon sea salt
1 egg
1 egg yolk
2 tablespoons whole milk
2 teaspoons vanilla extract
2 sticks butter, softened
$1^1/_4$ cups dark brown sugar
$^1/_4$ cup white sugar
6 ounces dark chocolate, chopped
6 ounces semi-sweet chocolate, chopped, or chocolate chips

Whisk together flour, baking soda, and sea salt. Set aside. In a small bowl, combine egg, egg yolk, milk, and vanilla, stirring until blended.

In a stand mixer (or in a large bowl with a sturdy hand mixer), whip the butter until pale and creamy. Add the sugars and mix on medium speed for five minutes. Lower the mixer speed, add the egg mixture, and then the dry ingredients. Continue to mix until the dry ingredients are entirely combined.

Fold in the chocolates with a sturdy wooden spoon. Refrigerate dough for at least an hour, or overnight.

Preheat oven to 350°F. Drop heaping tablespoons of dough two inches apart on a parchment paper–lined baking sheet. Bake for 13–15 minutes, or until just browned. Serve warm, with milk.

17

A daydream is a meal at which images are eaten. Some of us are gourmets, some gourmands, and a good many take their images precooked out of a can and swallow them down whole, absent-mindedly and with little relish.

—W. H. AUDEN

December 18, 1939

My dearest Mireille,

I confess that after hearing your glowing account of your trip to Ladurée with M. Roussard, I am not very surprised to hear that you have developed tender feelings for him.

However, I am curious to know if there have been any events that have led you to your certainty of matrimony. You must tell me at once if I'm to be a bridesmaid in the near future. A wedding for Maman to plan would be a blessing from the Lord.

Anticipating your arrival for the holidays. Maman has me looking at wallpaper samples when I'm not writing menus for tea parties.

À bientôt,

Cécile

January 15, 1939

My dear Cécile,

Please find enclosed six tea party menus for your personal use. I regret I could not write them up during my stay, but they should free up a little of your time *(if you do not wish your time freed, then by all means stash them in your bottommost desk drawer).*

And no, Gabriel and I have made no official declarations as yet, but we will.

Oh, Cécile, he is the most wonderful man. I'm sure you're tired of hearing me gush about him, but I cannot seem to help myself.

He doesn't think I'm unladylike or impractical for pursuing pastry. And his smile? He smiled at the cranky cheesemonger, and the woman couldn't help but smile back.

I love Gabriel for everything that he is, for his generosity and devotion to his family, his kindness—so many things. He is also a lovely kisser (although I shall not reveal any more than that).

Classes begin soon; Gabriel will be returning to work. I fear I will see him very little.

À bientôt,

Mireille

I looked up from the letters long enough to accept my cup of ginger ale and ice from the flight attendant. I smiled my thanks and returned my attention to the screen.

The slant of the next letter, with its strong decisive downward strokes told me that I'd finally reached one of Gabriel's letters. I leaned forward to read, even as my mind tumbled with questions about the man likely to be my biological grandfather.

February 1, 1939

Dear Mireille,

I have not had the pleasure of seeing your face for a week, and am saddened that I will not be able to see you for another week. And so, I have decided to write you a letter.

When we see each other, I feel . . . overwhelmed. When I am with you, I find myself enjoying those moments so much that I forget to be sensible. Because

I would not wish to change a moment of our time together, I have decided to "take to the pen," as my oldest brother would say.

Let me write of my family.

My parents, as you know, reside in the 4th arrondissement. My mother grew up in Poland as the daughter of a professor. Her father took a professorship at the Sorbonne, where my father was a student.

My oldest brother followed into the family tradition of scholarship. I wish I saw him more often, but his research keeps him busy in Poland. My younger brother, you know, has turned his nimble fingers to jewelry craft.

And myself? My parents laugh that I make pastry and yet found a way to teach as well.

You must know that my mother was raised a Messianic Jewess. My father was raised Protestant; my brothers and I were raised to know the old traditions, but attended services at the Protestant church in Paris. We live in the Marais district, home to much of Paris's Jewish community.

The political and social tensions for Jews, you know, are high. I am confident that France will remain safe, but I worry for my brother in Warsaw.

As much as I have grown to have an attachment to you, your smile—and your croissants—I want you to be aware of these things. Should you choose to end our acquaintance, I will understand.

With deepest regards,
Gabriel Roussard

I have grown to have an attachment to you, your smile—and your croissants, I read again. Obviously, the man had it bad.

February 3, 1939

Dear Gabriel,

Don't be ridiculous. I look forward to seeing you on Monday next. Prepare yourself, for I intend to be very serious indeed.

Mireille

I laughed out loud, earning a furtive glance of concern from the woman seated to my left. But I loved Mireille's response so much, I didn't care. I missed Grand-mère very much, but I had only ever known her as a grandmother. In her youth? I wish we could have had sleepovers and talked about pastry technique and boys, though perhaps not in that order.

She'd grown into a serious woman; while I never doubted her deep love for her family, I wouldn't have described her as vivacious. Did the shift occur after losing Gabriel, or was it just a side effect of time? I'd likely never know.

The next letter on the screen was addressed to Mireille.

February 16, 1939

Dearest Mireille,

Yes, your letter has been received. Maman and Papa withdrew into Papa's study for a length of time. Thank you for showing me how to hold a glass to a door so many years ago; that technique has served me well on several occasions.

They have their concerns, of course, and they feel you are being quite mysterious. Papa, for one, has carried hopes that you and Gilles would reconcile. Maman simply had hopes that you would marry well, but at least he's not a Belgian (because what could be worse, I suppose?).

Anyway, Maman is now writing you a letter (which you may receive before this one, due to sheer force of will) to inform you of their upcoming visit.

I am still contemplating if it's wise to join them. While they might be better behaved if I'm there, if the visit coincides with my "delicate time of the month," it may simply be too much to endure.

(That said, should you desire my presence, I could summon the necessary courage given a promise of lemon tartlets).

Bisous!
Cécile

As promised, the next letter was from my great-grandmother, written with great care to appear breezy.

February 25, 1939

My Darling Daughter,

    Your father and I were delighted to read your most recent letter. Our curiosity has gotten the best of us, and I have taken the liberty of writing to my sister Joséphine of a visit next Saturday and Sunday. If your M. Roussard could find it in his schedule to join us for dinner, that would bring us both great joy.

    We both miss you very much at the chateau. Mme. Bessette sends her regards, as do the staff, of course.

    Looking forward to seeing you, Joséphine, and Anouk soon.

    Regards,

    Your Maman

March 2, 1939

Dearest Cécile,

    Maman has indeed written, and they are indeed coming.

    She couldn't help but mention Gilles's mother in the letter, to remind me of him in case I had forgotten him by accident, rather than by choice.

    C'est la vie.

    I couldn't imagine asking you to come along if you are enduring your "ladylike trials." However, do keep in mind that this may be your one opportunity to meet Gabriel before our parents have him conveniently murdered. It must be very inconvenient for them that they cannot sell me to Gilles for several acres of land and a cask of Armagnac.

    The final choice is up to you, dearest, but do know that I have set to work on some lemon tarts that I might have no choice but to donate to the Ladies' League.

    Bisous!

    Mireille

March 12, 1939

Dearest Mireille,

Please forgive me, I have taken to my bed. I imagine Maman and Papa will enjoy the tarts.

Cécile

Poor Cécile, felled by her "ladylike trials." I smothered my own laughter and continued to read as my plane soared high over the earth.

18

Let the stoics say what they please, we do not eat for the good of living, but because the meat is savory and the appetite is keen.

—RALPH WALDO EMERSON

March 20, 1939

My very dearest sister Cécile,

Oh dear, oh dear, oh dear.

Take comfort in the fact that even your presence could not have prevented the difficulties that ensued during Maman and Papa's "holiday" in Paris.

Gabriel was able to join us for dinner by rearranging his schedule. To his credit, he was very charming and well spoken throughout dinner, no matter how Papa baited him. Maman even began to flirt with him (she couldn't help herself).

Afterward we parted ways with Gabriel, and Maman and Papa drove me back to Tante Joséphine's.

No one spoke the entire drive home. Tante Joséphine had retired to her rooms by the time we returned (an act of self-preservation, I am convinced). The next few hours (not an exaggeration) were spent explaining the many reasons why I could not contemplate an "attachment" to Gabriel, and why I should come home.

They admitted that he was "more gentlemanly than expected," and yet marriage was out of the question.

Before you ask, know that Gabriel hasn't asked me to marry him. And he might never, especially after meeting Maman and Papa.

But . . . I have no intention to return to the chateau. The only thing for me to do is complete the pastry program and find a job.

Naturally I haven't mentioned to Maman the fact that I'll have to find an apprenticeship. However, I would like to open a patisserie of my own. Surely Maman would not sneeze too much at that if I owned the patisserie myself?

You are right. I know what you would say without your having to say it.

Of course neither of them would ever approve.

I hope your womanly trials pass quickly, and without incident.

Bisous (and sighs),

Mireille

March 21, 1939

Dear Cécile,

I have more news. Maman and Papa departed on Sunday afternoon. Gabriel visited unannounced on Sunday evening. I told the maid I was going out before I left with him, not even stopping for a hat.

We walked together, he and I. Neither of us spoke specifically of the visit, but Gabriel very gently suggested that if I valued my relationship with my parents, it might be wisest if we ceased our courtship. He did not wish to damage our "familial bonds," as he put it.

Cécile, I am perplexed. I wish to be a good daughter, to honor our parents and their wishes. But their wishes for my life are the very opposite of all of my hopes. I have no desire—have never had a desire—to marry well and be chatelaine. If it's all the same to you, I am perfectly happy to pass that position to you, my sister.

While I had hoped that leaving for Paris might be a step in an independent direction, to Maman and Papa it is a temporary time away.

Yet while I am perplexed, I told Gabriel I did not wish to end our courtship. After I told him so, he said he had written to his parents about a visit of their own.

I'm so nervous at the prospect, my hands shake every time at the thought of it *(as evidenced by my penmanship. Deepest apologies). I might know how to make pastry, but I do not yet know how to be brave. I covet your prayers, Cécile, for I do not know the way.*

À bientôt,
Mireille

I reread the last line two, three times—they could have been words I'd written to Caterina. Reading the letters felt like reading a bittersweet romance novel. My heart swelled to read the sentiment shared between Mireille and Gabriel, and broke for the separation that loomed in their future.

And yet—did the impending sadness lessen the joy they shared? They were happy now. Couldn't that be enough?

Maybe that was what I needed to remember with Neil. Right now we were happy. Rather than wring my hands over what waited at the edge of the horizon, I could simply choose to enjoy the good things while they unfolded.

March 28, 1939

Dearest Mireille,

But of course I shall pray. I shall also buy a train ticket to France. If I'm going to be praying on the subject of a man, I should like to meet him.

Cécile

March 29, 1939

Dear Mireille,

My dear sister, I fear I have distressing news. Maman fell ill shortly after her return from Paris; what appeared to be a cold, the doctor has diagnosed as pneumonia.

Papa is beside himself. Maman is having difficulty taking cook's broth. I don't know what to do; I sit at Maman's bedside and pray.

I know you're in the middle of classes, but please come.

Cécile

The next document wasn't a letter at all, but a telegram I'd found stashed with the rest of the letters and also organized by date..

RÉPUBLIQUE FRANÇAISE
POSTES ET TÉLÉCOMMUNICATIONS

TÉLÉGRAMME
M. GABRIEL ROUSSARD
MAMAN IS SICK. GOING HOME IN MORNING. WILL WRITE SOON.
LOVE, MIREILLE

April 4, 1939

Dear Gabriel,

I have arrived at the chateau safely. While I am concerned for Maman, I can still feel the memory of our last kiss on my lips.

My hope is to get Maman to eat broth, and if that goes well, I'll move on to risotto, or a beef barley soup.

But that all depends on her taking broth. I had hoped that perhaps my sister had exaggerated her condition in her panic, but no. In the two weeks since I have seen her, she is much altered.

My father spends most of his time in the fields, checking the plants and walking the grounds.

I miss you. I pray for my mother's health, and that I may return to you soon.

Mireille

I could feel the worry on the page; I couldn't help but think of my own maman and her illness. If only a beef barley soup had such restorative powers . . . and yet hadn't I left my parents with a supply of foodstuffs?

Apparently I'd inherited my desire to heal through food, as surely as I'd inherited the D'Alisa nose and my yen for cream puffs.

Gabriel's response followed.

April 13, 1939

My darling Mireille,

Paris has not ceased to rain since you left. I took tea with your Tante Joséphine yesterday. She and Anouk are well, though they both miss you nearly as much as I do.

(I believe Anouk may miss you just as much, though for different reasons.)

The restaurant is doing well; the days are long. I think of you as I work, of your determination, of the way that you worked so hard to show up all of the stuffed shirts who considered themselves superior to you, and their faces once they figured out how wrong they were. I loved the look on your face as you discovered new techniques that improved your pastry—sheer joy.

I fell in love with you then.

I pray for your mother's health. Return to me, Mireille. Paris is bleak without you.

Gabriel

My heart full, I closed my laptop. If I continued longer, I'd probably fall to pieces the minute I saw Neil. Instead, I fitted my earbuds into place and closed my eyes, all while seeing Gabriel's last line behind my eyes.

Return to me. . . . Paris is bleak without you.

19

A man taking basil from a woman will love her always.

—Sir Thomas Moore

I texted Neil once the plane landed; a minute later my phone buzzed: "Pick you up in baggage claim. Can't wait to see you!"

I grinned and followed my fellow passengers to the baggage claim, laptop bag slung over one aching shoulder, handbag in a white-knuckled grasp.

Twenty minutes later there were no signs of Neil, but the baggage carousel had finally consented to release my suitcase. I extended the handle with a click and cast my gaze around the utilitarian space, hoping to see Neil somewhere in the crowd.

I checked my phone again; no messages. I thought about texting again, but decided against it.

My stomach muttered in hunger.

I found a bench and took a seat.

Sitting and waiting, I had no choice but to take in my surroundings. Whereas the Portland airport consisted of a sea of Caucasian faces with a smattering of representatives from South America, Asia, and the Pacific Islands, at the Memphis Airport I had to admit to myself that I'd never before seen so many African Americans.

A disturbing revelation for a self-conscious, politically correct Oregonian.

Another muttering of the stomach, and no sign of Neil.

In a burst of unchecked impulse fueled by hunger, I stood, grasped my belongings and strode out the glass doors.

The hot, humid West Tennessee air filled my lungs and clung to my skin. I felt sweat bead on my neck, my back, my hairline as I struggled to breathe.

My heart raced, my stomach shifted from muttering to yelling, and I felt my panic rise. Was it too late to turn around and go home?

"Juliette!"

I turned to see Neil running toward me, bouquet of flowers clutched in one hand, phone in the other.

He looked absolutely wonderful.

With renewed energy, I clung tight to my belongings as I strode to meet him halfway.

"I'm so sorry," he breathed once we were within speaking distance. "I got stuck and I tried to call but my phone freaked out."

"I'm fine," I said, closing my eyes as he wrapped his arms around me. As I breathed in his scent, I knew it was true.

"Let me help you," he said when we pulled apart, and within seconds Neil had my suitcase and laptop, while I had a bouquet of flowers to hold close.

He slung the laptop bag around the suitcase handle, pulling the two together behind him with one hand, holding my hand with the other. "Flight go okay?"

"It flew."

"You hungry?'

"Always." I cleared my throat. "When I travel I tend to eat. A lot. My subconscious self doesn't know where my next meal is coming from and tends to stockpile."

"Barbecue it is, then."

As we drove to the restaurant, I inwardly admitted that not driving myself had been a good idea. Not a single driver used a turn signal. Cars slid from lane to lane with inches in between, even at freeway speeds.

I'd never seen so many American sports cars on the freeway at one time—Mustangs, Corvettes, Camaros—all well represented. Neil narrated the sights as we zoomed past, though he paused after a few moments. "I'm talking your ear off, aren't I?"

"I wasn't complaining," I said, giving his hand a squeeze.

We pulled into the tiny parking lot that belonged to Corky's Barbecue on

Poplar Avenue and walked inside. The air smelled of meat; my stomach rumbled its appreciation.

Neil held the door open for me and I stepped inside, taking in the pig-themed décor and the tables on the opposite end of the hallway.

"Come in, come in," the host said when he spotted us, his voice warm and familiar. "There's a table for you." We were seated instantly, and our waitress swung by a moment later to take our drink orders, smiling all the while.

"Everybody's so, so nice," I commented once she'd stepped away. "Is that . . . normal?"

"For the restaurant or for the mid-south?"

I laughed. "Both?"

"Mid-south can be hit or miss, but here? Always."

"I feel like I'm at my uncle's place. You know, my uncle who's really, really into pigs."

Neil chuckled and walked me through his favorite items on the menu. From the detail he offered, I gathered he was a frequent diner.

I ordered the pork shoulder sandwich with a side salad and a side of fries, while Neil chose the beef brisket dinner.

"Don't worry," he said. "I'll share."

"You're so nice to me."

"Want to hear about the schedule for the week?"

I leaned forward, resting my chin in my hands. "Sure. What's the plan, coach?"

"Coach?"

"I'm tired. It's all I could think of. And I respect *Friday Night Lights*."

"Can't argue with that." He smiled. "Now, these are all suggestions. If you're too tired or if something sounds boring, we can change things up, okay?"

"Have some confidence, McLaren. I'm sure they're great plans."

He reached out and rested his hand on mine. "Tonight I take you over to Callan and Tarissa's. Tarissa will probably try to feed you."

I grinned. "I'm sure we'll be great friends."

"She sure hopes so. Just . . . know that before we met, she was on my case to date. For a long time. So the fact that we're together . . . she's pretty excited."

I felt my heart miss a beat. "Look . . . Neil," I said before I could stop myself, "I'm delighted to be here with you. I have missed you so much. Too much," I amended, shaking my head.

The words spilling from my mouth weren't words I had ever planned to say to Neil. But he was so hopeful, and I was so tired, I couldn't stop myself. "I want normal," I said. "And I don't know if we'll ever be able to have it."

"I know," Neil said quietly.

"But . . . when we're together, it's so good." I heard my voice crack. "I don't know what to do. I don't want to ruin what we have . . . you know, like I am. Right now. On our first date in ages."

"You're not ruining anything."

A quiet tear rolled down my cheek. "I'm crying in a restaurant decorated with pigs. It's at the very least off-brand."

Neil reached across the table and swiped the tear away. "I want normal too. I'm sorry, I'm sure the way I told you about Tarissa's excitement felt like . . . pressure. But they're my closest friends, and they know that we're still new, and Tarissa's a smart lady. She won't ask for your intentions or what kind of baby names you prefer."

I gave a wry smile. "Unless she decides to chase me off."

"She won't."

"I'm sorry." I unrolled my silverware and blew my nose on the paper napkin.

"Shh," Neil said, tucking my hair behind my ear. "I'm just glad you're here."

"You're too nice to me."

"Let's enjoy the time we have," Neil said. "And if you want to sit on my couch and watch TV all day, we can do that."

"You're funny."

"I'm serious. You're right, we're usually in tourist mode when we're together."

I gave a small shrug. "There hasn't been any help for it. Either we're exploring Portland—a worthy task—or Italy, or France . . ."

"Whatever you need, Jules. We can argue over a movie rental, mainline *Top Gear* or *Doctor Who,* play Scrabble until midnight."

"That all sounds perfect."

"So we'll do that."

I shook my head. "But I also want to see your city. It's important to you, the way Portland's important to me."

"Not that important. I think Portland loyalty runs extra deep. Texas-level deep."

"Yeah . . . probably. I'm just saying, I still want you to show me around. And then maybe we can play Scrabble or Go Fish or something."

"Or something." He smiled. "I think we can work something out."

"So tell me about your plans."

"I thought we could go to the outdoor sites tomorrow, especially since the weather's supposed to be a little cooler."

"What's your version of cooler?"

"Ninety degrees, rather than ninety-five to a hundred."

I forced a smile. "Okay."

Neil didn't miss it. "Portland weather is milder in the summer, isn't it?"

"Oh, it'll hit a hundred from time to time, but never more than a few days. And with less humidity," I added. "That's code for less sweat."

Neil shrugged. "You acclimate."

"I'll be fine," I said, despite my concern. The waitress interrupted my worryfest by arriving with our drinks. Short moments later, she returned with our food.

"Oh my goodness," I said, wiping a smear of barbecue sauce from my lip. "That is the most amazing meat I've ever had."

Neil grinned and forked a piece of his brisket. "Try this," he said, offering his fork.

I flushed pink as he placed it in my mouth. "That's really good too," I said, after chewing and swallowing. "And the sauce is amazing."

"You have sauce on your lip again."

"I have a feeling this is going to be the theme of the evening." I swiped at my mouth with my napkin. "So what outdoor sites are on your list?"

"The Rhodes campus is nice, great architecture. And the Dixon Gallery and Gardens, so I'm told, makes for a good date."

"So you're told?"

Now it was Neil's turn to blush. Naturally, on him it looked adorable. "I might have Googled 'romantic things to do in Memphis,'" he said.

"You might have?"

"Maybe."

"Good to know." I felt the knots in my shoulders begin to untangle. Apart, I'd forgotten just how easy company Neil could be. I loved my family, but so often a conversation with them could be like walking across a minefield without a map—something, anything could launch a passionate argument. But with Neil? We could simply enjoy being near each other.

Dinner flew by. Before I knew it, I was back in Neil's car, stifling yawns and clutching his right hand as we wove through traffic to reach Callan and Tarissa's house.

"Callan and Tarissa live in Germantown," he explained as we left the commercial buildings and drove down the wide, straight street lined with large homes and leafy trees. "It's one of the main suburbs," he said, "east of Memphis. It's pretty suburban."

"Where do you live?"

"I'm in Germantown too, about a mile away from Callan's. I like it. I'll take you there tomorrow. Just be forewarned—it's a bachelor's house."

"Not a lot of throw pillows?"

"A few throw pillows, but they were the ones that were displayed with the couch at the furniture store."

"Fair enough." A yawn escaped. I clapped my hand over my mouth. "Sorry."

"Don't be. You've been awake for a while."

I shrugged. "But I'm glad to be with you. I want you to know that."

He squeezed my hand. "I do."

We pulled in front of a lovely Georgian-style house with a circular drive. As we walked to the door with my luggage in hand, all I could think about was the fact that Neil and I hadn't kissed yet.

At the airport, we'd been surrounded by people and the carbon monoxide cocktail that was cigarette smoke and car exhaust. Then we'd been to the restaurant and back . . . and nothing.

I knew in the back of my mind that I was feeling tired and insecure, and that at some point Neil would probably kiss me and I didn't need to read anything into the timing. And yet, all of the knots that had untangled during dinner returned with a force. I felt deeply out of place and didn't relish the feeling—but hadn't Neil done the same thing when he'd visited me?

A glance at my phone told me I had no texts from home. Mom was fine, the restaurant was fine. Two fewer things to worry about for now.

But as we walked to the door, daisy-fresh waves of anxiety filled my mind. What if Neil's friends hated me? I'd never met these people, and I'd be staying at their house for the better part of a week. I'd be staying with people who didn't like me, and Neil hadn't even kissed me yet.

As if he knew that I was about to completely freak out while walking on his best friend's flagstone walkway, Neil squeezed my hand.

"You okay?"

"Sometimes I'm not very good with people," I whispered. "Sometimes they think I'm weird, or intense, or stuck up, or—"

Neil lifted my chin and kissed me hard, his lips telling me exactly what he thought about my concerns.

"Enough of that," he said when we came up for air, his voice quiet but intense. "You're perfect. They'll love you. Not as much as I love you, but enough. And if, for some reason, their brains are taken over by aliens and they aren't the people I've known and loved for the last six years, just say the word and I'll take you to a hotel. Any hotel. You can pick the hotel. You can stay at the Peabody and watch the ducks march every night."

"Ducks?"

"Either way, I'll take you to see the ducks."

"This conversation stopped making sense three or four sentences ago. The only marching Ducks I know about play musical instruments on football fields."

"Don't worry." He planted a kiss on my temple. "It will."

"I missed you."

He gave a crooked half smile. "I missed you too."

My heart swelled as I looked at the wonderful man in front of me, his gingery hair shimmering under the exterior floodlights. I wanted to grasp his hands in mine and beg him to move to Portland, to be with me.

But I knew he had a life here, a life and a job and friends, roots maybe not as deep as mine but deep enough that I had to respect them.

So I pasted on my bravest face, a face I was getting perhaps too good at. I hung on to his hand and walked the rest of the way to the front door.

Neil rapped three times and opened the door himself. "Tarissa fusses at me if I ring the bell," he said.

The door opened into a wide, high-ceilinged foyer. A sweeping staircase began at the right, leading to the second floor. There was an office behind french doors to my immediate right, with the living room and formal dining to my left.

"Is that them? Neil? Are you here?" A feminine voice sounded from a hallway that seemed to originate from behind the stairs.

"I'm here, I brought Juliette," Neil called back, winking at me.

Footsteps quickened. "Juliette!" Tarissa appeared through the hallway. She cut a striking figure in a mustard-toned shirtdress cinched with a wide leather belt, the yellow of the dress setting off her chocolatey complexion.

Her face brightened when she saw us. "Perfect timing! I just pulled the peach cornbread out of the oven." Tarissa's wide smile instantly put me at ease. She pulled me into a hug and then held me at arm's length. "Look at you! Just off a plane and looking so pretty. Come on back for some cornbread—Callan! Look who I found!"

"I'm guessing it was Neil and his friend, since we weren't expecting anyone else," Callan drawled, stepping forward and offering his hand. "It's nice to meet you. We're glad you've come to stay with us."

I smiled up at the man Neil called his best friend. Tall and broad-shouldered with glowing mahogany skin, he and Tarissa made a strikingly beautiful couple. "Thank you so much for having me," I said, my gratitude genuine. "Your house is lovely."

"Aw, thanks," said Tarissa. "You can stay forever. Do you want some decaf coffee?"

"I'd love some coffee."

"I would too," Neil said.

"You can serve yourself," Tarissa told him. "You know where everything is."

Neil shot me a glance. "They like you better. I've been demoted."

~ TARISSA'S PEACH CORNBREAD ~

3 ripe peaches, peeled and sliced

$1/4$ cup brown sugar

$2^{1}/4$ cups flour

$3/4$ cup yellow cornmeal

$1/4$ cup plus 2 tablespoons sugar

$1^{1}/2$ tablespoons baking powder

1 teaspoon sea salt

$1^{1}/2$ cups buttermilk, at room temperature

$1/2$ cup butter, melted and cooled

3 large eggs, beaten, at room temperature

Preheat oven to 400°F. Prepare a 9x13 baking dish by greasing it or lining it with parchment paper.

In a small bowl, stir together the peaches and brown sugar. Set aside.

In a medium-sized bowl, sift together the flour, cornmeal, sugar, baking powder, and salt. In a separate, smaller bowl, whisk together the buttermilk, butter, and eggs.

Stir the wet ingredients into the dry ingredients, mixing until the wet ingredients are well incorporated but the batter is still lumpy. Fold in the peaches. Pour the batter into the prepared pan.

Bake for 35–55 minutes, or until the cornbread is golden and a tester comes out clean.

Serve warm with lots of butter and honey.

20

For it is only in company that eating is done justice;
food must be divided and distributed if it is to be well
received.

—WALTER BENJAMIN

Neil, Callan, Tarissa, and I spent a happy evening chatting and eating Tarissa's peach cornbread. By ten o'clock, though, no amount of clenching my teeth or biting my cheeks could stop my yawns.

"I'm sorry, you guys," I said, another yawn careening around the bend. "It was a really early morning."

"Don't be!" Tarissa jumped up and took my plate and coffee cup away. "You've got to be exhausted. I'll take you upstairs, show you the guest room."

We made a strange little caravan to the second floor. Callan carried my luggage, Neil's grasp on my elbow kept me from falling over, and Tarissa narrated the tour from the front. Once I was settled, Callan and Tarissa said their good-byes, leaving Neil and me to have a moment to ourselves.

It would have been more romantic if I could stand up straight.

"You're cute when you're sleepy," he said, wrapping his arms around my waist. "Is this gonna work out for you?"

"Callan and Tarissa are terrific," I said. "I'm going to try to talk Tarissa into moving to Portland."

"Not Callan?"

"He'll do whatever Tarissa says."

Neil shrugged. "You're probably right. Sure, go ahead. Steal my friends." He smiled. "I'm glad you're here."

"Me too."

"Can I pick you up in the morning?"

I pretended to think about it first. "Sure. Are you sure it's not just because Tarissa promised to make a french toast casserole for breakfast?"

"I've had it. It's a good casserole. But no, that's not the only reason. Get a good night's sleep, and if you're up to it we'll visit the gardens tomorrow."

"That sounds like fun."

He tucked a stray piece of hair behind my ear. "I love you, Juliette." His hand cupped my cheek in a kinder, gentler version of the kiss we'd shared outside.

"I love being able to say good night to you," I said, snuggling into his shoulder, enjoying the feel of his hand in my hair.

"Are you going to read letters tonight?"

I snorted. "Me? I'll be asleep before my head hits the pillow."

"You'll have to catch me up on your grandmother's story tomorrow."

"Of course," I said with a nod. "It's been fascinating, and I still have so many more letters to go."

"Any answers?"

"Not really. But I've enjoyed reading about my grandmother as a young woman. She wrote good letters."

"So do you," he said. Another set of whispered good-byes, and Neil stepped from the room with a wave, closing the door behind him.

That night I dreamed of kisses, humidity, and cornbread.

The next morning I rose and enjoyed a long, hot shower, scrubbing off the remnants of the flight from my hair. I blew out my hair and applied makeup, skipping the foundation and sticking with powder—I had a suspicion that any foundation would melt and slide off my face anyway.

My outfit for the day included the floaty cotton sundress I'd worn for Nonno's birthday paired with comfortable yet respectable brown sandals. I left my hair loose, but decided to wear a hair band on my wrist next to my watch in case I needed to tie it up.

Neil waited downstairs at the breakfast table, chatting with Callan and Tarissa. While Callan and Tarissa were dressed for their respective workdays, Neil wore shorts and a short-sleeved, button-down shirt. His face lit up when he saw me, his grin warming me to my toes.

I hugged him good morning; he pressed a kiss to my temple.

"If I swoon," Tarissa said, fanning herself, "just ignore me."

Callan chuckled. "Would you like some coffee, Juliette?"

"Yes, please." I took a seat on the last remaining chair. "You might have to watch me, or I'll drink the whole pot."

Neil rubbed my back. "Want some breakfast?"

"Oh yes, that would be smart." I rose to serve myself but Neil held out a hand.

"I've got it," he said, plucking a plate from the countertop and striding to the stove. He returned a moment later with a plateful of french toast casserole with two sausage patties on the side. "Carbs and pork," he said when he slid the plate in front of me. "The perfect Memphis breakfast."

"It smells amazing," I said. "Thank you. And thank you, Tarissa, for making it." My eyes widened after a single bite. "If you share the recipe, I'll love you forever."

"Are you on Pinterest? I'll send you the pin," she assured me. "What are you two up to today?"

"I think we'll visit the botanical gardens this morning," Neil said, "and then the Dixon and finish at the museum when it gets warm."

Callan checked his watch. "You might want to get moving."

I cut a larger piece of french toast and shoveled it into my mouth.

"Well, that sounds very romantic," Tarissa said.

Neil grinned. "We'll visit my house, and then an old-fashioned dinner date tonight."

Tarissa clasped her hands to her heart and sighed. Callan patted her shoulder. "Don't worry. I'll take you out soon."

Tarissa arched an eyebrow. "Don't you go making promises you forget to keep."

He swooped in for a quick kiss. "Hush there. I never forget."

"Uh-huh. Juliette, would you like more food?"

I looked down at my plate to discover that I'd polished it off. "Oh no, I'm full. But it was wonderful, thank you."

"You ready to leave?" Neil asked.

"Are you going to make me eat and run like that?"

Tarissa held out a hand. "I've gotta run to get to the office, myself, and Callan's off to the lab. Oh! Before I forget—" Tarissa reached into a kitchen drawer and retrieved a key attached to a fob. "Here's a spare key for you, so if we're not here, you can just make yourself at home."

"Thanks so much!" I said, pocketing the key. "Hope your workdays go well."

"Someone has to continue the cause of science," Callan said. "Have fun today."

"And if you want to miss the heat," Tarissa said, pointing out the window, "you'd better run as fast as you can."

"Thanks again for breakfast," I said, carrying my dishes to the sink.

Following Tarissa's advice, I jogged upstairs to grab my purse before running back down, said farewells to Callan and Tarissa, and walked out the door with Neil.

The humidity greeted me like a too-tight hug from a difficult relative. We'd be walking in this? I looked at Neil.

He was handsome. I wouldn't do it for anyone else.

"Sorry," he said. "I don't think we'll be beating the heat much. But I brought these," he said holding up two water bottles full of ice water.

"Oh, thank you," I said. "I'll take one now, if you don't mind."

Despite the heat and humidity, we passed a romantic morning strolling through the Rhodes campus, admiring its architecture and the old trees.

After refilling our water, we walked through the Memphis Gardens. Neil stole kisses behind trees, under alcoves, over the footbridge. We also fed the koi fish. Judging from the size of the koi, we hadn't been the only ones.

For lunch we stopped by Café Eclectic, one of Neil's favorite haunts. It felt like a slice of the Pacific Northwest with its door covered in concert posters, its espresso machinery, and its hip wall décor.

I longed for a more adventurous order, but in the heat I couldn't muster enthusiasm for anything but salad. Still, the salad included walnuts, feta, and dried apricots.

Neil ordered a burger with sweet potato fries.

"This is the place I was telling you about in our e-mails," he said, taking a swig of sweet tea. "Their macaroni is really good. There's live music sometimes. It's fun."

"Reminds me of home," I said.

He smiled. "That's funny. Portland reminded me of here."

I saw the touch of insecurity in his eyes, and I knew that he wanted the city, his friends, his life, to make a good impression. I didn't know what to say; instead, I reached across the table for his hand. "I love that we're here together."

"You holding up okay?"

"Yeah," I said, hedging. "It's . . . warm." And I planned to ask Tarissa if I could wash my dress once I returned to the house. I'd sweated out the back long, long ago.

"The Dixon is air-conditioned. We don't have to walk through the gardens there if you don't want."

"I'm fine. But I'll let you know if I change my mind."

"Promise?"

"Promise."

"You've brought me up to date about the restaurant and your family, but I'm still waiting to hear about the letters you found at the chateau."

I leaned back to allow the waitress room to set my plate in front of me. Neil spread his napkin in his lap before digging into his burger.

"Mireille and Gabriel met while she was taking culinary classes and he was teaching for the term," I told him. "Afterward they began to see each other socially and fell for each other pretty quickly. She told Cécile all about it in her letters."

Neil took a bite out of his burger and nodded. "Go on."

"She was doing well in her classes, but her mother fell ill back at the château. Very ill. So she went home to help care for her. Right now the letters are between Mireille and Gabriel, all about how they miss each other while they're apart."

"Sound familiar?"

"Somewhat," I said. In truth, I understood the sentiments deeply. But Gabriel and Mireille, at least, were only separated by their circumstances. I assumed it would be temporary. Neil and I missed each other, and yet hadn't we walked into this relationship knowing what we were getting into?

"How many letters do you have left?"

"Oh, quite a few. I think I'm about a third of the way in. What's interesting about all of this is the completeness of the collection. I even found the telegram Mireille sent Gabriel that told him she was leaving for Montagnac."

"What do you think that means?'

"I don't know yet, not really. But the letters feel very . . . very curated, I think is the word. The collection is too complete for it to be an accident. If they were just Gabriel's letters to Mireille, or just Mireille's letters to Cécile, that would be one thing. But this? I haven't figured it out yet."

"Do you think Mireille hunted down every letter to do with Gabriel?" Neil asked. "After he died?"

"Maybe. It would make sense, I suppose." I shrugged. "I'm preparing myself for the fact that these letters will hold more questions than answers."

"I sort of thought you'd have read them all twice through by now."

I snorted. "In what, all of my spare time? And also, they're all in French. I have to read and translate at the same time. While my French is very, very good, it still takes longer than if I were reading them in English."

Neil placed a hand over mine. "I'm not criticizing. I'm sorry if it came out sounding that way."

"I don't know. I guess I thought I'd read them faster too. But I'm finding that there's just so much there, having to reframe everything I knew about my family history—it makes for dense reading. If I only read a little at a time, it's easier. Though," I added, "I did read quite a few letters on the plane out."

"Oh yeah?"

"Are you kidding? I got to sit down for hours at a time! It was amazing." I speared several leaves of lettuce onto my fork. "My hope is to get through another chunk on the flight back. Once the restaurant fully opens, free time will be harder to come by."

Neil squeezed my hand. "I'm just glad we got to see each other now."

We spent the afternoon exploring the Dixon gardens and art collection, admiring the fine art on the inside as much as the Neo-Georgian architecture and surrounding gardens.

After we'd wandered and canoodled to our heart's content, Neil drove me back to Callan and Tarissa's so I could change for our evening date.

Neil dropped me off with a kiss; I let myself in with the spare key Tarissa had given me that morning.

Had it been the same morning? I could hardly tell, my sense of time felt so altered.

I showered off the day's sweat and grime, washing my hair and scrubbing my skin. Afterward I spread a clay mask over my face in the hopes that maybe, maybe the sweat and heat wouldn't cause me to break out.

Once clean and dry, I changed into my trusty Italian black dress. I'd have to write to Letizia about that dress, let her know it'd seen its share of exploits even in such a short time.

She'd be pleased.

As I dried my hair and reapplied my makeup, I wondered again about Neil and the future of our relationship. I'd wanted so badly to live in the moment, but in truth, the moment felt so very overwhelming. A short glance at my phone revealed e-mails about the restaurant, requests for media information, questions or offers from suppliers. I lived in an unbiblical dread over news that my mother had taken a turn for the worse.

But tonight, Neil and I were going on a date, and I tingled with anticipation despite my nerves. I used a heavier line of eyeliner than usual, but stuck with a nude lipstick for practicality's sake.

I chose cognac-toned heeled sandals, and grabbed a long emerald-green cardigan for protection against aggressive air conditioning. As a finishing touch, I added a beaded amber necklace that my mother had given me two Christmases ago.

The garage door rumbled open beneath me—someone was home. After a last check in the mirror, I grabbed my clutch and headed downstairs.

Tarissa clasped her hand to her heart when she saw me. "That man had better propose to you," she said before closing her mouth abruptly. "I wasn't supposed to say that."

I couldn't help but smile. "We still have a lot to figure out," I said. "I think any marriage talk is a ways out."

"Neil's picking you up?"

"He is."

"Come sit with me in the kitchen. Would you like some tea?"

I almost declined the tea before remembering that Tennessee tea meant sweet, iced tea. "Sure. I'd like that."

"Neil told us your mom was sick." Tarissa reached into the cupboard for glasses. "I'm so sorry about that."

My smile wobbled. "Thanks. I just . . . with her . . ." I sank onto one of the kitchen stools. "It's difficult to make plans right now."

Tarissa poured the tea and handed me a tall glass. I could see the words behind her eyes, but she remained quiet.

"I'm glad he has you and Callan," I said. "I'd hate for him to be lonely."

"Oh, he's still lonely." Tarissa perched on the stool next to me and sipped her tea. "He and Callan are good for each other, though. I'm a Memphis girl, but Callan's from Chicago. He's had a hard time adjusting to the South, but his friendship with Neil has helped." She shrugged. "We might move to Chicago someday, but things are good for now."

"I know Neil appreciates having you both here."

Tarissa brightened. "You're so sweet—we enjoy him as well. Now, where's Neil taking you tonight?"

"Italian." I took a long drink of my tea. "That's good tea. I think the name of the restaurant was Amerigo?"

"Ooh, you'll like it. Get the cheese fritters."

"Cheese fritters at an Italian restaurant?"

"They're probably not that Italian," she admitted, "but so good nobody around here seems to care. They were featured in *Bon Appétit* magazine."

"That's cool. I will remember the cheese fritters."

A knock sounded at the door, followed by Neil's voice. "Hello? Juliette?"

"We're in the kitchen!" Tarissa called back. "Miss Juliette looks mighty pretty."

The heels of Neil's shoes sounded on the hardwood floors. I spun on my stool to see his approach. "Hi."

"Hi, yourself," he said, finally close enough to brush a short kiss on my lips. "I missed you."

"I'll leave the lights on for you," Tarissa said. "You've got your key for when you get back?"

"It's in my clutch," I answered. "Thanks for the tea."

"Anytime! You two go enjoy your dinner, have a little romance in your lives."

"Callan taking you out tonight?" Neil asked her teasingly.

"As a matter of fact, that's none of your business," Tarissa retorted, but from the glimmer in her eyes I suspected they had an evening planned.

She waved us out the door, and we returned to Neil's car, which he'd left running in the driveway with the A/C on.

"Ready for dinner?" Neil asked, leaning in for a more substantial kiss.

I mentally congratulated myself on the wisdom of the nude lipstick while twining my fingers in his hair.

21

The key to a great frittata is a very hot pan, because that, my friends, is what makes it fluffy.

—ALINE BROSH MCKENNA

For our evening out, Neil wore tropical-weight wool trousers with a beautiful drape, a striped button-down and a solid tie that brought out the coppery tones of his eyes. Upon our arrival, he retrieved a jacket from the backseat that matched his pants and carried it over his arm into the restaurant.

He looked wonderful; I couldn't stop looking at him.

While the exterior of the restaurant—a strip mall—didn't inspire, the interior surprised with dark wood and intimate lighting.

Several couples and families milled, waiting for their tables, but Neil and I were seated immediately at a corner table. Our bench seats met at a perfect ninety-degree angle, allowing us to sit as close as we liked.

Neil chose the lasagna while I elected to try the wild mushroom ravioli—only after placing an order for the cheese fritters—and I picked a bottle of wine I thought would suit them both, a red blend from the Umbria region of Italy.

"In hindsight," Neil said after the waiter left, "I've got a lot of nerve bringing you here after eating with your family in Italy."

"They'd be happy to hear that. There's a place for Italian-American food in cuisine, though. Part of the joy of food is seeing it interpreted and reinterpreted around the world. Some of the best French patisseries are actually in Japan."

Neil raised my hand to his lips and kissed my knuckles. "You look beautiful tonight, did I tell you that?"

"You did. Are you trying to get me off the topic of Japanese patisseries?"

"Never. I think they're romantic."

I laughed. "Okay, fine," I said, clasping his hand with both of mine. "I love you, Neil, and I'm so glad we're here together. I think you're even better than a Japanese patisserie."

"That's high praise—I'll take it," he said, leaning over to kiss me, a real kiss, right there in the restaurant. He pulled away and stroked my cheek with his hand. "I like you even better than Krispy Kreme."

"I'll walk with you inside," Neil said, after pulling into Callan and Tarissa's driveway later that night.

Callan and Tarissa must have been out for the evening; the house was dark and quiet. With an arm around my waist, Neil walked up the stairs alongside me, staying close by my side until we reached the door to my room.

He brushed hair from my face and tucked it behind my ear. "Sleep well, Juliette."

"Thank you," I said, "for tonight. It was . . . actually kinda perfect."

"I'm glad," he said, running a soft finger down my cheekbone. A good night kiss, and Neil saw himself to the door.

I lingered in my doorway, hating to see him go, but knowing I needed a full night's sleep before the following day. A quick wash and brush, and I climbed under the cozy blankets covering Tarissa's guest bed before falling into a deep, dreamless sleep.

When my phone rang in the dark, my eyes flew open and I sat bolt upright. I looked around for my phone, finding it on the nightstand.

"Hello?"

"Aunt Juliette?"

"Chloé?"

"Mom just went to the hospital with Grand-mère, and I'm home by myself and I'm scared Grand-mère's going to die and Mom's not answering her phone and I didn't know what to do."

My heartbeat raced at the news even as I knew I needed to help Chloé calm down. "Where's your Dad, honey?"

"He's on a work trip." The last word came out as a sob.

"I'm so sorry, sweetie."

"Are you at the hospital too? Could you come get me? Or stay here with me?"

My heart sank. "Oh, honey, I wish I could, but I'm in Memphis right now."

"Oh." She hiccupped. "I'm sorry."

I switched on the lamp next to my bed and glanced at the wall clock. If it was one thirty here, it was eleven thirty for Chloé. She had to be exhausted.

"Where are you in your house, sweetie?"

"Kitchen. I came downstairs for the phone."

"Want to take it someplace comfy? The living room or your bedroom?"

Chloé sniffed. "I guess I could take it back to bed."

"Snuggle up in bed, tuck your stuffed giraffe under your arm."

"Okay," she said a few minutes later. "I'm in bed. I have Giraffi."

"Good. I haven't had any calls from your mom or uncles, so I'm guessing that the hospital trip isn't a huge emergency," I said, praying for my words to be true. "People with cancer need different medical care than people without, so that can mean more hospital trips."

"I'm scared she's gonna die."

What could I tell her? "Me too. Cancer is scary, there's no way around it, and we don't know what the future holds. But," I added, "we have to pray. Which is hard—I wish my worrying would fix things. I have enough worry to fix all the things, all the time," I added with a half laugh.

"Can we pray together? Would you pray with me?"

"Of course," I assured her hastily, feeling guilt for not having suggested it first. We prayed for my mother's doctors, for her pain, for her safety. We prayed that we would feel less scared. Our words were simple, but as we traded prayers, I could hear Chloé's breathing regulate and her voice steady.

"Thanks, Aunt Jules," she said after our final amen. "I kinda wish you were here."

"Me too, sweetie. When I get back you'll get the biggest hug."

"You've been traveling a lot."

"I have," I said, fighting another stab of guilt. "It's true. But the restaurant is opening soon, and I'll be home for a long, long while after that."

"That's cool. I like your restaurant."

"I'm glad."

"I'd, like, want to go there for prom."

At her age, I would have been terrified to take my date to the family restaurant. But I loved her lack of self-consciousness as related to her family, and hoped that maybe it would survive the rest of her adolescence. "That sounds like a wonderful idea."

"I wish I could talk to my mom," she said, her voice soft and hesitant.

"The reception at the hospital is terrible, and she may have had to turn her phone off. Did you try your uncles?"

"They're not answering their phones, either."

"Want me to call Clementine? I bet she'd go over and hang out with you."

"No, I'll be okay."

"I'll bet she's awake. And she's gotten really good at Bananagrams lately too."

Silence. "I don't want to be a burden."

I very nearly laughed out loud. "Why don't I call you right back, okay, hon?"

"Okay."

First I tried to call Sophie, Alex, and Nico, but like Chloé, I couldn't get through.

So I dialed up Clementine. "What are you doing calling me?" she asked when she picked up. "You're supposed to be romancing and eating . . . and sleeping, considering the time over there."

"I know. Chloé called and woke me up."

"Everything okay?"

"Nelson's out of town, Sophie's at the hospital with my mom, and Chloé's home alone trying not to wig out. Look, I know it's late, but any way you could go over there and play Bananagrams or something with her for a bit?"

"Of course. I can take Gigi with me too, if you think she'd like that."

"Oh, she'd love it."

"I knew your mom was back in the hospital—Nico left about half an hour ago to meet them."

"Did he say what happened?"

"He got the call from Alex. It sounded like there was another fever, and they were concerned about a kidney infection, maybe? But I wasn't on the call, so don't take my word for it."

I opened my mouth to ask about the circumstances of Nico being nearby at eleven o'clock but decided instead to focus on the problems at hand.

"Chloé would love some company, I think. Sophie's phone's not working, but I'll send her a text so she knows that you're there."

"I'm getting Gigi's leash right now."

I released the breath I realized I'd been holding. "Thank you so much, Clementine. I owe you."

"Nonsense. I'm wearing my shoes, just threw the Bananagrams into my bag."

"Text me if you need anything?"

"I will. Go back to sleep."

"Sure," I said, knowing full well that it'd be at least an hour until I relaxed enough for sleep.

I called Chloé back and told her the plan, though I left out the bit about Gigi—Gigi could be a happy surprise.

Chloé sounded relieved to hear about Clementine, though she tried to cover it up beneath a veil of teenage nonchalance. We said our good nights, and I hung up.

Fully awake, I sent Neil a text letting him know that I needed a later start in the morning. What started out as a short text grew longer as I explained the complexities of the situation, but I hit Send and climbed into bed, forcing my breathing to slow and willing my muscles to unclench.

As I laid in my bed, I fought the guilt in swift, hand-to-hand combat. I should have been there. And yet I'd been able to do what I could from afar.

If only I'd been able to actually talk to one of my siblings. The uncertainty over my mother tied my brain into knots. I tried to breathe deeply, tried to pray, but I felt my psyche spiral deeper and deeper into panic.

I jumped when my phone rang again. This time, I looked at the caller information—Neil.

"I'm so sorry," I said when I picked up. "I didn't mean to wake you with my text."

"Shh, don't apologize," he said. "I just wanted to see if you were okay. I figured you were awake."

Hysterical laughter threatened to burst forth. "Yeah. Pretty sure. I'm just . . . I can't get through to anyone. My mom went in for a UTI last week, and it sounds like she's got a kidney infection."

"That's logical," Neil answered, "but treatable."

"I . . ." I only just stopped myself from telling him that I wished I'd been there. Sharing dessert was one thing—sharing guilt another. Neil didn't need that. "I'm worried about my mom. And I'm worried about Chloé."

"And you wish you could be there for them," Neil finished on my behalf.

"It's complicated. I'm just . . . Chloé was really frightened. I haven't heard her that upset since she got lost at Rose Parade years ago. But"—I took a deep breath to calm myself, though the more deep breaths I took the more light-headed I felt—"she's playing Bananagrams with Clementine. Clementine really is amazing. Chloé's in good hands. And Gigi's there too, so for tonight at least, she's taken care of."

"What about you?"

"Pardon?"

"Want me to come over? I don't have Bananagrams, but I've got a deck of cards around here somewhere. We can play that game of Go Fish you mentioned."

"You're sweet. I'll be fine, Neil," I lied. "I'll be okay."

"Promise?"

I left the line silent enough that Neil made up his mind. "I'll be over in a few minutes."

"Okay," I breathed.

When we both hung up, I rose and exchanged my sleep camisole for a proper bra and sweatshirt.

Neil arrived scant minutes later. How close did he live? I'd find out later. For now, I settled for being held in his arms.

He led me downstairs to the den. "I found the playing cards," he said, "but we could also watch *Doctor Who* on Netflix."

"Oh," I said, "truthfully, I'm not sure I have the brainpower for cards. Not even Go Fish."

"*Who* it is," he said.

Five minutes later we were snuggled up on the couch beneath the throw, his arm around my shoulders, my head against his chest.

We sat together, watching the TARDIS careen through space, time, and opening credits text.

I fell asleep seconds later.

Light streamed into the den windows when I next opened my eyes. A second's worth of contemplation reminded me how I'd wound up on the couch, and why Neil was still asleep next to me.

I couldn't help but smile at him. His head rested on the back cushion of the sofa, listing slightly to the side. He looked adorable.

The clock on the entertainment system read 6:42 a.m. So much for my attempt at sleeping in. Despite the unusual night, I felt surprisingly refreshed. But then—I'd spent half of it curled up with Neil.

As if he knew I'd been thinking of him, he sighed in his sleep before his head lolled to the opposite side.

I stood and stretched gently, testing my muscles for hidden aches. Finding none, I tugged my sweatshirt down before heading to the kitchen to rummage for breakfast.

Inside Tarissa's fridge I found plenty to work with—fresh eggs, jarred roasted red peppers, fresh spinach, potatoes, and a stray onion hiding in the corner.

I turned on the oven and hunted around for equipment.

After locating the knives and a cutting board, I made quick work of the onions, potatoes, and red peppers. Next I cracked the eggs into a small bowl and gave them a brief whisk.

In the spice cabinet I found dried thyme and parsley; I set the bottles aside.

I didn't hear anything from upstairs or from the den, so assumed everyone else was asleep, and cooked away. And really, it was easier that way—I'd adjusted to being on my own in the kitchen.

I sautéed the onions in butter, relishing the smell. Once they were nice and translucent, I added the potatoes and let them brown, and then placed the lid over the top to steam them soft. Fat, heat, and root vegetables—I loved the smells they released, the shade of gold they turned, the universality of their appeal.

Once the potatoes were done, I added the peppers and tossed them around the pan until they dried off. Next came the shower of salt, pepper, and herbs, a moment to let them toast, followed by the eggs.

I felt my spirits lift as I sprinkled cheese over the top. A frittata really was the perfect breakfast to serve when you had no idea when it was going to be eaten—traditionally they were meant to be served at room temperature. Tarissa and Callan had been so kind; making breakfast gave me a way to give back.

Once the eggs began to set and curl at the edges, I set the skillet into the oven and began to hand wash everything I'd used.

Neil shuffled into the kitchen while I rinsed the cutting board. "Hey, you," he said, wrapping his arms around my waist and kissing my cheek. "You were supposed to sleep in this morning."

"I woke up. There was light coming through the windows. And really, I've been keeping such strange hours with everything going on that I'm not as good at sleeping through the night as I used to be."

"I'm sorry."

I shrugged. "Glad to see you. Thanks for coming over last night."

"Of course. I finally got to see you in the middle of the night, rather than listen from far away." He stroked my hair. "You fell asleep fast."

"As it turns out, your chest is very comfortable," I answered with a prim lift to my chin.

He grinned. "Glad you got some rest, really. Especially since you're back here in your mothership."

I shrugged. "Everybody likes breakfast. The frittata will be done in about five minutes."

"No argument there." He glanced upstairs. "I can leave, you know, before Callan and Tarissa wake up."

I flushed. "Are you . . . embarrassed?"

"No, not at all—"

"This isn't Victorian England. I'm not 'compromised.' You don't have to marry me to protect me from social exile."

He rolled his eyes. "I just figured it was a situation that would need to be explained some, and if you didn't want to explain, that would be fine. I wouldn't want you to feel embarrassed in any way."

"I don't mind. Really. And I'd like your company. So if telling the whole story protects your virtue," I said, patting his arm, "I'm okay with it. And embarrassed? Are you serious? You met my family. I'm impervious. I'm a brick wall of nonembarrassment."

"Fine. You want coffee?"

"People keep asking me that. The answer is always, always going to be yes."

"Then I'll make you coffee." He planted another kiss on my cheek. "Want to go see the ducks this morning?"

"The ducks at the hotel you were telling me about? Sure. I'm always game for ducks. I'm from Oregon, I have Duck-ish loyalties."

"Perfect."

I gazed at Neil as he found the coffee beans, ground them down, and set the coffee maker. "This is nice," I said.

He looked up, our eyes meeting. "Yes, it is," he said.

I looked away before I said something I'd regret. I loved our time together and wanted to cherish every moment—no matter how short it turned out to be.

Footsteps sounded down the stairs. "I smell coffee," Callan said when he entered the kitchen.

"Oh! I've got to get the frittata out." I raced to the oven, grabbed the first mitt I found and hauled the pan onto the stovetop. "Gosh, that's gorgeous."

"Yes, it is," Callan agreed, before turning to study Neil's lounge attire. "Nice pants, bro."

"Neil spent most of the night," I said. "I ravished him. He's too embarrassed to admit it."

Neil covered his eyes with his hand. "I am never going to live this down."

Callan managed a straight face. "Ravished, huh?"

"Do you mind?" Neil asked, before telling the entire story.

I sighed once he'd made it through. "I liked my version better. Less tragic sounding."

"Have you heard anything from your family?" Callan asked.

"Clementine texted me when Chloé fell asleep, but otherwise no. They're either still there or all asleep. I'm functioning on the 'no news is good news' philosophy. If something happened, I would have heard about it," I said, praying deep in my heart that I spoke the truth.

"I'm sure you would have," Neil assured me.

I pasted a bright smile on my face, a skill that was fast becoming my most reliable superpower. "I'm sure everything's fine. Who's hungry for breakfast?"

~ LAST-MINUTE FRITTATA ~

The great thing about a frittata is that you can kind of clean out the fridge with it. While some kind of onion and starch is always a good idea, any kind of stray vegetables and ends of cheese can be thrown in as well. They're traditionally served at room temperature, but they're very good still warm from the oven.

1–2 tablespoons butter

1 onion or 2–3 shallots, diced fine

6–8 small fingerling potatoes, peels on, diced

$1\frac{1}{2}$ roasted red peppers, patted dry with paper towels and diced

2 handfuls of fresh spinach, washed, dried, and rough chopped

1 teaspoon fresh thyme leaves, or $\frac{1}{2}$ teaspoon dried

Pinch red pepper flakes

8 eggs, lightly beaten with $\frac{1}{3}$ cup whole milk

5 ounces mild cheese, such as fontina, grated
Salt and freshly ground pepper

Preheat the oven to 400°F.

Melt the butter in an oven-safe sauté pan or cast-iron skillet, using medium heat. Once the butter has melted, add the onions and sauté until translucent. Add the potatoes and season with salt and freshly ground pepper, stirring until the potatoes have browned. Cover and reduce heat to medium-low, and allow potatoes to steam until just cooked through, for about 5–7 minutes.

Add the roasted red peppers, tossing them with the onions and potatoes until they've dried. Add the red pepper flakes, thyme, and spinach, allowing them a moment to blend with the vegetables and butter.

Pour the egg mixture into the pan, and stir just enough to evenly distribute the vegetables. Sprinkle cheese on top.

Allow to cook for 3–5 minutes, until the frittata is set along the bottom and sides but is still liquid at the center.

Place the pan in the oven and bake for 5–10 minutes (time will depend on the amount of moisture remaining in the vegetables). The frittata is done when the eggs have set across the top and the edges have pulled away from the sides of the pan. Allow the frittata to set for five minutes.

Serve with a salad and rustic bread if you're partaking for lunch or dinner. For breakfast, serve with fruit and toast. Leftover frittata can be reheated or served cold.

Serves 6.

22

After violent emotion most people and all boys
demand food.

—RUDYARD KIPLING

After the frittata breakfast, I went upstairs to shower and get
ready for the day, and Neil went home to do the same. By nine
o'clock, the text messages started.

From Sophie: "Mom at ER for kidney infection pain and fever. They
changed her antibiotic to treat the kidney infection. Thanks for sending Clementine to watch Chloé. We'll talk when you're awake."

From Clementine: "Your niece is really good at Bananagrams. She went
back to bed after about an hour, I stayed the night. Your sister is really intense
but that woman knows how to pick a couch—best night's sleep I've ever had."

From Nico: "Mom's okay, hope you didn't get too worried last night. Clementine told me about it. Good idea to send her over. Talked to Chloé, she's
cool."

From Alex: "Sorry you can't vacation successfully. Hope you got some
sleep."

Nothing from my parents, which wasn't surprising since neither parent had
embraced texting as a form of communication. They both had cell phones, not
that either saw much use.

I started with a call to Alex. "Mom and Dad up? I didn't want to call and
wake them up if they're still asleep."

"I think they're asleep. I just walked through the main house to drop off
fresh coffee beans, and everything is still quiet."

"Glad they're sleeping at least. Is Mom . . . okay?"

"She's in pain. She was swearing in French at the nurses."

"That sounds funny and terrible at the same time."

He sighed. "It was. One of them spoke French back to her, told her she was sorry but doing the best she could, and if she wanted to she could call the doctor whatever name she wanted."

"I kind of love that."

"She turned out to be the best nurse."

Something in his voice piqued my curiosity. "Was she pretty?"

"Juliette. Seriously."

"She was," I said, amazed and disbelieving at the same time. "The pretty nurse at the ER speaks French and isn't intimidated by Mom."

"Juliette—"

"That's all. I'm done."

"It's not a good time for me to date, Jules. The divorce feels like it happened five minutes ago, and Mom's sick, and . . . it's a tough time."

My turn to sigh. "Don't I know it. I'm sorry—new topic."

"I'm out," he said, "unless you want to tell me about your trip."

"Oh, you know. The weather is bad, the company is good."

"Are you going to marry him?"

I rolled my eyes. "Not you too."

"Turnabout is fair play."

"I didn't say you should marry French-speaking nurse," I tossed back, my voice defensive. Secretly, though, my heart swelled at the opportunity to spar with my brother. After his divorce he'd gone from quiet to near silent. I'd missed him.

"Yeah, yeah," he retorted, sounding very mature. "It was implied."

We discussed his work for a couple of minutes, the catering jobs he'd managed to snag for the restaurant. Right as we began to say our good-byes, my phone beeped to indicate another call coming in.

Sophie.

"Soph's on the other line," I told Alex.

"I'll say a novena for you."

"You're funny. Not Catholic, but funny."

"Give Sophie my best."

"I will," I said, before saying good-bye and flipping the call over. "Hey, Soph. How are ya?"

"Fine. Tired. Fine." She exhaled hard. "These middle-of-the-night ER trips are tough."

"I'm so sorry, Soph. Is there anything I can do from here? I can order a pizza delivery for you in, you know, ten hours."

"Every time I meet her at the hospital," Sophie said, voice ragged, "I'm afraid we're going to lose her."

My heart cracked a little. "She's made it this far."

"People don't get over ovarian cancer, Etta. It's like diabetes, it becomes chronic."

"I know." I sat down on my bed. "I remember that oncology appointment. I'll be home soon, Soph."

"It's not like your being here will change things that much, though. I'll still be up and at the hospital every time Mom is."

I took a deep breath, doing my best not to bristle at her words. "Sometimes it's comforting to have someone to share the load with, though, and I'm happy to do that."

"You're right," Sophie said, her voice softer, contrite. "I'm sorry."

"And you're tired. It's okay. I'll see you when I get back."

By the time we hung up, I had a text from Caterina: "Talked to Alex. Having fun with the family medical emergencies while in another time zone?"

I snorted and texted her back. "And how."

My phone dinged a moment later. "Sorry, babe. Hugs."

I felt wrung out by the time Neil returned to pick me up. "You okay?" he asked, handing me a very large, very iced Starbucks to-go cup.

"Oh, thank you," I said, clutching the cold cup in my hands as if the cool condensation could sustain my soul. "I'm fine, I've just been on a phone-call and text binge with the family." I gave him the rundown. "So basically everybody's stable but stressed. Haven't talked to my mom yet, hoping to do that this afternoon."

He kissed my temple. "You're a good person."

"You're sweet. Are you ready to go?"

"I am—you?"

I held up my coffee. "I've got this. I can do anything."

Neil laughed and helped me into his car, and by ten fifteen we were speeding toward the Peabody hotel in downtown Memphis. We parked and walked inside, finding the foyer to be swarming with people.

"Oh good," Neil said. "It's not that crowded yet."

"No?" I asked incredulously.

"Just wait," he said.

At the center of the spacious lobby stood a large fountain, adorned at the top with an exuberant flower arrangement. We ordered mimosas and desserts at the lobby bar and carried them to a table with a view of the fountain.

Neil and I carried on a lively conversation about his work and the remodeling project at his house. As the minutes ticked by, the number of people only increased.

"Okay, you've got to tell me what's going on," I said, as adults with small children began to take seats near my feet. "Where are the ducks?"

"I can tell you," he said, "or it can be a surprise."

"The kids can't stop talking about ducks." I raised an eyebrow. "Are they in, like a . . . no, I have no ideas. I guess I'll just wait."

"You are so wise."

I grinned at him. "Thank you."

By the time the clock struck eleven, I felt certain half of Memphis had crowded inside the hotel in anticipation. And they were not disappointed.

A reveille played over the speakers, followed by a recording announcing that the famous Memphis Peabody ducks were on their way. The elevator opened, and a man in a formal uniform stepped forward, followed by . . . ducks.

"There are real ducks over there," I told Neil, pointing.

"Yup."

"That's the whole point, isn't it?"

Neil winked. "You catch on quick."

I watched in fascination as the uniformed gentleman gently herded five ducks—one male and four females—down the red carpet and up a small set of stairs at the base of the fountain. One by one, the ducks traveled up the stairs and jumped into the fountain. After landing, each duck began to paddle through the fountain water.

Flashes flashed. Children cried out in delight. Elderly ladies leaned over to one another and stage-whispered "Well, isn't that sweet" to each other.

After the majority of the crowd dispersed, Neil and I strolled over for a closer look.

"So they just swim around in the fountain all day?" I asked.

"The Duckmaster will come back for them at five."

I shot him an incredulous "The Duckmaster?"

"The guy in the uniform? That's his title."

"That's amazing."

"And sometimes people will come and be the guest Duckmaster."

"Oh my gosh. Have they ever had the Ducks football team come and be Duckmasters?"

"Considering that this is SEC territory, I would doubt it."

"Well . . . still. Ducks. If they wanted to be purely SEC about it they could have stuck some razorbacks into the fountain. Pigs swim too."

Neil threw back his head and laughed. "They do. You're right. Good job with the mascot memory."

"Well, it's impossible to miss the Razorback paraphernalia on the cars around here."

"Good point."

"And," I admitted, "my brother is really into football."

"Nico?"

"Alex, actually. Although in my parents' house, it's seriously still referred to as 'American football.' My dad's a huge soccer fan." I smiled in remembrance. "During the World Cup, Dad put a mini TV into the restaurant kitchen while he worked. If his team won, you could hear the cheering." I gave a half smile. "Those were the good days. Oh well." I straightened my shoulders. "Everything changes."

Neil gave my hand a squeeze. "I thought we could grab some lunch while we're out, maybe swing by the lab if you're interested, then stop by my house."

"I'd love that," I said, nodding. "And I'd love to visit your house."

So we did. After barbecue for lunch at Rendezvous, just a short walk from the Peabody, we drove to the wing of the hospital where Neil spent his days. I met co-workers and said hello to Callan, who ribbed Neil for playing hooky. The smiles were genuine, and from the subtext of each conversation I gathered that Neil's world revolved around his work and research.

What that research meant involved terminology and concepts above my pay grade, but I admired the passion he brought to his work. I understood it, even if our worlds were completely different. He loved his work the way that I loved restaurants, the way I loved working with food and seeing people enjoy what they tasted.

And if I were honest, truly honest with myself, he loved his work with a lack of reserve that I didn't see in my own work with the restaurant. Not that it meant that it wasn't worthwhile, or that it wouldn't change—after all, the restaurant hadn't even opened yet.

We drove to his home next—he was right, he lived minutes away from Callan and Tarissa's.

His home stood situated to the left on a large lot, surrounded by poplars. Built of brick, his house looked classic and cozy at the same time. "It's adorable," I said once we stepped out of the car.

"That's not the word I would pick," Neil said, locking the car behind us. "But I'm glad you like it."

The inside felt bright and breezy, with large windows bathing the interior with light. The décor could be described as sparse modern, but it suited him.

He gave me the tour, and we settled in the kitchen over glasses of iced tea, sitting next to each other on the stools by his kitchen island. "Fair warning," he said. "This tea started out life as powder."

"I'm brave," I said. "Mind if I step outside to try to call my parents?"

"By all means," Neil answered, "but you're welcome to stay inside the house. My office is just down the hall—it's air-conditioned in here."

"Good point." I followed him down the hall to his office, which faced the backyard with large windows. "This'll be perfect," I said, taking in the couch.

"Take your time."

I pulled out my phone and dialed my parents' house number. "Hello, Giulietta," my father said when he picked up the phone.

"Hi, Dad." I hated how tired he sounded. "I heard about your ordeal last night. How's Mom doing?"

"She's awake," he said. "She ate some breakfast. The doctors gave her new medicines. Would you like to talk to her?"

"Sure, in a minute." I sank onto Neil's office couch. "Are you okay?"

"It was a long night. Tomorrow will be better."

I found his optimism, while very much in character, sweet and more than a little heartbreaking.

"I hope so," I said.

"Me too. Are you enjoying the South?"

"It's different. I've eaten well."

"That's something," he said.

"I ate cheese fritters," I added, grinning.

"What are cheese fritters?" he asked, as if I'd just told him I'd eaten boogers.

Once I'd finished my description, he seemed more or less on board. "We shall try them when you're back. I'm curious. Okay," he said, his voice louder, "here is your mother."

"Bonjour, cherie," Maman said when she answered the phone. "How is Tennessee?"

"I'm eating cheese fritters and barbecue. I'm good. How are you feeling?"

"*Comme ci, comme ça.* They gave me very good medicine, the staff were very kind to me. One of the nurses even spoke French."

"I heard that. Alex told me."

"Alex told you, eh? That is very interesting."

"He admitted she was pretty too."

"Ah, oui, très belle. We could use a nurse in the family."

"Agreed. Anything I can do for you?"

"Juliette, ma cherie, enjoy your beau and have a good time," she said forcefully. "Do not worry about me."

She'd raised me to be obedient, to respect her words, but I didn't know how to not worry, not when she was battling cancer, not when she was visiting the ER in the middle of the night.

"I'll try," I said at last.

"*Non.* That is not good enough. You must promise, ma petite, that you will enjoy your time with your young man."

"I will, Maman." I sighed. "Can I at least bring you home some jam?"

"Of course. Bring me jam."

"I love you, Maman."

"*Je t'aime,* Juliette. You are loved. You are a special young woman. Now go show Neil how special you are."

"I think he knows."

"Go remind him, dearest," she said. Her wording reminded me of Mireille and Cécile's letters.

"Yes, Maman. Hug Papa for me, please."

"*Mais oui, ma petite, mais oui. Au revoir, cherie.*"

I hung up and wiped at my tears with the back of my hand. She was fine, I knew she was fine, and yet my worry pressed against my chest so tightly I could barely breathe. I tried to breathe, tried to pray. Little by little, my heart began to slow, my breathing deepened.

When I felt I could speak without warbling, I grabbed my iced tea and rejoined Neil in the kitchen.

"Hi," I said, giving a bright, if unfocused smile. "Sorry, I'm back."

Neil met me halfway and wrapped his arms around my waist. "Your parents? They're okay?"

"As okay as can be expected." I rested my hands around his shoulders and tilted my head up to him. We probably looked like two high schoolers during a slow dance. I decided to change the subject. "So . . . what about your parents? We're having dinner with them tomorrow, right?"

Neil studied my face before answering. "Yes." He stroked my hair. "They'll be here tomorrow early evening, and they'll join us for dinner. It's a quick flight in and out for them."

"They flew?" My eyes widened.

"It's a ten- to eleven-hour drive otherwise."

"But . . . I don't know, airfare . . ." I took a quarter-step backward; words bubbled up inside of me, and I swallowed them down deep.

Neil closed the distance between us. "Hey. They're a little intense, but I figured you'd understand."

"I get intense, but—"

"And from here they're going on to Nashville to visit my dad's best friend and visit the Grand Ole Opry. They love the Grand Ole Opry." Neil shrugged. "So you and me, we're just a stop to them."

"Just a stop," I repeated.

"I know it sounds like a big deal, but it's not. They'll come, they'll meet you, they'll stay the night at my place and then head out the next morning because my dad has golf plans."

"Your dad golfs? Good to know." I squinted at him. "Do you golf?"

"I don't, but not for my dad's lack of trying. Why?" Neil laughed. "Is that important?"

I waved a hand. "I have theories about men and golf, but it's neither here nor there. I just . . ." I disengaged myself from his hold and seated myself back on the kitchen stool. I tried once more to keep the words inside, but they wouldn't be stopped. "How serious do your parents think we are? How serious are we?"

"I love you. You love me." He shrugged, taking the seat next to me. "We're long distance for now, but we'll figure it out."

How? How would we figure it out? I wanted to throw my questions at him, but if growing up in my family had taught me anything, it was how to avoid a fight. I had a terrible feeling that too many questions too soon would bring our delicate, lovely little relationship tumbling to the ground.

And the truth was, as much as I wanted to ask the hard questions, I wasn't ready to hear the answers. So for now, I would wait. I would wait until I couldn't wait any longer.

"I'm really glad we're here, together," I said, clutching his hand.

He dismounted from his stool, stepping close. In one swift motion, his arm swept behind my back, his hand disengaged from mine long enough to lift my face to his.

It was a surprisingly smooth move from a guy who spent most of his time in a lab. My body began to tingle in anticipation even before his kiss landed.

And the kiss—how did he do it? How did he use his lips, his scent, his closeness, to make me believe that as long as we were together, everything would be all right? My eyes fell shut and my hands wrapped around his torso. We kissed until my body felt boneless and pliant. "You're really good at that," I said when I could speak.

Neil chuckled. "I have a good muse."

I looked into his eyes—and then the largest yawn I'd ever experienced escaped without permission. I clapped my hand over my mouth, but there was no hiding it.

Neil laughed out loud. "So I'm a boring kisser, then?"

"Oh, gosh. No. I'm just . . ." Another yawn.

"Want to go sit down on the couch? Watch something?"

"Sure," I said. "Just don't expect me to stay awake."

"I can take you back to Callan and Tarissa's, if you want."

"No," I said, with a shake of my head. "We don't have much time."

"I know," he said. So we sat on the couch, our hands woven together, my head against his shoulder. This time, I made it a whole episode before things got hazy and I fell asleep.

23

There is no technique, there is just the way to do it.
Now, are we going to measure or are we going to cook?

—FRANCES MAYES

I'd intended to make dinner for Callan and Tarissa, but Tarissa had plans of her own. "It's not every day I have a chef in my kitchen, and I'm gonna learn something from you," she said.

"Now I wish I'd picked something a little more sophisticated," I said, looking over my ingredients. I'd planned on a simple pasta primavera with grilled vegetables and shrimp—nothing that required a great deal of skill.

"That sounds good. Don't worry. I'm sure you know more than you think you know."

So I set to work. I set a pot of water to boil for the pasta before moving on to the vegetables. I chopped the red peppers, zucchini, and eggplant, showing Tarissa how I liked to cut them in order for them to grill properly. "You want them large enough to get grill marks and not fall through the grates. You should also pat them dry—you want as little water in the grill as possible."

Tarissa nodded. "That makes sense. I should take notes."

"If you like. Did Neil ever tell you that I gave a couple of cooking demos on our local morning television show, back in Portland?"

"No, he never breathed a word of that," she replied, affronted.

"That's nice of him. It went over well, but I was so nervous I threw up before the last one. I quit my job shortly after. It was the right thing to do. Now my co-worker Linn is in the spotlight, and she's great at it."

"Am I making you nervous?"

"Not yet," I answered with a cheeky smile. "Want to devein the shrimp?"

"That I can do. You couldn't grow up in my mama's house and not know shrimp."

"Perfect. Once they're deveined, we'll salt and pepper them, then toss them with some olive oil, salt, and pepper."

Once Tarissa settled in with the shrimp, I focused on cutting the zucchini and eggplant, getting meaty cuts with skin and cutting out the soft, seeded centers. Once they were ready, I threw them in a bowl with a splash of olive oil and stirred them around. Tarissa and I skewered the shrimp and vegetables with long bamboo skewers and took them outside to where Neil and Callan waited by the hot grill.

"The shrimp cooks just until it turns pink," I said as we laid the veggie skewers out. "Because it cooks quickly, we'll do the vegetables first."

While the men manned the skewers, I checked on the pasta water. Sure enough, the water bubbled away at a strong boil. "Perfect," I said, throwing a small handful of salt into the pot.

"I like salt as much as the next girl," Tarissa said, "but that looked like a lot."

"Oh, it is. But you want your pasta water salty—salty like the sea. You'll get more flavorful pasta in the end—it won't taste too salty, promise."

I dropped in the penne and gave it a stir. Over the next ten minutes I wore a path between the kitchen and the deck, checking on the pasta and looking over the vegetables.

Once the veggies were nearly done, I heated a skillet with some butter on the stove, then walked Tarissa through the steps of building a simple white sauce. "You don't want too much flour," I told her as I stirred the concoction with a whisk. "The flour will absorb too much flavor if you overdo it."

A splash of lemon juice, and the sauce was ready to go. I chopped up a generous amount of parsley and checked on the men.

Sure enough, the veggies had beautiful grill marks and the shrimp looked perfectly pink.

We carried everything inside, and I gave the veggies a quick chop before draining the pasta and throwing all of it together into the skillet. I finished with plenty of grated parmesan cheese, and we were ready to eat.

"You made that look easy," Tarissa said. "I could do that. You watch out," she told Callan. "I'm gonna make this again."

"I'm fine with that," he said, planting a sweet kiss on his wife's cheek.

We stayed out until well after dark, watching the fireflies dance.

Neil and I had agreed upon the wisdom of sleeping in the next morning. I took a light breakfast with Callan and Tarissa, then Neil arrived for coffee after. Tarissa encouraged him to take me to the Saddle Creek shops to walk and window-shop; afterward we drove to Poplar and spent the heat of the day in a cool movie theater.

At five Neil deposited me back at Callan and Tarissa's to change for dinner. I wore my navy sundress, pairing it with my green stone necklace and emerald-green heels.

I looked cute and sophisticated, but not too dressed up. I pulled the front of my hair back with bobby pins, and curled the ends of my hair.

As a last step, I borrowed some of Tarissa's nail polish, turning my nails a shiny pale pink.

"Have you met Neil's parents?" I asked Tarissa, once I'd decided I wasn't above a little digging.

"I did, once," she said. "Didn't spend much time with them."

No further elucidation. I was on my own.

Neil picked me up shortly after six, and we drove to the Macaroni Grill on Poplar Avenue.

He squeezed my hand as we crossed the parking lot. "Don't worry. They'll love you."

"What do you mean?"

He gave a soft chuckle. "I mean you're squeezing my hand to the point that it's getting tingly."

I forced myself to relax my grip and tossed him a saucy smile. "Maybe that's just our chemistry."

"Yes," he said, smiling. "I'm sure that's it."

We laughed together, but I couldn't relax—not really.

Four steps into the foyer and Neil made eye contact with a couple waiting inside, lifting a hand in a wave.

Showtime.

The closer we got, the more I could see the resemblance. Neil had inherited his dad's hair and height, but his mom's bone structure and eyes.

Neil greeted them both with hugs before stepping back and introducing me. "This is Juliette," he said, in a voice filled with pride. "Juliette, meet my parents—Bill and Vivianne McLaren."

"Nice to meet you, Bill," I said, shaking his hand when he offered. "Vivianne—such a pretty name."

Vivianne pressed a hand to her heart. "Aw, thank you, sweet pea. You can have a hug."

"Okay," I began to say, but the entire word didn't make it out before I was on the receiving end of the tightest hug I'd ever had.

"Table's ready," Neil announced before the breath returned to my body. We followed the waitress to one of the booths that overlooked the lower dining room.

Neil held my hand as we walked. "Everything will be fine," he whispered into my ear the instant before we slid into the booth.

I smiled into his eyes—I wanted him to be right.

To: Caterina, cdesanto@beneculinary.com
From: Me, jdalisa@twobluedoors.com

Well, I met the parents tonight. Just got back.

It went okay. Well, pretty much okay. I don't know. I'll write this out, and we can talk about it and figure out where things are on the okay-or-not scale.

We went to the Macaroni Grill, which isn't Dad's place by any means, but it's fine. I ordered a mixed green salad, and it was not so much a mixed green salad as much as it was a romaine salad with a sprig of frisée for décor. ONE SPRIG OF FRISÉE.

I thought maybe this was some kind of kitchen mishap. In hindsight that was very, very stupid. But my head was still in Portland, where if you get a mixed green salad, you can get up to five different kinds of leaves. I couldn't wrap my brain around anyone serving romaine with a SINGLE FRISÉE LEAF as a mixed green salad with a straight face.

So I asked the waitress if it was in fact the mixed green salad, and she said that yes, it was. And I couldn't help myself, I asked if the mixed greens usually included only the two greens. Call it morbid curiosity. And again, she said yes, it was.

I thanked her and she left me staring at my lone piece of frisée. I didn't even know what to do with it—eat it first? Save it for last? And that's when Neil's dad, Bill, announced that when he was a kid, he ate everything on his plate and never complained, but that it was a different time.

So yes, he basically called me an entitled millennial. I can't even imagine how Dad would have responded if someone had served him this salad—probably would have insinuated himself into the kitchen to have a conversation with the chef. Mom? Oh boy. She would have left altogether, because if the kitchen couldn't make salad, how could they handle chicken? All of this would be sprinkled with a choice insult or two—in French.

But me? Yes, I'm the spoiled millennial.

Neil tried to save the moment by explaining that I came from a restaurant family, that my father owned and ran a celebrated Italian restaurant in Portland, that I had a culinary degree and used to be a food writer and was now managing the new restaurant.

So then they asked what my management duties included, and Neil's mom, Vivianne, asked with wide eyes how that would work when I had a family.

OH YES. SHE DID.

When I explained how we grew up—fending for ourselves at home if we weren't running around the restaurant—well, let's just say they got quiet. And then Bill asked when I was planning to move to Tennessee.

That was the awkward moment when Neil and I stuttered in tandem that we were still figuring things out, that there were no plans yet to move. And then they talked about how Neil couldn't leave his job, how good of an opportunity he had in Memphis.

Neil talked about how important my job was in Portland, and how we weren't trying to make any permanent decisions right now, we were just enjoying spending time together.

The rest of the night was an awkward mixture of small talk and politics (suffice it to say, Bill and I do not agree on much, and Vivianne just agrees with whatever her husband says).

I mean, they're not terrible people. And frankly, it's not their fault they asked the questions that I've been wrestling with . . . though perhaps I would have been more content if they were questions they addressed privately with Neil, and not during a meet-and-greet dinner.

I'm so tired.

Anyway, I leave the day after tomorrow. Neil drove me home, of course, after dinner. We didn't talk much. I could call him . . . but I don't know what to say.

Cat, we're so good when we're together. I can see us having a life, a long life together. We're easy together. He's smart, he's stable, he's interesting—Neil is the complete package.

I feel angry at Neil's parents for treating us like two teenagers who think they'll stay in love forever even though they're seventeen and headed to two different state colleges, but I can't stay angry because they're not wrong.

And then I'll get on the plane, and I'll cry, and I've done this all before, and I'm tired of being unstable and emotional. Mom is sick, the restaurant is opening SOON, and I don't have time to be sad over my boyfriend.

And yet . . . it's Neil. I don't know what to do, Cat.

Juliette

P.S. I'm writing instead of calling because I'm at Callan and Tarissa's (and they're great, really, you'd be best friends with Tarissa), but I don't want to have this conversation about their friend, audibly, in their house, and it's too dark to go out on a walk.

To: Me, jdalisa@twobluedoors.com
From: Caterina, cdesanto@beneculinary.com

Oh, hon. Oh man. Oh. Oooooooohhhhhhhhh.
    Ouch.
    Sorry. I wish I had better words for you. Really. SO MUCH. And I wish I had more experience to pull from. Other than my decision to not date someone perpetually on the road (as we've discussed), dating Damian went smoothly. His mother took my face into her hands and told me that I was the best thing that had ever happened to him (he was, apparently, quite a handful as a child. I think she was delighted to have someone else take responsibility for him).
    But we were also in Chicago at the same time, and we agreed about our future. (This is back before we were married. The constant agreeing ends, like three minutes after the ceremony. Two if you're both Italian.)
    I wish so much that you and Neil could have had that, to have been in the same physical place, to be in agreement and at peace with what your future holds. Because if you don't feel comfortable with your current arrangement (which we've agreed is a legit concern)—no amount of hopes, dreams, and platitudes is going to change that. I think Neil's been pretty clear that he has no intention to leave Tennessee anytime soon. And unless you're ready to make the move—which I support, if that's your decision—you guys are kinda stuck until one of you changes your mind. And seriously, it's okay to take your time with a

relationship if it's healthy and self-sustaining. You don't have to make any decisions anytime soon.

Let's talk in person soon, you know, when you can. And I'll SEE you in person when I come for the grand opening. Bringing Damian and the boys this trip. I'm dressing them in matching outfits and NOBODY CAN STOP ME.

(Unless Damian intervenes and unpacks one of the outfits. Just one. That's how unstable this operation is. And who knows, I'll probably forget to pack one myself, so we'll wind up without any but MAYBE I'LL GO BUY NEW ONES IN PORTLAND WITHOUT SALES TAX, YES, THAT'S EXACTLY WHAT I'LL DO.)

The day the Italians found the Caps Lock . . . well, I don't know, but I feel it was significant.

I love you. Hoping and praying good things for you.

Cat

To: Caterina, cdesanto@beneculinary.com
From: Me, jdalisa@twobluedoors.com

Thanks for the hopes and prayers. Going to try to sleep. Probably won't sleep much. Wish I could beam myself up to Chicago, really. But that's just me wanting to run away from my problems.

I fly home day after tomorrow. Neil and I will have to talk tomorrow, then.

Looking forward to that. Not really.

Hugs, J

P.S. Hope Damian and the boys are well. I respect your problem-solving in regard to the matching outfits. Also: you are the best.

I closed my laptop and tried to sleep. Tried and failed. Thankfully Callan and Tarissa were gone when Neil and I returned to the house. He walked me to the door, we shared a good night kiss. I tried not to read anything into it, but my head replayed the scene in *Sabrina,* when William Holden explained to Humphrey Bogart about how good-bye kisses tasted different.

Ours wasn't a good-bye kiss. It was . . . a placeholder kiss. A kiss shared because neither of us wanted to go without, and yet neither of us knew what to do or what to think.

I didn't exactly feel better after e-mailing Caterina, but at least my thoughts seemed more ordered. If only I liked them more.

Rather than stew, I decided to quietly putter downstairs and make myself tea with Tarissa's instant hot water spout. I climbed the stairs afterward, settled into the chair in my room, and pulled out my computer to read Mireille's letters. If I remembered correctly, I'd left off with Mireille returning to the chateau to care for her mother.

April 24, 1939

Dear Gabriel,

Broth success! Maman has been able to take chicken and beef broth. Tomorrow I will make a chicken and garlic soup, or a beef and barley soup (I will likely make both and see which one she will eat).

Being with Cécile has been a comfort; my father has been difficult. And . . . my former fiancé has visited with his parents as well. His mother is, of course, no help—she acts as though she wants to be useful, but winds up gossiping about their friends. M. Bessette is a comfort to Papa, I suppose.

So there are no secrets between us, you should know that Gilles is trying to rekindle an attachment. This is a fruitless endeavor.

When I left our engagement and traveled to Paris, all I felt for weeks was relief. True and blissful relief.

But just a short time without you and . . . I ache to see you, to be near you. I work to be generous to my family, and as much as I am glad that I'm here and I can be helpful, I feel as though I've left my heart behind in Paris.

It is mine to be patient. And yours, I suspect.

Yours,
Mireille

~ Pasta Primavera for Four ~

Primavera is the Italian word for spring, but this version is decidedly summery. If a grill isn't an option, cut the vegetables a bit smaller and roast in a 425°F oven instead.

1½ red bell peppers (yellow or orange would work fine too), cut into quarters
2 medium-sized zucchini, cut into large pieces, seeded center cut away
1 eggplant, cut into large pieces, seeded center cut away
½ pound fresh shrimp, deveined with tails removed
Olive oil, for grilling and sauce
1 pound penne pasta
½ cup pasta water, reserved
1 cup parsley, chopped
1 cup parmesan cheese, grated
Juice from one lemon
½ cup pine nuts, toasted (optional)
1 tablespoon salt plus salt to season
Cracked black pepper

Dry the cut veggies with paper towels and coat with olive oil, salt, and pepper. Repeat the process with the shrimp, and fit each onto skewers.

Set the pasta water to boil with the tablespoon salt.

Grill the veggies and shrimp; cook the veggies until they soften and develop some char, about 3–5 minutes per side. Cook the shrimp until it turns pink and curls up.

While the vegetables and shrimp cook, boil the pasta until

al dente, about 9–11 minutes for penne. Drain, reserving ½ cup pasta water, and rinse the pasta in order to remove excess starch.

Once the veggies and shrimp are done, remove skewers and cut the veggies into smaller pieces. Toss the veggies, pasta, and parsley into the pasta pot together and stir; drizzle with olive oil and reserved pasta water. Add parmesan and stir again, followed with lots of cracked black pepper.

Serve immediately. Delicious with a squeeze of lemon over the top. Sprinkle with pine nuts if using.

24

I shouldn't think even millionaires could eat anything
nicer than new bread and real butter and honey for tea.

—DODIE SMITH

My heart squeezed as I read Mireille and Gabriel's love notes
through their separation. How long were they able to make it
work? What caused their separation in the end?

I continued reading, looking for answers.

May 7, 1939

Dear Mireille,

*I am gladdened to hear that your mother has begun to improve. Below you'll
find my mother's own favorite soup recipe, which has hastened many a recovery. I
do not make light of the severity of your mother's illness, only suggest that this soup
brought joy to my brothers and me.*

½ cup chopped onion
½ cup chopped celery
Two cloves garlic
1 cup chopped carrots (I like them still in rounds)
1 quart chicken stock
Three or four chicken thighs
Three bay leaves
Sprig thyme and dill
Handful chopped parsley
Salt, pepper to taste

Sauté the onion until translucent, and the garlic until fragrant. Add the celery and carrot and sauté until the celery softens a little. Add the chicken stock, thighs, thyme, and dill; bring to a boil, reduce, and simmer for an hour. Discard herbs, debone the chicken thighs, discard chicken skin and bones, chop cooked chicken. Add parsley and serve. Delicious with noodles, and also with matzo balls—I'll show you how to make them when you return.

You must know, Mireille, that I love you. I don't know what the future holds for us, but I do know that I love you, and I always will.

Gabriel

May 14, 1939

Dear Gabriel,

If you must know, I will always love you as well. I don't know what the future holds either, but the way you write, it sounds rather dour, though I look forward to discovering matzo.

Maman continues to improve. She took the chicken soup and beef and barley soup well, but the real success came with the risotto. When I walked into the room with the steaming bowl of risotto, she sat up from the scent of it! When she finished her bowl, her color had even seemed to improve.

It will be a few weeks before I can return to Paris—I know her well enough that once she begins to truly feel better, she'll make it difficult for me to leave.

I miss you terribly, but my heart warms to know that you've visited Tante Joséphine and my sweet Anouk.

When I return to Paris . . . I will say no more. We shall enjoy that time when it comes.

Mireille

May 22, 1939

Dear Gabriel,

Maman has improved greatly, but every time I speak of returning to Paris, she has a "spell" and must be accompanied to bed. I fear I may have to pack my trunks and return to Paris in the dead of night.

I have written to the culinary school of my intention to return for the next cycle of classes. I know I've missed enough of my classes to consider that term a wash. My only hope is that I'll be able to start again, without requiring the classes I missed.

I hope things are going well for you at the restaurant. I made a tarte tatin for Maman last night that she enjoyed very much. She can taste the difference in my pâté brisée, I know, but going back to pastry school? She'd still rather I didn't.

Cécile and I have begun to plot my escape. There is a horse involved.

I love you.

Mireille

June 3, 1939

Dear Mireille,

No horse necessary; I would be happy to come and spirit you away on foot. We could disappear to the Mediterranean together, the Alps, the Orient.

I have begun to think about leaving Paris. The political climate has become increasingly concerning for someone with my background. I've considered perhaps opening a patisserie of my own. My brother Benjamin speaks of leaving for America, though he is reluctant to give up his position at Van Cleef & Arpels.

Please write should you need to be rescued. I have no experience with balcony rescues, but have always believed I could try.

Avec amour,

Gabriel

June 17, 1939

My dearest Gabriel,

Are you asking me to run away with you? If so, the answer is yes. We can leave just as soon as I return to Paris, which should be on the 4 o'clock train on Monday the 26th. Neither of my parents is happy about it, but I've made my decision, and I'm prepared to climb out a window if necessary.

If you can bear it, I would be delighted to see you at the station.
Bisous,
Mireille

July 4, 1939

My dearest Cécile,

I hope Maman has continued in health since my departure. As much as I miss you, I am so very glad to be back in Paris.

Gabriel met me at the train station with a bouquet of hothouse flowers and a box of madeleines.

I am to meet his parents next week. Please pray for me, dearest—I am so very nervous! We are beginning to make plans for the future. Nothing official, only discussing hopes for the future and what it might look like. If he asks me, I mean to marry him. He is the very best man I have ever met.

I am not a romantic, at least not like that silly Veronique Jeunet. If necessary, I could live without Gabriel—my lungs would continue to take in air, my heart would continue beating. I could manage. But I do not wish to. I look into the future and envision a life without him, and it pales in comparison to a life that we might share together.

Do visit soon. I miss your face so very much.
Mireille

July 16, 1939

My dear Mireille,

Flowers and madeleines at the train station? I must meet this man. I have spoken to Maman about a trip to Paris. More specifically, I told her that I am in desperate need of two new frocks. It is a sad statement about my frocks that she could not have agreed fast enough. You'd tell me the truth if I looked shabby, wouldn't you?

Cécile

July 27, 1939

Dearest, most fashionable Cécile—

For heaven's sakes, if your frocks are old, mine must be antediluvian. Be of peace knowing you are a fashion plate. And even if some of your frocks are a few years old, no one would know it—you have a classic eye.

M. and Mme. Roussard invited me to dine at their home last week.

While I am certain Papa would find a reason to look down his nose at them, Gabriel's parents are by no means poor. Their house is lovely, and they employ a housekeeper who made a wonderful meal.

I don't even know why I'm beginning with that. Perhaps I'm trying to set the stage. I hardly knew what to expect when I arrived.

(In case you are wondering, I wore my navy dress with the tulip skirt and looked both chic and appropriate.)

Gabriel's mother, Ruth, is very elegant. She has fine, delicate features and Gabriel's lovely eyes (I suppose Gabriel has her eyes, but I saw them first on him). Gabriel's father, Théodore, is a retired professor and is still devoted to his scholarship.

We had a lovely dinner, though at times it felt, perhaps, a little awkward. I do not gather that Gabriel is in the habit of bringing young ladies to the home as dinner guests.

M. Roussard asked about the chateau, its history, and if I was to be in charge of its care in the future. Mme. Roussard asked about my pastry studies, and what I planned to do with them, and if I was also planning to settle down and have a family in the future.

In short: many difficult questions with complicated answers. I am not the intellectual that they had hoped for, I think, though why they would believe their pastry-making son would court a scholar, I do not know.

The conversation also turned briefly to the oldest brother in Warsaw, who would soon be moving to Paris with his family. I fear that they are not moving as much as they are fleeing for their safety. Such difficult times we live in.

The Roussards also asked if I had been to America, and if I would consider moving there in the future. I shook my head and said no, I would miss France and all of its strange, elegant ways. M. Roussard admonished that the political unrest in Germany was unlikely to stay in Germany, and that all of Europe could be swept into Herr Hitler's political agenda.

He is a learned man, so I must believe that he has reason to think such things. France is no stranger to war, of course, but I had hopes that perhaps it would not happen again so soon.

All of this discourse made for an unsettling dinner, though they were very kind when we parted, assuring me that I was welcome to return and they were certain they would see me again soon.

Gabriel and I took a cab back to Tante Joséphine's. The dinner had left him worried as well. He told me that he believes a move to the south, to Marseille, could be beneficial for the future.

I know that he is concerned about his brother in Warsaw, and his mother's status as a Jewess. He told me that he is considered to be a Jew as well, since it is, apparently, passed on through the mother.

But while he has dark eyes and hair, so have many Parisians without a single Jewish ancestor. With his French surname, I do not fully understand his concerns. But I told him that if he thought it wise to go to Marseille, that it was a lovely enough city, though parts of it stink of fish.

A little worried and confused tonight. I shall bake (and eat) a batch of . . . something . . . in consolation. Looking forward to seeing you!

Mireille

I sighed. At least Mireille's meeting of the parents went better than my own. Mireille and Gabriel seemed so ready to give up everything for each other. Would Neil and I ever be ready to do the same?

25

Better than any argument is to rise at dawn and
pick dew-wet red berries in a cup.

—WENDELL BERRY

I rose and dressed early. We'd agreed the night before to attend church
together. It seemed like a good idea at the time, but now I wasn't so
sure. After last night, I had no idea where we stood in our relationship—did I
want to meet his church community?

My options included going or pleading a headache. My shoulders felt so
tight I knew a headache couldn't be too far off. But I dressed for church anyway, choosing a light silk sundress in a blue floral print, ballet flats, and a
beaded coral necklace.

Callan and Tarissa were already up, dressed, and caffeinated by the time I
made it downstairs. "How'd dinner go?" Tarissa asked when she saw me, her
eyes bright.

I accepted the cup of coffee from Callan. "It went fine," I said, busying
myself with adding cream and sugar to the brew. "My pasta was good, I enjoyed the sauce."

"Oh good," Tarissa answered. "And his parents?"

"Tarissa," Callan warned, "don't pry."

"Mr. McLaren has strong opinions. Mrs. McLaren is very nice." I tested
the coffee for sweetness. "I think they're joining us for church this morning
before driving to Nashville."

Tarissa arched an eyebrow. "Were they rude?"

"Tarissa," Callan repeated.

"What?" She threw up her hands. "They were rude to you, Callan. I don't
know how Neil turned out so well."

Callan's jaw worked as he considered his words. "Neil's dad had difficulty accepting a black man in a professional job. He's surely a product of his own upbringing," he continued, his voice rising to prevent Tarissa's interruption, "and I feel pity for him."

Tarissa snorted.

"That's good of you," I said, meaning it.

He shrugged. "Getting angry about it doesn't change anything. But they did raise Neil, and he is a fine man and a good friend."

"Neil's a good man," I agreed. "Mr. McLaren . . . to be blunt, he doesn't see how we can have a future." I paused and considered my words, trying to choose what I could say and what I shouldn't. "And Mr. McLaren wasn't wrong, really, that's the problem. Neil and I haven't discussed it yet, though."

Callan gave a decisive nod. "Then we'll leave you to figure out your own problems."

Tarissa gave an unhappy grunt; Callan gave her an affectionate swat in return. I smiled as I took another sip of coffee. Theirs was a true love match—they reminded me of Caterina and Damian, the way they were easy with each other.

A few minutes later, Neil knocked on the door and let himself in. He greeted all of us, me with a brief kiss, before we separated to go to our cars. Unsurprisingly, Neil, Callan, and Tarissa attended the same church in Collierville.

The McLarens waited in the backseat of Neil's BMW, parked in the driveway with the engine and A/C running. Neil opened the front passenger seat for me and I slid in, saying my hellos at the same time.

With his parents present, Neil and I made small talk, but otherwise the church drive remained as quiet as our drive the night before—at least between us. The McLarens commented on the houses we drove past, reflections on their food the night before, and the fact that Neil's church met in a gym.

"It echoes," Vivianne noted, "but the chairs are comfortable enough. They have the good folding chairs—not those terrible metal ones. The plastic ones are more ergonomic."

"That's good," I said, nearly counting down the minutes until we arrived. If only Neil and I were alone, we could talk. As much as I wasn't looking forward to the conversation we needed to have.

Callan and Tarissa parked next to Neil's car; once we all climbed out, Tarissa kindly stuck near me, acting as a buffer.

I followed everybody inside, waiting when any of the three regulars paused to shake a hand or exchange hugs.

Inside the gym, we found seats and sat down. I guessed there were about three hundred people milling around before the music started and things began to settle. We'd cut it close enough that the beginning of the music stalled anyone curious enough to find out who I was—at least, before the meet and greet.

Neil reached for my hand and held it tightly within his own. I looked up at him but his gaze remained fixed on the stage.

I restrained a sigh. If we were in Portland, I would have suggested leaving church to go and work out our problems over strong coffee.

But I wasn't ignorant; I knew Tennessee culture meant you went to church on Sunday morning, and if you didn't you were probably a godless heathen. So Neil and I sat next to each other, miserable. At least I was miserable—and from Neil's expression he didn't look like he was about to launch into a Snoopy dance.

I did my best to focus on the music, and shook plenty of hands and smiled brightly when everyone followed instructions to greet their neighbors, even though I seemed in particular to be everybody's neighbor. Everyone was friendly and kind, and soon enough we settled into the three-point sermon, followed by closing worship.

Afterward Bill and Vivianne told us that they needed to get on the road to Nashville, and if Neil could kindly drive them back to their car at his home, that would be perfect. I wondered to myself why they hadn't simply driven their rental car to church, but mine was not to know.

So we said our good-byes to Callan and Tarissa, walked back to the car, and piled in. Neil said little, but Bill and Vivianne parsed the sermon and discussed the fact that the pastor had been casually dressed in chinos and a polo shirt.

Coming from Portland, land of plaid and flip-flops, I didn't feel any contribution to the conversation would be appreciated.

At Neil's house the McLarens took a moment to retrieve their luggage, which was otherwise packed and ready to go. They said their good-byes, with hugs and pats on the cheek. Neil and I stood in the driveway, watched, and waved as they drove away.

Neil's gaze remained fixed on the road, even after they'd gone. "I'm sorry about dinner last night."

My breath hitched. "It wasn't your fault."

"They're my parents," he maintained, turning toward me. "I agreed they could come. Made the reservations." He shook his head, turned. "It's too hot to stand around outside. Want to go for a drive?"

"Sure," I said. "Let's drive."

I followed Neil to the car, already toasty though the A/C had only been off five minutes.

"They were blunt," I allowed, as Neil pulled out of the driveway, "but your parents weren't wrong." All of the words I'd kept locked away for so long came tumbling out. "I want us to be together. I do. And I wish I knew how it could happen. But . . . your life is here, and my life? I can't leave right now. My mom, the restaurant—"

"I know. And I wouldn't want you to leave, not now. In a year or two, though, who knows?"

My eyebrows flew upward. "A year or two? I feel . . . I feel like we're in limbo. And limbo was never my party game—I've always been too all-or-nothing for my own good. The idea of us stuck in a long-distance limbo, I hate it, I really hate it."

Neil turned onto a wooded lane and pulled the car over. "I don't like it either. We just started, though. Don't you think we can take a little time?"

"When we started this thing—even before—I told you I was a mess. My career, my living situation, even my mom's health," I said, my voice catching. "It's all in a weird stage of transition, everything changing all of the time."

"I know. I'm saying we can take things slow."

"But why? Why can't something, just one thing, be easy and decided? No more limbo, no more in-between places. If we know we want to be with each other, that we're good together, then let's choose each other. Let's work through

life's problems together. And if we can't work through things together, then . . ."
I took a deep breath and barreled through the end of my thought. "Then
maybe we need to move on."

Neil's voice quavered with emotion as he spoke. "Is that an ultimatum?
Now or never?"

"No, Neil," I said, even as I knew that it really was something of an ultimatum. What was I doing? What was wrong with me? I searched for words.
"I'm afraid of living in limbo too long. I'm afraid that maybe, maybe we don't
want the same things."

"How long have you felt like this?"

"I don't know," I answered truthfully. "Probably a while but I didn't want
to admit it to myself. "I don't know what to do."

"Me either," Neil said softly. His hand closed around mine.

"I sound like a crazy person."

"No, you don't."

"That's being generous."

"Okay, maybe a little." His mouth quirked into a small smile. "But I get it.
And I don't disagree with you. Having you here—I don't know what I'll do
when you're not upstairs at Callan and Tarissa's, when you're not next to me.
After Europe I just wanted to be with you all the time. I still want that. But
both of our lives are complicated, and I don't see any easy fixes for that."

Selfish me wanted him to say he'd move to Portland, that he'd leave without a second thought. Instead, he pulled back onto the road and we drove
around in the quiet; no music, only the sound of the car on the road.

After a while the fields turned back into housing developments, and we
paused at a traffic light. "Where do we go from here?" Neil asked.

My stomach rumbled loud enough to be heard over the street noise. "How
do you feel about lunch?"

Neil chuckled, a low, soft sound that made my heart squeeze. "Sure."

"Are you hungry?"

"Not really."

I studied his face and read between the lines. "Sorry. I eat when I'm
stressed. It's probably genetic."

A wry smile. "Don't worry about it."

We drove to Panera, where I ordered a sandwich, salad, and cookie.

Neil drank a cup of coffee while I ate.

Once I'd finished eating a somewhat embarrassing amount of food, I set my fork down and looked up at Neil. "You asked a good question earlier. About where we go from here."

"I say we take time to think," Neil said. "Your opening is next week?"

"Yes."

He set his coffee mug down. "I'd already hoped to fly out for it. We'll think for a week, talk about it in Portland."

"Are you sure? Do you have the time, with your job, to fly out so soon?"

"Your restaurant is a priority for you," Neil answered firmly. "That makes it a priority for me."

I opened my mouth to argue, but decided against it. "If that's what you'd like to do, I'd love to see you there, show you the restaurant. It's beautiful."

"Of course it is."

"So we'll give it a week and then talk?" I repeated, wanting to make sure I had my relationship facts straight. This was the sort of conversation that took on a life of its own once it began to replay in my head.

"A week," he echoed.

I wrestled with the idea in my head. On one hand, I knew that my situation wouldn't change over the course of the week, a month—any foreseeable length of time. I wasn't going to wake up and suddenly be ready to move to Tennessee, or be fine with the fact that my loved one and I lived largely separate lives.

Instead, everything depended on Neil. Either he followed the call westward or the two of us would move on to different relationships, different people, different lives.

The thought depressed me, but I saw no help for it. We were so good together, but it required actually being together. Others might be talented at being apart, but I knew in my heart it wasn't for me.

I wished I could handle the distance, be the kind of low-maintenance girlfriend who could be content with texting and e-mails, but I had as much power over those feelings as I did my dislike of licorice. As much as I wanted to remain open-minded to all foods, I couldn't help but spit out anything that tasted of licorice.

We spent the rest of the afternoon at the zoo. At some point when I wasn't looking, he must have checked in with Callan.

"We're invited to join them for dinner tonight," he said. "And they're planning on watching a movie afterward. Not sure what, but I know Callan's been angling for a rewatch of *The Avengers*."

"Noble goal. That sounds fine," I said, my heart breaking just a little. Using his friends for a buffer wasn't how I'd pictured our last night together in Memphis.

But what had I pictured? After all, I'd flown out unsure about where we'd stood. In my head, though, I thought it would go well or go badly—I hadn't considered that there might be a middle ground.

Neil and I picked up a bottle of wine to take to dinner before returning to Callan and Tarissa's.

The evening passed pleasantly enough, with Tarissa's running commentary on how to fry chicken, the finer points of SEC football loyalties, and her ranking of Marvel's franchises, from *The Avengers* to *Thor*. I wanted to stay in touch with her, but if Neil and I broke up, I didn't want her to feel conflicted—Neil needed all of the loved ones around that he could get.

When the movie ended, I walked with Neil out to his car. "I need to get upstairs and pack," I said. "Are you sure you want to drive me to the airport in the morning? I can take a cab."

"Of course I'll take you," Neil said. "I'll be here at five thirty."

"Okay." I hugged my arms to myself.

He stepped closer. I could see the emotions behind his eyes, his thoughts.

And then he reached for me, pulling the two of us together. One hand held me close at the waist, the other around the back of my head, fingers entwined in my hair.

My arms wrapped around him, and I accepted his kiss.

He tasted of cayenne pepper and buckwheat honey.

We'd shared so many kisses—but this kiss? Desperation, sorrow, and something else combined into a potent cocktail of nonverbal communication. His hand left my hair and cupped my cheek, my chin. My hand toyed with his stubbly ginger beard.

The desperation faded slowly, and his caress became wistful. We parted a moment later, both of us breathless.

"This . . . this thing we're doing? You and me. This is real, Juliette," he said, his voice hoarse and uneven. "No matter what happens to us in the future. I want you to remember."

My heart twisted. "I love you, Neil."

"And I love you," he answered, breathing a final kiss onto my lips.

I kissed him back, wondering if my heart could be patient, if our love would truly be enough.

If Tarissa noticed my mussed hair and clearly kissed lips, she graciously chose not to mention them. Since I was leaving so early in the morning, I said my good-byes that night, thanking them earnestly for their hospitality and kindness during my visit.

"I'm not supposed to say this," Tarissa said, ignoring Callan's snort, "but I hope you two work it out. Next time you come out, we're going shopping, hear?"

"Of course," I promised. "And if you make it west to Portland, let me know—I'll give you the insider's tour."

"Travel safe," Callan said. "Come back and see us if you can."

After the hugs and well-wishes, I retreated to my room to pack.

Once again I had no expectations of sleep. Instead, after I tucked away my belongings, I opened up my laptop to read about Mireille and Gabriel.

August 15, 1939

Dearest Mireille—

   Thank you again for the lovely visit. I had such a wonderful time seeing you and Tante Joséphine (and sweet Anouk, of course), but most of all I adored getting to meet your Gabriel.

*He was sweet and kind and funny, and simply by seeing him look at you, I
know he loves you very much.*

*These are difficult times, and I know they worry you. Your feelings are
rational. But you've managed to find someone extraordinary to love, and I believe
that to be very special.*

Go with God, dearest.

Cécile

Oh, Anouk—reading about her made me miss Gigi more than ever. I
loved Cécile's words—*you've managed to find someone extraordinary to love,
and I believe that to be very special.*

The next letter I had to enlarge in order to be able to read. The text slanted
into itself, the letters elegant but shaky.

September 2, 1939

Dear Antoinette,

*You should know that Mireille has eloped with her young man. I did not
stand up at the wedding, but neither did I stand in her way.*

*Before you tell me that I should have tried to separate them, I'm going to ask
you to sit down and light a cigarette.*

*They're young. They're in love. The harder you might have tried to keep them
apart, the harder they would have worked to stay together. This way, we know where
they are, that they are safe, and heaven help us all—that they're happy.*

And no, I couldn't send her to a convent. They don't run like they used to.

*Cheer up. You'll have grandchildren soon, unless I miss my guess. I would
expect some joyful news in ten months or so.*

*And I've seen the apartment. It's small, and it's shabby, but it's in an
excellent neighborhood. I've told Mireille that I'm redecorating, and I've sent
her a good selection of furniture.*

*Be happy for her, or at least give a show of joy. She's too precious for us to lose
over an imprudent marriage.*

Joséphine

I read the letter twice to be sure I'd interpreted it correctly. They eloped! And Tante Joséphine approved, even if she tried to cover it in her letter.

If Gabriel and Mireille could overcome such circumstances, surely Neil and I could overcome ours as well?

With a full heart, I closed the laptop and decided to try to sleep for a few hours after all.

26

Anybody can make you enjoy the first bite of
a dish, but only a real chef can make you enjoy
the last.

—François Minot

*N*eil picked me up the next morning, before daybreak, and drove
me to the airport.

We said little. I'd dreamed about our kiss the night before, though in my
dream we stood on the steps of Tara at the time. There might have been super-
heroes fighting over our heads as well.

Neil pulled up to my airline's departures gate and stepped out of the car,
leaving the engine running. He pulled my suitcase from the trunk and handed
it to me, our fingers meeting at the handle.

"I'll see you next week," he said.

I pulled him into a hug. "I love you," I said, before pulling back to study
his face. "You're a good man, Neil McLaren."

The early morning light cast a glow on his features. I touched his hair, the
line of his eyebrow, his beard. I wanted to memorize his face, not just how it
looked but how it felt under my fingertips.

Neil's hand reached for mine; we shared a sweet, soft kiss.

I pulled away first and looked up into his eyes.

"I'll see you next week," he repeated.

"Okay." I nodded. "Good-bye, Neil."

Too soon, we parted ways.

I didn't cry during the flight to LAX, or the flight to PDX. My heart felt
so many things; I had no room for tears. Instead, I read letters.

September 3, 1939

Dearest Maman and Papa—

I am writing to let you know that Gabriel and I have eloped.

We now live in a lovely little apartment, not very far from Tante Joséphine. It has large windows and wonderful light, and a great deal of beautiful moulding. It does need a small touch of paint, but there are plans to remedy that shortly. We'd love to have you visit soon.

Love to all.

Mireille

September 3, 1939

Dearest Cécile—

Well, I've done it. I've married Gabriel.

I suppose we've eloped. That's what I told Maman in her letter, which is short and probably doesn't make a great deal of sense (however, I have no desire to write another draft).

Marrying someone on purpose, but without a great deal of preparation— that's elopement, oui?

I am delighted that you were able to meet Gabriel during your visit.

Unbeknownst to me, he had been considering marriage for a while. He secured the apartment and moved out of his parents' home, with hopes that we would share it together after our marriage.

The apartment is in a wonderful neighborhood, and has wonderful light.

Aesthetically, aside from a few architectural details, it's not good, but it does have an extraordinarily large kitchen. By Paris standards, it's palatial (which means it has more than a meter of countertop and a working stove).

Between his jobs at the restaurant and teaching, Gabriel makes a comfortable enough living. He has also saved much of his income for many years, and has invested wisely. We are comfortable, if not wealthy.

However, we are talking about opening a patisserie together, once I've finished my classes.

Did I mention I've restarted my classes? The term started up again, and I'm covered in flour once more and couldn't be happier. I cook all day, and then Gabriel and I bake together in the evenings.

(There are other activities, dear sister, but I shall not be indelicate, other than to say it's much more fun than Mme. Proulx makes it out to be when she's tipsy and maudlin over former lovers.)

We're so very happy, Cécile. I feel drunk on joy.

I must be a complete bore. Please, do excuse me. Know that I wish you such a happiness, dearest.

Mireille Roussard

September 13, 1939

Dear Mme. Roussard,

How surprising to write such a name, and yet only a simpleton could be surprised at the reality of it. Very best of wishes, dear sister. I wish you nothing but happiness and joy.

Cécile

September 14, 1939

Dear Mireille,

Your mother and I were very surprised to receive your letter, and disappointed in its contents. In light of your decisions, we will no longer be able to correspond or keep society.

Enclosed, please find a check for the remains of your inheritance from your grandfather, which you are legally entitled to.

Of course, should you come to your senses, I feel confident in the abilities of my notaire to annul the union.

Regards,

Papa

September 28, 1939

Dearest Cécile,

I do hope you are able to receive this letter. Papa has written to tell me, very politely, that I'm excommunicated from the family. He sent my inheritance from our Grand-Papa and a line about annulling the marriage.

Despite that unpleasantness, Gabriel and I remain deliriously happy. I love my pastry classes, though I do not know how much longer we will be able to afford them. Gabriel is speaking to the head of the school about a reduced fee, since I am the wife of an instructor.

Anouk despairs while Gabriel and I are gone, but lately I have discovered that there is a very kindly elderly woman upstairs with a very nice sofa, so Anouk has taken to sitting on either her lap or her sofa cushions while I am away. Mme. Ledoyen enjoys the company, as well as the sweets I bring her in thanks.

The apartment is coming along; I've painted it myself, and where it was the color of day-old, unbaked yeasted dough, it is now crisp and clean.

Tante Joséphine has been to visit twice. While she has a brusque, curt exterior, inside I believe she's made of custard. If I'm right, she's become quite fond of Gabriel, Anouk, and me. She's even sent her driver around to collect Anouk a few times—I believe she enjoys the company Anouk provides (though I hope to contribute superior conversation myself, Anouk is a devoted listener).

While we have chosen to forgo a full-time maid—to the horror of both Gabriel's parents and Tante Joséphine, we do have a lovely woman who comes to clean once a week and keep us from perishing in our own filth.

I hardly know how to sign off this letter, only to say that I hope you are well, and that I would love very much to hear of your adventures and trials at the chateau and in the village. This depends, of course, on your being able to receive it. If necessary, I shall attempt a sort of creative delivery.

Bisous!
Mireille

October 9, 1939

Dear Mireille—

I'm pleased to report I did receive your letter, though I've learned there's wisdom in getting to the mail before Maman or the housekeeper.

I'm sorry about Maman and Papa. They've said nothing to me on the subject, other than I'm to be much wiser about choosing a mate. It's possible Maman will pick him out and do her best to keep me in sight until the vows have been spoken and I've been, er, taken to the marriage bed.

Horrors.

I wish I had happier—or more interesting—news to share. The chateau is fine, but Papa is struggling under the workload. He's sleeping poorly, I believe, and has had more difficulty working in the lavender fields the way he prefers. To make matters worse, the foreman quit, so he's had more hours in the hot sun than Maman or I would prefer.

Gilles has attempted to pitch in where he can, but his time is limited.

Maman is even more determined, now, for the two of us go to Marseille or Paris, ostensibly to be in the city for a little while, but really to find me a husband. She has friends, of course, and several of those friends have sons.

You can imagine how she plans for this to happen. If only I enjoyed cocktail parties the way you do, the future might not look so grim.

Cécile

October 21, 1939

My dearest Cécile,

In truth, I never much enjoyed the cocktail parties, but I became quite skilled at pretending I did. The secret is the cocktail laugh. Practice it in the woods by the chateau, or better yet near the horses. If you can laugh without frightening the horses, you've succeeded. Armed with that laugh, everyone will think you're charming, refined, and clever, and not making a list in your head of everything else you'd rather be doing.

In some circles, I know it is the burden of the married siblings to help throw their younger brothers and sisters into the path of a prospective spouse, but I spend all day with cranky bakers who I don't feel would suit you at all. The sad truth is that I believe I have the only one worth having.

Also, you might be disowned if you married someone I introduced you to. So you might consider other options.

I'm very sorry to hear of Papa's trials with the fields and the chateau, though I am glad that Gilles has been able to be of some help, despite everything. I don't wish him to suffer, truly, but when I think of how I nearly married him, and how I almost missed Gabriel . . .

There I go, writing like an idiot newlywed. Begging your forgiveness again, dearest. I'm sure I'll improve once Gabriel has done something unforgiveable, such as . . . no, I can't think of anything. Come home late and forget to kiss me hello? Perhaps that. It won't be enough to bring about the annulment that Papa hopes for.

Thank you for keeping me up to date on the chateau. I really do wish Maman and Papa the best, and I shall be praying about you and Maman and your husband hunt. It might be a little amusing, don't you think?

Mireille

November 2, 1939

Dearest Mireille—

I can only assume that the idea of the "husband hunt" is amusing to you because you have your husband. From here, it seems quite dismal.

Maman is planning a social tour, scheduling visits with all of her friends. She will take me to visit these friends (mind you, these are only friends with sons), where she hopes to present me at various cocktail parties.

I can't think of anything worse, though the specter of not seeing you at holidays feels bleak at present. So if you can spare a moment in your domestic bliss, think of your sister who's about to be paraded like a show pony.

But I miss you dearly, so please continue to tell me of your newly wedded bliss. One of us deserves to be happy.

Cécile

November 18, 1939

My dear Cécile,

*Maman always hung the idea of such a tour over my head, but never man-
aged. I'm sorry that she's doubly determined to parade you around, though you are
far lovelier than any show pony.*

*My days have been busy. I've started a new term. I'm beginning to feel this
is the one that is going to do me in. We've been working on several pastries, and
I'm having a difficult time getting the canelé just right. Either the outsides are
perfectly crisp and golden but the insides are a bit dry, or the insides are perfect but
the outside is underdone. The instructor, I believe, feels he is above teaching a
woman, so you can imagine how well that's going. So every night, very late when
Gabriel is home, we make canelé together. It's getting better, though still frustrating.*

I fear the neighbor is getting tired of the baskets of canelés we bring her.

*We visit Gabriel's parents once a week. They still haven't gotten over the shock
of our marriage, but they're still speaking to us, which is nice.*

*His younger brother Benjamin has begun to pursue a young woman from
church. (Gabriel's parents are relieved he's given up on the shop girl he was interested
in previously.) He's gone from the family home more than usual, and his parents are
secretly both delighted and hopeful for a wedding in the next six months.*

*They've also had a letter from their oldest son in Warsaw. He's to arrive
with his family soon. Mme. Roussard is hopeful that they will move into their
home—it really is spacious enough to accommodate an additional family of
six—and has been industriously making room for them.*

*The political tensions directed toward Jews has Gabriel quite concerned. His
parents and younger brother remain largely unconcerned, and I understand their
reasoning—the Jews have faced one kind of disdain or persecution for thousands of
years. But Gabriel is concerned that the wave of unrest in Germany and Poland
will spread to France. He's been talking about leaving France for Great Britain or
America.*

*I have no great desire to leave for Great Britain (the English are just so . . .
English), and even less desire to live in America. As my husband, though, these*

are his decisions. At the very least, he's been talking about leaving Paris and moving into the countryside.

What would we do there? I don't know. There's already one boulangerie in the village. Could it accommodate two? Or would we return to run the chateau— would my Gabriel become a farmer?

This is all speculation.

Mireille

November 30, 1939

Dear Mireille—

In an attempt to get out of this tour, I've taken stock of the local young men. Gilles, objectively, is the best choice, but obviously out of the question, though I am fond of his sister.

There's the baker's son, Jérôme, who's nice enough but rather vague. There's Maurice Duguay, but he's both too old and too fat, though his house is lovely.

Then there's Richard Caron, who's rather dreamy, to be honest.

I gasped, clasping my hand to my heart. Grand-oncle Richard! I only met him twice—once when he and Grand-tante Cécile came to visit Grand-mère, the second during a trip to the chateau. As the youngest of the cousins, I often found myself alone after unsuccessfully trying to tag along. Grand-oncle Richard took me to the stables or read me books. Growing up with a busy chef father and my only grandfather across the ocean in Montalcino, I loved the attention. I loved it so much that I soon let my siblings run off on their own adventures, just so I could have Richard to myself.

And now I got to read, in Cécile's hand, how she found him dreamy.

He inherited his father's carpentry business, and Maman had him to the house for some repairs to the south staircase and some of the door casings in the east wing.

He's very kind, though at my age I'm beneath his attention.

I grinned. Oh, she'd get his attention, all right.

With so much of Grand-mère's life remaining a mystery, I enjoyed knowing that somebody's story ended happily.

No, I'm sure I'll find some pompous though witty son of a country lord who has few skills but an excellent stable full of horses, and I'll spend my life decorating and redecorating his family home.

Does that thought depress you as much as it depresses me?

Cécile

December 6, 1939

My dearest Cécile,

Of course that thought depresses me—that's why I fled for Paris and pastry. But beware the cost, dearest.

Not much to report here—it's flour, butter, sugar, eggs on repeat around here. Anouk is completely bored of me.

I remember Richard Caron. He's not too old—perhaps twenty-seven or twenty-eight? Not yet thirty, at least. And you're eighteen soon. Those aren't insurmountable numbers. But if your heart is set on a man obsessed with horses, by all means proceed.

Mireille

December 20, 1939

Dearest Cécile—

I couldn't wait to write to you. You'll never guess! Gabriel and I are expecting! I visited the doctor today, and he confirmed my suspicions.

Gabriel and I visited Tante Joséphine to share the news.

My dearest, my heart is so full of joy I cannot contain it. I've been baking macarons for days for happiness (also, they've been the only food that sounded appetizing). I've not written to them as yet, but perhaps with this news, Maman and Papa might acknowledge my marriage and accept Gabriel, who has been the best of husbands.

I am full of joy, but also terrified. I'm trying to continue with classes (which will pause ever so briefly for the holidays), but hiding my illness has not been easy. And after the baby arrives—I cannot think of that just yet.

I wish you could visit, dearest. I miss you terribly. Paris for Christmas is truly beautiful, but it doesn't hold a candle to your company.

With great joy (and a little fear),

Mireille

I'm convinced my fate turned on a strawberry tartlet.

—DORIE GREENSPAN

I reread the last letter from Mireille a second time. Pregnant. I checked the dates—it couldn't have been my mother, and it certainly wasn't Henri, her younger brother. I read on.

January 4, 1940

Mireille,

My very dearest sister in all the world—

My heart is full of joy for you! How wonderful! Oh, you and Gabriel will have the most deliciously adorable babies—his eyes, your smile. I'm swooning already.

You know this means I'll have to learn to knit more than scarves and lap-blankets.

And as for the future—pastry or no pastry, I wish you all happiness.

Oh, dearest, I'm so happy for you. Really and truly. Perhaps I might be able to come to Paris under the pretense of visiting Tante Joséphine.

Cécile

I smiled. Their joy shone through the page. The flight attendant arrived with the drinks tray. I waved her on and continued.

January 21, 1940

Dearest Cécile—

I know I asked for you to visit soon, but if you did you'd find me the very worst hostess. I'm trying to hide my symptoms when I'm at class—working with food—and while some days I'm successful, I accidentally vomited in the hallway yesterday.

This was not a proud moment for me.

I snorted, drawing a curious glance from the woman seated next to me.

I don't know how long I'll be permitted to continue with classes, but I'm working hard to stay on top of my workload.

I sent a letter to Maman and Papa with the news. I have not had a letter back, as yet.

Our apartment is, of course, quite small, but we do have a room to transform into a nursery while still maintaining a guest room. Tante Joséphine is beginning her campaign for a nursemaid/nanny. While there are aspects of the idea that are admittedly wonderful, we can barely afford our housekeeper.

Gabriel's parents are likewise pleased. Stoic, but pleased. Mme. Roussard smiled and gave me a delightfully awkward little hug. M. Roussard gave a pleased nod.

Did I tell you that Benjamin's courtship of Alice, the young woman from church, is going well? They're really quite sweet together. She's brunette and delicate and very nice. I hope that he marries her, she'd make a nice sister-in-law.

(Do not fear being displaced, though, sister mine. No one could ever take your place in my heart. And besides, Alice lacks your élan—she has terrible taste in hats.)

With great affection,
Mireille

February 3, 1940

Dearest Mireille,

I had no concerns over being replaced, for I feel confident in the deep regard we hold for each other.

I cannot say if your letter has been received, I'm afraid. I can say that Papa is in poor health again. Gilles has been here more often, helping on the farm. I do not believe our parents have shared your news with him, and I suspect it's for the best. They do benefit from his aid, and would be loath to part with it.

I visited the village today, partly for errands and partly for the fresh air. Curiously enough—do you know who said hello and tipped his hat? M. Caron!

I'm sure he was merely being solicitous, but it did seem amusing after writing about him so recently.

Please tell—have you and Gabriel begun to discuss names for your baby yet?

Cécile

(which would sound lovely on a tiny baby, don't you think?)

February 17, 1940

Dearest Cécile,

Names! No, we haven't discussed names, but I will have more time in the weeks to come to consider them, since I had to quit the pastry program yesterday.

The director of the program, who knows Gabriel and knows that we married, figured out that a recently married woman with an uncertain stomach was likely pregnant. He and Gabriel had a meeting to discuss my "situation," and while it was stated that there was nothing wrong with a young married woman being with child, the director made it clear that the pastry school was not the place for me.

As much as I'm glad to be ill in the privacy of our home, I'm heartbroken about classes. I feel as though I'll never be able to finish my training, that my life will be ordinary.

I've watched enough friends have babies and be wrapped up in that life—at least, wrapped up in telling the nanny what to do—and they seem to enjoy it. I just never imagined myself a mother. I'm trying not to resent this tiny baby we've made for taking away a future that perhaps ought never to have been mine to begin with. Gabriel knows I'm saddened from the loss of pastry school and is quite happy to teach me himself—he is more than proficient, of course. But it's not how I'd imagined it. I'd so looked forward to seeing my name on that certificate.

Enough about me. I'm sorry to hear that Papa is ill again. Give him my best;

he doesn't have to know it's from me. And as difficult as things were with Gilles, I'm grateful for his help.

And you and your M. Caron—what luck! Though I'm not surprised you've caught his eye. You really are very pretty, dearest. He'd be foolish (or blind) not to notice your many feminine attributes.

Mireille

March 7, 1940

Dear Cécile,

I'm afraid I have some very sad news. Mireille lost the baby yesterday.

I dislike the term "lost" because I don't want it to sound as though it's in any way her fault. The doctor has seen her and believes she will be well, in time, and we have no reason to believe she won't be able to have another child.

Mireille is despondent and has not left her bed. She wanted to write but has not yet been able, thus my letter.

You must be busy, and I hate to impose (especially in light of how difficult my father-in-law is being), but if it would be possible for you to visit Mireille here in Paris, it might help. While I don't believe much but time will lift her spirits, I do know that having you near would be beneficial for her.

Kind regards,

Gabriel Roussard

RÉPUBLIQUE FRANÇAISE
POSTES ET TÉLÉCOMMUNICATIONS

TÉLÉGRAMME

M. GABRIEL ROUSSARD

WILL ARRIVE ON 2 PM TRAIN.

CÉCILE

28

When I walk into my kitchen today, I am not alone.
Whether we know it or not, none of us is. We bring
fathers and mothers and kitchen tables, and every
meal we have ever eaten.

—MOLLY WIZENBERG

*M*y heart ached with the news of Mireille's miscarriage. I paused,
not knowing whether to continue with the letters.

But I also knew that once my plane landed, my time would be spoken for
more often than not. I braced myself and read on.

April 2, 1940

Dearest Cécile,

*Thank you again for your visit. Anouk and I took a walk to the park today.
I saw nannies and mothers with children and went home in tears, but at least I
had a little fresh air beforehand.*

*Poor Gabriel. He has a wife who cries over the smallest things, in bed, over
breakfast, while cooking.*

*What I haven't told him is that I worry that my doubts about leaving my
studies somehow caused the baby to fade away. I know it's not reasonable, but there
it is. Now that the baby is gone, it's all I want in the world.*

*Mme. Brisbois at church heard, I don't know how, and patted my hand and
told me that it was the Lord's will.*

Cécile, I nearly slapped her.

I have read the Scriptures, likely not as much as I should, but enough that I do not believe such a thing is the doing of the Lord. Gabriel led me away in time that I did not cause Mme. Brisbois harm, which is likely for the best.

This is a terrible letter. I apologize. I only wished to thank you for your visit.

Much love,
Mireille

April 15, 1940

My very dearest sister,

Of course it's not your fault. And I'm very sorry about Mme. Brisbois and her unkind words. I am praying for joy in your life, not that it will make up for this sadness, but perhaps lessen it just the tiniest bit.

And as always, I enjoyed seeing you, even though the circumstances were unhappy. Again I was reminded of what a wonderful man you married. And I'm not just saying that because he makes amazing pain au chocolate (truly, though, it is the best I've ever tasted).

I'm sorry I don't have better words of comfort. At times like these, I feel so very young and naive. I cannot fathom the road that you walk, but my love is with you always.

Cécile

April 23, 1940

Dearest Cécile,

Please know that I treasure your words of comfort. Thank you, thank you, so many times thank you for your kindness and patience with me.

Gabriel has been very kind, and we are planning to take a holiday soon, perhaps to the sea.

I cannot return to the pastry school, so I remain at home. I bake, but all food tastes like ash in my mouth. Perhaps it is time I tried my hand at being a proper housewife.

Everyone (no, not everyone. But it feels very much like everyone) is telling me that there will be other babies, not to be discouraged.

To be merely discouraged feels like a very distant country. I must be doing this all wrong. I must be doing everything wrong.

Mireille

May 4, 1940

Dearest Mireille,

Sending you imaginary hugs. Also, you'll find enclosed in the parcel some cunning lace handkerchiefs, which I found in the shop in the village and thought were quite pretty, along with cuttings of our latest crop of lavender and a jar of new honey.

Rather than tell you all over again how sorry I am about your sadness, instead I shall tell you about the goings-on at the chateau. Papa is better, though still not at his best. I fear he is growing old and will be unable to carry on with his work in the fields the way he would prefer.

Maman has given up redecorating the chateau in favor of redecorating me. To be fair, she does have good taste. At her insistence, my hair is a bit shorter, curled, and set, and I admit I look very chic.

I wore one of my new dresses into town—and I saw M. Caron again! And this time he not only tipped his hat, but asked how I was, and after everyone at the chateau.

He smiled at me; I feel so foolish, but he really is so handsome. I must steel myself. You married purely for love; I doubt I will be lucky enough to do the same.

Holding tea at the chateau in two weeks. If you or Gabriel have any new recipes to send my way, please do——I could use a novelty pastry to give someone something to talk about that's not politics or my marriage prospects.

I love you, dearest sister. And my heart breaks for your sadness. I hope that in time, your heart might find joy in life again.

À bientôt,

Cécile

May 17, 1940

Dearest Cécile—

You are too good to me. I still feel as though there is a stone in my chest where my heart should be, but I am eating more, and Gabriel made me laugh yesterday. You should have seen him celebrate after, he was so proud of himself.

Tante Joséphine and I took tea yesterday. It was the first time we've spent time together since the miscarriage.

She was very kind. Very kind, but also firm in a way that, I believe, was necessary. She insisted that I take time to heal, but advised me to start classes again the next term.

"You come from Guérin stock, on your mother's side," she said. "Guérins never give up."

We took a short walk with Anouk (who has been quite concerned through all of this, seldom leaving my side) and didn't speak much, but the breeze and the sunshine felt restorative, in the smallest way.

The world moves on, no matter how I feel about it. Gabriel's older brother has arrived in the city with his wife and their four children. From the sound of it, they had a narrow escape from Warsaw.

When we visited for dinner last, his wife put the children to bed after the meal and the adults retired to the library, where Nathan told us about the conditions and persecution of Polish Jews. While their parents feel that their status as French citizens protects them from such harsh treatment, Nathan is uncertain. He feels deeply that if France is invaded by Germany, no amount of French citizenship will stop the social and political campaign against Jews.

He, along with fellow professors at the university, has been studying the propaganda distributed against Jews throughout much of Europe, focusing on Central and Eastern Europe. He feels certain that if Germany marched on France, Paris would fall.

Again, M. Roussard and Benjamin disagreed with him, citing trade agreements and France's value as, if not an ally, at least a country with a border worth respecting.

Gabriel did not speak, but I could tell even then that he was listening to each word, measuring its value. He hasn't spoken of it since, but I know his mind has continued to dwell on the subject.

So you see, the world really is much larger than my sorrows. Do not fear, dearest. I'll be myself again soon. I am anxious to hear more about M. Caron. I have every hope and prayer that you will love your husband the way I love Gabriel.

Mireille

June 3, 1940

Dear Mireille,

Maman has officially scheduled our tour. She has a calendar, and has confirmed with each friend we shall be staying with.

I tried your advice about the laughter, but I keep startling the horses. It's not funny, Mireille—the groom suggested I stop visiting the stables, because the horses seem agitated after I leave. I'm so embarrassed.

I'm glad your visit with Tante Joséphine was so beneficial. Give her my love when you see her next. Concerned to hear about your brother-in-law's news. What do you think it means for Gabriel's family in Paris, and you and Gabriel by extension?

Life is quiet here, save the hum of the honeybees in the lavender. Awaiting your letters. Our little corner of the world can feel very small sometimes.

Cécile

29

Pray for peace and grace and spiritual food, for wisdom
and guidance, for all these are good, but don't forget
the potatoes.

—JOHN TYLER PETTEE

*R*eading the letters between the sisters made me miss Caterina
and Sophie, Cat most acutely. I hadn't seen her for months now,
and while that wasn't unusual, with all that had happened I felt it more deeply.

When the plane landed, I found a text from Neil, hoping for my safe travels. I told him I'd landed safely, and shifted to send a text to Clementine, letting
her know I'd be out shortly.

After the long journey home last time, I skipped past my siblings and
asked if Clementine would mind picking me up in my car.

"See you soon," Clementine texted back.

I picked up my luggage from the baggage claim and strode outside, looking for my car with Clementine behind the wheel.

Sure enough, just ahead I spotted it—not hard, since an old red Alfa
Romeo tends to stand out. I jogged toward it, dragging my suitcase behind. I
waved hello, threw my suitcase into the trunk, and jumped into the passenger
seat. "Hey," I said, to the back of Clementine's head, "thanks for—"

I shrieked in surprise. It wasn't Clementine in the driver's seat at all.

"Hello, stranger," said my sister Cat, grinning cheekily. "Good flight?"

I threw my arms around her. "What are you doing here? I didn't think you
were flying in until Thursday!"

"I missed you, Mom's got an appointment on Wednesday, and I meant to
buy tickets a long time ago and forgot. Damian was game for an early trip—it
worked out."

"You have no idea how glad I am to see you."

"Back atcha." She checked the mirrors pulled out into the through-lane. "So—flight go okay?"

"Just fine. I'm over planes, though. If I visit you in Chicago, I'm taking the train."

"That's so retro of you."

"How are the boys?"

"Jet-lagged and cranky, but enjoying an afternoon with Dad and Damian." I leaned my head back. "You guys staying with Mom and Dad?"

"For now. I'm keeping an eye on the boys. Any cold symptoms and we'll decamp to a hotel, but for now, yes. I expect them to come home with five new French words each and a sense of pastry entitlement."

"Once Mom gets ahold of them? Five conversational words and two songs. The pastry thing you'll just have to live with."

Caterina patted my leg. "I know. Tell me about the last of your time with Neil."

I told her about our one-week time frame, zoo trip, and movie night with Callan and Tarissa.

"So let me get this straight. You basically gave him an ultimatum, you're both thinking things over, he's flying out for the opening, and then you'll figure out where your relationship goes from there?"

I propped my elbow against the car door and rested my head in my hand. "I'm worried I killed it, Cat. I'm worried I said too much, that he'll think it over and be gone forever."

"But you're not loving the long-distance thing. Are you thinking of moving out there anytime soon?"

"I can't leave Mom. And with the restaurant just about to open—leaving Portland isn't an option."

"And you've explained this to Neil, right?"

"Right. I was completely honest with him. Probably too honest."

"And you've been up-front with him that long-distance is no good, and that moving right now isn't an option. So there's really nothing for you to think about—it's on him to decide if he's willing to consider relocation, if he wants your relationship to continue."

I winced. "That sounds selfish."

"Eh," Cat said with a Gallic shrug, "at this point in the relationship, there's little room for altruism. Hanging on to a relationship that's not going to work for you in an effort to be unselfish is a terrible idea."

"But breaking up would be . . . awful."

"Yeah," Cat said softly. "So basically you're spending your week waiting to find out if Neil will move to Portland."

I thought it over and nodded. "Pretty much."

"That sounds awful."

"It is."

"Does he seem like he might be willing to move? And if you're done talking about it, that's okay."

"No, it's fine. The thing is, he's pretty settled. He's got a job he likes and good friends in Callan and Tarissa. His work is important, and he's passionate about it. He doesn't see the need for things to change the way I do. I don't think he makes friends easily, but when he does they're long term. Romantically, I think he's that guy who's happy to date for two or three years before any conversations happen about the future."

Caterina snorted. "I've heard about those guys. I didn't marry one, but rumor has it they exist."

"Basically," I said. Caterina and Damian had met and married within a year—no grass had grown beneath their feet. "And he's a scientist. He runs tests over long periods of time. I don't know that he'd ever move that fast."

"Hard to say," she answered.

I raised an eyebrow. "What?"

"What do you mean, *what*?"

"You're thinking something you're not saying."

"I just . . . I get lots of couples in my classes, I hear lots of stories. You can tell the couples who are into each other. Most of the time, if they're the marrying kind, there's not a lot of indecision on the guy's behalf. I think something clicks in a guy's brain and he wants to get a lady off the market before anybody else snatches her up. But everybody's different. So I don't want to generalize."

I rolled my eyes. "You do too want to generalize."

"I'm worried you want different things, that he's just not ready." she said softly. "But I don't know him, I've never met him. I can't say."

"It's okay," I said. "I asked. He says he loves me. I believe him—I do. I just don't know if it's enough."

"Hope you didn't mind the subterfuge," Clementine said when we got back to the apartment. "Caterina couldn't wait to surprise you."

"Ciao, Gigi," Caterina said, bending down to greet the dog. Gigi, in turn, couldn't figure out who to greet first, and ultimately decided to roll over on her belly, and allow her admirers to come to her.

Caterina obliged, then stood to take in her surroundings. "You've done a great job with this place. It looks like you, but in a way that Grand-mère would approve of. I don't know what I'm saying—it looks freshened."

"Thanks," I said with a smile. "It took work. Did Nico or Clementine show you the restaurant?"

"No, but I love the blue paint."

We walked downstairs alongside the building, and I led her into the restaurant from the back. "Kitchen looks great—nice layout," Caterina said as we walked though. "And the dining room—oh, Juliette," she breathed. "It's lovely."

"Thanks," I said, smiling. "It looks so peaceful when it's sleeping."

Caterina cackled. "You are so right. You excited about the opening?"

"I think so, yeah?"

"Okay, well . . . just remember, you don't have to spend the rest of your life here."

I snorted. "I think I'm committed for a while."

"For a while, but not the rest of your life. Nico can find another manager if you ever feel the need to move on to a new dream."

"What would I do? I left my job to be here."

"Your dreams are up to you. Gosh." She wrinkled her nose. "That sounds like a stupid motivational poster. Whatever, I'm just rambling that I want good things for you. If this is what you want, stay forever. And if not, just remember that you can do anything you want."

"Yes ma'am."

"Planning on dinner tomorrow with the family—do you think that'll work for you?"

"It should, yes."

"And I want to take you shopping before the opening, my treat."

"You don't have to—"

"I *want* to, thank you very much."

I grinned. "Fine then. Be like that." I threw my arm around her shoulders. "You have *no idea* how happy I am that you're here."

"I know. I'm delightful," she answered with a wink. "There's extra food in your fridge. Eat at your leisure and put your feet up. This is your last chance to relax, you know."

"Oh, I know." I ran my hands over my eyes. "I'm trying not to think about it too hard."

After an exchange of continental kisses and hugs, Caterina left to rejoin her family. I ate, sharing with Clementine before taking Gigi for a walk. My head and heart were so full, I hardly knew how I thought or felt, only that the sun felt good on my face and for once I was so very glad to be home.

When I arrived at my parents' house later that night, Caterina, Damian, and the boys had all turned in for the night, but my parents were still awake and sociable. My father made coffee and the three of us sat on the back deck around the brazier, admiring the stars.

"I'm glad you stopped by," my mother said, squeezing my hand. "Such a good daughter. Did you have a nice time with Neil?"

"It was good to see him," I said carefully. "We're not sure where the relationship is headed, but we like each other very much. He'll be out for the opening, so I'll see him then."

My parents exchanged glances.

"You do not know if you love each other?" my father asked. "I am confused."

"I love him," I said softly, "and he loves me, but he's in Memphis. I can't move to Memphis, and he may not be able to move here. So . . . it may not work out."

"Why wouldn't he leave Memphis?" my father persisted. "There are tornados in Memphis."

"He has a good job there, and good friends. It's complicated."

"I think not so complicated," he answered gently.

"If he doesn't choose to move for you, he's foolish," Maman said. "And you're too smart to put up with a foolish man."

"I feel selfish asking him to move for me," I admitted.

"Bah." Maman waved a hand. "No more worrying. If you love this man, you'll find a way to be with him. It's the way. Now. Let us talk of the restaurant opening. Do you feel ready?"

I thought it over for a moment. "Yes. I think so. The last pieces are pretty much in place, and Clementine's ice cream maker will arrive on Wednesday."

"Clementine will be making ice cream?" My father sat up straighter. "I look forward to that."

We chatted for a few minutes longer about whatever we could think of. I tried bringing up Maman's health—the ER trips had spooked me—but my attempts were neatly evaded each time. Life was short, and my mother had no interest in discussing her illness. When Maman began to yawn and slouch in her seat, however, I said my good-byes in order to let them get their rest.

I used the last of my energy to read a few more letters before sleep that night.

June 24, 1940

My dearest Cécile,

    The Germans have arrived in Paris. Gabriel's youngest brother has decided to marry Alice, and given the political uncertainty, they are planning on a simple wedding in two weeks.

Many of the Jews in the 9th arrondissement have fled. Tante Joséphine considered leaving, but decided that she was too old to leave her home, and so has stayed.

And indeed the city has remained quiet. If anything, business has been good because the soldiers, they like to eat.

I have begun my pastry courses again, which has been a pleasant distraction. Now I attend class, and after cooking all day I go home and cook some more. There is an advantage to being married to a pastry chef—Gabriel has been able to help me when he is home. But he has begun to work later at the restaurant, and with me at the school during the day, we see very little of each other. Never fear—he has taken to leaving short notes for me to assure me of his affection.

How are the affairs at the chateau? I hope the men that Papa hired have worked out sufficiently. Has Maman changed her mind about your tour, with the war going on?

Silly me. As if she'd change her plans to marry you off because of a war.

Bisous!

Mireille

I couldn't help but laugh. I hadn't heard very many stories about my great-grandmother, but she sounded like a handful. And, perhaps, a little like Sophie—single-minded in her pursuit of perfect domesticity.

Cécile's response came next.

July 20, 1940

Dearest Mireille,

Yes, I regret to report the tour is on, and I don't know what might bar its way. I shall regret the departure, though. I've begun to come up with excuses to drive into the village to accidentally run into M. Caron.

Oh well. We leave in two weeks. At least we'll take the train. I've always found trains exciting. Perhaps the change of scenery will be enjoyable.

Nothing much else to report. Gilles's mother has been visiting often, telling us of Gilles's business success in Paris. I didn't even know he'd left for Paris, and from the way you've spoken of him, I didn't think he'd ever leave here. It doesn't take a great genius to deduct that she's still put out that you broke off the engagement. I am pleased you were not stuck with her as a mother-in-law.

Oh—and the latest foal is really quite lovely. Not only is she the loveliest shade of reddish brown, but she isn't at all frightened when I practice my laugh nearby. I've named her Coco.

À bientôt,
Cécile

September 1, 1940

Dearest Cécile,

I am glad you've returned safely from your trip. I confess I felt quite worried about you these past several weeks..

One of the reasons I feel particularly high strung is that we are expecting again.

Was this my mother? I mulled the dates over in my head. My mom was born in '41, so likely yes? I read on to learn more.

I can hardly believe it myself, but already my body is swelling and growing with alarming speed. Yet again I've had to drop out of school, and I believe this time it's for good. I am very, very ill, so ill that I've become gaunt in places even while the rest of me balloons. I look nearly comical these days, though it concerns Gabriel to the point that he's become obsessively committed to helping me put weight back on.

He sees my sickness as a puzzle to overcome. White rice and bread I can't hold down at all, but a sturdy wheat bread helps. Porridge, too, has been successful.

If Gabriel cooks meat—even the freshest, loveliest cuts—I have to go and sit with Mme. Ledoyen, who clucks her tongue at me as she knits away at a suspiciously tiny sweater.

It would be sweet if I felt more confident. Because of the miscarriage, I become frightened at every twinge. This baby is full of twinges. The doctor has come and gone, telling me that nothing's wrong, that the pregnancy is proceeding smoothly enough despite my illness.

Still, I have not begun to work on the nursery. It remains the way it was, when Gabriel began to tidy and paint it last time.

It's still early days. I'll write Maman once it seems certain this baby will arrive safely. I feel she'd want to know, even if she does not return correspondence.

Mireille

For her sake, I hoped so. Surely this one was my mother—this time, the dates lined up. I set the letters aside, switched off my light, and dreamed of Paris.

30

A great meal is an experience that nourishes more than your body.

—Ruth Reichl

I swung by the toy shop on NW 23rd before dinner on Tuesday for last-minute gifts for Luca and Christian. Bedlam waited inside my parents' house when I arrived. Something had burned—I could smell it from the outside—Nico and Caterina were arguing at top volume, Luca and Christian ran through the house with Chloé right behind.

I paused on the threshold.

"I used to think my family was loud," came a voice behind me. I turned to see Adrian just behind me. He seemed to have become a fixture at our family dinners.

"Either you're very quiet or they drowned you out," I observed.

Adrian shrugged. "Probably both. These are my quiet shoes. Didn't meant to startle you."

"Don't worry about it. I'm fine."

"How was Memphis?"

"Good." I pasted a bright smile on my face. "It's pretty, lots of nice architecture. Leafy trees. And the barbecue was good—you were right about Corky's. I brought you back sauce, forgot to bring it with me."

"I'm sure we'll work something out. You live pretty close to my workplace."

"True."

"Neil's all right?"

"Yeah. He's good." I looked back toward the entryway. "We should probably go in."

"You're ready?"

"I've learned a few things in the last twenty-eight years, and the most important one?" I held up the presents for the boys. "The art of distraction." I stepped inside, lifting the gifts high. "I've got presents for two little boys—if there are two little boys here, I've got presents for them."

Sure enough, I had my nephews clinging to my knees within seconds, Chloé close behind. Nico and Caterina gave up their argument to say hello and watch the boys open their presents.

"Well played," Adrian noted admiringly.

Clementine arrived a few minutes later bearing leftover desserts from her catering gig. My father led us out to the deck, where we dined on a crispier-than-intended roast duck.

We ate al fresco, taking advantage of the warm evening. I thought back to the fireflies I'd seen at Callan and Tarissa's.

After dinner I hung back to clean up, only to see Adrian had stayed behind as well. "I thought you could use a hand," he said.

"Thanks."

We gathered cups and silverware in silence for a moment before he spoke again. "I think your family's pretty cool. The way they've included me— Clementine too. They're good people."

"There's always room at the table," I said. "That's the motto I grew up with. The only thing keeping my dad from accepting every reservation request at D'Alisa & Elle was the fire marshal's capacity limit."

Adrian laughed. "I can see that. Caterina and Damian—they're cool too. You're a lot like your sister."

"You think so? That's a high compliment." I lifted the tablecloth from the table and moved to shake it out over the edge of the deck. "Caterina's pretty amazing. She's who I want to be when I grow up."

"You're not grown up?"

I shrugged and began to fold the cloth. "Cat has . . . a confidence about who she is, where she's going in life. She writes her own story. I'm"—I paused to search for the right words—"I don't know. Still trying to figure that out."

"She does have a head start. Their boys are cute."

"Yeah," I said, smiling. "Luca and Christian are great kids."

"Twins run in the family?"

"Not really," I answered, choosing my words carefully as I set the gathered the dishes on my arm to carry inside. "They had a hard time getting pregnant. They knew going in that fertility treatments could result in multiples. Caterina joked that she wanted triplets." I leaned against the deck railing. "They were really happy when the boys arrived safely. Caterina is . . . she's brave. Brave in a way I wish I was."

"You're no slouch yourself," Adrian said as he lifted half of the dishes off my stack and placed several drinking glasses on top. Ordinarily I would have worried about things falling, but I could tell from the way he stacked and gathered that he'd bussed his share of tables.

I thought of my relationship with Neil as we headed toward the house. "I don't know about that. But the restaurant's opening, so I guess we'll find out soon enough."

While I expected Adrian to find something else to amuse himself with, he stayed and helped me wash the dishes.

Oddly enough, none of my other family members arrived to pitch in, instead staying preoccupied elsewhere.

We made quick work of the dishes anyway, discussing the opening, the menu, and the finer points of Memphis barbecue until each dish had been taken care of.

Neil and I caught up over the phone the following afternoon, while I hung artwork and he drove home from the lab. He'd launched into an explanation of his lab work involving antibiotic resistance and narrow spectrum therapies, which I followed to a point before I found myself well in over my head.

"Wow," I said, hoping that was the right response. I really didn't know. "Well, I'm off to my mom's doctor appointment. My sisters are going too. We're making an event out of it."

"Hey," he said, "I'm sorry, Juliette. You're a good daughter and a good friend."

"Thanks. I think you're kind of great."

"Don't make light of it—you look out for your people, Jules. I love you. Let me know how your mom's appointment goes."

We said our good-byes and hung up. I tucked Gigi away in her kennel and grabbed my purse before heading downstairs to check in with Clementine.

Downstairs, however, Clementine was nowhere to be found.

My heart began to pound. The ice cream maker had been scheduled to arrive today and would need to be signed for. Our opening summer menu depended on being able to make ice creams and gelatos in quantity—we wouldn't have time to ship a second machine out.

I reached for my phone and dialed Clementine. No answer.

I dialed a second time—this time, I heard her voice at the other end of the line, and then explained the situation. "Oh no. I marked that on my calendar for tomorrow. Juliette, I'm so sorry."

"Where are you?"

"I'm catering desserts, one of my last gigs before the opening," she answered miserably. "And I'm in Vancouver. Even if I wanted to get there quickly, I couldn't. I'm so, so sorry."

"Mistakes happen," I said, recalling the great potato fiasco from two months before. The only problem was I didn't know how to solve this one.

"I'll make some calls, see what I can do. Your mom's appointment is today, right?"

"It is. It's . . . soon." As in, forty minutes away, and I still needed to drive and park.

"Give me five minutes."

I didn't have to. She called back in two. "Nico's on shift at D'Alisa," she said, "and Adrian's not answering his phone. Kenny's on shift too. I'm so sorry, Etta."

"I'll figure something out," I said, even though I had no idea how. "Don't worry about—"

Just then I heard the back door slam and footsteps. "Hello?" Adrian's voice sounded down the back hallway.

"Adrian's here!" I squealed into the phone.

"Yay! Gotta go—I've got cakes to prep. I'll make it up to both of you, I promise."

"Don't worry about it," I told her before hanging up. "Adrian!" I called in my next breath. "You're here?"

"I'm here. I have shallots," he said, glancing down at the crate of shallots in his arms. "What's up?"

"Can you stay?" I pleaded. "The ice cream maker's being delivered and Clementine was going to be here to sign for it but marked it wrong and she's on a catering job, and my mom's chemo appointment is in, like half an hour, and I promised I'd be there—"

"I'll sign for it," he said, putting the crate down on the counter. "Don't worry about it."

"Really?" Elated, I threw my arms around him in the quickest of hugs. "Thanks so much, you're the best." My face flushed as I realized what I'd done. And how solid his arms had felt beneath mine. "Traffic," I said. "I've got to—"

"Go on, get out of here," he said, looking away. Was he blushing? Or was he flushed from carrying around shallots? "I'll take care of it."

"Perfect," I said, backing away before I could speculate further. "Thanks so much. Bye!"

I raced out, ultimately making it to the appointment early enough to distract Sophie from badgering the receptionist. Between Caterina and me, we were able to sail without an altercation into what they called the "chemo lounge," with its overstuffed recliners, televisions, and IV stands.

Mom looked fragile, but buoyed by our presence. Caterina told story after story about the boys' antics and the odd personalities that came through her classes. Soon enough, Mom had finished her drip and we headed out.

"I'm glad you girls could make it," she said as we stepped out into the sunshine. "I feel I could get through anything with you, *mes filles.*"

I slung my arm around her narrow shoulders. "I'm just glad I was able to make it. I almost got stuck at the restaurant waiting for Clementine's ice cream maker."

"Did it arrive early?" Caterina asked. "That never happens to me."

"No, Adrian came in at the last minute and offered to stay."

Three pairs of eyes swiveled to stare at me.

"What? He'd just picked up a crate of shallots for Nico. It worked out."

"Of course." Maman patted my arm. "He is a sweet boy. Be sure to tell him thank you for me."

Caterina and I went shopping that evening. We parked near NW 23rd and Lovejoy and walked southward, up the hill. We ducked in and out of boutiques, browsing and chatting, stopping halfway through for ice cream at Salt & Straw.

"So. In all of our conversations," Caterina began as we sat outside with our ice cream cones, "you never mentioned how good-looking Adrian is."

"Didn't know it was worth mentioning."

"Those curls?"

I gave her that. "He does have good hair."

"That's better than 'good hair.' Josh Groban wants that hair."

"When I met him, you have to understand," I said, "he was . . . flirtatious to the point of smarmy."

"Huh. I wouldn't have gotten that."

"He's changed."

"Did he? I don't find that people ever change all that much. Which isn't to say people can't change, only that they don't usually choose to."

"That's deep." I brushed my hair back out of my face.

"Maybe he was always an okay guy who liked you, but didn't know how to show it. Just because a guy's not eight anymore, doesn't mean he's necessarily any good at knowing what to do with his feelings."

"Maybe. He never asked me out—it was nothing."

"Would you have accepted?"

"Of course not."

"He doesn't strike me as stupid. No man wants to be turned down."

"I'm with Neil. It doesn't matter."

"True." Caterina stood up and looked around. "Are you ready to walk? I'm ready."

We finished our cones and resumed our stroll.

"Have you talked to Neil recently?" Caterina asked. "When's he flying out?"

"Probably not until Saturday morning, he said. He's trying to wrap some things up at work this week before he leaves."

"Sounds logical."

"I wish it were sooner, but it is what it is. Ooh, look—" I stopped in front of one shop window. "Let's go in there."

A swingy black dress later, we strolled back down the hill toward the car. "I love it," I told my sister for the thirtieth time. "Thank you so much. And tell Damian thanks too."

"You're welcome. There's no such thing as too many black dresses, and that one fit you perfectly."

I wrapped my arms around her in a sloppy hug. "You're the best. I wish you were here always. I know you've got your grown-up life in Chicago, but a girl can dream. I feel like I can manage life better when you're around."

"I'm only a phone call away. And you're managing life just fine—give yourself some credit."

"Thanks," I said, thinking of Grand-mère's letters, the restaurant, Neil. "I feel pretty overwhelmed . . . most of the time."

"Hang in there," Caterina said as we approached the car. "The restaurant will be open soon, and you'll be too busy to feel overwhelmed."

I barked out a laugh. "Thanks a lot."

In bed that night, with Gigi curled up beside me, I pulled out my grandmother's letters. Evenings had become "Mireille time"—and the more I read, the more I wanted to know the end of the story, hoped that there might be a happy ending waiting for her, one way or another.

September 12, 1940

Dearest Mireille,

I am cautiously hopeful on your behalf, with the baby. I am so sorry about the dreadful Germans in the city at such a time! I regret this is a short letter— Maman has me running errands today, and I wanted to dash off a response sooner rather than later, even if it wasn't nearly long enough. My love and prayers are with you. I'm delighted to be home, and more delighted that you may soon have a baby to fill your life with more joy.

Bisous,
Cécile

October 1, 1940

Dearest Cécile,

The doctor visited today. He believes it's possible I'm carrying twins!

I drew back in shock. Twins? I read the line twice over—there was no mistaking it. But if this pregnancy was the one resulting in my mother, either the doctor was wrong, or something had happened. There were three years between her and my oncle Henri.

Can you believe such a thing? I almost can, because I am so very large, and I am quite certain about the timing.

The sickness has passed, which I'm glad for—as bad as my sickness was last time, this was far more severe. Now that I am better, I bake at our apartment or Tante Joséphine's to practice my technique.

I try to stay busy because Gabriel is gone so often. He is teaching at the pastry school and working evenings at the restaurant. He is conscious of us having money set aside for when the babies come.

It is far enough along, I have decided to write Maman and Papa and tell them of the babies. While there is still a part of me that hardly believes it to be true, there is another part of me, a deeper part, that tells me that they will arrive whether I'm ready or not.

Perhaps they're talking to me from the womb. I suppose it could happen.

Please tell me how things are after your trip—are you receiving letters from admirers? Have you seen any more of M. Caron?

À bientôt,

Mireille

I smiled and put the letters down for the night. My stomach curled in anxiety about Mireille's future, but reading about Cécile and Richard never failed to put a smile on my face.

31

We seldom report of having eaten too little.

—THOMAS JEFFERSON

On Thursday, I discovered I had nothing to do. The restaurant thrummed with readiness. The last of the details had been attended to, and what needed to be done rested on Nico's shoulders and not mine.

So I found myself with a strange window of free time. Gigi and I took a long walk, her fur growing dingy from the dirt, her tongue extended with joy. I thought about Mireille—I'd continued to think of her less as my grand-mère, more as a friend, or a character in a novel.

Gigi and I enjoyed our walk; when we got home I left her to snooze on the floor while I tapped out a brief e-mail to Élodie. I updated her on what I knew about Gabriel and Mireille in Paris, and promised that I'd likely know more soon.

And then I realized I had a few more hours to myself.

I wanted to read more letters—I knew that for sure—but I'd hardly spent any time in my own kitchen for weeks.

I brightened when I found Rainier cherries in the fridge, with their sunset-colored skin. Nearby sat a tub of mascarpone, and I knew then I could make simple *crostini*. I washed and pitted the cherries, and then sliced a stray baguette on the bias. While the slices toasted, I mixed the mascarpone with a bit of honey for sweetness and lemon zest for acidity. Once the slices were hot and crisp, I spooned the mascarpone mixture over the top, added a few leaves of lemon thyme, and topped each one with a heaping spoonful of sliced cherries.

A single bite tasted of summer.

I took a glass of iced tea, a couple of cherry crostini, and a napkin with me to the chair in the front window, and sat down to read letters on my laptop.

October 10, 1940

Dearest Mireille,

    If I never attend another party for the rest of my life, I will die a contented woman.

    And unfortunately yes, there were letters from "admirers." I'm probably being melodramatic by using quotation marks, but I feel they admire my family and social standing more than they actually admire me. I laughed my awkward laugh at the party, dearest. I can't help but be suspicious of a gentleman who would continue his attentions after such a sound.

    I'm glad to be reunited with Coco, who still welcomes me near. That is a comfort, and I reward her for it with apples (she was kind even before I began bringing the apples, lest you believe I purchased her affection in the first place). One of the hands is training her to a bit and to ride—I'm going to ask Papa for her to be mine.

    Much love,
    Cécile

P.S. I regret to say I spotted M. Caron in the village with a brunette. That's all on that subject that I shall commit to paper.

Shame on Grand-oncle Richard, existing near a brunette! I couldn't help but giggle at Cécile's horror. I knew her history too well to be particularly concerned.

October 25, 1940

Dearest Cécile,

    The city has me on edge. There was a census taken this month by the government, requesting (demanding, more like) Jews to register. Because of their surnames and Protestant beliefs, Gabriel and Benjamin did not register. Nathan did not either, though it pained him, as he has chosen to follow much of his mother's ways. In the end, his wife—who came from a prominent Jewish family in

Poland—convinced him to hide their identity for the time being, as Esther did in the palace of Xerxes.

The scriptural reference assuaged his spirit, although he argued that Daniel and his compatriots chose to stand apart in the court of Nebuchadnezzar. In the end, they agreed that the safety of their children was paramount. Gabriel breathed easier once his brother told him he'd chosen to continue to hide their heritage.

Gabriel also found Nathan a job. Linguistics professorships are difficult to come by at best in the city, and not with any more ease during the academic year. They also agreed that to continue as a professor might be dangerous—he specialized in Hebrew at the university in Warsaw. Now he drives a delivery truck for the suppliers used by Gabriel's restaurant. It is far beneath him intellectually, and yet he's taken to it with cheer.

Did I tell you about Benjamin's wedding? I cannot even remember what we have to catch up on. He designed her wedding ring, as he designed mine (with Gabriel's input). Their ceremony was small but lovely; she wore a beautiful ivory suit, which she informed me could be worn and repurposed as separates. Her practicality can be dreary sometimes, but she is a good fit for Benjamin, who is highly pragmatic himself. Indeed it seems I married the dreamer of the family.

Please tell me how you are—any enjoyable correspondence from your gentlemen?

Bisous,
Mireille

November 5, 1940

Dearest Mireille,

Oh, my gentlemen. They write such fascinating missives! One of them wrote about his racing car and how he hopes the war will not affect his racing season in Montenegro.

Another wrote at length about his interests in botany. It's fascinating. I've had trouble sleeping lately, and while reading War and Peace did not help, his letter did.

This is not to say that botany cannot be interesting, and yet from this young man it made me terribly drowsy.

I would probably like these men more if I didn't find myself thinking so often about M. Caron. Papa hired him to perform some repairs on the barn, and Maman wants a new trellis in the garden, so it appears he'll be nearby often.

No word on the identity of the brunette in the village. I didn't know her, but then I didn't see her face either.

Maman asks after my correspondents often. I've passed the letters to her when I'm done with them—I suspect she enjoys them more than I do.

The amount that she pesters me, I suspect she won't rest until I've chosen a suitor, at which point Maman would invite that gentleman and his mother to visit the chateau.

Can you imagine anything worse?

Aside from having the Germans in Paris, and all of that?

Oh, dearest, please accept my hyperbole in the manner intended.

Cécile

November 14, 1940

Dearest Cécile,

You are right. That sounds dreadful, and hardly hyperbolic.

Not much to report here. Every morning I wake up and find myself somehow larger than the night before. Anouk hardly knows what to make of my changing shape, but she's trying to make the best of it. The fact that I'm moving more slowly during walks, I think, is her greatest trial.

Gabriel's begun to come home even later from the restaurant than usual.

In fact, I think his brother Nathan sees more of him than I do, since he's been taking deliveries around. I came home early from baking at Tante Joséphine's one day, arms full of baked goods to share with our neighbors, and found him and Nathan at the apartment together. From the stack of coffee cups in the sink, they'd been in deep discussion for quite some time.

I suspect Gabriel may be planning a patisserie of his own, and he and his brother are thinking of going together in the business. But when I ask, he evades me (this is, of course, in the off-chance that we see each other).

Oh well. When he's ready to confide in me, he will. But it's a potentially concerning endeavor, should the Germans and Vichy government decide to consider them Jewish because of their mother's heritage.

Coco sounds absolutely delightful. I'm sorry none of your suitor letters are satisfactory, however.

Have you tried distracting mother with decorating? I remember the dining rooms appeared a bit dated when I visited last (it didn't, really, but you could suggest a new fabric for the drapes. The rest will take care of itself).

Bisous,
Mireille

December 2, 1940

Dearest Mireille,

You're quite brilliant—the drapery distraction worked like a charm! We have a trip to Marseille planned for fabric. Fabric, I can shop for. And there are the holidays to consider as well. We must be festive, even in these times, at least that is Mother's endeavor.

I'm sorry to hear that Gabriel's been so scarce lately. Any other gentleman I might suspect had . . . other interests, but of course I could never think such a thing of Gabriel.

You didn't ask about M. Caron, because I suspect you were trying to be delicate.

He's been quite solicitous, though reservedly so—especially if Maman or Papa are anywhere nearby. A storm brought a tree down and into a window in the south wing. Nobody was hurt, save a very old, very ugly chaise that's been damaged beyond repair by the water. At any rate, M. Caron has been conducting the repairs. He has the loveliest eyes, and when he smiles at me I wonder if perhaps I was mistaken about the brunette in town all those months ago.

But just when I begin to wonder, someone will walk by and he will tuck his smile away, making me think I imagined it in the first place.

Did you ever do such a thing? Imagine smiles? Please tell me.

Gilles has returned from Paris and visited Papa last week. I sat with him while he waited for Papa. He asked after you in Paris, and by the way he asked I realized he did not know you'd married.

I shouldn't have been surprised since Maman and Papa have been difficult about it, and I suppose you didn't feel the need to write Mme. Bessette to tell her the news. At any rate, I told him you'd married a lovely man, a pastry chef, and looked forward to starting a family. He asked after your husband's name, and when I told him, he seemed to recognize it. Gabriel has quite a name for himself—even Gilles has dined enough in Paris to recognize it, or so he said. He nodded very somberly and said he wished you all happiness.

I know you were quite pleased to be away from him, but he did seem genuinely glad to hear you were well and happy, even if you're stuck in a city with Germans. That was very nice of him, don't you think?

Forgive me, I'm still dwelling on M. Caron and the fallen tree. It's just as well we'll be going to Marseille for a few days. Perhaps he'll be done by the time we get back.

Bisous,
Cécile

December 15, 1940

Dearest Cécile,

Yes, perhaps getting away from M. Caron and to Marseille will be beneficial. I can't believe you'll be there and back again without one—or three—cocktail parties and conversations with pampered, moneyed boys.

However, it's also possible that M. Caron has romantic desires that he feels he cannot act on because of Maman and Papa. Have you flirted with him much? When Maman and Papa are not in the house?

Try it and see what happens. If he is kind and responsive—and flirts back—perhaps once he's done with the work at the house, you might venture back to the village and see if he's more forward (weather permitting).

And if not . . . well, there's always your botanist gentleman.

I'm glad Gilles has continued to keep Papa company, though I do wish our parents might decide to accept my marriage. I'm carrying their grandchildren, after all.

No, I don't worry about Gabriel. When we do see each other, he is . . . attentive. Because we're both ladies, I won't explain in further detail. But I am not concerned about him straying to another woman. Not when he is so very expressive of his affection.

I only wish he were a little more communicative. Oh well.

Missing you deeply during this Advent season, but wishing you (and our parents as well) a joyful Christmas all the same.

Bisous,
Mireille

December 24, 1940

My very dearest Mireille,

Joyeux Noël! I miss you terribly as well. Christmas isn't the same without you, but I have determined to be joyful just the same.

You are so very wise! Not only did I have three cocktail parties awaiting me in Marseille—more on that subject later—but I waited until Maman went to tea with Mme. Proulx (I pleaded a headache, which was true. What was also true was that I may have knocked my head rather gently against my bedroom wall a few times before telling her so), and Papa was in his office.

I found M. Caron outside working on the window casing. I offered him a cup of hot tea, spiked with your lavender syrup. We discussed the weather for a moment before he complimented me on my coat dress (which really is quite fetching, and chosen for that purpose). I complimented the window and asked after his work.

He invited me to his workshop in the village, if I was interested in seeing some of his finer work.

You're not here to answer immediately, but I feel fairly certain that this was a very positive exchange? Invited to his workshop?

I'm young, and I've seen very little of the world. But we are surrounded by war, and in such times especially, I suspect M. Caron would make a more practical husband than any race car driver or amateur botanist.

Or etymologist. I met one of those in Toulouse, and his letters arrived shortly after. If I weren't anticipating your letters, I could hide from the arrival of the post.

Cécile

I smiled at Cécile's letter—her letters always made me happy, while Mireille's made me anxious. Scraping a bit of sweet mascarpone from my plate, I stretched my legs to tidy the kitchen before settling for another string of letters.

~ FRESH CHERRY CROSTINI ~

These are simple to assemble, and perfect for a no-bake summer appetizer or dessert! The mascarpone pairs beautifully with fresh, sweet cherries. A cherry-pitting tool will make quick work of the pits, but you can also use a chopstick or a bobby pin. If you have trouble finding mascarpone, ricotta is also delicious.

1 cup mascarpone
1 tablespoon honey
Zest of one small lemon
$1/2$ of a fresh baguette, sliced on the bias
2–3 sprigs fresh lemon thyme (optional)
1 cup fresh cherries, washed, pitted, and halved

Stir mascarpone, lemon zest, and honey together.

Toast baguette slices, either in batches or on a cookie sheet in a 375°F oven.

Spread mascarpone mixture over each baguette slice. Sprinkle thyme leaves over the top. Place cherries over the top and press into the filling. Serve immediately.

Makes about 8 slices.

32

Think in the morning. Act in the noon. Eat in the
evening. Sleep in the night.

—WILLIAM BLAKE

When I returned to the letters, I skimmed a bit. Mireille grew—and grew and grew—while Cécile continued to fall in love with Richard. I breezed through several missives, but when my eyes hit the word "Vichy" I stopped to read the entire letter more carefully.

March 7, 1941

Dearest Cécile,

The Germans and Vichy government have been repossessing businesses owned by Jews and preventing them from government positions. I shouldn't be very surprised—after all, we heard about what happened in Poland from Nathan. The government had the census information. I'm shocked and horrified, but not as shocked as I wish I were.

Which means . . . I believe it will get worse. Won't it? Can't it?

I want to leave, but Gabriel feels adamant that we stay. And so . . . we stay.

I can feel the babies—and there's certainly two in there—grow restless. It won't be long. I don't know what to do—I don't really want to give birth in Paris, not while such horrible things happen. And yet travel sounds like a terrible idea, and Gabriel insists we will remain safe in the city.

There are no options that I like, essentially. Gabriel continues to work late, though with the arrival of the babies, he is becoming conscious of trying to be nearer more often.

I hesitate to take walks through the streets these days, and Anouk grows restless.

My world is dreary, save the anticipation of the babies (I've begun to believe I might be able to hold one of them, though the nursery is still a shambles). Please tell me of your M. Caron. I'm anxious to hear stories that aren't my own.

Mireille

My shoulders tensed as I read; Gigi sensed my distress and hopped up to my lap to join me—though she also brought her ball with her, just in case I was interested in a game to help me unwind.

As I threw the ball, I racked my brain for details about Paris during the war years. I could have looked up some of the information online, but what mattered, at least with the letters, was how these events would affect Mireille.

After a few trips across the room after the ball, Gigi settled under the couch with her toy, content to chew it out of sight. I took a deep breath and continued.

March 19, 1941

Dearest Mireille,

I am so sorry to hear of the strife in Paris. Word trickles here, through newspapers and rumors. I used to long for the city, and yet the longer the war drags, the more I am glad to be so far away.

Though right now being away from the city means being away from you, and that's the last thing I want.

You are correct—after these many months, I finally managed to steal away to visit Richard's workshop. Yes, he is Richard, because, dearest sister, he kissed me!

I visited his workshop, where he showed me the fine woodwork creations in his shop. He has pieces of beautiful inlay, designs with flowers and scroll motifs. He does so much more work than the repairs and construction, but he says that in the village, that's what keeps him fed and clothed. His father and uncle taught him the trade. His father showed him how to build and repair, while his uncle taught him the fine woodwork techniques that he applies in his own pieces.

I cannot tell you, sister, how very handsome he looks in his shop, little bits of

*shaved wood in the nooks and crannies of his shirt and pants. He stands taller there,
with more confidence. It is that confidence, I believe, that encouraged him to
attempt a kiss.*

I'm so glad he did. Now it is my turn to be ladylike and undescriptive.

*He asked to take me on a picnic next week, can you imagine? I'm over the
moon and concerned about the weather, all at the same time.*

With great excitement,

Cécile

March 31, 1941

My dearest Cécile,

*I am so delighted for you! I cannot wait to hear of your picnic. Please spare
as few details as possible.*

*I've been cleaning everything lately, despite the fact that I can't bend over
without a great deal of effort. The one area I've had difficulty with, though, is the
nursery. It's ironic, though Gabriel is understanding. After the miscarriage, that
room has become a difficult place. I only wish to place two healthy babies in
there—I don't care if there are no rugs or pictures on the wall.*

*However, there will be both if Tante Joséphine has anything to say or do on the
subject. She's agitated about the war, understandably, and I think preparing for the
babies has become a pleasant distraction. And as always, I value her company,
though I do miss you most acutely of late.*

Mireille

I remembered back to Caterina's pregnancy. Damian's mother set up most
of the boys' nursery while Caterina was in the hospital after the delivery—
throughout her pregnancy, Cat had struggled between her excitement and fear
that the twins might not make it safely into the world and out of the NICU.
She didn't step foot into the boys' nursery until she and Damian carried their
newborns inside.

Grand-mère hadn't mentioned her own delay at the time, but considering
all of the things she'd kept to herself, I wasn't surprised.

April 10, 1941

Dearest Mireille,

Our picnic was lovely, thank you! I'd rather share in person, but it's unlikely we'll have a great deal of time together. I made your chouquettes and packed them in a basket. They looked quite pretty.

You remember the little forest outside of the village, with the little bridge over the rill? There's a small clearing nearby, and that's where we made our picnic. The weather cooperated, though I made sure to wear my good walking shoes in case of mud (this turned out to be wise). Richard made chicken sandwiches and brought some early fruit, and we had a feast. Afterward we walked along the rill, crossed the bridge, and wandered through the trees. He was quite . . . affectionate. I had thought him reserved and mild-mannered, but as it turns out, he's actually quite passionate after an outdoor lunch.

Did I mention he packed hot mint tea as well? He really is practical.

I don't know what his intentions are—it's really too soon. But even after this short time, I can tell you I've lost my heart to him completely. No cocktail party attendee could ever compare! I love him so much, the calluses on his hands from his trade, his craftsman's eye for detail, his appreciation of beauty.

Oh, and the brunette? His sister, visiting. I'm such a ninny. Mistaking a sister for a lady friend—isn't that the worst of clichés?

Praying for the last days/weeks of your pregnancy. I've decided to make a trip in three weeks or so—I'm going to see those babies while they're fresh and new. I don't care what Maman has to say about it, though I suspect she'll be jealous. Missing you terribly, but cannot wait to see you!

Bisous,
Cécile

June 5, 1941

Dearest Cécile,

You cannot know how much I miss you! Alice and Gabrielle miss you too.

Alice and Gabrielle—Gabrielle and Alice. My heart stopped when I read
the names. So my mother, certainly, and a twin sister I'd never heard about.

Did my mother know she'd had a twin? And whatever could have happened to her? My heart twisted with dread. Considering the times, it was unlikely any outcome could merely have been unfortunate. There were simply too
many opportunities for tragedy.

*They're eating and sleeping with vigor, but they're happiest when someone's
holding them, and they're quite aware that there are fewer people to attend to
their every whim.*

*You'd hardly know they were sisters! Every time I look at Alice, I see
Gabriel's face looking back at me, only in tiny baby form with the loveliest, most
feminine lips. Somehow Gabrielle favors me, of course. She has the Chancelier look
about her.*

*I can't stop staring at them. After carrying them and feeling them within me
for so long, seeing them outside feels so strange and yet so natural. And yet another
part of me cannot believe they are here, that they survived.*

*Anouk, of course, continues to have mixed feelings about them. She thinks
they smell delicious, possibly even better than chicken. But she resents having
competition for my lap. I'm sure they'll be the best of friends.*

*Thank you for all of your help with Tante Joséphine and the nursery. In the
end, letting her put her stamp on the room was certainly the wise thing to do. And to
be honest, Gabriel and I are on a budget, and Tante Joséphine would never have
been content with the pieces I chose. Letting her spend the equivalent of two months
of our food budget on the room brought her joy and kept the peace.*

*She continues to visit often, which has been helpful. I wish you could see the
little jackets she's knitted for them! Light pink for Gabrielle, dark pink for Alice.
I complimented her on her sense—there's no reason why both girls couldn't wear
pink. She agreed heartily. Apparently when she and Maman were girls, their
parents dressed Maman in pink and Tante Joséphine in blue, and she resented it
so much that when she married she had half of her trousseau made up in shades
of pink.*

My heart feels so full, though I miss you terribly. I want you to know that

I treasure your letters. Your letters, and my letters to Gabriel, I keep in my drawer, and when I feel sad I go back and reread them, even the sad ones, because they remind me where I've been, and how far we've all come.

We have a telephone of course, but there's something about the written word, don't you think?

Anyway, I'm delighted things are going so well with your Richard. Neither of us knows the future, but I wish you every happiness.

On a less happy note (much less, actually), Gabriel is distressed, sleeping poorly, if at all, with deep circles under his eyes (he would be sleeping poorly even if the girls weren't waking up several times per night to say hello and ask for a meal). Friends he grew up with, Jewish friends, are without work and means of supporting themselves. We don't have much extra (and I don't have my full strength back), but we're both baking bread to feed those without.

The world feels so overwhelming sometimes, but then I look at Alice and Gabrielle sleeping and work my hardest to enjoy the beautiful moments when they happen.

À bientôt,
Mireille

There were more letters, but they'd certainly become sporadic on Mireille's end, and they were mainly chronicles of the babies. The girls ate, they slept, and they woke—often. But by April of 1942, it seemed Cécile's life faced a significant shift.

April 9, 1942

Dearest Mireille,

Richard and I have begun to discuss the future. Can you believe such a thing? With his flat feet (and I have seen them, they are indeed quite flat), the French army never wanted him in their ranks. I have no idea how to broach the subject of our future together with Maman and Papa, especially considering the unspeakable way they've treated you. They can hardly cease speaking to both of their daughters, can they? Perhaps if Richard and I marry, they'll be forced to speak to each of us.

Someone will have to inherit the chateau—Maman would never tolerate it going to a cousin.

Is there a way that Richard and I can keep the chateau going, make it profitable as a farm and estate? I believe it's possible. Richard would need help to keep up with the repairs, which are a large part of the property's maintenance, but he's more capable than most. He's no farmer by trade, but has the strength to tend the fields and gardens with the hands if necessary. It is a great deal of work for one man, though. I don't know. I only know that there are possibilities.

I pray for you, Gabriel, and your sweet girls in Paris. You all have my love.

Love and prayers,

Cécile

I read longer, continuing as Cécile told her parents she wished to marry Richard, and how she threatened to elope just as Mireille had. In the end, faced with losing both daughters—and being left with no one to manage Chateau de l'Abeille—they consented. Mireille and Gabriel readied for the wedding but couldn't travel when the twins came down with a frightening case of whooping cough.

In the end, the twins mended, Cécile and Richard married in a small ceremony, and Richard moved into the chateau, promptly making himself indispensable. They were happy, though the happiness in Mireille's letters sounded as fragile as spun sugar.

June 13, 1942

Dearest Cécile,

We are well enough. The city is beautiful with the blooms and at odds with the war and arrests. Jewish men have been arrested for the last few months, leaving the women and children—many of whom have already suffered through unemployment—with very little support. There are charitable organizations trying to meet their needs, but this is difficult for practical and political reasons. My heart is heavy for them.

The girls are healthy, growing, and walking everywhere. Gabriel is so very precious with them—last night they both fell asleep on his chest. I'm a poor artist, but enclosed you'll find a sketch of the moment. Maman had hopes I might have a talent for art—you remember the art lessons I had when I was younger? Well, I'm glad for them if only they give me the opportunity to remember times like these. I do want to have us sit for a family portrait soon. Gabriel has a place in mind, and hopefully we'll attend to it within a week or so. Tante Joséphine brings her camera, of course, when she visits, so there are those pictures as well.

It's been difficult without word from Maman and Papa, and yet Tante Joséphine has been like a mother to me these past two years. I treasure her time and her wisdom.

I apologize for the lack of correspondence lately! You're thought of and missed. My brain seems scattered in a dozen places. I tried to bake the other day and switched baking soda and baking powder.

It didn't end well.

Bisous!

Mireille

I laughed out loud. The baking soda/powder swap—I'd been guilty of that a time or two. Despite her attempt at humor, I couldn't help but feel as though something terrible waited in the shadows.

I scrolled through the next several letters. They were breezy and unnoteworthy, full of stories of the girls as they learned to walk and explore, visits from Tante Joséphine—who sounded delightful—and Cécile's early married days with Richard. Mireille sent Cécile romantic advice that had me fanning my face, and stories of the toddlers that had me cackling in laughter at their antics. Cécile enjoyed all aspects of her new life, taking an active role in the chateau and looking for ways to make it self-sufficient, planting food and learning to preserve her harvest.

Their lives were happy, but I knew in my heart it couldn't last forever. I turned off my light and went to bed before their lives changed, letting them be happy just a little bit longer.

33

All cooks, like all great artists, must have an
audience worth cooking for.

—ANDRE SIMON

That evening I visited my parents, Caterina, Damian, and the boys,
trying to make the most of family time before the restaurant swallowed my life whole.

Maman and I sat outside until the evening grew cool and she turned in for
the night. Caterina joined me on the patio after the boys went to bed.

"Are you ready for tomorrow?" Caterina asked as we watched the summer
sky turn colors.

"Oh, about as ready as I'll ever be."

"When's Neil arriving?"

I winced. "About four tomorrow. He'll come straight from the airport."

"That's some fun flying."

"He'll be dead on his feet, that's for sure."

"But you'll be glad to see him."

"I will," I said, not even trying to conceal my smile.

"You guys talk recently?"

"We did, earlier today. One of his co-workers is going to an immunology
and infectious disease conference in Florida for him so that he'll be able to
come."

"I'm sure he'll be disappointed to miss out on the conference," Caterina
said, her voice dry.

I laughed. "They're presenting a big project, so it's kind of a huge deal. But
Neil isn't a conference guy, so he's fine with missing it."

"What's the project?"

"They're working a lot with antibiotic resistance. He's passionate about it."

"Rightly so. Scares me to think of the boys getting an infection in their lifetime that won't be treatable."

"Neil's part of a huge initiative working on new therapies."

"You guys have any other conversations about, you know, your relationship?"

"No." I looked away. "I think we've both avoided it."

"Hang in there." She reached out and grabbed my hand. "Someday you'll be settled down and worried about an entirely different set of things."

I laughed and rolled my eyes. "I shall cherish your words of wisdom."

She gave a sage nod. "I'm here for ya, babe."

Knowing I only had a few letters to go, I settled in for the night, ready to find out as much as I could about Mireille and Gabriel, my mom, and the mysterious baby Alice.

I found a few more letters cataloguing the growth and development of the girls—nothing new. But when I came to a letter addressed in Mireille's handwriting to her aunt Joséphine, a knot formed at the base of my stomach and I bent to carefully read each word.

July 22, 1942

Dear Tante Joséphine,

I hardly know how to write this letter. First, the girls and I and Anouk are safe. I do not feel I can give the specifics at this time. But know that my beloved has died, in circumstances I can hardly believe.

Yes, his death is related in more ways than one to recent events.

The girls and I are in a place we know well, where we have been cautiously welcomed. There will be more travels, for we are not yet out of harm's way.

This is an untidy letter, and I hope one day to explain fully. I apologize. You saw my sweet love more than everyone else in the family, even Cécile. I know he loved you and came to think of you as his very own aunt.

Love and deep regards,
Mireille

I read the letter through three times; by the third, I realized I'd been crying from shock. It made no sense, but the more I read it, the more I could tell that was the point. Recent events? I opened up my Internet browser, searched for "Paris Jews WWII July 1942," and found my answer.

The Vel' d'Hiv Roundup—it had to be. The two days, July 16 and 17, when the Nazis directed a roundup of French Jews with the assistance of the French police.

The police recorded 13,152 arrests. The detainees were held in internment camps—including the Vélodrome d'Hiver—with little food, water, or sanitation before being shipped off to internment camps and finally Auschwitz.

Barely coherent, I strode into my room for my picture of Grand-mère and me upon my graduation from culinary school. Her smile spread across her face with limitless joy. In that moment, she was happy. I clung to that smile, clung to the idea that at some point she healed enough to smile.

I had no idea how, though—how did someone get over a loss like that? A husband and, somehow, a daughter.

She knew at the time that she was by no means the only woman to sustain brutal losses during the war. All things considered, I felt staggering relief that Gabriel hadn't been one of the men arrested in Paris and deported to Auschwitz.

So many questions remained, though. What had become of baby Alice? How was it possible to learn so much and be left knowing so little?

My thoughts turned to the key and the closet at the chateau that I'd found, the one Sandrine hadn't been able to open. Were there answers behind that door? Or did Cécile remember if Mireille had indeed made it safely to the chateau? And what did Mireille mean when she said that Gabriel's death had to do with the Vel' d'Hiv Roundup in more ways than one?

The letters had left my nerves sharp and jumpy; I turned to my kitchen.

It took a few hours and a large batch of strawberry ice cream, but after a while I felt my muscles begin to untangle and my lids grow heavy.

For the first night in many, I picked up a silly romance novel before bed and fell asleep and tried not to dream of internment camps.

~ SOOTHING STRAWBERRY ICE CREAM ~

Because of the nature of the process, it's very helpful to have all of your ice cream ingredients measured and ready before starting. That way you'll have everything ready to go the instant you need it. The French term for having your ingredients measured and set out is *mise en place,* which translates to "put in place." You will also need an ice cream maker.

2 pounds (about 6 cups) of very ripe strawberries, rinsed,
    hulled, and sliced
1⅓ cups sugar, divided, plus ¼ cup sugar
Zest of 3 lemons (organic lemons preferred)
2 egg yolks
2 cups heavy cream
1 cup half and half
1 cup whole milk
2 teaspoons vanilla bean paste
Juice of 3 lemons

Place the strawberries in a bowl and mash them with ¼ cup of the sugar, mashing until the strawberries are pulpy with some small chunks of berry remaining. Alternately, pulse berries in a food processor a few times, until the berries have broken down but have not liquefied. Set berries aside.

Put the zest and ¹/₃ cup sugar in a food processor; process for about 30 seconds or until the zest has blended into the sugar.

Whisk egg yolks together in a small mixing bowl and set aside.

Mix the cream, half and half, milk, remaining cup of sugar, vanilla, and lemon zest mixture into a saucepan over medium heat.

Heat for 6–8 minutes or until the mixture is almost simmering. Do not allow the mixture to boil; stir continuously with a flat-bottomed utensil, scraping the bottom of the pan.

Once the cream mixture has reached a near-simmer, remove from the burner immediately. Slowly pour a cup of the hot cream into the egg yolks while stirring with a fork; continue to whisk until smooth. Then slowly pour the egg yolk mixture into the hot cream and return the pan to the burner, over medium-low heat. Cook, stirring constantly, until it's thick enough to coat the back of a spoon, about 6–8 minutes.

Strain the custard into a bowl through a cheesecloth or fine sieve. Place a dishtowel over the bowl and allow the mixture to reach room temperature, about an hour.

When the custard is lukewarm, add the lemon juice; whisk until smooth. Add the strawberries. Cover and refrigerate until chilled.

Mix according to the ice cream maker's instructions. Allow to set in the freezer for two to three hours.

Makes about 6 servings.

34

One of the secrets, and pleasures, of cooking is to learn
to correct something if it goes awry; and one of the lessons is to grin and bear it if it cannot be fixed.

—JULIA CHILD

I shouldn't have been surprised when the call came at two in the
morning. "I'm sorry to wake you," my father said, his voice rough
and tired. "But we're headed to the hospital. Your mother's been very ill."

I told him I'd meet them there and hung up. Unlike the last late-night ER
run I'd made so long ago, before Memphis, this time I didn't even try to pack
snacks. My dad's voice—it frightened me. I dressed, tied my hair back, and
tucked Gigi into her kennel with a kind word and a treat.

Alex met me at the front of the ER. "She's in the back, they admitted her."

"What happened?" I asked as he led me through the hospital labyrinth.

"She started vomiting and hasn't been able to stop. Haven't figured why
yet."

"That's not good," I said.

"No."

I held his arm as we walked down the hallway, striding and turning until
I heard the sound of my father's voice and my mother's dry, painful retching.

There were new nodes on my mom's liver. The tests had taken hours, and the
doctor had assured us that a proper radiologist might have different thoughts,
and that she'd be scheduled for a full body scan on Monday. One look at his
face, though, told us that the imagery revealed new cancer, that Mom's cancer
journey had just become more complicated.

Sophie and Nico stayed until the medications kicked in. My father sat next to my mother's bed, holding her hand as if he worried his grasp might break her. Alex fell asleep in his chair, his head resting between the wall and the room divider.

Mom gazed at me from where her head rested against the flat hospital pillow. "You can go home, cherie. Get some rest, you have a big day tomorrow."

"I won't be able to sleep anyway," I said. "I'd rather be here."

"Well, it's good to see your face. You've been busy lately."

"I know. I'm sorry I haven't been around to the house as much."

"No," she corrected gently. "You've been busy. I'm not upset at all. I'm so proud of you, of your work with the restaurant. And I think your grandmother would be too."

Something in my head whispered to my heart—it was now or never. "About Grand-mère . . ." I took a deep breath. "I found something. A photo. More than that . . ." Another breath. "I found letters at Chateau de l'Abeille, letters between Grand-mère and Grand-tante Cécile, and letters between Grand-mère and a man named Gabriel Roussard."

Before I could talk myself out of it, reason with myself that there had to be a better time, a better place—certainly a better preamble—the entire story spilled out like an overturned bottle of olive oil. My parents listened closely, asking a few questions for clarification but otherwise letting me tell them about the photo, the box hidden in Grand-mère's trunk, the letters that answered questions and created new ones, the discovery of new and unfamiliar branches on the family tree.

"I just . . . I wanted you to know," I said, ending with a rush of breath.

Maman patted my hand. "Such secrets you've carried," she said. "That's a great deal to take in."

"I didn't want to say anything until I knew more. But the more I learned . . ." I lifted a shoulder. "I have no idea what happened to Alice, or how Gabriel died."

"He looked like our Nico, this Gabriel?"

"I'll show you the photo. It's uncanny. Tomorrow I'll show you the letters."

"Tomorrow you'll be opening a new restaurant."

"It won't take a moment," I began, but she stopped my words with the gentlest squeeze of the hand.

"I trust you, Juliette. And we will find Alice if we're meant to find Alice. Tante Cécile might remember something, or she might not."

"I should have told you sooner," I said. "Or later. I don't know . . ."

Her head rocked gently against her pillow in disagreement. "I loved my mother, Juliette, and I loved my father too. These letters you've found, yes, they change many things—but they don't change everything."

I released the breath I'd been holding, the one it seemed I'd held since the moment I'd found Gabriel's photo. "Okay."

"Be at peace, cherie," she said, reaching out to cup my face the way she did when I was a child. "Be at peace."

"I love you, Maman."

"Je t'aime, Juliette. Now, would you do something for me?"

I gave a half smile. "You know I will."

She fixed me with her best, most effective Mom gaze. "Go home and sleep."

I called Neil on the way home, thankful for the first time that he was two hours ahead and very much awake.

"Is everything okay?" he asked upon answering. Both of us knew I never chose to be awake at 6 a.m.

I told him about my mom, her liver scans, the cancer, the letters. By the end, tears ran down my face and my hands gripped the steering wheel with a manic tension.

"I'm sad and scared. I'm glad she knows now," I said, trying to summarize my stream of consciousness, "but she's so sick, and I'm scared." A deep breath. "But she'll be okay. We'll get through this. They'll change her treatment, she'll get better, and we'll find out what became of Alice and Gabriel."

"I hope so," Neil said. "I want her to get better too. She's your mom, and you love her. But mets on the liver are difficult. She needs her strength and liver mets can make it very difficult for her to hold food down."

"There are medications. They'll figure it out."

"They might. But . . . you might want to prepare yourself."

I braked too hard at the stoplight. "She's going to be okay, Neil. She's going to beat this."

"Even in the best-case scenarios, ovarian cancer is a chronic condition. And at the stage she's at—"

"No, stop!" I yelled. "She's not going to die, don't you dare say she'll die. I can't lose her. We can't lose her."

"Juliette—" Neil's frustrated voice filled the car.

"You think she's going to die. You do, don't deny it."

"I hope she makes a full recovery, I do, honey. But I also don't want you to be surprised if it doesn't work out that way. The statistics for her age, type, and stage are . . . challenging."

"Listen to me, Neil McLaren," I said, barely managing any control. "I don't care about statistics. I care about my mom. So I will hope and pray and scrape together as much faith as I can that we will all get through this."

"I'll be leaving for the airport in a few minutes," he said. "We can talk about this later. I just need you to believe me that I want the best for you and your family."

He may have wanted my mom to make it, to go into remission, but I could hear in his voice that he didn't believe she would be okay.

In that split second, every bit of me that longed for his arrival evaporated. I didn't want to see his pitying face or listen to a speech about statistics.

I didn't know if I could love a man who believed my mom would die.

"No," I said. "Don't do it."

"What?"

My voice shook. "Just . . . stay home, Neil."

"You're asking me not to come?"

"I'm telling you I don't want to have this argument again, in person."

"Work is crazy for the next few months, Jules. If I don't come out now, we won't see each other for a while."

"You're telling me my mom is going to die. I can't look at you, knowing that you think that. I'm sorry, and I wish it were different, but that's where it's at."

"Juliette, no. I'm sorry. Please listen to me—I want the best for your mom, and your family, and you. I really do."

"But you don't believe it's possible."

"I— I'm sorry."

"Please, Neil. I can't look at your face, knowing that's what you believe."

"You can't look at me," he repeated, his voice wooden.

"I'm sorry."

"So that's it then? Are we done?"

"Neil, I—"

"You're telling me not to get on a plane that's taking off in two and a half hours." His voice turned rough, frustrated. "Is this what you want, Juliette? Tell me."

I'd finally pulled into my driveway and parked my car, exhaling deeply as I shifted the car into park. "It's not what I want," I said at last. "I didn't wake up wanting this to happen. I didn't wake up wanting to hear that my mom was in the ER again, either. It just *is,* Neil. I'm sorry."

Silence. "Then it's good-bye, I guess."

We hadn't hung up yet. I could undo it. My eyes squeezed shut, and I thought about Neil's face in Provence, in the sun, in the lavender fields. For a moment, I doubted.

But then I thought about that same face here, at the restaurant, with my parents, believing more firmly in my mother's mortality than in her healing.

My eyes flew open. "Good-bye, Neil," I said, my voice shaky but firm. "I wish you all the best, I really do."

And then I hung up, ending my last conversation with Neil McLaren.

Neil McLaren, the man I thought I might love forever.

After the phone call, I went upstairs, took Gigi out, and went straight to bed. Gigi didn't mind and settled on my pillow with a contented sigh.

I woke up hours later, unsettled. A few moments later, the memories came back—the ER, the call, the liver nodes, the breakup. My head rested against the pillow as I cried; large wet tears running down my face, spreading into my pillowcase.

If only the cancer hadn't spread. If only I hadn't called Neil. If only I weren't so deeply, profoundly tired.

One look at my phone showed that Neil hadn't tried to call or text back. We were done. I squeezed my eyes shut and tried to remember our good-bye in Memphis, but even as I pictured his face, my anger returned.

How could he have been cruel about my mom's condition? Every time my emotions ran toward sadness, I remembered what he'd said, and angry indignation swept away the sadness.

We were done. It was for the best.

I rose, resolved, and prepared for the day. I spent the morning organizing the paperwork, PR, and social media for the opening, and the afternoon arranging the fresh flowers for the tables, making sure the dining room looked perfect and ready to go.

Nico, Adrian, Clementine, and Kenny worked in the kitchen, prepping meats, cutting produce, and getting ready for the evening crush. I smiled, listening to the shouts and clangs that made it past the heavy kitchen doors—our little restaurant was finally coming to life.

I went upstairs to change into the dress Caterina had purchased for me. The black dress featured a pleated wrap-style bodice and an easy A-line skirt, trimmed in crocheted black lace, and finished with crocheted lace cap sleeves. The dress managed to be sophisticated enough for an evening seating while still being pretty and breezy.

I skipped a necklace and chose instead a pair of Grand-mère's pearl earrings and a pearl ring my mother gave me when I turned twenty-five. I braided my hair into two braids, tied them in a knot, and pinned the ends away. A nude lipstick kept me from looking like an extra from *Mad Men*.

I packed up my lipstick and blotting papers to stash in the downstairs office, along with a bottle of water and my cell phone.

Soon enough the waitstaff arrived and I went back over the menu with them, making sure they knew all of the ingredients in every dish, where we sourced our meats and fish, and which wines to pair. When we were done, I turned on the music and opened the door, letting in the summer breeze along with our first diners.

Sure enough, they were real live people, unrelated to any of the kitchen staff. I welcomed them inside and settled them with menus in the care of Mallory.

And so the evening proceeded as a stream of curious Portland foodies entered the restaurant until we were full, and then proceeded to congregate on the porch and sidewalk while they waited for tables.

I sent Braeden out with blackberry-flavored Italian sodas and candied nuts for those who waited.

My heart swelled to see so many strangers and familiar faces mixed together. Everyone from the test run had come, and then some—and from the smiles, I knew they liked what they found.

While I had my hands full running between the front and back, checking in with Nico about how the kitchen fared, I nearly tripped when I saw one of the men by the door. The height, the hair—it looked just like Neil.

But he turned, and I realized he clearly wasn't. His eyes didn't laugh, his chin had no opinions. I felt relieved and disappointed all at once, my heart so full of unexpected emotions, it threatened to overflow.

I asked Mallory to watch the front while I stepped into the office.

The reality of the night at the hospital and my argument with Neil washed over me again. The cancer wasn't getting better. Neil and I were over. The initial numbness swept away, replaced by wracking sobs that tore my chest apart.

I barely heard the knock at the office door. "Juliette? Is everything okay?"

"I'm fine," I gasped.

The door opened, Adrian's face appeared. When he saw my tear-streaked face, he stepped inside quickly and closed the door behind. "What happened? What's wrong?"

I swiped at my face. "I'm fine. It's okay. You can go back. I'm—I'm sure the kitchen's swamped."

"No, you're not fine. And I've got a minute. We're right between the sittings. What happened? Is your mom okay? Do you need me to get Nico?"

I shook my head. "No," I said, and hiccupped.

"You're worrying me." And before I realized what was happening, he wrapped his arms around me, holding me close to his chest.

I tensed, and then relaxed despite myself. After the last twenty-four hours, being held by someone, anyone, felt so very good.

"My mom. They found nodes on her liver last night."

"Nico said you guys were at the ER again."

"It's bad. And Neil and I broke up," I told Adrian, feeling my nose tingle from a lack of oxygen. I forced myself to take deeper breaths. "He was just a short time away from getting on the plane to come here, tonight, but he said . . . he said I should prepare myself. That Mom might not get better, that she might . . ." I couldn't finish the sentence. "I got so angry with him. I'm still angry."

"Understandable."

"And I told him not to get on the plane." I shook my head and wiped away more tears. "I'm the worst."

"You're not the worst."

I sniffed. "I can't believe we ended things on the phone like that."

"He's a fool."

"No, he's not, that's what makes it worse." So, so much worse. Another deep breath, but with the increased oxygen came the avalanche of emotions, and I felt another sob build in my chest.

"Shh," Adrian said, holding me even tighter. I leaned further into the embrace, holding on to his arms like a drowning woman.

His hand stroked my hair, and I sighed and leaned in closer. His lips touched the crown of my forehead, my cheeks, my lips.

Adrian's kiss began gently, tentatively, and when I didn't pull away, it became the kiss of a man finally receiving something long-awaited, fear and joy mixed together.

Without thinking, I found myself kissing him back, responding to the feel of his hands in my hair, his generous mouth, and the scent of a spicy soap that mingled with the aromatics of the kitchen.

His kiss quieted my tears, ended my weeping, calmed me until I realized what I was doing. I pulled away, unsteadily. "What are we— I've got to go. I've got a whole restaurant out there."

Adrian just stared back at me, his eyes unfocused. "Yeah. You're right."

"What was I . . . I just . . ." I shook my head and looked away, unable to look into his eyes, his huge, startled eyes. "My makeup bag's around here somewhere. I have to get back out there. This was a mistake."

"No, it wasn't," Adrian said, his voice more resolute than I'd ever heard. "I know what mistakes are, and that wasn't one of them."

I finally looked up at him. "I have to go."

He reached out and wiped the last tear from my face, then walked out of the office, closing the door behind him.

After he left, the office seemed small and stifling. I found my makeup bag and repaired my face, erasing the mascara smudges and tear trails; the only thing I couldn't fix were my reddened eyes.

Once I looked pulled together enough not to arouse suspicion, I left the office and reentered the dining room. To my relief, everyone seemed relaxed and at ease—nothing had fallen apart, no one had stormed out.

"There you are!"

I whipped around to find Caterina right behind me. "Hi."

"We've been here for ten minutes. Mallory said you stepped out. Everything all right?"

"Yeah." I took another look around the dining room to confirm my assessment. "Everything's fine. Everything's running smoothly." I took a deep breath and smiled. "I'm so glad you guys were able to make it."

"The boys are all set with the sitter, and we're delighted to be here. Mom and Dad are coming later. Mom's not feeling well." She squinted at me. "You look weird."

"Thanks," I said dryly. "We'll talk about it later."

"Where's Neil? He made it, right?"

"Long story; he's not here." My gaze flitted away.

"That's quite the talk we'll have later," she said, eyebrow raised.

I cleared my throat. "You have no idea. Do you think if I call Mom and Dad and tell them to stay home—do you think they'd listen?"

"Not a chance."

The rest of the evening sped by. People ate, people left. I saw smiles all around, assurances that they'd enjoyed their meal. Marti winked and pointed finger guns at me. "Good job, kid," she'd said. Linn gave me a huge hug and made me promise we'd hang out soon, even if it meant the two of us getting drinks together after hours.

"We'll make it work," she promised.

My siblings stayed for hours, eating a proper European meal course after course, with plenty of wine and conversation to hold them until the appearance of the next course. My parents arrived in time for a generous platter of Clementine's desserts, presented by Clementine herself.

"I'm sorry we could not come sooner," my mother said.

I shook my head violently. "I'm delighted you were able to make it out at all. If you need to go home, it's fine."

"For a little while, I can manage. Ah!" She brightened. "I had a call from Sandrine. She's coming for a visit in a couple weeks."

"Oh! That's wonderful! Is Auguste joining her?"

"No, someone has to stay with the guests."

For a split second I wondered about the timing—not ideal for Sandrine, in the middle of tourist season. Of my mother's cousins, Sandrine was the one she'd remained closest to, even after leaving France. With my mother very ill, I shouldn't have been surprised that Sandrine would make a trip happen. "Well, I'm looking forward to seeing her," I said.

My parents stayed another hour and then left for home. The rest of the family—Alex, Sophie and Nelson and young Chloé, Caterina and Damian—stayed until closing.

I helped the waitstaff clean the dining room and prepare the restaurant for the next day. This would be our lives—the adventure of the dining room, and doing it all over again, day after day.

Nico opened a bottle of champagne in the kitchen to commence the staff's celebration, but I pleaded exhaustion and retreated for the upstairs apartment.

I took Gigi outside and then changed into sweats and let my hair down. The warmth of the day lingered, but I craved the comfort of a cup of hot tea.

The knock at the door sounded while I waited for the water to boil.

Finding Adrian on my doorstep sent my heart pounding.

"Hi," I said, pushing my hair from my face.

"I won't be long," he said, "but we didn't get to finish our conversation earlier. I just wanted to say that I know you and Neil just broke up, and that he was very important to you. But you also need to know, Juliette, that you're important to me. And if you need time, I'll wait. I'll wait however long you want. I'm not going anywhere—I'll just be downstairs when you're ready." He cleared his throat. "Well, I'll be going home after this. But I'll be back tomorrow morning. You know what I mean. It sounded better in my head."

I looked at him, and in that moment I saw the man who had helped me move, who'd taken care of the dining room mouse, who'd waited at the restaurant for an ice cream maker just because I'd asked. He'd been there all along, I realized, waiting.

We might have stood there forever, in my entryway, but the sharp whistle of the teakettle broke the moment.

"Water's done," I said, trying to catch my breath.

"You should probably get that," he said, his voice tense but hopeful. "I'll see you tomorrow."

35

Happiness. Simple as a glass of chocolate or tortuous
as the heart. Bitter. Sweet. Alive.

—JOANNE HARRIS

ow," Caterina said over a late brunch Saturday morning. "I
mean, I can't say I'm surprised, but wow." She nodded. "Good
for Adrian."

My elbows on the table, I rested my head in my hands. "Are you kidding?
I'm panicking over Mom, Neil and I break up. He had no business kissing me."

"Did you kiss him back?"

"I was vulnerable. And what do you mean you're not surprised?"

Caterina shrugged. "I got a vibe when he was at dinner last, that he had a
thing for you."

"News to me. I mean . . . I thought he might have liked me, back when we
met, but then I was dating Neil and I stopped paying attention."

"Seems like you're up to date now. Did you like kissing him?"

"That's completely beside the point. I feel like . . . I feel like if I broke up
with Neil and then kissed Adrian, does that mean that what Neil and I had
didn't matter to me?"

"I think . . . love and attraction are complicated." She shrugged. "We can
talk circles around this like schoolgirls, and if that's what you want, we can do
that. But the way I see it, you and Neil aren't together, Adrian's thrown his hat
in the ring, and the rest is really up to you and what you want. If you enjoy
kissing Adrian, date him."

I slouched in my seat. "He hasn't asked me on a date."

"Whatever. He will." She patted my hand. "This was a good talk. It's been
an eventful few days."

"No joke." I sighed and leaned my forehead in my hand. "I'm worried about Mom. More than worried—I'm terrified we're going to lose her."

"Me too," Caterina said quietly. "But my worrying about it isn't going to help anything. We hope, we pray, we do what we can do."

"I know." I reached into my bag for the legal envelope I'd brought with me. "I need to tell you something, Cat. These," I said, pushing the envelope across the table, "are scans of Grand-mère's letters from before her marriage to Grand-père."

"I didn't know about these." She opened it up and peered inside. "Are they in any particular order?"

"They are."

She pulled out the first letter with care. "Nineteen thirty-nine, wow. She was so young then, wasn't she?" Caterina looked up, studied my face. "What aren't you telling me?"

"I found this photo in her prep table, the one I inherited last spring."

She took the photo from my hands. "That's . . . Wait." Caterina looked up at me. "This is old."

"It is."

"So . . . not Nico?"

"Not Nico," I said. I think . . . I know actually . . . it's our grandfather, Cat. Our biological grandfather."

Caterina's face turned serious. "I know you, Etta. I know you wouldn't tell me that if you weren't one hundred percent positive."

"I am."

"Should I ask you to explain it to me, or should I read the letters?"

I thought about it for a moment. "Read the letters. They'll do a better job explaining than I could. Mom knows. I told her at the ER the other night."

"How's that for timing."

"I didn't want to say anything until I knew for sure. But with Mom so sick—"

"You had your reasons. Where did you find the letters?"

"The chateau, when I was back there last month."

Caterina opened her mouth and closed it again. "Okay. I'll read them. I trust you." She reached out and clutched my hand. "I'll read them, and then we'll chat. Don't worry."

The service that night ran smoothly despite even larger numbers than the night before, as word of mouth began to spread. I knew that it wouldn't always be easy, that we'd have to market and fight to keep crowds as the novelty wore off.

After our kiss the night before and the words that followed, I didn't know what to expect from Adrian. When he showed up for work, he tossed a warm smile my way before throwing on his jacket and setting up at his station.

After the service that night, we closed up and the four of us—Clementine, Nico, Adrian, and I—all headed upstairs for coffee and the pizza Nico had ordered. We laughed and chatted and came down off the adrenaline high.

I found myself admiring Adrian's generous smile and easy laugh, the way he tossed a ball for Gigi until she flopped on the floor with a contented sigh.

Mom went in for a full body scan on Monday, followed by an appointment on Tuesday to discuss the results with her oncologist. I sat in the waiting room with the rest of my siblings—we were deemed too many in number to join my parents for the actual appointment.

Not that we fit very well in the waiting room either. We filled one corner, Nico and Alex sharing a car magazine, Sophie reading a book, Caterina texting Damian about the boys, and me answering e-mails and press inquiries about the restaurant.

At long last my parents emerged from behind the office doors; my father looked drawn and pale, my mother fragile yet resolute.

They sat near us, and we circled around to hear the news.

"The cancer has indeed spread to the liver," Maman began. "It's also spread to two new lymph nodes."

"Is there a new treatment plan?" Sophie asked.

"There will be new chemo," Papa said, "and another surgery."

"The surgery and chemo might work," Maman said. "Or it might not. If it does not, we will have . . . less time together."

"How much less?" Nico asked quietly.

"One month," Maman answered. "Maybe six."

My breath caught in my chest, and my vision blurred. For the first time in so many months, I allowed my brain to try to piece together life without my mother at the table. The thought made my head feel as though the two halves were splitting apart—I couldn't begin to conceive of the idea, not without feeling as though everything were breaking and splitting apart.

"We will pray," Caterina said in a resolute voice, grasping Maman's hand. I leaned against Caterina and reached for their joined hands. Alex murmured a soft prayer. I couldn't hear the particulars, but I figured God could hear it fine, and that was good enough for me.

Nico and I drove back to the restaurant together. The radio played, but we said little.

"I broke up with Neil because he told me Mom might not make it," I said at last, as we neared home. "He told me I should prepare myself."

Nico swore softly under his breath. "You did the right thing."

"He might not be wrong."

"Doesn't matter."

"I love you, bro."

"You're not half-bad, Juliette." He tossed me a half smile. "That Neil guy is an idiot."

"No, he's not. It was . . . more than that," I said. "It wasn't just that argument."

"It never is."

The Tuesday-night dinner crowd was laid back and thinner than the weekend, for which I was grateful. My head wasn't in it, though I smiled and charmed and managed the floor as if my heart weren't breaking.

Afterward Clementine, Adrian, and Nico hung out in the apartment, where we finished off the last of the dessert selection and experimented with wine pairings. The notes from the pairings would later be framed and hung in my kitchen. What mattered most, though, is that after a late night of laughter, the world seemed slightly less bleak.

That night set the pattern for the next week. Some nights, we put on a movie and simply enjoyed the sensation of being off our feet. Other nights, Clementine or Nico would beg off earlier, or take Gigi out for a walk, leaving Adrian and me to our coffee and conversation. I learned about his parents (divorced), his siblings (one brother, one sister), and his travels (Spain, Thailand, Texas). He asked about growing up at D'Alisa, my years in culinary school, my time at the newspaper.

He made me laugh, but he didn't try to kiss me. I kept my distance.

Caterina, Damian, and the boys flew home to Chicago, and I missed them deeply.

The breakup with Neil still wrung my heart. There had been no texts, no e-mails, and no phone calls. We'd quit each other cold turkey. I couldn't help but remember how similar it had been with Éric—one argument, and I never heard from him again.

Focusing on work kept me from falling apart. For the time being, Nico, Frank, and I decided to keep the restaurant open six days a week, at least for the first three months. Frank had pushed for seven, but Nico and I agreed that we wanted Sunday dinners with our parents. If the business remained steady over the next three months, we'd look at adding lunch and hiring more staff to give the core staff a respite.

I spent my days keeping track of the numbers, staying on top of our ordering, and managing the restaurant's social media. I managed the background music and the flower arrangements on the tables, finding indie artists and unusual blooms to bring variety to our establishment. If I had a window of time, I'd visit my mom. Sometimes we talked, other times I found myself holding her steady as she vomited into a basin.

In the evenings I put on a dress or smart separates and kept everything moving efficiently at the front of the house, making sure the food made it to the tables quickly and without drama.

One Friday Adrian and I took Gigi for a leisurely evening walk after work, in the dark.

"I like the city like this," he said. "Peaceful."

"It's nice."

Adrian cocked his head to the side. "Want to have a picnic with me tomorrow? I'll cook. You can bring Gigi, if you want."

"She'd like that."

"And you?"

I tilted my head and shot him a sideways smile. "I'd like it too."

Sandrine arrived in Portland just as the blackberries began to ripen on the vines. She brought a breath of fresh, lavender-scented air, settling into my parents' guest room and immediately making herself useful in the kitchen and tidying the areas of the house my father and Sophie hadn't been able to attend to.

She reminded us she'd been a nurse until the management of the chateau had fallen into her hands. Auguste had quit his job tending the Tuileries Garden in Paris and returned to Chateau de l'Abeille beside his wife.

Naturally she asked about Neil once we had a moment alone.

"We had a disagreement," I said carefully. I hadn't told my mother the true nature of the argument, and I couldn't risk Sandrine passing it along.

"*C'est tragique,*" she said, "but it happens. This Adrian? Your brother's friend? He makes you happy, does he not?"

"He does," I said, an easy smile spreading across my face. "It's not at all serious—I can't even think about anything long term right now—but Adrian's good company."

Sandrine shrugged. "Bon idea. He is handsome."

"And he's sweet, when you get to know him. He makes sure I eat during the dinner shift."

"Ah! That is a good quality in a man. But you miss Neil, don't you?"

I looked away, stung. "I shouldn't."

"You loved each other."

"We did." I shook my head. "How is Grand-tante Cécile?"

"She is good, well enough. Auguste dotes on her, and I'm not sure she knows I am gone."

"I'm sorry. That must be difficult."

"We all have our difficulties in life, lose people in different ways."

"I have a key," I said, changing the subject before my eyes could finish tearing up. "I found it in Grand-mère's things. It's probably a long shot, but I wonder if it might fit that odd closet of yours."

"Mais oui, the mystery closet. I can take it home with me when I leave, see if it happens, or if the house rebels."

We laughed together.

"How long are you planning to stay?" I asked.

Another shrug. "*Je ne sais pas.* I had thought a week or two, but perhaps longer," she said, her eyes cutting down the hall to where Maman slept. "I do enjoy Portland, you know. So much coffee, so serious about everything, so much protesting—it is practically French."

I laughed the way I was meant to, and forced myself not to read into her words. "It's wonderful having you here," I said. "And not just because of your croissants."

She read the worry on my face anyway. "It is in God's hands. And this is not our only world. I know one day I will be in heaven, and my mother will know my face."

"You're right."

She wrapped her arm around my shoulders. "Be at peace, Juliette. There are grand plans for us yet."

Readers Guide

1. When Juliette is on the phone with Neil, she tells him that she wants her job and she wants him too. Do you think having both is possible?

2. As she travels through Europe with Neil, Juliette feels as though their relationship exists best in a bubble. Have you ever had a relationship or friendship that formed under specific circumstances? Did it translate into everyday life?

3. Back at home, Juliette struggles to balance her work life and her family life. What do you do to establish work-family balance? In what ways do your methods need to be fluid?

4. The letters reveal Mireille's great love for Gabriel and the tragic events that unfold during the German occupation of France. Why do you think Mireille never told Gabrielle about her father or her sister?

5. Juliette travels to Memphis and is surprised by how different it feels from her world. Where have you travelled that felt far from home? Would you consider moving to such a place for another person?

6. The more Juliette gets to know Adrian, the more her opinion of him changes. When in your life have you found your opinion about someone changing?

7. What do you think about Juliette's telling Gabrielle about the letters? Would you have waited or told her sooner?

8. Juliette has family ties in both France and Italy, and she enjoys the local cuisine and culture as she travels. Which country calls to you more? If you had to choose between Rome or Paris, Provence or Tuscany, which would you choose, and why?

9. The food in *Reservations for Two* is a character all on its own. What kinds of recipes send you to the kitchen? Which recipes from this book would you consider trying?

10. Juliette decides to hope for good things, even when doing so doesn't make sense. When have you had similar moments in your life?

Acknowledgments

I have many people to acknowledge and thank, but here's a little secret: writing this book was not terribly easy, and I have blocked much of it out. So if you're reading this and we had a lovely conversation and I forgot to thank you, your treasure in heaven shall be even greater.

My agent Sandra Bishop is always at the top of these lists, and I'm so glad to have her.

Many thanks to my editor, Shannon Marchese, whose thoughts and insights into each character proved invaluable, as always.

Thanks to Laura Wright, who shepherded this book (and the last) through copyediting.

I've said it before, but authors are some of the loveliest people you'll ever meet. I'm so thankful for the supportive prayer and community provided by Carla Stewart and Katie Ganshert, the plot chats with Sarah Varland, the shop talk with Carla Laureano and Elizabeth Byler Younts, and the Bingo with Allison Pittman, which perhaps didn't apply directly to the book but fed my soul just the same.

Giant thanks to Shiloh the Girl Band (a.k.a. Rachel McMillan and Melissa Tagg). You guys are the best, both in person and online, and you brighten every day.

Many thanks to Kara Christensen and Rachel Lulich, whose feedback I appreciate so much.

Merci beaucoup as well to Malika Renard and Diane Schwieger, for their (often late-night) French assistance. Grazie mille to Alessandra Gardino for her invaluable Italian translations, cultural input, travel advice, and tiramisu recipe.

Super huge thanks to my recipe testers, Noël Chrisman and Aimee Madsen. This book tastes better because of you.

And speaking of, many thanks to the winner of the recipe contest, Heidi Toth, whose strawberry ice cream recipe fits the text so perfectly.

Many thanks to my family, who have always been so supportive of my crazy job.

And to Danny, who has to live (and work) with a woman on deadline, and who is so very wonderful at picking up Indian takeout and listening to the particulars of people who don't actually exist. The character of Neil is based loosely on him, but the real Danny is so much better—I am so thankful for him.

About the Author

HILLARY MANTON LODGE is a storyteller at heart. She is the author of *Plain Jayne,* a Carol Award finalist, and *Simply Sara,* an ECPA best-selling book. A graduate of the University of Oregon's School of Journalism, Hillary discovered the world of cuisine during an internship at *Northwest Palate* magazine. In her free time she enjoys experimenting in the kitchen, watching foreign films, and exploring her most recent hometown of Portland, Oregon. She shares her home with her husband, Danny, and their Cavalier King Charles Spaniel, Shiloh.

COMING MAY 2016

Look for the Conclusion
to the Two Blue Doors Series

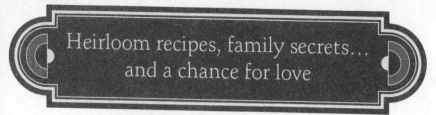

Heirloom recipes, family secrets...
and a chance for love

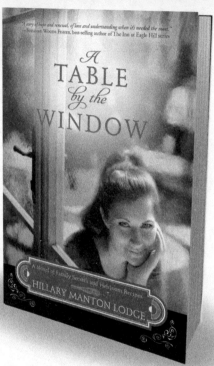

A TABLE by the WINDOW

HILLARY MANTON LODGE

Food writer Juliette D'Alisa can't avoid her culinary
heritage. With pressure from brother Nico to leave
her career and start a new restaurant, Juliette finds
relief talking to online love interest and non-foodie
Neil McLaren. That is until a photo leads to family
secrets and life gets stickier than ever before.

Read an excerpt from this book and more at
www.WaterBrookMultnomah.com!